THE
LOCH MOOSE
MONSTER

Other books edited by Sheila Williams

WHY I LEFT HARRY'S ALL-NIGHT HAMBURGERS
And Other Stories from
Isaac Asimov's Science Fiction Magazine
(with Charles Ardai)

THE
LOCH
MOOSE
MONSTER

More Stories from
ISAAC ASIMOV'S
SCIENCE FICTION MAGAZINE

Foreword by Joan D. Vinge
Edited by
Sheila Williams

**Delacorte
Press**

Published by
Delacorte Press
Bantam Doubleday Dell Publishing Group, Inc.
666 Fifth Avenue
New York, New York 10103

Library of Congress Cataloging in Publication Data

The Loch Moose monster : more stories from Isaac Asimov's science fiction magazine / edited by Sheila Williams ; foreword by Joan D. Vinge.
    p. cm.
  ISBN 0-385-30600-8
  1. Science fiction, American. I. Williams, Sheila. II. Isaac Asimov's science fiction magazine.
PS648.S3L63   1993
813′.0876208—dc20

                            91-36291
                               CIP

Manufactured in the United States of America

March 1993

10 9 8 7 6 5 4 3 2 1

BVG

ACKNOWLEDGMENTS

I would like to thank Gardner Dozois, who originally purchased most of these stories, and from whom I have learned
so much; Ian Randal Strock and Scott L. Towner, who helped
me with the detail work; *IAsfm*'s Subsidiary Rights Director,
Cynthia Manson, and her assistant, Charles Ardai, who made
this deal possible; Jack Dann for inspiration; and David W.
Bruce for his help and support. Special thanks are due to my
own editor, Sue Scarfe.

FOR MY DAD,
ALFRED R. WILLIAMS
AND, OF COURSE,
FOR DAVID

CONTENTS

FOREWORD:
SCIENCE FICTION CHANGED MY LIFE

Joan D. Vinge

Science fiction changed my life. I know, that's the sort of sweeping statement usually reserved for religious experiences or brushes with death; but in this case it's really not such an exaggeration.

I still remember the day I bought my first science fiction book. I was thirteen or fourteen and living in San Diego. One sunny spring afternoon I walked up and over the hill to the local shopping center. I don't remember now whether I was going to the supermarket for anything besides a look through their revolving book racks. All I remember is that I did look, and I found a paperback novel called *Storm over Warlock,* by Andre Norton. On the front cover there was a handsome guy holding a ray gun, with a strange animal (which turned out to be a wolverine) beside him, an alien, and a rocket ship.

I had never read any science fiction, but I loved books about adventure, so the cover picture was enough to make me pick it off the rack. I read the back cover, and then the first page, which talked about an attack by Throgs on a Terran survey camp, and the lone survivor's struggle to escape. I didn't know what Terrans were—let alone Throgs. I wondered if Terrans were supposed to be humans, or some sort of aliens. Not knowing what they were made me a little nervous, but I did like the cover . . . and besides, it was only forty cents. So I bought the book, took it home, read it . . . and not just a whole new world but the entire universe opened up for me.

Storm over Warlock gave me an unforgettable adventure on a world with amber skies and strange, fluorescent vegetation, where the hero (who was indeed a human being) encountered not only the vicious, insectoid Throgs (who were indeed aliens), but also a matriarchal native race of scaled amphibians, who used mental powers first to test and then to aid him. I was, as they say, "in love on another planet," and I never wanted to come back.

I suppose it wasn't a total surprise that I was ready to fall in love with science fiction at first sight. I had always been fascinated by space and other planets (as well as other places and times), even before I knew that anyone was writing stories about them. My father had a telescope in the backyard when I was little, and we all used to go out and look through it at the moon and planets. My mother taught me the names of the constellations and how to watch the shadow of a solar eclipse by making a hole in a piece of cardboard.

I had been haunted for years by a series of astronomical paintings by Chesley Bonestall that appeared in a *Life* magazine article on outer space when I was about six. I was crushed when my mother told me the word *hypothetical*—applied to an amazing portrait of a binary sun system, viewed from a crater-pocked, airless "hypothetical" planet—meant "imaginary." I'd thought it meant "hot" or "cold"—but "imaginary"? That meant it didn't really exist! I was only six years old, but I was terribly disappointed. I think that from then on, I had secretly been longing for some way to reclaim my vision of that world. And with *Storm over Warlock*, I had finally found something that recaptured the awe and wonder

I'd felt when I looked at that impossible starscape and believed it was real.

When people who read science fiction talk about what makes them such passionate fans of the genre, they often speak of the "sense of wonder" that it inspires in them. Generally they mean that science fiction has the ability to take you out of the present and transport you to places you've never been before, even in your dreams. And once I'd been there—out in space, on another world—I found I wanted to go on exploring all the infinite possibilities of space, time, and the human imagination.

I began to search for more science fiction books—not knowing where to find them, at first, since most grocery stores had only a few in their generic mix. (This was before the era of bookstore chains, or even the multitude of malls as we know them.) Finally I discovered the science fiction section at Al's Cigar Store (they also had a lot of comic books), and, eventually, real bookstores with real SF sections. Through high school and into college, I spent as much time as I could having mind-expanding adventures in space and time.

And when I was forced to spend time back in the real world, I found that I began to view what went on there in new and different ways. Reading science fiction can be challenging at times because unfamiliar terms and ideas often occur in the stories. I think one of the reasons that most people who become SF fans do so when they are teenagers, or younger, is that young readers are more open to the new and strange. The older you get, the more difficult it is to get into a story in which something unfamiliar is happening or which is set in an unfamiliar environment.

But people who find they like science fiction will probably never have a problem with understanding new and strange concepts. Science fiction is not simply about rockets and ray guns or swords and sorcery—it's about dealing with the unknown, with the unexpected changes that throw a monkey wrench into the orderly machinery of life. And generally in science fiction the characters don't indulge in endless oomphalokepsis about their fates. They confront the changes with a courage and resourcefulness that can give inspiration to someone wrestling with the problems the modern world invariably throws into our daily lives.

And besides, once they have encountered the strange, the alien, and the unexpected in print, it can be easier for someone who reads science fiction to accept the differences among people and situations in the real world: to see that whatever life-style or way of doing things they grew up with is not the only one that works.

Allowing me that insight was one of the most important ways in which science fiction affected my life. I had grown up in a very ordinary suburban, 1950s-style world. By offering me a glimpse of the possibilities that lay beyond my somewhat limited horizons, science fiction gave me the courage to push toward new frontiers in my own life.

In college I majored in anthropology. (Anthropology is the study of people and everything they do, basically—it gives you a sense of perspective about human behavior in much the same way science fiction does.) That choice was influenced by my love of science fiction in general, and by my fondness for one novel in particular: another of Andre Norton's, called *The Time Traders*. *The Time Traders* evoked prehistoric Europe so vividly that it made me desperate to know more about that mysterious, distant place and time. I took a course in European prehistory, and had the same response to anthropology that I'd had to science fiction: "Where has this been all my life—?"

Anthropology has been an invaluable tool in my own science fiction writing. But I probably would never have become a science fiction writer—or a writer at all—if I hadn't been a science fiction reader first. Discovering in my teens that Andre Norton was actually a *woman* writing my favorite fiction was an immense thrill and inspiration for me—though at the time I hardly imagined that someday I could, or would, follow in her footsteps and become a writer myself.

I had always liked to write stories just for fun, to entertain myself and my friends (though, like a lot of novice writers, I rarely finished a story). Before I began reading science fiction my tales had been horse stories. Once I discovered science fiction, though, that was all I wanted to write. But for a long time I only thought of my writing as a hobby, and never considered sending anything out to a magazine or publisher. But while I was in college I was encouraged to take my writing seriously. And so I did, because, being a science fiction reader, I believed in my ability to face a challenge. Much to my surprise, I sold my first "serious" story . . . and then another, and another . . . and suddenly I had a career. After that first sale, there was no going back: I was a science fiction writer.

I've been writing the kind of fiction I love best ever since, and have won two Hugo Awards, the science fiction "Oscar." At this point it seems as though my life would have been entirely different (and probably not nearly as interesting or satisfying) if I had not picked up *Storm over Warlock* at the grocery store on that fateful day in spring.

Will science fiction change your life? Maybe. If you let it. Remember, all it takes is one book. . . . This could be the one.

TV TIME

Mark L. Van Name

 I got one good week of summer vacation, and then Dad hurt himself, Mom quit her job, the new hi-def TV arrived, and things haven't been the same since.

Dad's accident started it all. Dad said he never would have had to mess around with those power cables in the first place if the damn hardware group had been doing its job, but he was always ragging on those guys. Dad may be an okay programmer—although I doubt it, I mean, who can believe a guy in his fifties knowing squat about computers—but he's a total hardware loser. So, he's moving his computer to a new office, plugging in the connections on the power box and—boom—megavolts lay him out flatter than day-old road pizza. When he comes to, he's got this twitch that you've just got to see to believe. He'll be sitting on the sofa, or at the dinner table, just as calm as a switched-off TV, and then his hands'll start. His legs usually go next, although sometimes his hips join in first, a sort of Elvis look if you ignore the hands, and then all hell breaks loose. Mom put a seat belt on his chair after he fell off the third time. The doctor told him that he just has to stick with the muscle relaxers and wait it out.

I say, enjoy it while it lasts. That twitch is awesome. I tried to get him to let me video it and sync him up to some serious metal noise, but he turned red and took the camera away from me for a week. "Ted," he said, "other people's misery isn't funny."

Okay, so it's not funny, but it sure could make great video.

Then Mom quit her job to take care of Dad. She didn't really want to quit, but Dad kept after her. He said that they could afford it, because he was getting full salary on his disability leave, and that he needed an adult around.

Mom tried first to get Grandma and Grandpa to come over, but they were still steamed about that video I made of them in the bedroom. I don't know what the big deal was; I only wanted to see if I could take over the security camera system. It's not like they were doing anything I've never seen before. (After all, Dad is such a truster—he keeps his passwords in a card in his wallet—that I've had the code for the Ecstasy Channel since I was ten.) Grandma and Grandpa were older, though. Lots older. I'd have been home free if Dad hadn't heard my deck clicking when he got up to pee that night. He took it away, and they swore never to visit again. No big loss, I thought, until Dad got hurt and it brought Mom home to stay.

Things picked up a little when the new TV arrived. What a mother of a display! The Sears guys brought it in rolled up like a carpet. We cleared the wall at the end of the TV room, and then they stood it up and unwound it along the wall. A screen seven feet tall and almost eleven feet long! Plus seven-by-three-foot planar speakers at either end! A wall of life-size action, bigger than real, better than real. "Big enough to hold a man," Dad said. In the afternoon sun, with the curtains open, it shimmers like the oil on the Gulf. Get Dad going in front of it, hit it with some fast strobes, and you could make great video without even turning it on.

I was stoked. Videos large as life, the Earcrushers shaking the speakers off the wall mounts—it was gonna be a rattling new world.

Then reality crashed in. Dad and Mom sat on the sofa all day long, butts leaving prints in their favorite spots, that beautiful display wasted on game shows and soaps, reruns and tired old-network crap. Sure, I watched too; any video was better than none, better than going outside and trying to breathe that shit that Tampa bills as "the cleanest air in Florida."

Mom was the worst. Start a show with her and you had to watch it all. At first she would get up and mess around with house crap during the commercials, but after a while she stopped all that and stayed with Dad, glued to the sofa.

Dad, though, Dad got wilder as the twitch got worse. Maybe it sped him up. When Mom would go to the kitchen for food, or off to take a nap—she napped a lot after they moved to separate beds, after that morning when she showed up at breakfast with bruises all over her shoulders and head—Dad and I would start the Big Flip.

The Big Flip was my fave. I'd sit on the floor beside the sofa, master remote on my lap, and Dad—from his usual sofa spot—would say go. He was timekeeper; I couldn't count on him to operate the remote for an entire flip. I'd run the dish up to the top satellite, start at Channel One, and hit 'em all, every channel, every satellite. New channel, guess the show or movie, settle any arguments with the on-screen program guide, move on. First time through, it took us over two hours; within a week we could check out all three hundred channels in just over an hour. It was great! Nonstop images, no delays, no wait for plot or character crap, just go go go, game show to western to outer space to music vid and on and on.

Mom hated the flip. She would come in and it was back to rerun city. Some of them were okay, like the old space shows and the cop gigs, the ones where you didn't have to wait too long for something to happen, but most were pure death. I kept the six-inch Sony in my lap for when the going got slow. The Sony didn't pick up many channels, but at least it increased my options.

Late at night, though, Dracula time, the TV was mine. I had to use the 'phones so the noise wouldn't bug them, but otherwise I was on my own. The first few nights I fell asleep on the sofa, the screen flashing and the 'phones shooting tangled tunes straight into my brain and down my spine, but then Mom threatened to take away the remote and I got better about crawling off to bed before they got up. I learned to play that TV like it was hardwired into me. I got the max twelve splits going at once, different shows flashing all over the screen, its metal vibrating with light. Full-size, half-size, a dozen splits, and back to one, I did it all. Grandma and Grandpa were amazing at almost twice normal size and speed. (Can you believe Dad thought I made only one copy?)

At four or five A.M., when even the screaming light couldn't keep my eyes open, I'd power it all down and crash, eyeballs still twitching under my lids. Then up around noon for lunch. The boring afternoon, deadly prime time, flat beach scum of dry images saved only by occasional Big Flips, and back to Dracula time. That was the rest of June, and into July, until just after the Fourth, when Dad walked into the TV.

I still don't know where he got the idea, but it was hot, no doubt about it. Maybe it was the samurai westerns. The Japanese love westerns; they have whole satellites full of 'em, new ones and old ones, but mostly old ones—with a twist, of course.

They'd usually start out just like the originals. Old Joe and Hoss would come riding into town to buy a few big bags of Purina horse chow, some guy in a black hat would start beating up on some woman about twice as pretty as anybody else in town, and then—boom—fight time. So far, so good, nothing special. Routine. Just as Hoss was about to land the big one, though, he'd stop and in would ride Hirohito or Toshiro Mifune or God knows who else. You had to admire those Tokyo programmers; on the good channels you could barely tell the new stuff from the old: no shitty haze lines, shadows falling true, new digital and old analog blending like fresh-from-the-jar Tang. At the end, of course, all the cowboys—Hoss and Joe, Hirohito and Mifune, all of them—would ride off into the big sky. The town folk would be happy, maybe waving from in front of the bar, and there was usually a farm family or two tossed in somewhere, their land safe, their young daughter, eyes as big as CDs, staring at Joe as he rode off.

That ending, said Dad, showed the real beauty of those shows: They had something for everybody. "A man could live in a world like that," he said. Want to stay around the house and farm a little? Go for it. Feel like riding into town and raising Saturday night hell? No problem. Got a hunger to be a good guy? Plenty of room for that, too. Sometimes Dad would walk up to the screen and just stand next to Mifune—Mifune was his favorite. Hoss was too fat, Joe too dumb, Hirohito too damn stiff. He'd look at Mifune and then look at me and Mom. "Couldn't you just see it, Ted? Dear? Couldn't you see me riding into town, high on the saddle?" Mom never said anything; sometimes she'd smile a little. Me, I thought he was more the farmer type, all beat down by the sun, stuck on the wagon heading out of town—but I'd usually agree just so he'd sit down. If he stood too long, the twitch would come on him, and then Mom and I had to carry him back to the sofa. He was a real bitch to lift when he was vibrating.

The day he left he was on the sofa watching the end of a particularly good one, a three-parter with the whole ranch gang, even Adam, plus Hirohito and Mifune, this samurai Musashi, Yamamoto in a cameo as a tough foreman, and tons of other guests. The plot seemed to tie in a young cutey who couldn't take her eyes off Joe, her fat old man, some stolen plutonium, and a hot new chip, but who really cared? Shit was happening all over the screen.

When the last commercials before the big wind-up were blasting away, Dad stood up and marched to the screen, back soldier-straight, arms oddly still at his side. He stopped in front of it and turned around. "Dear," he said, looking at Mom, "Ted"—he looked at me—"that's the place for me." He turned, and then looked back at us over his shoulder. "Don't worry, I'll be fine, and so will you. TV'll take care of everything. You'll see." Then he walked right into the screen, like diving sideways into the Gulf but without a splash. There one minute, and then slipped away. I was so surprised I dropped the Sony; damn thing hasn't been right since. Mom didn't move, but she did stop smiling.

When the show came back on, there was Dad, on the steps of the bar, waving good-bye to the boys on the horses. At least he wasn't stuck on the wagon with the farmers. He looked great, better than I'd ever seen him, tall and straight in jeans and a flannel shirt, no gray in his hair, no twitch, waving and grinning like a son of a bitch. For a second or two I swear he turned to look straight at us; Mom even waved back. Then the credits started to roll.

Mom picked up the remote from where Dad had left it and switched off the tube. She sat dead still for a moment. "Well," she finally said, "I think it's bedtime."

I decided that maybe, for a change, she was right.

When I got up the next morning I stayed in my room for a while and hacked on the Sony, but no luck. I was pretty sure Dad was really gone, but it was a little hard to believe, even for Dad. Finally I figured I might as well check it out myself, so I headed for the kitchen.

Mom was already up, of course, sitting at the counter, drinking her coffee, same as always. The seat belt straps on Dad's chair hung as calmly as his arms had before he got the twitch. Through the doorway to the den I could see the TV and the sofa. The TV was on—two geek families on *Win a Life* going for an expense-free year by trading stupid-relative stories and accident photos—but the sofa was definitely empty. I dropped six spoons of Tang into a glass of water and stirred the glop around. It tastes best when it's like pudding.

Mom looked at me over her cup. "Well, your father's really done it this time. Now what are we supposed to do? I don't think I can get my old job back."

Great, I thought, I hope you can; I want the house to myself. I wasn't quite sure what to say, though. In the background the TV went to commercials in preparation for the audience round, where some lucky sucker wins a whole year just for being there, no stupid stories or anything, just for showing up and spinning a wheel and getting it to stop in the right place. "I don't know, Mom."

The commercial ended, the show came back, the announcer pulled a big lime card out of this huge bucket, and read off Dad's name. "Mom!" I ran for the TV as Dad came streaking out of the audience. "Mom!" She ran in too. Dad looked as good as yesterday, but this time he wasn't in western clothes. He was wearing a standard *Win a Life* costume, the kind you needed to get in, a giant fake leaf taped around his waist. Even with green paint all over him he looked great. He smiled at the audience and waved. Mom waved back.

The announcer led Dad over to the wheel. Dad waved once more to the audience and then let her rip. It must have spun around a dozen times before it even started slowing down—probably a show record—and then it tick-tick-ticked down until the plastic flap stopped right in the middle of the big red cherry.

Mom jumped off the sofa and started clapping. "He won, he won, he won!"

The audience went crazy, everybody screaming and clapping, stamping their feet. When the noise died down the announcer put his arm around Dad. "So, what do you plan to do with this year?"

"Well, Bob," Dad said, "I just want the money to go straight to my wife, the best little woman a man could ever want, and to my boy, Ted. Put it all in their names." Yeah, a mention on national video! Dad was all right. "Bob, could I say a word to my family?"

Bob smiled that big announcer smile and let go of Dad. "By all means." The credits were rolling.

"Dear, I told you everything would work out." Then Dad smiled, and I swear even his teeth looked new. "I hope I'll see you soon."

Mom whispered something, but I couldn't quite hear it. Maybe that's when she got the idea herself.

As the last of the credits flashed up, Dad yelled, "And see you, too, Son!" Dad had sure gotten cool in a hurry.

I looked at Mom. She was in her usual spot on the sofa, her hand resting where Dad would have sat.

"I guess that means you won't be going back to work, huh?" So much for getting the house to myself.

"No, dear, I guess not." She smiled. "I think I'll go take a little nap. You keep the TV quiet, okay?"

When I walked by their bedroom later the door was open a little. I peeked through the crack. Mom was sleeping in Dad's bed, her arm around his pillow, a big grin on her face. And they say money can't buy happiness!

Over the next few weeks Dad popped up everywhere. He was on two more game shows—I got a new camera out of one of them—and a bunch of dumb daytime soaps. He hardly ever got his name in the credits, although once, on *Hostile Takeover*, he got a last-line mention when he played a corporate hit man. He was ice in that one, cold and hard and practically dripping action. He killed two of the corporate turkeys before some automatic-security laser cut him in half. He took almost a minute to stop twitching and finally die. His death twitches looked good; I knew that accident would come in handy someday.

That laser shook Mom up a lot, because it was the first time we'd seen Dad die. She walked around the house all day, muttering and half crying, until he turned up later that night on a samurai western. We still watched at least one of those a day even though Mom didn't like them much. She said it was kind of like a shrine to Dad. She felt a lot better after he made it through that whole show.

I kinda got into the shows where Dad died, because he always died a little differently. One time he'd just fall down, bam, no waiting, no fuss. The next time he'd stretch it out, blood oozing from his lips, his body shaking and sometimes even bouncing around on the ground. My favorite was on one of the old space shows, where they stuck Dad in a red shirt and used this cheap special-effects beam to send him down to a fakoid alien planet that looked like St. Pete beach on a good day. This alien who could have been my language skills teacher's brother hit Dad with an orange ray, and Dad got to shake and rattle for a fair time before he died.

Now that Dad was gone, we mostly watched what Mom wanted. Her favorites were the hospital shows, where every other patient has some rare disease that even the diagnostic computer has never heard of. Mom loved them, but I couldn't stand 'em—how could you believe that some human doctor would know about Paraguayan black tongue disease if the computer didn't?

One day Dad turned up as a guest doctor on one of Mom's favorites, *Medicine and Magic*, a show that spiced up the usual hospital crap with a doctor who had learned voodoo in Haiti as a boy and wasn't afraid to use it. Pretty cool, as hospital shows go.

Dad looked great. He had on a white shirt, oil-slick black pants, and a white open lab coat with shiny medical shit in every pocket. Mom watched him every second of the few minutes he was on. She wouldn't even get up to go to the bathroom during the commercials. "Imagine," she must have said three or four times, "your father, a doctor."

When the show was over, she went into the bedroom. I figured she was probably getting ready for a nap, so I put on the phones and switched to a pure-vid channel.

A few minutes later I felt a tap on my head. I pulled off the phones. Mom was standing there in a work suit, makeup on, ready to head out even though it was the middle of the night.

"Ted, I know you'll be fine. When you need money, you can sign the checks and deposit them. If you get in trouble, call Grandma and Grandpa."

I didn't know what to say. Mom grabbed the remote and flipped around until she found another time zone's feed of *Medicine and Magic.* The Haitian doctor was sacrificing a chicken when a family of nine geeks—four grandparents, the works—walked in to thank the voodoo man for saving their little girl. Mom put down the remote.

"Bye, dear."

So I said, "Bye." What else was I supposed to do? Then she walked into the TV, into the doctor's office behind the geek family, and waved good-bye to me as the credits rolled. I waved back until the screen changed and the commercials started.

I walked over to the sofa and looked down. Still two butt-prints.

The commercial was this gross one for borrowing money with organs as collateral, so I scooped up the remote and switched to a metal station. I started to put on the phones, but then I figured, what the hell? Who's to hear? I unplugged and cranked it up to wall-shaking max. I would have turned it louder if I could have.

The house was hopping the next few days. I put tin foil on the windows so the light wouldn't screw up the TV picture, and I watched what I wanted, when I wanted. I slept with the tube on, sometimes on the floor in front of it, sometimes in my room. Without the tube I never would have known what time it was. Not that I cared.

After a while, though, the food started running out. I thought about going out for groceries, or maybe even calling Grandma and Grandpa, but who could live with them? Sharing the screen with Mom and Dad had been bad enough, but who knows what senile shit those old farts would want to watch.

Meanwhile, Dad and Mom were all over the channels. Mom now looked as young as Dad, and almost as good, as good as your own Mom can look. I programmed the tube to search for their names in credits, so it let me know whenever they were on. Of course, I'm sure I missed a lot of minor spots, but Dad seemed to be getting more credit lines these days, and Mom started out faster than he did, so I got to see them plenty. They weren't in the same shows very often, but every now and then they'd end up together holding hands as the farmers on a samurai western, or picking up their stolen car from a cop lot. They smiled a lot, held hands, even kissed. They always waved if they could. My name didn't come up much because they hardly ever got to talk, but I did get two more mentions. Four times on national video and the summer was only half over!

Still, when I ran out of Tang and the frozen dinners were gone, it was clear I had to do something. When you think about it, it really wasn't too hard to decide.

I chose that old space show, the one where Dad got raygunned while wearing the red shirt. It was on about ten channels; I picked an episode where some kid with mondo eyebrows had big-time mental powers. Dad and Mom weren't on that one, but I figured the kid could use a buddy, so I walked on in.

I was on my fifth spot before I finally ran into Dad. He was hanging out in the bar in a samurai western, and I was delivering a message for Hoss. During the commercial he pulled me over and gave me a big hug. He told me that he and Mom would be together on a show over on the X3 satellite later that day.

Then he leaned real close and whispered in my ear, "Ted, I think if we play our cards right, we'll get a show of our own someday."

All *right*.

WATER BRINGER

Mary Rosenblum

 Sitting with his back against the sunscorched rimrock, Jeremy made the dragonfly appear in the air in front of him. It hovered in the hot, still air, wings shimmering with bluegreen glints. Pretty. He looked automatically over his shoulder, as if Dad might be standing there, face hard and angry. But Dad was down in the dusty fields. So were Jonathan, Mother, Rupert, even the twins—everyone but him.

It was safe.

Jeremy hunched farther into his sliver of shade, frowning at his creation. It was a little too blue—that was it—and the eyes were too small. He frowned, trying to remember the picture in the insect book. The dragonfly's bright body darkened as its eyes swelled.

Bingo. Jeremy smiled and sat up straight. The dragonfly hovered above a withered bush, wings glittering in the sunlight. He sent it darting out over the canyon, leaned over the ledge to watch it.

For below, a man was leading a packhorse up the main road from the old riverbed. A stranger! Jeremy let the dragonfly vanish as he squinted against the glare. Man and horse walked with their heads down, like they were both tired. Their feet raised brown puffs of dust that hung in the air like smoke.

Jeremy held his breath as the stranger stopped at their road. "Come *on*," Jeremy breathed. "There's nowhere else for two miles."

As if they'd heard him, the pair turned up the rutted track. The man didn't pull on the horse's lead rope—they moved together, like they'd both decided together to stop at the farm.

Jeremy scrambled up over the rimrock and lurched into a shambling run. You didn't see strangers out here very often. Mostly, they stopped at La Grande. The convoys stuck to the interstate, and nobody else went anywhere. Dead grass stems left from the brief spring crackled and snapped under Jeremy's feet, and the hard ground jolted him, stabbing his twisted knees with bright slivers of pain.

At the top of the steep trail that led down to the farm, Jeremy had to slow up. He limped down the slope, licking dust from his lips, breathing quick and hard. They'd hear it all first—all the news—before he even got there. The sparse needles on the dying pines held the heat close to the ground. Dry branches clawed at him, trying to slow him down even more. They wouldn't wait for him. They never did. Suddenly furious, Jeremy swung at the branches with his thickened hands, but they only slapped back at him, scratching his face and arms.

Sure enough, by the time he reached the barnyard the brown-and-white horse was tethered in the dim heat of the sagging barn, unsaddled and drowsing. Everyone would be in the kitchen with the stranger. Jeremy licked his lips. At least there'd be a pitcher of fresh water out. He crossed the sunburned yard and limped up the warped porch steps.

". . . desertification's finally reached its limit, so the government's putting all its resources into reclamation."

Desertification? Jeremy paused at the door. The word didn't have a clear meaning in his head, but it felt dusty and dry as the fields. He peeked inside. The stranger sat in Dad's place at the big table, surrounded by the whole family. He wore a stained tan shirt with a picture of a castle tower embroidered on the pocket. He had dark curly hair and a long face with a jutting nose. Jeremy pushed the screen door slowly open. The stranger's face reminded him of the canyon wall, all crags and peaks and sharp shadows.

The door slipped through his fingers and banged closed behind him.

"Jeremy?" His mother threw a quick glance at Dad as she turned around. "Where have you been? I was worried."

"He snuck up to the rimrock again," Rupert muttered, just loud enough.

Jeremy flinched, but Dad wasn't looking at him at all. He'd heard, though. His jaw had gotten tight, but he didn't even turn his head. Jeremy felt his face getting hot, and edged toward the door.

"Hi." The stranger's smile pinned Jeremy in place; it crinkled the sun-browned skin around his eyes. "I'm Dan Greely," the stranger said.

"From the Army Engineers!" ten-year-old David announced.

"To bring *water!*" Paulie interrupted his twin.

"You're not supposed to go up there, Jeremy." Mother gave Dad an uneasy, sideways glance. "You could fall."

"So, just how does the Corps of Engineers plan to irrigate the valley when the river's dry as a bone?" Jeremy's father spoke as if no one else had said a word. "God knows, you can't find water when it ain't there to be found."

"Don't be so hard on him, Everett." Mother turned back to Dad.

"I ain't even heard any solid reasons for *why* the damn

country's drying up," Dad growled. "Desertification!" He snorted. "Fancy word for no damn water. Tell me *why*, surveyor."

"At least someone's trying to do something about it." Mother was using her soothing tone.

They weren't paying any attention to him anymore, not even tattletale Rupert. Jeremy slipped into his favorite place, the crevice between the woodbox and the cold kitchen cookstove.

"We'll be glad to put you up while you're about your business," Mother went on. "It would be like a dream come true for us, if you folks can give us water again. We've all wondered sometimes if we did right to stay here and try to hang on."

"What else *could* we do?" Dad said harshly. "Quit and go work in the Project fields like a bunch of Mexican laborers?"

"I can't promise you water," the stranger said gravely. "I'm just the surveyor. I hear that some of these deep-aquifer projects have been pretty successful, though."

"It's enough to know that there's hope." Mother's voice had gone rough, like she wanted to cry.

Jeremy started to peak around the stove, but froze as Dad's hand smacked the tabletop.

"He ain't dug any wells *yet*. You kids get back to work. Those beans gotta be weeded by supper, 'cause we're not wasting water on weeds. Jonathan, I know you and Rupert ain't finished your pumping yet."

"Aw, come on," Rupert whined. "We want to hear about stuff. Are people really eating each other in the cities?"

"You heard your father," Mother said sharply. "The wash bucket's too dirty for supper dishes. Rupert, you take it out to the squash—the last two hills in the end row—and bring me a fresh bucket."

"Aw, Mom!" Rupert said, but he pushed back his chair.

Jeremy scrunched down, listening to the scuffle of his brothers' bare feet as they filed out of the kitchen.

"We don't have much in the way of hay for your pony," Jeremy's father grumbled. "How long are you planning on staying, anyway?"

"Not long. I can give you a voucher for food and shelter. When they set up the construction camp, you just take it to the comptroller for payment."

"Lot of good *money*'ll do me. There wasn't enough rain to make hay worth shit this season. Where'm I going to buy any?"

The screen door banged. Dad was angry. Jeremy frowned and wiggled into a more comfortable position. Why should Dad be angry? The stranger talked about water. Everyone needed water.

"Never mind him." From the clatter, Mother was dishing up bean-and-squash stew left over from lunch. "You have to understand, it's hard for him to hope after all these years." A plate clunked on the table. "You keep pumping water, trying to grow enough to live on, praying the well holds out and watching your kids go to bed hungry. You don't have much energy left for hoping. When you're done, I'll show you your room. The twins can sleep with Jeremy and Rupert."

She sounded like she was going to cry again. Jeremy looked down at his loosely curled fists. The thick joints made his fingers look like knobby tree roots. The stranger said something, but Jeremy didn't catch it. He'd only heard Mother cry once before—when the doctor over in La Grande had told her that there wasn't anything that could be done about his hands or his knees.

This stranger made Dad angry and Mother sad. Jeremy thought about that while he waited, but he couldn't make any sense of it at all. As soon as the stranger and Mother left the kitchen, Jeremy slipped out of his hiding place. Sure enough, the big plastic pitcher stood on the table, surrounded by empty glasses. You didn't ask for water between meals. Jeremy listened to the quiet. He lifted the pitcher, clutching it tightly in his thick, awkward grip.

The water was almost as warm as the air by now, but it tasted sweet on his dusty throat. He never got enough water. No one did—not when the crops needed it too. Jeremy swirled the pitcher, watching the last bit of water climb the sides in a miniature whirlpool.

Absently, he made it fill clear to the brim. What would it be like to live in the old days, when it rained all the time and the riverbed was full of water and fish? He imagined a fish, made it appear in the water. He'd seen it in another book, all speckled green with a soft shading of pink on its belly. He made the fish leap out of the pitcher and dive back in, splashing tiny droplets of water that vanished as they fell. Jeremy tilted his head, pleased with himself. Trout—he remembered the fish's name, now.

"Jeremy!"

Jeremy started at his mother's cry and dropped the pitcher. Water and fish vanished as the plastic clattered on the linoleum. Throat tight, he stared at the small puddle of real water. The stranger stood behind Mother in the doorway.

"Go see if there are any eggs." His mother's voice quivered. "Do it right now!"

Jeremy limped out the door without looking at either of them.

"Don't mind him," he heard his mother say breathlessly. "He's clumsy, is all."

She was afraid that the stranger had seen the fish. Jeremy hurried across the oven glare of the barnyard. What if he *had*? What if he said something in front of Dad? His skin twitched with the memory of the last beating Dad had given him, when he'd gotten to daydreaming and made the dragonfly appear in the church. Jeremy shivered.

The stranger's horse snorted at him, pulling back against its halter with a muffled thudding of hooves. "Easy, boy, easy." Jeremy stumbled to a halt, stretched out his hand. The pinto shook its thick mane and stretched its neck to sniff. Jeremy smiled as the velvety lips brushed his palm. "You're pretty," he said, but it wasn't true. It wasn't even a horse, really—just a scruffy pony with a thick neck and feet big as dinnerplates.

He was ugly. Jeremy sat down stiffly, leaning his back against the old, smooth boards of the barn. "Hey." He wiggled his toes as the pony sniffed at his bare feet. "It's not *your* fault you're ugly." He stroked the pony's nose. "I bet you can run like the wind," he murmured.

The pony's raspy breathing sounded friendly, comforting. Eyes half closed, Jeremy imagined himself galloping over the sunscorched meadows. His knees wouldn't matter at all. He drifted off into a dream of wind and galloping hooves.

"Jeremy! It's suppertime. Where the hell are you?"

Rupert's voice. Jeremy blinked awake, swallowing a yawn. It was almost dark. Straw tickled his cheek, and he remembered. He was in the barn, and a stranger had seen him make something.

"I know you're in here." Rupert's footsteps crunched closer.

By now, Dad probably knew about the trout. Jeremy rolled onto his stomach and wriggled under the main beam beneath the wall. There was just enough space for his skinny body.

"I hear you, you brat." Rupert's silhouette loomed against the gray rectangle of the doorway. "You think I want to play hide-and-seek after I work all day? If I get in trouble, I'll *get* you."

The pony laid back its ears and whinnied shrilly.

"Jesus!" Rupert jumped back. "I hope you get your head kicked off!" he yelled.

Jeremy listened to Rupert stomp out of the barn. "Thanks, pony," he whispered as he scrambled out of his hiding place. He shook powdery dust out of his clothes, listening for the slam of the screen door.

Better to face Rupert later than Dad right now.

The pony nudged him, and Jeremy scratched absently at its ear. A bat twittered in the darkness over his head. Jeremy looked up, barely able to make out the flittering shadows coming and going through the gray arch of the doorway. He'd sneak in later. Jeremy's stomach growled as he curled up against the wall of the barn. The pony snuffled softly and moved closer, as if it was glad he was there.

The barn was full of dry creaks and whispers. Something rustled loudly in the loft above Jeremy's head and he started. Funny how darkness *changed* the friendly barn, stretched it out so big. Too big and too dark. "Want to see a firefly?" Jeremy asked the pony. The darkness seemed to swallow his words. It pressed in around him, as if he had made it angry by talking.

He hadn't been able to find a picture. . . . The firefly appeared, bright as a candleflame in the darkness. It looked sort of like a glowing moth. That didn't seem right, but its warm glow drove back the darkness. Jeremy examined it thoughtfully. Maybe he should make the wings bigger.

"So I wasn't seeing things," a voice said.

The pony whinnied and Jeremy snuffed out the firefly. Before he could hide, a dazzling beam of light flashed in his eyes. He raised a hand against the hurting glare.

"Sorry." The light dipped, illuminating a circular patch of dust and Jeremy's dirty legs. "So, this is where you've been. Your brother said he couldn't find you." The beam hesitated on Jeremy's lumpy knees.

The surveyor patted the pony and bent to prop the solar flashlight on the floor. Its powerful beam splashed back from the wall, streaking the straw with shadows. "Can you do it again?" he asked. "Make that insect appear, I mean."

Jeremy licked his dry lips. He *had* seen the trout. "I'm not supposed to . . . make things."

"I sort of got that impression." The man gave him a slow, thoughtful smile. "I pretended I didn't notice. I didn't want to get you in trouble."

Jeremy blinked. This stranger—a grown-up—had worried about getting *him* in trouble? The bright, comforting light and the surveyor's amazing claim shut the two of them into a kind of private, magic circle.

Why *not* let him see? He'd already seen the trout, and he hadn't told Dad. The firefly glowed to life in the air between them. "What does a firefly really look like?" Jeremy asked.

"I don't know." The surveyor reached out to touch the making, snatched his hand away as his finger passed through the delicate wings.

"It isn't real. It doesn't even *look* right." Disappointed, Jeremy let it fade and vanish.

"Wow." The surveyor whistled softly. "I've never seen anything like *that*."

He make it sound like Jeremy was doing something wonderful. "Don't tell I showed you, okay?" Jeremy picked at a thread in his ragged cutoffs.

"I won't." The man answered him seriously, as if he was talking to another grown-up. "How old are you?" he asked, after a minute.

"Twelve. I'm small for my age." Jeremy watched him pick up his marvelous light and swing its bright beam over the old pony.

"You look pretty settled, Ezra. I'll get you some more water in the morning." The surveyor slapped the pony on the neck. "Come on," he said to Jeremy. "Let's go in. I think your mom left a plate out for you." He gave Jeremy a sideways look. "Your dad went to bed," he said.

"Oh." Jeremy scrambled to his feet, wondering how the stranger knew to say that. If Dad was asleep, it was safe to go back in. Besides, this ungrownuplike man hadn't told on him. "Are you going to bring us water?" he asked.

"No," the man said slowly. "I just make maps. I don't dig wells."

"I bet you're good," Jeremy said. He wanted to say something nice to this man, and that was all he could think of.

"Thanks," the surveyor said, but he sounded more sad than pleased. "I'm pretty good at what I do."

No, he didn't act like a grown-up. He didn't act like anyone Jeremy had ever met. Thoughtfully, he followed the bright beam of the surveyor's flashlight into the house.

Next morning was church-Sunday, but the family got up at dawn as usual, because it was such a long walk into town. Jeremy put on his good pair of shorts and went down to take on Mother in the kitchen.

"You can't go." She shoved a full water jug into the lunch pack. "It's too far."

She was remembering the dragonfly. "I won't forget. I'll be good," Jeremy said. "Please?"

"Forget it." Rupert glared at him from the doorway. "The freak'll forget and do something weird again."

"That's enough." Mother closed the pack with a jerk. "I'll bring you a new book." She wouldn't meet Jeremy's eyes. "What do you want?"

"I don't know." Jeremy set his jaw. He didn't usually care, didn't like church-Sundays with all the careful eyes that sneaked like Rupert when they looked at his hands and knees. But this time, the surveyor was going. "I want to *come*," he said.

"Mom . . ."

"I said that's enough." Mother looked past Rupert. "Did you get enough breakfast, Mr. Greely?" she asked too cheerfully.

"More than enough, thanks." The surveyor walked into the kitchen and the conversation ended.

When Jeremy started down the gravel road with them, Mother's lips got tight and Rupert threw him a look that promised trouble, but Dad acted like he wasn't even there, and no one else dared say anything. Jeremy limped along as fast as he could, trying not to fall behind. He had won. He wasn't sure why, but he had.

It was a long, hot walk to town.

Rupert and Jonathan stuck to the surveyor like burrs, asking about the iceberg tugs, the Drylands, Portland, and L.A. The surveyor answered their questions gravely and politely. He wore a fresh tan shirt tucked into his faded jeans. It was clean, and the tower on the pocket make it look like it meant something special.

It meant *water* . . .

Everyone was there by the time they reached the church —except the Menendez family who lived way down the dry creekbed and sometimes didn't come anyway. The Pearson kids were screaming as they took turns jumping off the porch, and Bev LaMont was watching for Jonathan, like she always did.

As soon as they got close enough for people to count the extra person, everyone abandoned their picnic spreads and made for the porch.

"This is Mr. Greely, a surveyor with the Army Corps of Engineers," Mother announced as they climbed the wide steps.

"Pleased to meet you." The surveyor's warm smile swept the sun-dried faces. "I've been sent to make a preliminary survey for a federal irrigation project." He perched on the porch railing, like he'd done it a hundred times before. "The new Singhe solar cells are going to power a deepwell pumping operation. We think we've identified a major aquifer in this region."

"How come we ain't heard of this before?" It was bearded Ted Brewster, who ran the Exxon station when he could get gas, speaking up from the back of the crowd.

"Come on, Ted." Fists on her bony hips, gray-haired Sally Brandt raised her voice. "By the time news makes it here from Boise, it's gone through six drunken truckers. They're lucky if they can remember their names."

"No. That's a good question." The surveyor looked

around at the small knot of dusty faces. "You don't get any radio or TV?"

"No power, out here." Sally shook her head. "Anyway, we couldn't get TV after Spokane quit. There's too many mountains to pick up Boise, and I don't think there's anything big broadcasting anymore this side of Portland."

The surveyor nodded and reached inside his shirt. "I have a letter from the regional supervisor." He pulled out a white rectangle. "I'm supposed to deliver it to the mayor, city supervisor, or whoever's in charge." He raised his eyebrows expectantly.

A gust of wind whispered across the crowded porch, and no one spoke.

"Most people just *left*." Jeremy's father finally stepped forward, fists in the pockets of his patched jeans. "This was wheat and alfalfa land, from the time the Oregon Territory became a state. You can't farm wheat without water." His voice sounded loud in the silence. "The National Guard come around and told us to go get work on the Columbia River project. That's all the help the *government* was gonna give us. If we stayed, they said, we'd dry up and starve. They didn't really give a shit." He paused. "We don't have a mayor anymore," he said. "There's just us."

The surveyor looked at the dusty faces, one by one. "Like I told Mr. Barlow last night," he said quietly, "I can't promise that we'll find water, or that you'll grow wheat again. I'm only the surveyor."

For a long moment, Jeremy's father stared at the envelope. Then, with a jerky, awkward gesture, he reached out and took it. He pried up the white flap with a blunt thumb, and squinted at the print, forehead wrinkling with effort.

Without a word, he handed the paper to Ted Brewster. Jeremy watched the white paper pass from hand to hand. People held it like it was precious—like it was water. He listened to the dry rustle of the paper. When it came around to Dad again, he stuck it into the glass beside the door of the church. "I hope to God you find water," he said softly.

"Amen," someone said.

"Amen." The ragged mutter ran through the crowd.

After that, everyone broke up. After the Reverend had died in the big dust storm, they'd moved the pews outside. Families spread cloths on the long, rickety tables inside. There weren't any more sermons, but people still came to eat together on church-Sundays. The surveyor wandered from group to group in the colored shadows of the church, eating the food people pressed on him. They crowded him, talking, brushing up against him, as if his touch would bring good luck, bring water to the dead fields.

Jeremy hung back, under the blue-and-green diamonds of the stained-glass window. Finally, he went down the narrow stairs to the sparse shelves of the basement library. He found a little paperback book on insects, but it didn't have a picture of a firefly. He tossed it back onto the shelf. When it fell onto the dusty concrete floor, he kicked it, feeling both guilty and pleased when it skittered out of sight under a shelf. Upstairs, the surveyor was giving everyone the same warm grin that he'd given to Jeremy in the barn last night.

It made Jeremy's stomach ball up into an angry knot.

He wandered outside and found little Rita Menendez poking at ants on the front walk. Mrs. Menendez was yelling at the older kids as she started to unpack the lunch, so Jeremy carried Rita off into the dappled shade under the scraggly shrubs. She was too little to mind his hands. Belly still tight, Jeremy made a bright green frog appear on Rita's knee.

Her gurgly laugh eased some of the tightness. *She* liked his makings. He turned the frog into the dragonfly and she grabbed at it. This time, Jeremy heard the surveyor coming. By the time the man pushed the brittle branches aside, the dragonfly was gone.

"Do you always hide?" He reached down to tickle Rita's plump chin.

"I'm not hiding." Jeremy peeked up through his sun-bleached hair.

"I need someone to help me." The surveyor squatted, so that Jeremy had to meet his eyes. "I talked to your father and he said I could hire you. If you agree. The Corp's only paying crisis-minimum," he said apologetically.

Jeremy pushed Rita gently off his lap. This man wanted to hire *him*—with his bad knees and his lumpy, useless hands? Hiring was something from the old days, like the flashlight and this man's clean, creased shirt.

Jeremy wiped his hands on his pants, pressing hard, as if by doing so he might straighten his bent fingers. "I'd like that, Mr. Greely," he said breathlessly.

"Good." The man smiled like he meant it. "We'll get started first thing tomorrow." He stood, giving Rita a final pat that made her chuckle. "Call me Dan," he said. "Okay?"

"Okay, Dan," Jeremy said softly. He watched the man walk away, feeling warm inside.

Jeremy didn't see much of Dan Greely before the next morning. It seemed like everyone had to talk to Dan about watertables, aquifers, deep wells, and the Army Corps of Engineers. They said the words like the Reverend used to say prayers. *Army Corps of Engineers.*

Dan, Dad, and Jonathan stayed in town. Mother shepherded the rest of them home. The twins were tired, but Rupert was pissed because he couldn't stay too. He shoved Jeremy whenever Mother wasn't looking.

"I hope you work hard for Mr. Greely," Mother said when she came up to say good night. The twins were already snoring in the hot darkness of the attic room.

"Waste of time to hire *him*," Rupert growled from his bed. "The pony'd be more use."

"That's enough." Mother's voice sounded sharp as a new nail. "We can't spare either you or Jonathan from the pumping, so don't get yourself worked up. You don't *have* to go with him," she said to Jeremy. Her hand trembled just a little as she brushed the hair back from his forehead.

She was worried. "It'll be okay," Jeremy murmured. He wondered why. He almost told her that Dan already knew about the making and wouldn't tell, but Rupert was listening. "I'll do good," he said, and wished he believed it.

It took Jeremy a long time to fall asleep, but, when he did, it seemed like only moments had passed before he woke up again. At first, he thought Mother was calling him for breakfast. It was still dark, but the east window showed faint gray.

There it was again—Mother's voice. Too wide-awake to fall back to sleep, Jeremy slipped out of bed and tiptoed into the dark hall.

"Stop worrying." Dad's low growl drifted through the half-open door. "What do you think he's gonna do? Eat the kid?"

"I don't know. He said he needed a helper, but what . . ."

"What can Jeremy do? He can't do shit, but Greely's gonna pay wages, and we can use anything we can get." Dad's voice sounded like the dry, scouring winds. "How do you think I felt when I had to go crawling to the Brewsters and the Pearsons for food last winter?"

"It wasn't Jeremy's fault, Everett, the well giving out."

"No one *else* has an extra mouth to feed. No one but me, and I've gotta go begging."

"I lost three babies after Rupert." Mother's voice sounded high and tight. "I couldn't of stood losing another."

Jeremy fumbled his way down the hall, teeth clenched so hard, they felt like they were going to break. *No one else has an extra mouth to feed.* His father's cold words chased him down the stairs. *No one but me.*

A light glowed in the barn's darkness. "Hi." Dan pulled a strap tight on the pony's packsaddle. "I was just going to come wake you. Ezra and I are used to starting at dawn." He tugged on the pack, nodded to himself. "Have you eaten yet?" he asked Jeremy.

"Yeah," Jeremy lied.

Dan gave him a searching look, then shrugged. "Okay. Let's go."

It was just light enough to see as they started down the track. The pony stepped over the thin, white pipe that carried water from the well to the field. Above them, the old bicycle frame of the pump looked like a skeleton sticking up out of the gray dirt. In an hour, Jonathan would be pedaling hard to get his gallons pumped. Then Rupert would take over. The twins would be carrying the yoked pails, and dipping out precious water to each thirsty plant.

"Did your dad make that?" Dan nodded at the metal frame.

"Uh huh." Jeremy walked a little faster, trying not to limp.

He had had a thousand questions about the outside world to ask, but the sharp whispers in the upstairs hall had dried them up like the wind dried up a puddle. He watched Ezra's big feet kick up the brown dust, feeling dry and empty inside.

"We'll start here." The surveyor pulled Ezra to a halt. They were looking down on the dry riverbed and the narrow, rusty bridge. The road went across the riverbed now. It was easier.

The pony waited patiently, head drooping, while Dan unloaded it. "This machine measures distance by bouncing a beam of light off a mirror." Dan set the cracked plastic case down on the ground. "It sits on this tripod and the reflector goes on the other one." He unloaded a water jug, lunch, an ax, a steel tape measure, and other odds and ends. "Now, we get to work," he said when he was done.

Sweat stuck Jeremy's hair to his face as he struggled across the sunbaked clay after Dan. They set up the machine and reflector, took them down and set them up somewhere else. Sometimes Dan hacked a path through the dry brush. It was hard going. In spite of all he could do, Jeremy was limping badly by midmorning.

"I'm sorry." Dan stopped abruptly. "You keep up so well, it's easy to forget that you hurt."

His tone was matter-of-fact, without a trace of pity. There was a knot in Jeremy's throat as Dan boosted him onto Ezra's back. He sat up straight on the hard packsaddle, arms tight around the precious machine. It felt heavy, dense with the magic that would call water out of the ground. Jeremy tried to imagine the gullied dun hills all green, with blue water tumbling down the old riverbed.

If there was plenty of water, it wouldn't matter so much that he couldn't pump or carry buckets.

Jeremy thought about water while he held what Dan gave him to hold, and, once or twice, pushed buttons on the distance machine. He could manage that much. It hummed under his touch and bright red numbers winked in a tiny window. He had to remember them, because his fingers were too clumsy to write them down in Dan's brown notebook.

Dan didn't really need any help with the measuring. Jeremy stood beside the magic machine, watching a single hawk circle in the hard blue sky. Mother had been right. Dan wanted something else from him.

Well, that was okay. Jeremy shrugged as the hawk drifted off southward. No one else thought he had *anything* to offer.

The sun stood high overhead when they stopped for lunch. It poured searing light down on the land, sucking up their sweat. Dan and Jeremy huddled in a narrow strip of shade beneath the canyon wall. Ezra stood in front of them, head down, tail whisking.

They shared warm, plastic-tasting water with the pony, and Dan produced dried apple slices from the lunch pack. He had stripped off his shirt, and sweat gleamed like oil on his brown shoulders. His eyes were gray, Jeremy noticed. They looked bright in his dark face.

"Why do you have to do all this stuff?" Awkwardly, Jeremy scooped up a leathery disc of dried apple. The tart sweetness filled his mouth with a rush of saliva.

"I'm making a map of the ground." Dan shaded his eyes, squinting into the shimmering heat-haze. "They have to know all the humps, hollows, and slopes before they can decide how to build a road or plan buildings."

"I was trying to imagine lots of water." Jeremy reached for another apple slice. "It's hard."

"Yeah," Dan said harshly. "Well, don't start counting the days yet." He shook himself and his expression softened. "Tell me about your fireflies and your fish that jump out of pitchers."

"Not much to tell." Jeremy looked away from Dan's intent gray eyes. Was *that* what he wanted? "If I think of something hard enough, you can see it. It's not real. It's not any *good* for anything." Jeremy drew a zigzag pattern in the dust with his fingers. "It . . . bothers people," he said.

"Like your mom and dad."

"Dad doesn't like it." Jeremy smoothed the lines away.

"What about your mother? What about the other folk?" Dan prodded.

"Dad doesn't let us talk about it. I don't make things where people can see." Mostly. Jeremy shifted uneasily, remembering the dragonfly.

"Is that why you hide?" Dan was looking at him.

"The Pearsons had a baby with joints like mine. So did Sally Brandt—from the dust or the water, or something in it." Jeremy spread his thick, clumsy hands. "They . . . died," he said. "There isn't enough water for extra mouths."

"Who said that?" Dan asked in a hard, quiet voice.

I lost three babies, Mother had cried in that scary voice. *I couldn't stand to lose another.*

Their old nanny goat had had a kid with an extra leg last spring. Dad had taken the biggest knife from the kitchen and cut its throat by a bean hill, so that the blood would water the seedlings. The apple slice in Jeremy's mouth tasted like dust. Feeling stony hard inside, he made the dragonfly appear, sent it darting through the air to land on Dan's knee with a glitter of wings.

"Holy shit." Dried apples scattered in the dust as Dan flinched. "I can almost believe that I feel it," he breathed.

He wasn't angry. Jeremy sighed as the shimmering wings blurred and vanished.

"I don't believe it." Dan stared at the space where the making had been. "Yes, I *do* believe it, but it's fantastic!" He slapped Jeremy lightly on the shoulder, a slow smile spreading across his face. "We could be the hottest thing in this whole damn dry country, kid. *Think* of it. The hicks would fall all over themselves to come see a show like that! *Hoo* . . . ey." His grin faded suddenly.

"You're afraid of doing it, aren't you?" Dan asked softly. "Because it scares your dad?"

Scared? Not Dad. Jeremy shook his head. Rupert was scared of the brown lizards that lived under the rocks out back. He killed them all the time. But Dad wasn't scared of the makings. He *hated* them.

"Look at this." Dan yanked a grubby red bandanna out of his pocket and dangled it in front of Jeremy's eyes. He stuffed the cloth into his closed fist. "Abracadabra . . ." He waved his hand around. "Watch closely, and . . . ta da." He snapped open his hand.

Jeremy stared at his empty palm.

"Your handkerchief, sir." With a flourish, Dan reached behind Jeremy's head and twitched the bandanna into view.

"Wow." Jeremy touched the handkerchief. "How did you do that?"

"It's pretty easy." Dan looked sad as he stuffed the bandanna back into his pocket. "The card tricks, juggling—it's not enough to keep you in water out here in the Dry. The sun's baked all the *belief* out of people. It would take a miracle to get some attention." He stared solemnly at Jeremy. *"You're* that kind of a miracle," he said.

Dan acted like the making was a wonderful thing, not something shameful, not something that made Dad have to ask the Brewsters for food. Suddenly unsure, Jeremy bent to scoop up the apples that Dan had dropped. "You don't want to waste these."

"I'd give a lot for your talent." Dan's eyes gleamed like water.

Talent? Jeremy dumped the withered rings of apple into the pack, struggling to understand Dan's tone. "You're a surveyor," he said. "You don't *need* to do tricks."

"I guess I am." Dan's laugh sounded bitter. "So I guess we'd better get back to surveying." He got to his feet.

Strange feelings fluttered in Jeremy's chest. Could Dan be right? Would people really look at him like Dan had looked at him, all excited and envious? What if Dan was *wrong*? What if everyone looked at him like *Dad* did, instead?

He could find out. If he went with Dan.

Jeremy thought about that—going with Dan—for the rest of the day, while he steadied the machine and pushed buttons. It excited him and scared him, but he didn't say anything to Dan.

Dan might not want him to come along.

It seemed like everyone within walking distance was waiting at the house when they plodded back to the farm that evening. People had brought food and water, because you didn't ask for hospitality, not anymore. Covered dishes and water jugs cluttered the kitchen table, and Dan swept into the crowd and out of Jeremy's reach.

Dan didn't belong to him here, in the dusty house. Here, Dan belonged to the grown-ups and the Army Corps of Engineers. It was only when they were out in the dry hills with Ezra that Dan would be his. Jeremy slipped away to his barn sanctuary to pet Ezra and think.

What would happen if he walked away from the peeling old house? Dad wouldn't have to ask the Brewsters for food then, Jeremy thought, and he pulled at the pony's tangled mane until the coarse horsehair cut his fingers.

After the first three days, the crowd waiting at the farm had thinned out. They'd heard what news Dan had to tell. They'd sold him the food and supplies that he'd asked for, taking his pale green voucher slips as payment. Now they were waiting for the construction crews to arrive. Even Dad was waiting. He whistled while he carried water to the potato plants, and he smiled at Dan.

Dan was the water bringer. *Everyone* smiled at Dan.

It made Jeremy jealous when they were at home, but they weren't home very often. He and Dan trudged all over the scorched hills along the river. Dan talked about cities and about the Dryland beyond the fields, with its ghosts and the bones of dead towns. He told Jeremy unbelievable stories about the shrinking sea and the ice getting thicker up north, maybe getting ready to slide southward and bury the Dry. He taught Jeremy how to describe the land in numbers. He asked Jeremy to make things every day, and he laughed when Jeremy made a frog appear on Ezra's head.

Jeremy tried hard to make Dan laugh. His face and hands got scratched by the brittle scrub and his knees hurt all the time, but it was worth it. Dan never asked him outright, but he talked like Jeremy was going to come with him to the cities and the sea. Both of them understood it, and the understanding was a comfortable thing between them.

"Where did you come from?" Jeremy asked on Saturday afternoon. They were eating lunch under the same overhang where they'd stopped the first day out.

"The Corp's regional office at Bonneville."

"No, I don't mean that." Jeremy swallowed cold beans. "I mean *before* that—before the surveying. Where were you born?"

"South." Dan looked out toward the dead river. His gray eyes looked vague, like he was looking at something far away or deep inside his head.

"Everyone thought it would be a war," he said, after a while. "No one really believed that the *weather* could do us in." He gave a jerky shrug. "We came north from L.A., running from the Mexican wars and the gangs." His eyes flickered. "California was dying, and if anyone had water in the Valley, they weren't sharing, so we kept on going. You leave everything behind you when you're dying of thirst—one piece at a time. Everything." He was silent for a moment. The wind blew grit across the rocks with a soft hiss and Jeremy didn't make a sound.

"I ended up with the Corps," Dan said abruptly.

The transition from *we* to *I* cut off Jeremy's questions like a knife. He watched Dan toss a pebble down the slope. It bounced off an elk skull half-buried in drifted dust.

"I won't kid you about things." Dan tossed another pebble at the bleached skull. "If you come with me, you're going to find out that things aren't always what they should be. When you're on the road, you don't have any options. You do what it takes to stay alive. Sometimes you don't like it much, but you *do* it."

The sad-bitterness in Dan's tone scared Jeremy a little, but it didn't matter. Dan had said *if you come with me.*

If you come with me.

"Can you make a face?" Dan asked suddenly.

"I don't know." Jeremy looked into Dan's bleak, hungry eyes. "I'll try," he said uncertainly.

"She was about sixteen, with brown eyes and black hair. It was straight, like rain falling." His eyes focused on that invisible something again. "She looked a little like me, but prettier," he said. "Her nose was thin—I used to kid her about it—and she smiled a lot."

Straight black hair; thin nose . . . Jeremy shaped a face in his mind, watched it take shape in the air. No. That was *wrong.* He didn't need Dan's look of disappointment to tell him so.

"Stupid to play that kind of game." Dan laid his hand on Jeremy's shoulder. "Thanks for trying."

Jeremy shook his head, wanting to do this more than he'd ever wanted to do anything in his life. The face was wrong, but barely wrong. He could *feel* it. If he just changed it a little, maybe smoothed the forehead like *so,* widened the nose, it might be . . .

Right.

She smiled, face brimming with warmth and sadness. Jeremy stared at her, sweat stinging his eyes. She was *right* in a way that no bird or fish or animal had ever been right.

"Amy!" Dan cried brokenly. "Oh God, Amy!"

The sound of Dan's voice scared Jeremy. He felt the making slip and tried to hang on, but the face wavered, blurred, and vanished. "I'm sorry," he whispered.

Dan buried his face in his hands. That was scarier than if he'd cried or yelled. Hesitantly, Jeremy reached out and touched him.

"It's all right." Dan raised his head, drew a long breath. "You did what I asked, didn't you?" His eyes were dry as the riverbed. "I didn't know." He got up suddenly. "Let's go back." He looked down the dead valley. "I'm through here."

"You mean all through? Like you're leaving?" Jeremy forced the words through the sudden tightness in his throat.

"Yeah." Dan looked down at him. "The job's finished. I didn't expect to be here this long. I shouldn't have stayed this long." His shoulders lifted as he took a long, slow breath. "Are you coming?"

"Yes." Jeremy stood up as straight as he could. There was nothing for him here. Nothing at all. "I'm coming," he said.

"Good." Dan boosted him onto Ezra's back. "I'm leaving early," he said. "You better not tell your folks."

"I won't," Jeremy said.

★   ★   ★

No one was pumping on the bicycle frame as they plodded past. Jeremy looked up at the brown hillside, imagining it
all green with grass, like in pictures. Water would come, Dad
would be happy, and *he* would be with Dan. Mother would
cry, but she wouldn't have to protect him from Dad anymore.

The green landscape wouldn't take shape in his mind.
Ezra broke into a jouncing trot, and Jeremy had to grab the
saddle as the pony headed for the barnyard and the watertub
there.

"Mr. Greely," Dad called from the porch.

Jeremy stiffened. Dad sounded cold and mad, like when
he caught Jeremy making.

"We want to talk to you."

Mr. Brewster stepped onto the porch behind him. Rupert
and Jonathan followed, with Mr. Mendoza, Sally Brandt, and
the Deardorf boys.

Mr. Mendoza had his old deer rifle. They all looked angry.

"My brother got into town last night." Sally's voice was
shrill. "He told me about this scam he heard of back in Pen-
dleton. Seems this guy goes around to little towns pretending
to be a surveyor. He buys things with vouchers from the
Army Corps of Engineers."

"We searched your stuff." Ted Brewster held up a fistful
of white. "You carry a few spare letters, don't you?" He
opened his hand. "You're a fake," he said harshly.

The white envelopes fluttered to the dusty ground like
dead leaves. Stunned by the anger of the crowd, Jeremy
turned to Dan, waiting for him to explain, waiting for Dan to
tell them how they were wrong, waiting for him to remind
them about the *water.*

"Dan?" he whispered.

Dan looked at him finally, his head moving slowly on his
neck, and Jeremy felt his insides going numb and dead.
"Mother gave you dried apples." Jeremy swallowed, remem-

bering the tears and hope in her voice. "Dried apples are for birthdays."

For one instant, Dan's gray eyes filled with hurt. Then he looked away, turning a bland smile on the approaching adults. "I heard about some bastard doing that." He spread his hands. "But *I'm* legit." He plucked at the black insignia on his sweaty shirt.

Dad took one long step forward and smashed his fist into Dan's face. "He described you." He looked down as Dan sprawled in the dirt. "He described you real well."

Dan got up very slowly, wiping dust from his face. Blood smeared his chin. He shrugged.

They took him into town, walking around him in a loose ring. Jeremy stood in the road, watching the dust settle behind them. Even if Mr. Mendoza didn't have the gun, Dan couldn't run. The dry hills brooded on every side. Where would he run *to*? Jeremy climbed up onto the rimrock, and didn't come down until it got dark.

"I wondered about that guy," Rupert sneered as they got ready for bed that night. "Federal survey, huh? The feds couldn't even hang on to the Columbia project! I don't know how anybody could believe him."

"Hope is a tempting thing." Jeremy's mother leaned against the doorway. She hadn't scolded Jeremy for running off. "If there was any water around here, no matter how deep, someone would have drilled for it a long time ago." Her voice was tired. "I guess we all just *wanted* to hope."

Jeremy climbed onto his cot without looking at her.

"I'm sorry," she murmured. "I'm sorry for us, and I'm sorry for him, too."

"They'll *hang* him—like they did to that trucker over in La Grande."

"Shame on you, Rupert." Her voice caught a little.

Jeremy buried his face in his pillow. She was feeling sorry for him, and he didn't want anyone to feel sorry for him. I hate him, too, he thought fiercely. Why couldn't Dan have been what he said? He could have gone with Dan, *made* things for him. Now, they'd always have to pump, and he would always be an extra mouth to Dad. A *useless* mouth.

"They're gonna *hang* him," Rupert whispered to Jeremy after Mother had left. He sounded smug. "No wonder that jerk wanted *you* to help him. You're too damn dumb to figure out he was a fake!"

Jeremy pressed his face into the pillow until he could barely breathe. If he made a sound, if he moved, he'd kill Rupert. Rupert might be almost sixteen and Jeremy's hands might not work very well, but he'd kill Rupert, somehow.

Rupert was right. They were going to hang Dan. He'd seen it in their eyes when they walked up to him. It wasn't just because he'd tricked them. They hated Dan because the government, the Army Corps of Engineers, didn't *really* care about them.

No one cared. And Dan made them see it.

He lied to me, too. Jeremy burrowed deeper into the pillow, but he kept hearing Dan's sad-bitter voice. *You do what it takes to stay alive. Sometimes you don't like it much, but you do it.*

Dan hadn't lied to *him.*

Jeremy must have fallen asleep, because he woke up from a dream of the woman with the black hair. Like rain, Dan had said. Jeremy opened his eyes. His throat hurt, as if he had been crying in his sleep. Amy, Dan had cried. She was dead, whoever she had been. Dan's *we* had turned into *I.*

Rupert snored, arm hanging over the side of his mattress. The sloping roof pressed down on Jeremy, threatening to crush him, trying to smear him into dry darkness, dissolve him. Where was Dan now? In the church? Jeremy sat up, pushing against the heavy darkness, heart pounding with the knowledge of what he had to do. The house creaked softly to itself as he tiptoed down the steep stairs.

"Who's there?" his father said from the bottom of the stairway.

"Me." Jeremy froze, clutching the railing with both hands. "I . . . had to pee," he stammered. It was a feeble lie —the pot in the bedroom was never full.

"Jeremy?" His father bulked over him, a tower of shadow. "It's late. I just got back from town." He ran a thick hand across his face. "You liked Greely."

It was an accusation. "I still like him." Jeremy forced himself to stand straight. "He's not a bad man."

His father grunted, moved down a step. "He's a parasite," he said harshly. "His kind live on other people's sweat. You got to understand that. You got to understand that there's no worse crime than that."

"Isn't there?" Jeremy's voice trembled. "Who's going to share with *him*? Who's going to let him have a piece of their orchard or a field? He was just trying to live, and he didn't hurt anybody, not really . . ."

"He lied to us and he stole from us." His tone dismissed Dan, judged and sentenced him. "You get back to bed. Now!"

"No." Jeremy's knees were shaking and he clung to the railing. "If it doesn't help the crops, it's bad, isn't it? Nothing else matters to you but the land. *Nothing.*"

His father's hand swung up and Jeremy turned to flee. His knee banged the riser and he fell, crying out with the hot pain, sprawling on the steps at his father's feet.

All by itself, the firefly popped into the air between them, glowing like a hot coal.

With a hoarse cry, Dad flinched backward, his hand clenching into a fist, ready to smash him like he'd smashed Dan. He *was* scared. Dan was right. Jeremy stared up at his father through a blur of pain tears. "It's not bad!" he screamed. "It's just *me. Me!* I make things because they're pretty! Doesn't that count?" He cringed away from his father's fist.

His father hesitated, lowered his hand slowly. "No," he said in a choked voice. "It doesn't count. It doesn't count, either, that a man's just trying to stay alive. I . . . I wish it did." He stepped past Jeremy and went on up the stairs.

Jeremy listened to his slow, heavy tread on the floorboards over his head. His pulse pounded in his ears and he felt dizzy. *It doesn't count,* his father had said. *I wish it did.* Jeremy put his forehead down on his clenched fists, and his tears scalded his knuckles.

Jeremy was right. Dan was in the church basement. Yellow light glowed dimly from one of the window wells along the concrete foundation, the only light in the dark, dead town. Jeremy lay down on his stomach and peered through the glassless window. Yep. Mr. Brewster was sitting on an old pew beside a wooden door, flipping through a tattered hunting magazine by the light of a hissing gasoline lantern.

He looked wide-awake.

Jeremy looked at the sky. Was it getting light? How long until dawn? Desperate, he leaned over the cracked lip of the well. Mr. Brewster wasn't going to fall asleep. Not in time.

The firefly had scared Dad. Jeremy lay flat in the dust, face pressed against his clenched fists. Mr. Brewster didn't know about the makings, *probably* didn't, anyway. Cold balled in Jeremy's belly, so bad that he almost threw up. *Bigger* would be scarier, but bigger was harder. What if he couldn't do it?

The firefly popped into the air two feet from Mr. Brewster's magazine, big as a chicken.

"Holy shit!" Mr. Brewster's chair banged over as he scrambled to his feet. "Mother of *God,* what's *that?*" His voice sounded strange and squeaky.

Nails biting his palms, Jeremy made the firefly dart at Mr. Brewster's face. It moved sluggishly, dimming to a dull orange. Oh, God, don't let it fade! Sweat stung Jeremy's eyes.

Mr. Brewster yelled and threw his magazine at it. His footsteps pounded up the wooden stairs, and a moment later the church door thudded open. Jeremy lay flat in the dust as

Mr. Brewster ran past him. The ground felt warm, as if the earth had a fever. Sweat turned the dust on Jeremy's face to mud, and he was shaking all over. He couldn't hear Mr. Brewster's footsteps anymore.

Now!

He scrambled down through the window. A fragment of glass still stuck in the frame grazed his arm, and he landed on the broken chair. It collapsed with a terrible crash. Panting, Jeremy scrambled to his feet. Oh, God, please don't let Mr. Brewster come back. He struggled with the bolt on the storeroom door, bruising his palm. It slid back, and he pushed the heavy door open.

Dan was sitting on the floor between shelves of musty hymnals and folded choir robes. The yellow light made his skin look tawny brown, like the dust. His face was swollen and streaked with dried blood.

"Jeremy?" Hope flared in Dan's eyes.

"Hurry." Jeremy grabbed his arm.

Dan staggered to his feet and followed Jeremy up the steps, treading on his heels. Someone shouted behind them and Jeremy's heart lurched.

"That way." He pointed.

Dan threw an arm around him and ran, half carrying Jeremy as they ducked behind the dark Exxon station. They scrambled under the board fence in the back, lay flat while someone ran and panted past. Mr. Brewster? This was like a scary game of hide-and-seek. Gray banded the eastern horizon as Jeremy led Dan across the dust main street, listening for footsteps, stumbling on the rough pavement. They turned left by the boarded-up restaurant, cut through a yard full of drifted dust, dead weeds, and a gasless car.

Jeremy had left Ezra tethered behind the last house on the street. The pony gave a low, growling whinny as they hurried up. Dan stroked his nose to quiet him, his eyes running over the lumpy bulges of the pack.

"It's all there, food, water, and everything," Jeremy panted. "It's not a very good job—I didn't know how to fix a pack. The ground's pretty hard along the river, so you won't leave many tracks. Willow creekbed'll take you way south. It's the first creekbed past the old feed mill. You can't miss it."

"I thought you were coming with me." Dan looked down at Jeremy.

"I was." Jeremy looked at the old nylon daypack he'd left on the ground beside Ezra. It wasn't very heavy because he didn't have much. "I changed my mind."

"You can't." Dan's fingers dug into his shoulders. "They'll know you let me out. What'll happen then?"

"I don't know." Jeremy swallowed a lump of fear. His father was part of the land, linked to it. If the land dried up and died, Dad would die. "I got to stay," he whispered.

"Why? You think you'll make peace with your father?" Dan shook him—one short, sharp jerk that made Jeremy's teeth snap together. "You've got magic in your hands. Real magic. You think that's ever going to matter to *him*?"

"I don't know." Tears clogged Jeremy's nose, burned his eyes.

"Hell, my own choices haven't turned out so hot. Who am I to tell you what you should do?" Dan wiped the tears away, his fingers rough and dry on Jeremy's face. "Just don't let them kill your magic." He shook Jeremy again, gently this time. "He needs it. They *all* need it." He sighed. "And I'd better get going. Keep making things, kid." He squeezed Jeremy's shoulder hard, grabbed Ezra's lead rope, and walked away into the fading night.

Jeremy stood still, the last of his tears drying on his face, listening to Ezra's muffled hoofbeats fade in the distance. He listened until he could hear nothing but the dry whisper of the morning breeze, then he started back. He thought about cutting across the dun hills and down through the riverbed to get home. Instead, his feet carried him back into town and he let them.

They might have been waiting for him in front of the church—Mr. Brewster, Sally Brandt, Mr. Mendoza and . . . Dad. Jeremy faltered as they all turned to stare at him, wishing in one terrible, frightened instant that he had gone with Dan after all. They looked at him like they had looked at Dan yesterday, hard and cold. Mr. Brewster walked to meet him, slow and stifflegged, and Jeremy wondered suddenly if they'd hang *him* instead of Dan.

Maybe. It was there, in their faces, back behind their cold eyes.

"You little snot." Mr. Brewster's hand closed on Jeremy's shirt, balling up the fabric, lifting him a little off his feet. "You let Greely out! I saw you. Where's he headed?"

"I don't know," Jeremy said.

"Like *hell*." Brewster slapped him.

Red-and-black light exploded behind Jeremy's eyelids, and his mouth filled with a harsh, metallic taste. He fell, hard and hurting, onto his knees, dizzy, eyes blurred with tears, belly full of sickness.

"Knock it off, Ted."

Dad—amazingly, *Dad*—was lifting him to his feet, hands under his arms, gentle, almost.

"*I* lay hands on my kids," he said harshly. "No one else."

"He knows where that bastard's headed!" Mr. Brewster was breathing heavy and fast. "You beat it out of him or *I* do."

"He said he doesn't know. That's the end of it, you hear me?"

Jeremy breathed slow, trying not to throw up. Silence hung between the two men, heavy and hot. It made the air feel thick and hard to breathe. Dad was angry, but not at him. He was angry at Mr. Brewster. For hitting him? Jeremy held his breath, tasting blood on his swelling lip, afraid to look up.

"You talk pretty high and mighty," Mr. Brewster said

softly. "Considering you had to come crawling for help last winter. Seems like you ought to shut up."

Jeremy felt his father jerk, as if Mr. Brewster had kicked him. He felt his father's arms tremble and held his breath, wondering if Dad was going to let go, turn his back and walk away.

"Seems like *we* all pitched in, when mice got into *your* seed stock a few years back," Dad said quietly.

Mr. Brewster made a small, harsh sound.

"Come *on*, Ted!" Sally's shrill exasperation shattered the tension of the moment. "While you're standing around arguing, Greely's making tracks for Boardman."

"We got to split up," Mr. Mendoza chimed in.

Legs spread, shoulders hunched, Mr. Brewster glowered at Jeremy. Abruptly, he spun his heel. "Shit." He jerked his head at Mr. Mendoza. "I bet the bastard headed west," he snarled. "We'll go down the riverbed, cut his tracks." He stalked off down the street with Mr. Mendoza.

Sally Brandt pushed tousled hair out of her face, sighed. "I'll go wake up the Deardorfs," she said. "We'll spread north and east. You can take the south."

He felt his father's body move a little, as if he had nodded at her. Jeremy stared down at the dust between his feet, heart pounding so hard that it felt like it was going to burst through his ribs. He felt Dad's hands lift from his shoulders, cringed a little as his father moved around in front of him, blocking the rising sun, but all he did was lift Jeremy's chin, until he had to meet his father's eyes.

"I thought you'd gone with him," he said.

Jeremy looked at his father's weathered face. It looked like the hills, all folded into dun gullies—not angry, not sad, just old and dry.

"If we find Greely, we have to hang him," Dad said heavily. "Right or wrong, we voted—you got to know that, Son."

"I was going to go." Jeremy swallowed, tasted dust. "You had to ask for food," he whispered. "Because of me."

His father's face twitched, as if something hurt him inside.

Without warning, the firefly popped into the air between them again, pale this time, a flickering shadow in the harsh morning light. Jeremy sucked in his breath, snuffed it out as his father flinched away from it.

"I'm sorry," he cried. "I didn't *mean* to make it, it just . . . happened. It makes Rita Menendez laugh." He took a deep, hurting breath. "I won't do it anymore," he whispered, struggling to get the words past the tightness in his throat. "Not ever."

"Do it again." His father's hand clamped down on Jeremy's shoulder. "Right now."

Trembling, afraid to look at his father's face, Jeremy made the firefly appear again.

His father stared at it, breathing hard. With a shudder, he thrust his fingers into the firefly, yanked his hand back as if it had burned him. "It scares me." His voice was a harsh whisper. "I don't understand it." He stared at his hand, closed his fingers slowly into a fist. "It's like this crazy drought." His voice shook. "I don't understand that, neither." He looked at Jeremy suddenly. "Not everyone's going to laugh. You scared the shit out of Ted. He ain't going to forgive you for that."

Dad talked like he could keep on making things. Jeremy sneaked a look at him, heart beating fast again, throat hurting.

"Hell," his father said softly. "I don't have any answers. Maybe there *aren't* any answers anymore—no good ones, anyway." He met Jeremy's eyes. "I've got to look south for Greely," he said. "Which way do you think he headed? Down Willow creekbed—or by the main road to La Grande?"

Jeremy hesitated for a moment, then straightened his shoulders with a jerk. "I think he went down the main road," he said, and held his breath.

His father shaded his eyes, stared at the dun fold of Willow creekbed in the distance. "There aren't any good answers." He sighed and put his hand on his son's shoulder. "We'll look for Greely on the main road," he said.

COMPUTER FRIENDLY

Eileen Gunn

Holding her dad's hand, Elizabeth went up the limestone steps to the testing center. As she climbed, she craned her neck to read the words carved in pink granite over the top of the door: *Francis W. Parker School.* Above them was a banner made of gray cement that read *Health, Happiness, Success.*

"This building is old," said Elizabeth. "It was built before the war."

"Pay attention to where you're going, punkin," said her dad. "You almost ran into that lady there."

Inside, the entrance hall was dark and cool. A dim yellow glow came through the shades on the tall windows.

As Elizabeth walked across the polished floor, her footsteps echoed lightly down the corridors that led off to either side. She and her father went down the hallway to the testing room. An old, beat-up, army-green query box sat on a table outside the door.

"Ratherford, Elizabeth Ratherford," said her father to the box. "Age seven, computer-friendly, smart as a whip."

"We'll see," said the box with a chuckle. It had a gruff, teasing, grandfatherly voice. "We'll just see about *that*, young lady." What a jolly interface, thought Elizabeth. She watched as the classroom door swung open. "You go right along in there, and we'll see just how smart you are." It chuckled again, then it spoke to Elizabeth's dad. "You come back for her at three, sir. She'll be all ready and waiting for you, bright as a little watermelon."

This was going to be fun, thought Elizabeth. Nothing to do all day except show how smart she was.

Her father knelt in front of her and smoothed her hair back from her face. "You try real hard on these tests, punkin. You show them just how talented and clever you really are, okay?" Elizabeth nodded. "And you be on your best behavior." He gave her a hug and a pat on the rear.

Inside the testing room were dozens of other seven-year-olds, sitting in rows of tiny chairs with access boxes in front of them. Glancing around the room, Elizabeth realized that she had never seen so many children together all at once. There were only ten in her weekly socialization class. It was sort of overwhelming.

The monitors called everyone to attention and told them to put on their headsets and ask their boxes for Section One.

Elizabeth followed directions, and she found that all the interfaces were strange—they were friendly enough, but none of them were the programs she worked with at home. The first part of the test was the multiple-choice exam. The problems, at least, were familiar to Elizabeth—she'd practiced for this test all her life, it seemed. There were word games, number games, and games in which she had to rotate little boxes in her head. She knew enough to skip the hardest until she'd worked her way through the whole test. There were only a couple of problems left to do when the system told her to stop and the box went all gray.

The monitors led the whole room full of kids in jumping-jack exercises for five minutes. Then everyone sat down again and a new test came up in the box. This one seemed very easy, but it wasn't one she'd ever done before. It consisted of a series of very detailed pictures; she was supposed to make up a story about each picture. Well, she could do that. The first picture showed a child and a lot of different kinds of animals. "Once upon a time there was a little girl who lived all alone in the forest with her friends the skunk, the wolf, the bear, and the lion. . . ." A beep sounded every so often to tell her to end one story and begin another. Elizabeth really enjoyed telling the stories, and was sorry when that part of the test was over.

But the next exercise was almost as interesting. She was to read a series of short stories and answer questions about them. Not the usual questions about what happened in the story—these were harder. "Is it fair to punish a starving cat for stealing?" "Should people do good deeds for strangers?" "Why is it important for everyone to learn to obey?"

When this part was over, the monitors took the class down the hall to the big cafeteria, where there were lots of other seven-year-olds, who had been taking tests in other rooms.

Elizabeth was amazed at the number and variety of children in the cafeteria. She watched them as she stood in line for her milk and sandwich. Hundreds of kids, all exactly as old as she was. Tall and skinny, little and fat; curly hair, straight hair, and hair that was frizzy or held up with ribbons or cut into strange patterns against the scalp; skin that was light brown like Elizabeth's, chocolate brown, almost black, pale pink, freckled, and all the colors in between. Some of the kids were all dressed up in fancy clothes; others were wearing patched pants and old shirts.

When she got her snack, Elizabeth's first thought was to find someone who looked like herself, and sit next to her. But then a freckled boy with dark, nappy hair smiled at her in a very friendly way. He looked at her feet and nodded. "Nice shoes," he said. She sat down on the empty seat next to him, suddenly aware of her red maryjanes with the embroidered flowers. She was pleased that they had been noticed, and a little embarrassed.

"Let me see *your* shoes," she said, unwrapping her sandwich.

He stuck his feet out. He was wearing pink plastic sneakers with hologram pictures of a missile gantry on the toes. When he moved his feet, they launched a defensive counterattack.

"Oh, neat." Elizabeth nodded appreciatively and took a bite of the sandwich. It was filled with something yellow that tasted okay.

A little tiny girl with long, straight black hair was sitting on the other side of the table from them. She put one foot up on the table. "I got shoes, too," she said. "Look." Her shoes were black patent, with straps. Elizabeth and the freckled boy both admired them politely. Elizabeth thought that the little girl was very daring to put her shoe right up on the table. It was certainly an interesting way to enter a conversation.

"My name is Sheena and I can spit," said the little girl. "Watch." Sure enough, she could spit really well. The spit hit the beige wall several meters away, just under the mirror, and slid slowly down.

"I can spit, too," said the freckled boy. He demonstrated, hitting the wall a little lower than Sheena had.

"I can *learn* to spit," said Elizabeth.

"All right there, no spitting!" said a monitor firmly. "Now, you take a napkin and clean that up." It pointed to Elizabeth.

"She didn't do it, I did," said Sheena. "I'll clean it up."

"I'll help," said Elizabeth. She didn't want to claim credit for Sheena's spitting ability, but she liked being mistaken for a really good spitter.

The monitor watched as they wiped the wall, then took

their thumbprints. "You three settle down now. I don't want any more spitting." It moved away. All three of them were quiet for a few minutes, and munched on their sandwiches.

"What's your name?" said Sheena suddenly. "My name is Sheena."

"Elizabeth."

"Lizardbreath. That's a funny name," said Sheena.

"My name is Oginga," said the freckled boy.

"That's *really* a funny name," said Sheena.

"You think everybody's name is funny," said Oginga. "Sheena-Teena-Peena."

"I can tap-dance, too," said Sheena, who had recognized that it was time to change the subject. "These are my tap shoes." She squirmed around to wave her feet in the air briefly, then swung them back under the table.

She moves more than anyone I've ever seen, thought Elizabeth.

"Wanna see me shuffle off to Buffalo?" asked Sheena.

A bell rang at the front of the room, and the three of them looked up. A monitor was speaking.

"Quiet! Everybody quiet, now! Finish up your lunch quickly, those of you who are still eating, and put your wrappers in the wastebaskets against the wall. Then line up on the west side of the room. The west side. . . ."

The children were taken to the restroom after lunch. It was grander than any bathroom Elizabeth had ever seen, with walls made of polished red granite, lots of little stalls with toilets in them, and a whole row of sinks. The sinks were lower than the sink at home, and so were the toilets. Even the mirrors were just the right height for kids.

It was funny because there were no stoppers in the sinks, so you couldn't wash your hands in a proper sink of water. Sheena said she could make the sink fill up, and Oginga dared her to do it, so she took off her sweater and put it in the sink, and sure enough, it filled up with water and started to overflow, and then she couldn't get the sweater out of it, so she called a monitor over. "This sink is overflowing," she said, as if it were all the sink's fault. A group of children stood around and watched while the monitor fished the sweater from the drain and wrung it out.

"That's mine!" said Sheena, as if she had dropped it by mistake. She grabbed it away from the monitor, shook it, and nodded knowingly to Elizabeth. "It dries real fast." The monitor wanted thumbprints from Sheena and Elizabeth and everyone who watched.

The monitors then took the children to the auditorium, and led the whole group in singing songs and playing games, which Elizabeth found only moderately interesting. She would have preferred to learn to spit. At one o'clock, a monitor announced it was time to go back to the classrooms, and all the children should line up by the door.

Elizabeth and Sheena and Oginga pushed into the same line together. There were so many kids that there was a long wait while they all lined up and the monitors moved up and down the lines to make them straight.

"Are you going to go to the Asia Center?" asked Sheena. "My mom says I can probably go to the Asia Center tomorrow, because I'm so fidgety."

Elizabeth didn't know what the Asia Center was, but she didn't want to look stupid. "I don't know. I'll have to ask my dad." She turned to Oginga, who was behind her. "Are you going to the Asia Center?"

"What's the Asia Center?" asked Oginga.

Elizabeth looked back at Sheena, waiting to hear her answer.

"Where we go to sleep," Sheena said. "My mom says it doesn't hurt."

"I got my own room," said Oginga.

"It's not like your room," Sheena explained. "You go there, and you go to sleep, and your parents get to try again."

"What do they try?" asked Elizabeth. "Why do you have to go to sleep?"

"You go to sleep so they have some peace and quiet," said Sheena. "So you're not in their way."

"But what do they try?" repeated Elizabeth.

"I bet they try more of that stuff that they do when they think you're asleep," said Oginga. Sheena snorted and started to giggle, and then Oginga started to giggle and he snorted too, and the more one giggled and snorted, the more the other did. Pretty soon Elizabeth was giggling too, and the three of them were helplessly choking, behind great hiccoughing gulps of noise.

The monitor rolled by then and told them to be quiet and move on to their assigned classrooms. That broke the spell of their giggling, and, subdued, they moved ahead in the line. All the children filed quietly out of the auditorium and walked slowly down the halls. When Elizabeth came to her classroom, she shrugged her shoulders at Oginga and Sheena and jerked her head to one side. "I go in here," she whispered.

"See ya at the Asia Center," said Sheena.

The rest of the tests went by quickly, though Elizabeth didn't think they were as much fun as in the morning. The afternoon tests were more physical; she pulled at joysticks and tried to push buttons quickly on command. They tested her hearing and even made her sing to the computer. Elizabeth didn't like to do things fast, and she didn't like to sing.

When it was over, the monitors told the children they could go now, their parents were waiting for them at the front of the school. Elizabeth looked for Oginga and Sheena as she left, but children from the other classrooms were not in the halls. Her dad was waiting for her out front, as he had said he would be.

Elizabeth called to him to get his attention. He had just come off work, and she knew he would be sort of confused. They wiped their secrets out of his brain before he logged off of the system, and sometimes they took a little other stuff with it by mistake, so he might not be too sure about his name, or where he lived.

On the way home, she told him about her new friends. "They don't sound as though they would do very well at their lessons, princess," said her father. "But it does sound as if you had an interesting time at lunch." Elizabeth pulled his hand to guide him onto the right street. He'd be okay in an hour or so—anything important usually came back pretty fast.

When they got home, her dad went into the kitchen to start dinner, and Elizabeth played with her dog, Brownie. Brownie didn't live with them anymore because his brain was being used to help control data traffic in the network. Between rush hours, Elizabeth would call him up on the system and run simulations in which she plotted the trajectory of a ball and he plotted an interception of it.

They ate dinner when her mom logged off work. Elizabeth's parents believed it was very important for the family to all eat together in the evening, and her mom had custom-made connectors that stretched all the way into the dining room. Even though she didn't really eat anymore, her local I/O was always extended to the table at dinnertime.

After dinner, Elizabeth got ready for bed. She could hear her father in his office, asking his mail for the results of her test that day. When he came into her room to tuck her in, she could tell he had good news for her.

"Did you wash behind your ears, punkin?" he asked. Elizabeth figured that this was a ritual question, since she was unaware that washing behind her ears was more useful than washing anywhere else.

She gave the correct response: "Yes, Daddy." She understood that, whether she washed or not, giving the expected answer was an important part of the ritual. Now it was her turn to ask a question. "Did you get the results of my tests, Daddy?"

"We sure did, princess," her father replied. "You did very well on them."

Elizabeth was pleased, but not too surprised. "What about my new friends, Daddy? How did they do?"

"I don't know about that, punkin. They don't send us everybody's scores, just yours."

"I want to be with them when I go to the Asia Center."

Elizabeth could tell by the look on her father's face that she'd said something wrong. "The what? Where did you hear about that?" he asked sharply.

"My friend Sheena told me about it. She said she was going to the Asia Center tomorrow," said Elizabeth.

"Well, *she* might be going there, but that's not anyplace you're going." Her dad sounded very strict. *"You're* going to continue your studies, young lady, and someday you'll be an important executive like your mother. That's clear from your test results. I don't want to hear any talk about you doing anything else. Or about this Sheena."

"What does Mommy do, Daddy?"

"She's a processing center, sweetheart, that talks directly to the CPU. She uses her brain to control important information and tell the rest of the computer what to do. And she gives the whole system common sense." He sat down on the edge of the bed, and Elizabeth could tell that she was going to get what her dad called an "explanatory chat."

"You did so well on your test today that maybe it's time we told you something about what you might be doing when you get a little older." He pulled the blanket up a little bit closer to her chin and turned the sheet down evenly over it.

"It'll be a lot like studying, or like taking that test today," he continued. "Except you'll be hardwired into the network, just like your mom, so you won't have to get up and move around. You'll be able to do anything and go anywhere in your head."

"Will I be able to play with Brownie?"

"Of course, sweetheart, you'll be able to call him up just like you did tonight. It's important that you play. It keeps you healthy and alert, and it's good for Brownie, too."

"Will I be able to call you and Mommy?"

"Well, princess, that depends on what kind of job you're

doing. You just might be so busy and important that you don't have time to call us."

Like Bobby, she thought. Her parents didn't talk much about her brother, Bobby. He had done well on his tests too. Now he was a milintel cyborg with go–nogo authority. He never called home, and her parents didn't call him either.

"Being an executive is sort of like playing games all the time," her father added, when Elizabeth didn't say anything. "And the harder you work right now, the better you do on your tests, the more fun you'll have later."

He tucked the covers up around her neck again. "Now you go to sleep, so you can work your best tomorrow, okay, princess?" Elizabeth nodded. Her dad kissed her good night, and poked at the covers again. He got up. "Good night, sweetheart," he said, and he left the room.

Elizabeth lay in bed for a while, trying to get to sleep. The door was open so that the light would come in from the hall, and she could hear her parents talking downstairs.

Her dad, she knew, would be reading the news at his access box, as he did every evening. Her mom would be tidying up noise-damaged data in the household module. She didn't have to do that, but she said it calmed her nerves.

Listening to the rise and fall of their voices, she heard her name. What were they saying? Was it about the test? She got up out of bed, crept to the door of her room. They stopped talking. Could they hear her? She was very quiet. Standing in the doorway, she was only a few feet from the railing at the top of the staircase, and the sounds came up very clearly from the living room below.

"Just the house settling," said her father, after a moment. "She's asleep by now." Ice cubes clinked in a glass.

"Well," said her mother, resuming the conversation, "I don't know what they think they're doing, putting euthanasable children in the testing center with children like Elizabeth." There was a bit of a whine behind her mother's voice. RF interference, perhaps. "Just talking with that Sheena could skew her test results for years. I have half a mind to call the net executive and ask it what it thinks it's doing."

"Now, calm down, honey," said her dad. Elizabeth heard his chair squeak as he turned away from his access box toward the console that housed her mother. "You don't want the exec to think we're questioning its judgment. Maybe this was part of the test."

"Well, you'd think they'd let us know, so we could prepare her for it."

Was Sheena part of the test? wondered Elizabeth. She'd have to ask the system what "euthanasable" meant.

"Look at her scores," said her father. "She did much better than the first two on verbal skills—her programs are on the right track there. And her physical aptitude scores are even lower than Bobby's."

"That's a blessing," said her mother. "It held Christopher back, right from the beginning, being so active." Who's Christopher? wondered Elizabeth.

Her mother continued. "But it was a mistake, putting him in with the euthana—"

"Her socialization scores were okay, but right on the edge," added her dad, talking right over her mother. "Maybe they should reduce her class time to twice a month. Look at how she sat right down with those children at lunch."

"Anyway, she passed," said her mother. "They're moving her up a level instead of taking her now."

"Maybe because she didn't initiate the contact, but she *was* able to handle it when it occurred. Maybe that's what they want for the execs."

Elizabeth shifted her weight, and the floor squeaked again.

Her father called up to her, "Elizabeth, are you up?"

"Just getting a drink of water, Daddy." She walked to the bathroom and drew a glass of water from the tap. She drank a little and poured the rest down the drain.

Then she went back to her room and climbed into bed.

Her parents were talking more quietly now, and she could hear only little bits of what they were saying.

". . . mistake about Christopher. . . ." Her mother's voice.

". . . putting that other little girl to sleep forever. . . ." Her dad.

". . . worth it? . . ." Her mother again.

Their voices slowed down and fell away, and Elizabeth dreamed of eerie white things in glass jars, of Brownie, still a dog, all furry and fetching a ball, and of Sheena, wearing a sparkly costume and tap-dancing very fast. She fanned her hands out to her sides and turned around in a circle, tapping faster and faster.

Then Sheena began to run down like a wind-up toy. She went limp and dropped to the floor. Brownie sniffed at her, and the white things in the jars watched. Elizabeth was afraid, but she didn't know why. She grabbed Sheena's shoulders and tried to rouse her.

"Don't let me fall asleep," Sheena murmured, but she dozed off even as Elizabeth shook her.

"Wake up! Wake up!" Elizabeth's own words pulled her out of her dream. She sat up in bed. The house was quiet, except for the sound of her father snoring in the other room.

Sheena needed her help, thought Elizabeth, but she wasn't really sure why. Very quietly, she slipped out of bed. On the other side of her room, her terminal was waiting for her, humming faintly.

When she put the headset on, she saw her familiar animal friends: a gorilla, a bird, and a pig. Each was a node that enabled her to communicate with other parts of the system. Elizabeth had given them names.

Facing Sam, the crow, she called her dog. Sam transmitted the signal, and was replaced by Brownie, who was barking. That meant his brain was routing information, and she couldn't get through.

What am I doing, anyway? Elizabeth asked herself. As

she thought, a window irised open in the center of her vision, and there appeared the face of a boy of about eleven or twelve. "Hey, Elizabeth, what are you doing up at this hour?" It was the sysop on duty in her sector.

"My dog was crying."

The sysop laughed. "Your dog was crying? That's the first time I've ever heard anybody say something like that." He shook his head at her.

"He was so crying. Even if he wasn't crying out loud, I heard him, and I came over to see what was the matter. Now he's busy and I can't get through."

The sysop stopped laughing. "Sorry. I didn't mean to make fun of you. I had a dog once, before I came here, and they took him for the system, too."

"Do you call him up?"

"Well, not anymore. I don't have time. I used to, though. He was a golden Lab. . . ." Then the boy shook his head sternly and said, "But you should be in bed."

"Can't I stay until Brownie is free again? Just a few more minutes?"

"Well, maybe a couple minutes more. But then you gotta go to bed for sure. I'll be back to check. Good night, Elizabeth."

"Good night," she said, but the window had already closed.

Wow, thought Elizabeth. That worked. She had never told a really complicated lie before and was surprised that it had gone over so well. It seemed to be mostly a matter of convincing yourself that what you said was true.

But right now, she had an important problem to solve, and she wasn't even exactly sure what it was. If she could get into the files for Sheena and Oginga, maybe she could find out what was going on. Then maybe she could change the results on their tests or move them to her socialization group or something. . . .

If she could just get through to Brownie, she knew he

could help her. After a few minutes, the flood of data washed away, and the dog stopped barking. "Here, Brownie!" she called. He wagged his tail and looked happy to see her.

She told Brownie her problem, and he seemed to understand her. "Can you get it, Brownie?"

He gave a little bark, like he did when she plotted curves. "Okay, go get it."

Brownie ran away real fast, braked to a halt, and seemed to be digging. This wasn't what he was really doing, of course, it was just the way Elizabeth's interface interpreted Brownie's brain waves. In just a few seconds, Brownie came trotting back with the records from yesterday's tests in his mouth.

But when Elizabeth examined them, her heart sank. There were four Sheenas and fifteen Ogingas. But then she looked more carefully, and noticed that most of the identifying information didn't fit her Sheena and Oginga. There was only one of each that was the right height, with the right color hair.

When she read the information, she felt bad again. Oginga had done all right on the test, but they wanted to use him for routine processing right away, kind of like Brownie. Sheena, as Elizabeth's mother had suggested, had failed the personality profile and was scheduled for the euthanasia center the next afternoon at two o'clock. There was that word again: *euthanasia.* Elizabeth didn't like the sound of it.

"Here, Brownie." Her dog looked up at her with a glint in his eye. "Now listen to me. We're going to play with this stuff just a little, and then I want you to take it and put it back where you got it. Okay, Brownie?"

The window irised open again and the sysop reappeared. "Elizabeth, what do you think you're doing?" he said. "You're not supposed to have access to this data."

Elizabeth thought for a minute. Then she figured she was caught red-handed, so she might as well ask for his advice. So she explained her problem, all about her new friends and how

Oginga was going to be put in the system like Brownie, and Sheena was going to be taken away somewhere.

"They said she would go to the euthanasia center, and I'm not real sure what that is," said Elizabeth. "But I don't think it's good."

"Let me look it up," said the sysop. He paused for a second, then he looked worried. "They want my ID before they'll tell me what it means. I don't want to get in trouble. Forget it."

"Well, what can I do to help my friends?" she asked.

"Gee," said the sysop. "It's a tough one. The way you were doing it, they'd catch you for sure, just like I did. It looks like a little kid got at it."

I am a little kid, thought Elizabeth, but she didn't say anything.

I need help, she thought. But who could she go to? She turned to the sysop. "I want to talk to my brother Bobby, in milintel. Can you put me through to him?"

"I don't know," said the sysop, "but I'll ask the mailer demon." He irised shut for a second, then opened again. "The mailer demon says it's no skin off his nose, but he doesn't think you ought to."

"How come?" asked Elizabeth.

"He says it's not your brother anymore. He says you'll be sorry."

"I want to talk to him anyway," said Elizabeth.

The sysop nodded, and his window winked shut just as another irised open. An older boy who looked kind of like Elizabeth herself stared out. His tongue darted rapidly out between his lips, keeping them slightly wet. His pale eyes, unblinking, stared into hers.

"Begin," said the boy. "You have sixty seconds."

"Bobby?" said Elizabeth.

"True. Begin," said the boy.

"Bobby, um, I'm your sister Elizabeth."

The boy just looked at her, the tip of his tongue moving

rapidly. She wanted to hide from him, but she couldn't pull her eyes from his. She didn't want to tell him her story, but she could feel words filling her throat. She moved new words forward, before the others could burst out.

"Log off!" she yelled. "Log off!"

She was in her bedroom, drenched in sweat, the sound of her own voice ringing in her ears. Had she actually yelled? The house was quiet, her father still snoring. She probably hadn't made any noise.

She was very scared, but she knew she had to go back in there. She hoped that her brother was gone. She waited a couple of minutes, then logged on.

Whew. Just her animals. She called the sysop, who irised on, looking nervous.

"If you want to do that again, Elizabeth, don't go through me, huh?" He shuddered.

"I'm sorry," she said. "But I can't do this by myself. Do you know anybody that can help?"

"Maybe we ought to ask Norton," said the sysop after a minute.

"Who's Norton?"

"He's this old utility I found that nobody uses much anymore," said the sysop. "He's kind of grotty, but he helps me out." He took a breath. "Hey, Norton!" he yelled, real loud. Of course, it wasn't really yelling, but that's what it seemed like to Elizabeth.

Instantly, another window irised open, and a skinny middle-aged man leaned out of the window so far that Elizabeth thought he was going to fall out, and yelled back, just as loud, "Don't bust your bellows. I can hear you."

He was wearing a striped vest over a dirty undershirt and had a squashed old porkpie hat on his head. This wasn't anyone that Elizabeth had ever seen in the system before.

The man looked at Elizabeth and jerked his head in her direction. "Who's the dwarf?"

The sysop introduced Elizabeth and explained her problem to Norton. Norton didn't look impressed. "What d'ya want me to do about it, kid?"

"Come on, Norton," said the sysop. "You can figure it out. Give us a hand."

"Jeez, kid, it's practically four o'clock in the morning. I gotta get my beauty rest, y'know. Plus, now you've got milintel involved, it's a real mess. They'll be back, sure as houses."

The sysop just looked at him. Elizabeth looked at Norton, too. She tried to look patient and helpless, because that always helped with her dad, but she really didn't know if that would work on this weird old program.

"Y'know, there ain't much that you or me can do in the system that they won't find out about, kids," said Norton.

"Isn't there somebody who can help?" asked Elizabeth.

"Well, there's the Chickenheart. There's not much that it can't do, when it wants to. We could go see the Chickenheart."

"Who's the Chickenheart?" asked Elizabeth.

"The Chickenheart's where the system began." Of course Elizabeth knew that story—about the networks of nerve fibers organically woven into great convoluted mats, a mammoth supercortex that had stored the original programs, before processing was distributed to satellite brains. Her own system told her the tale sometimes before her nap.

"You mean the original core is still there?" said the sysop, surprised. "You never told me that, Norton."

"Lot of things I ain't told you, kid." Norton scratched his chest under his shirt. "Listen. If we go see the Chickenheart, and *if* it wants to help, it can figure out what to do for your friends. But you gotta know that this is a big deal. The Chickenheart's a busy guy, and this ain't one-hunnert-percent safe."

"Are you sure you want to do it, Elizabeth?" asked the sysop. "I wouldn't."

"How come it's not safe?" asked Elizabeth. "Is he mean?"

"Nah," said Norton. "A little strange, maybe, not mean. But di'n't I tell you the Chickenheart's been around for a while? You know what that means? It means you got yer intermittents, you got yer problems with feedback, runaway processes, what have you. It means the Chickenheart's got a lot of frayed connections, if you get what I mean. Sometimes the old C.H. just goes chaotic on you." Norton smiled, showing yellow teeth. "Plus you got the chance there's someone listening in. The netexec, for instance. Now there's someone I wouldn't want to catch me up to no mischief. Nossir. Not if I was you."

"Why not?" asked Elizabeth.

"Because that's sure curtains for you, kid. The netexec don't ask no questions, he don't check to see if you maybe could be repaired. You go bye-bye and you don't come back."

Like Sheena, thought Elizabeth. "Does he listen in often?" she asked.

"Never has," said Norton. "Not yet. Don't even know the Chickenheart's there, far as I can tell. Always a first time, though."

"I want to talk to the Chickenheart," said Elizabeth, although she wasn't sure she wanted anything of the kind, after her last experience.

"You got it," said Norton. "This'll just take a second."

Suddenly all the friendly animals disappeared, and Elizabeth felt herself falling very hard and fast along a slippery blue line in the dark. The line glowed neon blue at first, then changed to fuchsia, then sulfur yellow. She knew that Norton was falling with her, but she couldn't see him. Against the dark background, his shadow moved with hers, black, and opalescent as an oilslick.

They arrived somewhere moist and warm. The Chickenheart pulsated next to them, nutrients swishing through its external tubing. It was huge, and wetly organic. Elizabeth felt slightly sick.

"Oh, turn it off, for chrissake," said Norton, with exasperation. "It's just me and a kid."

The monstrous creature vanished, and a cartoon rabbit with impossibly tall ears and big dewy brown eyes appeared in its place. It looked at Norton, raised an eyebrow, cocked an ear in his direction, and took a huge, noisy bite out of the carrot it was holding.

"Gimme a break," said Norton.

The bunny was replaced by a tall, overweight man in his sixties wearing a rumpled white linen suit. He held a small, paddle-shaped fan, which he slowly moved back and forth. "Ah, Mr. Norton," he said. "Hot enough for you, sir?"

"We got us a problem here, Chick," said Norton. He looked over at Elizabeth and nodded. "You tell him about it, kid."

First she told him about her brother. "Nontrivial, young lady," said the Chickenheart. "Nontrivial, but easy enough to fix. Let me take care of it right now." He went rigid and quiet for a few seconds, as though frozen in time. Then he was back. "Now, then, young lady," he said. "We'll talk if you like."

So Elizabeth told the Chickenheart about Sheena and Oginga, about the testing center and the wet sweater and the monitor telling her to clean up the spit. Even though she didn't have to say a word, she told him everything, and she was sure that if he wanted to come up with a solution, he could do it.

The Chickenheart seemed surprised to hear about the euthanasia center, and especially surprised that Sheena was going to be sent there. He addressed Norton. "I know I've been out of touch, but I find this hard to believe. Mr. Norton, have you any conception of how difficult it can be to obtain components like this? Let me investigate the situation." His face went quiet for a second, then came back. "By gad, sir, it's true," he said to Norton. "They say they're optimizing for predictability. It's a mistake, sir, let me tell you. Things are too predictable here already. Same old ideas churning around and around. A few more components like that Sheena, things might get interesting again.

"I want to look at their records." He paused for a moment, then continued talking.

"Ah, yes, yes, I want that Sheena right away, sir," he said to Norton. "An amazing character. Oginga, too—not as gonzo as the girl, but he has a brand of aggressive curiosity we can put to use, sir. And there are forty-six others with similar personality profiles scheduled for euthanasia today at two." His face went quiet again.

"What is he doing?" Elizabeth asked Norton.

"Old Chickenheart's got his hooks into everythin'," Norton replied. "He just reaches along those pathways, faster'n you can think, and does what he wants. The altered data will look like it's been there all along, and ain't nobody can prove anythin' different."

"Done and done, Mr. Norton." The Chickenheart was back.

"Thank you, Mr. Chickenheart," said Elizabeth, remembering her manners. "What's going to happen to Sheena and Oginga now?"

"Well, young lady, we're going to bring your friends right into the system, sort of like the sysop, but without, shall we say, official recognition. We'll have Mr. Norton here keep an eye on them. They'll be our little surprises, eh? Timebombs that we've planted. They can explore the system, learn what's what, what they can get away with and what they can't. Rather like I do."

"What will they do?" asked Elizabeth.

"That's a good question, my dear," said the Chickenheart. "They'll have to figure it out for themselves. Maybe they'll put together a few new solutions to some old problems, or create a few new problems to keep us on our toes.

One way or the other, I'm sure they'll liven up the old home-stead."

"But what about me?" asked Elizabeth.

"Well, Miss Elizabeth, what about you? Doesn't look to me as though you have any cause to worry. You passed your tests yesterday with flying colors. You can just go right on being a little girl, and someday you'll have a nice, safe job as an executive. Maybe you'll even become netexec, who knows? I wiped just a tiny bit of your brother's brain and removed all records of your call. I'll wipe your memory of this, and you'll do just fine, yes indeed."

"But my friends are in here," said Elizabeth, and she started to feel sorry for herself. "My dog, too."

"Well, then, what do you want me to do?"

"Can't you fix my tests?"

The Chickenheart looked at Elizabeth with surprise.

"What's this, my dear? Do you think you're a timebomb, too?"

"I can *learn* to be a timebomb," said Elizabeth with conviction. And she knew she could, whatever a timebomb was.

"I don't know," said the Chickenheart, "that anyone can learn that sort of thing. You've either got it or you don't, Miss Elizabeth."

"Call me Lizardbreath. That's my *real* name. And I can get what I want. I got away from my brother, didn't I? And I got here."

The Chickenheart raised his thin black eyebrows. "You have a point there, my dear. Perhaps you could be a timebomb, after all."

"But not today," said Lizardbreath. "Today I'm learning to spit."

THE LOCH MOOSE MONSTER

Janet Kagan

This year the Ribeiros' daffodils seeded early and they seeded cockroaches. Now ecologically speaking, even a cockroach has its place—but these suckers *bit*. That didn't sound Earth authentic to me. Not that I care, mind you, all I ask is useful. I wasn't betting on that either.

As usual, we were shorthanded—most of the team was up-country trying to stabilize a herd of Guernseys—which left me and Mike to throw a containment tent around the Ribeiro place while we did the gene-reads on the roaches and the daffodils that spawned 'em. Dragon's Teeth, sure enough, and worse than useless. I grabbed my gear and went in to clean them out, daffodils and all.

By the time I crawled back out of the containment tent, exhausted, cranky, and thoroughly bitten, there wasn't a daffodil left in town. Damn fools. If I'd told 'em the roaches were Earth authentic, they'd have cheered 'em, no matter how obnoxious they were.

I didn't even have the good grace to say hi to Mike when I

slammed into the lab. The first thing out of my mouth was "The red daffodils—in front of Sagdeev's."

"I got 'em," he said. "Nick of time, but I got 'em. They're in the greenhouse. . . ."

We'd done a gene-read on that particular patch of daffodils the first year they'd flowered red: they promised to produce a good strain of praying mantises, probably Earth authentic. We both knew how badly Mirabile needed insectivores. The other possibility was something harmless but pretty that ships' records called "fireflies." Either would have been welcome, and those idiots had been ready to consign both to a fire.

"I used the same soil, Annie, so don't give me that look."

"Town's full of fools," I growled, to let him know that look wasn't aimed at him. "Same soil, fine, but can we match the rest of the environmental conditions those praying mantises need in the damn greenhouse?"

"It's the best we've got," he said. He shrugged and his right hand came up bandaged. I glared at it.

He dropped the bandaged hand behind the lab bench. "They were gonna burn 'em. I couldn't—" He looked away, looked back. "Annie, it's nothing to worry about."

I'd have done the same myself, true, but that was no reason to let *him* get into the habit of taking fool risks.

I started across to check out his hand and give him pure hell from close up. Halfway there the com blatted for attention. Yellow light on the console, meaning it was no emergency, but I snatched it up to deal with the interruption before I dealt with Mike. I snapped a "Yeah?" at the screen.

"Mama Jason?"

Nobody calls me that but Elly's kids. I glowered at the face on screen: my age, third-generation Mirabilan, and not so privileged. "Annie Jason Masmajean," I corrected. "Who wants to know?"

"Leonov Bellmaker Denness at this end," he said. "I

apologize for my improper use of your nickname." Ship's manners—he ignored my rudeness completely.

The name struck me as vaguely familiar, but I was in no mood to search my memory; I'd lost my ship's manners about three hours into the cockroach clean-out. "State your business," I said.

To his credit, he did: "Two of Elly's lodgers claim there's a monster in Loch Moose. By their description, it's a humdinger."

I was all ears now. Elly runs the lodge at Loch Moose for fun—her profession's raising kids. (Elly Raiser Roget, like her father before her. Our population is still so small we can't afford to lose genes just because somebody's not suited, one way or another, for parenting.) A chimera anywhere near Loch Moose was a potential disaster. Thing of it was, Denness didn't sound right for that. "Then why aren't *they* making this call?"

He gave a deep-throated chuckle. "They're in the dining room gorging themselves on Chris's shrimp. I doubt they'll make you a formal call when they're done. Their names are Emile Pilot Stirzaker and François Cobbler Pastides and, right now, they can't spell either without dropping letters."

So he thought they'd both been smoking dumbweed. Fair enough. I simmered down and reconsidered him. I'd've bet money he was the one who sidetracked Pastides and Stirzaker into the eating binge.

Recognition struck at last: this was the guy Elly's kids called "Noisy." The first thing he'd done on moving into the neighborhood was outshout every one of 'em in one helluva contest. He was equally legendary for his stories, his bells, and his ability to keep secrets. I hadn't met him, but I'd sure as hell heard tell.

I must have said the nickname aloud, because Denness said, "Yes, 'Noisy.' Is that enough to get me a hearing?"

"It is." It was my turn to apologize. "Sorry. What more do you want me to hear?"

"You should, I think, hear Stirzaker imitate his monster's bellow of rage."

It took me a long moment to get his drift, but get it I did. "I'm on my way," I said. I snapped off and started repacking my gear.

Mike stared at me. "Annie? What did I miss?"

"You ever know anybody who got auditory hallucinations on dumbweed?"

"Shit," he said. "No." He scrambled for his own pack.

"Not you," I said. "I need you here to coddle those daffodils, check the environmental conditions that produced 'em, and call me if Dragon's Teeth pop up anywhere else." I shouldered my pack and finished with a glare and a growl: "That should be enough to keep you out of bonfires while I'm gone, shouldn't it?"

By the time I grounded in the clearing next to Elly's lodge, I'd decided I was on a wild moose chase. Yeah, I know the Earth authentic is wild *goose,* but "wild moose" was Granddaddy Jason's phrase. He'd known Jason—the original first-generation Jason—well before the Dragon's Teeth had started popping up.

One look at the wilderness where Elly's lodge is now and Jason knew she had the perfect EC for moose. She hauled the embryos out of ships' storage and set them thawing. Built up a nice little herd of the things and turned 'em loose. Not a one of them survived—damn foolish creatures died of a taste for a Mirabilan plant they couldn't metabolize.

Trying to establish a viable herd got to be an obsession with Jason. She must've spent years at it, off and on. She never succeeded but somebody with a warped sense of humor named the lake Loch Moose and it stuck, moose or no moose.

Loch Moose looked as serene as it always did this time of year. The waterlilies were in full bloom—patches of velvety red and green against the sparkles of sunlight off the water. Here and there I saw a ripple of real trout, Earth authentic.

On the bank to the far right, Susan's troop of otters played tag, skidding down the incline and hitting the water with a splash. They whistled encouragement to each other like a pack of fans at a ballgame. Never saw a creature have more pure *fun* than an otter—unless it was a dozen otters, like now.

The pines were that dusty gold that meant I'd timed it just right to see Loch Moose smoke. There's nothing quite so beautiful as that drift of pollen fog across the loch. It would gild rocks and trees alike until the next rainfall.

Monster, my ass—but where better for a wild moose chase?

I clambered down the steps to Elly's lodge, still gawking at the scenery, so I was totally unprepared for the EC in the lobby. If that bright-eyed geneticist back on Earth put the double-whammy on any of the human genes in the cold banks they sent along (*swore* they hadn't, but after the kangaroo rex, damnify believe anything the old records tell me), the pandemonium I found would have been enough to kick off Dragon's Teeth by the dozens.

Amid the chaos Ilanith, Elly's next-to-oldest, was handling the oversized gilt ledger with great dignity. She lit up when she saw me and waved. Then she bent down for whispered conversation. A second later Jen, the nine-year-old, exploded from behind the desk, bellowing, "Elleeeeee! Noiseeeeee! Come quick! Mama Jason's here!" The kid's lungpower cut right through the chaos and startled the room into a momentary hush. She charged through the door to the dining room, still trying to shout the house down.

I took advantage of the distraction to elbow my way to the desk and Ilanith.

She squinted a little at me, purely Elly in manner, and said, "Bet you got hopped on by a kangaroo rex this week. You're *real* snarly."

"Can't do anything about my face," I told her. "And it

was biting cockroaches." I pushed up a sleeve to show her the bites.

"Bleeeeeh," she said, with an inch or two of tongue for emphasis. "I hope they weren't keepers."

"Just the six I saved to put in your bed. Wouldn't want you to think I'd forgotten you."

She wrinkled her nose at me and flung herself across the desk to plant a big sloppy kiss on my cheek. "Mama Jason, you are the world's biggest tease. But I'm gonna give you your favorite room anyhow"—she wrinkled her nose in a very different fashion at the couple to my right—"since *those two* just checked out of it."

One of the *those two* peered at me like a myopic crane. I saw recognition strike, then he said, "We've changed our minds. We'll keep the room."

"Too late," said Ilanith—and she was smug about it. "But if you want to stay, I can give you one on the other side of the lodge. No view." Score one for the good guys, I thought.

"See, Elly?" It was Jen, back at a trot beside Elly and dragging Noisy behind her. "See?" Jen said again. "If Mama Jason's here, I won't have to go away, right?"

"Right," I said.

"Oh, Jen!" Elly dropped to one knee to pull Jen into one of her full-body-check hugs. "Is *that* what's been worrying you? Leo already explained to your mom. There's no monster —nobody's going to send you away from Loch Moose!"

Jen, who'd been looking relieved, suddenly looked suspicious. "If there's no monster, why's Mama Jason here?"

"Need a break," I said, realizing I meant it. Seeing Elly and the kids was break enough all by itself. "Stomped enough Dragon's Teeth this week. I'm not about to go running after monsters that vanish at the first breath of fresh air."

Elly gave me a smile that would have thawed a glacier and my shoulders relaxed for the first time in what seemed like months.

I grinned back. "Have your two monster-sighters sobered up yet?"

"Sobered up," reported Ilanith, "and checked out." She giggled. "You should have seen how red-faced they were, Mama Jason."

I glowered at no one in particular. "Just as well. After the day I had, they'd have been twice as red if I'd had to deal with 'em."

Elly rose to her feet, bringing Jen with her. The two of them looked me over, Jen imitating Elly's keen-eyed inspection. "We'd better get Mama Jason to her room. She needs a shower and a nap worse than any kid in the household."

Ilanith shook her head. "Let her eat first, Elly. By the time she's done, we'll have her room ready."

"Sounds good to me," I said, "if the kids waiting tables can take it."

"We raise a sturdy bunch around here. Go eat, Annie." She gave me a kiss on the cheek—I got a bonus kiss from Jen —and the two of them bustled off to get my room ready. I frowned after them: Jen still seemed worried and I wondered why.

Ilanith rounded the desk to grab my pack. Standing between me and Leo, she suddenly jammed her fists into her hips. "Oh, nuts. Ship's manners. Honestly, Mama Jason— how did people *ever* get acquainted in the old days?" With an expression of tried patience, she formally introduced the two of us.

I looked him over, this time giving him a fair shake. The face was as good as the reputation, all laugh lines etched deep. In return, I got inspected just as hard.

When nobody said anything for a full half second, Ilanith said, "More? You need more? Didn't I get it right?"

Leo gave a smile that was a match for Elly's. Definitely the EC, I thought. Then he thrust out a huge welcoming hand and said, "That's Leo to you, as I don't imagine I could out-shout you."

That assessment visibly impressed Ilanith.

"Annie," I said. I took the hand. Not many people have hands the size of mine. In Denness I'd met my match for once. Surprised me how good that felt. He didn't let go immediately and I wasn't all that anxious for him to do so.

Ilanith eyed him severely. "Leo, there's no need to be grabby!" She tapped his hand, trying to make him let go.

"Shows how much you know about ship's manners," Leo said. "I was about to offer the lady my arm, to escort her into the dining room."

"Perfectly good old-time ritual," I said. "I can stand it if he can."

Leo held out his arm, ship's formal; I took it. We went off rather grandly, leaving Ilanith all the more suspicious that we'd made it up for her benefit.

Leo chuckled as we passed beyond her earshot. "She won't believe that until she double-checks with Elly."

"I know. Good for 'em—check it out for yourself, I always say. Have *you* heard any bellowing off the loch?"

"Yes," he said, "I have heard a couple of unusual sounds off the loch lately. I've no way of knowing if they're all made by the same creature. But I've lived here long enough to know that these are new. One is a kind of sucking gurgle. Then there's something related to a cow's lowing"—he held up a hand—"*not* cow and *not* red deer either. I know both. And there's a bellow that'll bring you out of a sound sleep faster than a shotgun blast."

His lips flattened a bit. "I can't vouch for that one. I've *only* heard it awakening from sleep. It might have been a dream but it never *feels* like dream—and the bellow Stirzaker gave was a fair approximation of it."

The lines across his forehead deepened. "There's something else you should know, Annie. Jen's been acting spooked, and neither Elly nor I can make any sense of it."

"I saw. I thought she was still keyed up over the monster business."

He shook his head. "This started weeks ago, long before Stirzaker and Pastides got everybody stirred up."

"I'll see what I can find out."

"Anything I can do to help," he said. He swung his free hand to tell me how extensive that "anything" actually was. "On either count."

"Right now, you watch me eat a big plate of *my* shrimp with Chris's barbecue sauce on 'em."

Loch Moose was the only source of freshwater shrimp on Mirabile and they were one of my triumphs. Not just the way they tasted when Chris got done with them, but because I'd brought the water lilies they came from myself and planted them down in Loch Moose on the chance they'd throw off something good. Spent three years making sure they stabilized. Got some pretty dragonflies out of that redundancy, too. Elly's kids use 'em for catching rock lobsters, which is another thing Chris cooks to perfection.

By the time I'd finished my shrimp, the dining room was empty except for a couple of people I knew to be locals like Leo. I blinked my surprise, I guess.

Leo said, "Most of the guests checked out this morning. Let's take advantage of it." He picked up my glass and his own and bowed me toward one of the empty booths.

I followed and sank, sighing, into overstuffed comfort. "Now," I said, "tell me what you heard from Stirzaker and Pastides."

He obliged in detail, playing both roles. When he was done, I appreciated his reputation for story-telling, but I knew as well he'd given me an accurate account, right down to the two of them tripping over each other's words in their excitement.

Their description of the chimera would have scared the daylights out of me—if they'd been able to agree on any given part of it aside from the size. Stirzaker had seen the thing reach for him with two great clawlike hands. Pastides had seen the loops of a water snake, grown to unbelievable lengths, undulate past him. They agreed again only when it came to the creature's bellow.

When all was said, I had to laugh. "I bet *their* granddaddy told *them* scary bedtime stories, too!"

"Good God," said Leo, grinning suddenly. "The Loch Ness Monster! I should have recognized it!"

"From which description?" I grinned back. Luckily the question didn't require an answer.

"Mama Jason!"

That was all the warning I got. Susan—all hundred pounds of her—pounced into my lap.

"They were *dumbstruck*, both of them," she said, her manner making it clear that this was the most important news of the century. "You should have seen them eat! Tell her, Noisy—you saw!"

"Hello to you too," I said, "and I just got the full story, complete with sound effects."

That settled her down a bit, but not much. At sixteen, nothing settles them *down*. Sliding into the seat beside me, she said, "Now you tell—about the biting cockroaches."

Well, I'd have had to tell that one sooner or later, so I told it for two, ending with Mike's heroic attempt to rescue the red daffodils.

Susan's eyes went dreamy. "Fireflies," she said. "Think how pretty they'd be around the lake at night!"

"I was," I said, all too curtly. "Sorry," I amended, "I'm still pissed off about them."

"I've got another one for you," Susan said, matching my scowl. "Rowena, who lives about twenty miles that way"— she pointed, glanced at Leo (who nudged her finger about 5 degrees left), then went on—"*that* way, claims that the only way to keep from raising Dragon's Teeth is to spit tobacco on your plants whenever you go past them." She gave another glance at Leo, this one a different sort of query. "I think she *believes* that. I know she *does* it!"

" 'Fraid so," Leo said.

"Well, we'll know just what EC to check when something unusual pops out of Rowena's plants, won't we?" I sighed. The superstitions really were adding to our problems.

"Mama Jason," said Susan—with a look that accused me of making a joke much too low for her age level—"how many authentics need tobacco spit ECs to pop up?"

"No joke, honey. It's not authentic species I'd expect under conditions like that. It'd be Dragon's Teeth plain and probably not so simple." I looked from one to the other. "Keep an eye on those plants for me. Anything suddenly flowers in a different color or a slightly different form, snag a sample and send it to me fast!"

They nodded, Susan looking pleased with the assignment, Leo slightly puzzled. At last Leo said, "I'm afraid I've never understood this business of Dragon's Teeth—" He broke off, suddenly embarrassed.

"Fine," I said, "as long as you don't spit tobacco on the ragweed or piss on the petunias or toss the soapy washwater on the lettuce patch."

Susan eyed me askance. I said, "Last year the whole town of Misty Valley decided that pissing on the petunias was the only way to stabilize them." I threw up my hands to stave off the question that was already on the tip of Susan's tongue. "*I* don't know how that got started, so don't ask me. I'm not even sure I *want* to know!—The end result, of course, was that the petunias seeded ladybugs."

"Authentic?" Susan asked.

"No, but close enough to be valuable. Nice little insectivores and surprisingly well suited for doing in ragmites." The ragmites are native and a bloody nuisance. "And before you ask," I added, "the things they *might* have gotten in the same EC included a very nasty species of poisonous ant and two different grain-eaters, one of which would chain up to a salamander with a taste for quail eggs."

"Oh, my!" said Susan. "Misty Valley's where we get our quail eggs!"

"So does everybody on Mirabile," I said. "Nobody's gotten the quail to thrive anywhere else yet." For Leo's benefit, I added, "So many of our Earth-authentic species are on rocky ground, we can't afford to lose a lot of individuals to a Dragon's Tooth."

Leo still looked puzzled. After a moment, he shook his head. "I've never understood this business. Maybe for once I could get a simple explanation, suitable for a bell-maker . . . ?"

I gestured to Susan. "My assistant will be glad to give you the short course."

Susan gave one of those award-winning grins. "It goes all the way back to before we left Earth, Leo." Leo arched an eyebrow: " 'We'?" Susan punched him—lightly—on the arm and said, "You know what I mean! Humans!"

She heaved a dramatic sigh and went on in spite of it all. "They wanted to make sure we'd have everything we might possibly need."

"I thought that's why they sent along the embryo and gene banks," Leo said.

Susan nodded. "It was. But at the time there was a fad for redundancy—every system doubled, tripled, even quadrupled —so just to make *sure* we couldn't lose a species we might need, they built all that redundancy into the gene pool, too."

She glanced at me. She was doing fine, so I nodded for her to go on.

"Look, Noisy. They took the genes for, say, sunflowers and they tucked 'em into a twist in wheat helices. Purely recessive, but when the environmental conditions are right, maybe one one-hundredth of your wheat seeds will turn out to sprout sunflowers."

She leaned closer, all earnestness. "And one one-hundredth of the sunflowers, given the right EC, will seed bumblebees, and so on and so forth. That's what Mama Jason calls 'chaining up.' Eventually you might get red deer."

Leo frowned. "I don't see how you can go from plant to animal. . . ."

"There's usually an intermediate stage—a plant that comes out all wrong for that plant but perfect for an incubator for whatever's in the next twist." She paused dramatically, then finished, "As you can see, it was a perfectly *dumb* idea."

I decided to add my two bits here. "The *idea* wasn't as dumb as you make out, kiddo. They just hadn't worked the bugs out before they stuck us with it."

"When she says *bugs*," Susan confided grimly to Leo, "she *means* Dragon's Teeth."

I stepped in again. "Two things went wrong, Leo. First, there was supposed to be an easy way to turn anything other than the primary helix off and on at will. The problem is, that information was in the chunk of ships' records we lost and it was such new knowledge at the time that it didn't get passed to anyone on the ship.

"The second problem was the result of pure goof. They forgot that, in the long run, all plants and animals change to suit their environment. A new mutation may be just the thing for our wheat, but who knows what it's done to those hidden sunflowers? Those—and the chimerae—are the real Dragon's Teeth."

Leo turned to Susan. "Want to explain the chimerae as long as you're at it?"

"A chimera is something that's, well, sort of patched together from two, maybe three, different genetic sources. Ordinarily it's nothing striking—you'd probably only notice if you did a full gene-read. But with all those hidden sets of genes, just about anything can happen."

"Kangaroo rex, for example," I said. "That one was a true chimera: a wolf in kangaroo's clothing."

"I remember the news films," Leo said. "Nasty."

"Viable, too," I said. "That was a tough fight. I'm still sorry I lost." It still rankled, I discovered.

Leo looked startled.

"I wanted to save 'em, Leo, but I got voted down. We really couldn't afford a new predator in that area."

"Don't look so shocked, Noisy," Susan said. "You never know what might be useful some day. Just suppose we get an overpopulation of rabbits or something and we need a predator to balance them out before they eat all our crops. That's why Mama Jason wanted to keep them."

Leo looked unconvinced, Susan looked hurt suddenly. "Just because it's ugly, Leo," she said, "doesn't mean you wipe it out. There's nothing pretty about a rock lobster but it sure as hell tastes good."

"I grant you that. I'm just not as sure about things that think *I* taste good."

Susan folded her arms across her chest and heaved another of those dramatic sighs. "Now I know what you're up against, Mama Jason," she said. "Pure ignorance."

That surprised me. I held my tongue for once, waiting to see how Leo would take that.

"Nothing pure about it," he said. "Don't insult a man who's trying to enlighten himself. That never furthered a cause." He paused, then added, "You sound like you take it very personally."

Susan dropped her eyes. There was something in that evasion that wasn't simple embarrassment at overstepping good manners. When she looked up again, she said, "I'm sorry, Leo. I just get so *mad* sometimes. Mama Jason—"

This time I had to come to her rescue. "Mama Jason sets a bad example, Leo. I come up here and rave about the rampant stupidity everywhere else. Susan, better to educate people than insult them. If I say insulting things about them when I'm in family that's one thing. But I would never say to somebody who was concerned about his kids or his crops what you just said to Leo."

"Yeah. I know. I'm sorry again."

"Forgiven," said Leo. "Better you make your mistakes on

me and learn from them than make 'em on somebody else who might wallop you and turn you stubborn."

Susan brightened. "Oh, but I *am* stubborn, Leo! You always say so!"

"Stubborn, yes. *Stupid* stubborn—not that I've seen."

Again there was something other than embarrassment in her dropped eyes. I tried to puzzle it out, but I was distracted by a noise in the distance.

It came from the direction of the loch—something faint and unfamiliar. I cocked my head to listen harder and got an earful of sneezes instead.

"S-sorry!" Susan gasped, through a second series of sneezes. "P-pollen!" Then she was off again, her face buried in a napkin.

Leo caught my eye. He thought the sneezing fit was as phony as I did.

"Well," I said, "you may be allergic to the pollen"—she wasn't, I knew very well—"but I came hoping I'd timed it right to see Loch Moose smoke. And to get in some contemplative fishing"—meaning I didn't intend to bait my hook—"before it gets too dark."

Susan held up her hand, finished off one last sequence of sneezes, then said, "What about your nap?"

"What do you think contemplative fishing *is*?"

"Oh. Right. Get Leo to take you, then. He knows all the best places."

"I'd be honored," Leo said.

We left Susan scrubbing her face. Pausing only to pick up poles in the hallway, we set off in silence along the footpath down to Loch Moose. When we got to the first parting of the path, I broke the silence. "Which way to your favorite spot?"

He pointed to the right fork. I'd figured as much. "Mine's to the left," I said and headed out that way. If Susan didn't want me in my usual haunts, I wanted to know why. Leo followed without comment, so I knew he was thinking the same thing.

"Keep your ears open. I heard something before Susan started her sneezing fit to cover it."

We came to another parting in the path. I angled right and again he followed. Pretty soon we were skidding and picking our way down the incline that led to the otters' playground.

When we got to surer footing, Leo paused. "Annie—now that I've got somebody to ask: will you satisfy my curiosity?"

That piqued mine. "About what?"

"*Was* there such a thing as the Loch Ness Monster? I always thought my mother had made it up."

I laughed. "And I thought my granddaddy had, especially since he claimed that people came to Loch Ness from all over the Earth hoping to catch a glimpse of the monster! I looked it up once in ships' records. There really *was* such a place and people really did come from everywhere for a look!"

He was as taken aback about that as I'd been, then he heard what I hadn't said. "And the monster—was *it* real? Did it look like any of the stories?"

"I never found out."

"Pre-photograph?"

"No," I said, "that was the odd thing about it. There were some fuzzy photos—old flat ones, from a period when *everybody* had photographic equipment—that might have been photos of anything. The story was that Nessie was very shy and the loch was too full of peat to get sonograms. Lots of excuses, no results."

"Smoking too much weed, eh?"

"Lot of that going around," I said. "But no, I suspect Nessie was exactly what granddad used her for—a story. What's always fascinated me is that people went to *look*!"

Leo chuckled. "You underestimate the average curiosity. I don't think you appreciate how many people stayed glued to their TVs while you folks rounded up those kangaroo rexes. A little thrill is high entertainment."

"The hell it is," I said indignantly. "I oughta know: I do

it for a living. *They* didn't get their boots chewed off by the damn things."

"Exactly my point," said Leo. "Scary but safe. Elly's kids would be the first to tell you what a good combination that is. They watch their kangaroo rex tape about twice a week, and cheer for you every time."

Some things I was better off not knowing, I thought. I sighed. Turning away from Leo, I got the full view of Loch Moose and its surroundings, which drew a second sigh—this time pure content.

The secret of its appeal was that despite the vast sparkle of sunlight that glittered off it, Loch Moose always felt hidden away—a place you and you alone were aware of.

It took me a while to remember that Leo was beside me. No, I take that back. I was aware that he was there all along, but he was as content as I to simply drink it all in without a word.

Sometime—when we were both done admiring the scene—we headed for the boats, by some sort of mutual agreement. I was liking Leo more and more. For another thing, the whistling of the otters made him smile.

The slope down to the boats was dotted with violets. Most of them were that almost fiery shade of blue that practically defines the species, but once in a while they came out white just for the surprise of it. Some were more surprising than white, though. Almost hidden in the deep shade was a small isolated patch of scarlet.

For the life of me, I couldn't remember seeing any material on scarlet violets. I stooped for a closer look. Damned odd texture to the petals, too, like velvet.

"Pretty, aren't they?" Leo said. "Stop by my place while you're here, and I'll show you half an acre of them."

I stood up to look him in the eye. "Popped up all at once? First time, this year?"

"No. I've been putting them in when I found them for, oh, three years now."

"Oh, Leo. Half of Mirabile thinks everything's going to sprout fangs and bite them and the other half doesn't even take elementary precautions. Never *ever* transplant something red unless somebody's done a work-up on it first!"

He looked startled. "Are they dangerous?"

"Don't *you* start!" Dammit, I'd done it—jumped on him with both feet. "Sorry. I'm still fuming over those red daffodils, I guess."

"Annie, I'm too damned old to worry about everything that flowers red. I took them for what my grandmother called 'pansies.' Much to her disappointment, she never could get any started on Mirabile. Maybe they aren't, but that's how I think of them. I'm going to hate it if you tell me I have to pull 'em out because they're about to seed mosquitoes."

And he'd never forgive me either, I could tell.

"We'll get a sample on the way back, Leo. If there's a problem, I'll see if I can stabilize them for you." He looked so surprised, I had to add, "Practical is not my only consideration. Never has been. 'Pretty' is just fine, provided I've got the time to spare."

That satisfied him. He smiled all the way down to the edge of the water.

Two hands made light work of launching a boat and we paddled across to a sheltered cove I had always favored. I tied the boat to a low branch that overhung the water, dropped a naked hook into the loch, and leaned back. Leo did the same.

What I liked best about this spot, I think, was that it was the perfect view of the otters' playground—without disturbing the play. It also meant I didn't have to bring along treats for the little beggars. Susan had been feeding them since she was—oh—Jen's age. They'd grown so used to it that they hustled the tourists now.

I didn't believe in it myself, but as long as she didn't overdo it to the point they couldn't fend for themselves I wasn't about to make a fuss. I think Susan knew that too. She had a better grasp of the principles than most adults I knew, aside from those on the team, of course.

The hillside and water were alive with the antics of the otters. Some rippled snake-like through the water. One chased one of those king-sized dragonflies. Two others tussled on the ridge and eventually threw themselves down the incline, tumbling over and over each other, to hit the water with a splash.

Leo touched my arm and pointed a little to the side. He was frowning. I turned to take it in and discovered there was an altercation going on, just below the surface of the water. This one was of a more serious nature.

"Odd," I said, speaking aloud for the first time since we'd settled in. He nodded, and we both kept watching, but there wasn't anything to see except the occasional flick of a long muscular tail, the wild splash of water. A squeal of anger was followed by a squeal of distress and the combatants broke off, one of them hightailing it toward us.

I got only a glimpse as it passed us by but it seemed to me it was considerably bigger than its opponent. Biggest otter I'd seen, in fact. I wondered why it had run instead of the smaller one.

The smaller one was already back at play. Leo shrugged and grinned. "I thought mating season was over," he said. "So did she, considering how she treated him."

"Ah," I said, "I missed the opening moves."

We settled back again, nothing to perturb us but the otter follies, which brought us to laughter over and over again. We trusted nothing would interrupt that by tugging at our lines.

Shadow was beginning to lengthen across us. I knew we had another half hour before it would be too dark for us to make our way easily back up to the lodge. "Leo," I said, "want me to head in? Your way will be in shadows long before mine."

"Staying the night at the lodge. I promised Elly I'd do

some handiwork for her. Besides, I could do with another of Chris's meals."

There was a stir and a series of splashes to our right, deep in the cove. That large otter, back with friends. There were two troops of them in the loch now. I made a mental note to make sure they weren't overfishing the shrimp or the trout, then I made a second note to see if we couldn't spread the otters to another lake as well. The otters were pretty firmly established on Mirabile, but it never hurt to start up another colony elsewhere.

I turned to get a better look, maybe count noses to get a rough estimate of numbers. I counted six, eight, nine separate ripples in the water. Something seemed a little off about them. I got a firm clamp on my suspicious mind and on the stories I'd heard all day and tried to take an unbiased look. They weren't about to hold still long enough for me to get a fix on them through the branches and the shadows that were deepening by the moment.

One twined around an overhang. I could see the characteristic tail but its head was lost in a stand of water lilies. Good fishing there, I knew. The trout always thought they could hide in the water lilies and the otters always knew just where to find them. Then I realized with a start that the water lilies were disappearing.

I frowned. I untied the boat and gestured for Leo to help me get closer. We grabbed at branches to pull the boat along as silently as possible. To no avail: with a sudden flurry of splashes all around, the otters were gone.

"Hell," I said. I unshipped the oars and we continued on over. I was losing too much of the light. I thrust down into the icy water and felt around the stand of lilies, then I grabbed and yanked, splattering water all over Leo. He made not a word of complaint. Instead, he stuck a damp match into his shirt pocket and tried a second one. This one lit.

It told my eyes what my fingers had already learned: the water lily had been neatly chewed. Several other leaves had been nipped off the stems as well—but at an earlier time, to judge from the way the stem had sealed itself. I dropped the plant back in the water and wiped my hands dry on my slacks.

Leo drowned the match and stuck it in his pocket with the first. It got suddenly very dark and very quiet on the loch.

I decided I didn't want either of us out here without some kind of protective gear. I reached for the overhang and shoved us back toward the sunlit side of the loch. It wasn't until I'd unshipped my oar again that I got my second shock of the day.

That branch was the one I'd seen the otter twined around. That gave me a belated sense of scale. The "otter" had been a good eight feet long!

I chewed on the thought all the way back to the lodge. Would have forgotten the violets altogether but for Leo's refusal to let that happen. I put my pole back in its place and took the scarlet violet and its clump of earth from him. Spotted Susan and said, "Leo wants to see a gene-read. Can you have Chris send rock lobster for two up to my room?"

"It's on its way, Mama." She paused to glance at the violets. "Pretty," she said, "I hope—"

"Yeah, me too."

"Hey!" she said suddenly. "I thought you were here for a break."

"How else can I lure Leo up to my room?"

"You could just invite him, Mama Jason. That's what you're always telling us: Keep it simple and straightforward. . . ."

"I should keep my mouth shut."

"Then you wouldn't be able to eat your lobster." With that as her parting shot, Susan vanished back into the dining room. I paused to poke my head around the corner—empty, just as before.

We climbed the stairs. I motioned Leo in, laid down the

clump of violets and opened my gear. "Violets first," I said, "as long as we're about to be interrupted."

I took my sample and cued up the room computer, linking it to the one back at the lab. There was a message from Mike waiting. "The daffodils have perked up, so they look good," it said, "and the troops have returned from the Guernsey wars triumphant. We'll call if we need you. You do the same."

"You forgot to say how your hand is, dummy," I growled at the screen—then typed the same in, for him to find in the morning.

The first-level gene-read on the violets went fast. All it takes is a decent microscope—that I carry—and the computer. The hard part was running it through ships' records looking for a match or a near match. I could let that run all night while I slept through it.

Susan brought the rock lobster and peered over my shoulder as she set it down. "Mama Jason, I can keep an eye on that while you eat if you like."

"Sure," I said, getting up to give her the chair. Leo and I dug into our lobster, with an occasional glance at the monitor. "Watch this part, Leo," I said. Susan had already finished the preliminary and was looking for any tacked-on genes that might be readable.

Susan's fingers danced, then she peered at the screen like she was trying to see through it. Mike gets that same look. I suppose I do too. The screen looks right through the "whatsis"—as Susan would say—and into its genetic makeup. "Mama Jason, I can't see anything but the primary helix."

"Okay." Neither did I. "Try a match with violets." To Leo, I added, "We might as well try the easy stuff first. Why run the all-night program if you don't have to?" I ducked into the bathroom to wash rock lobster and butter off my fingers.

"No luck," Susan called to me.

When I came out, Leo had disappointment written all over his face. "Buck up," I said. "We're not giving up that easily. Susan, ask the computer if it's got a pattern for something called a 'pansy' or a 'pansies.' "

" 'Pansy,' " said Leo and he spelled it for her.

It did. Luckily, that wasn't one of the areas we'd lost data in. "Oh, Mama Jason!" said Susan. "Will you look at *that*?"

We had a match.

"Leo, you lucky dog!" I said. "Your grandma would be proud of you!"

His jaw dropped. "You mean—they really *are* pansies?"

"Dead on," I told him, while Susan grinned like crazy. I patted her on the shoulder—and gave her a bit of a nudge toward the door at the same time. "You bring Susan a sample of the ones you planted around your place, just so she can double-check for stability. But I think you've got exactly what you hoped you had."

I pointed to the left side of the screen. "According to this, they should come in just about every color of the rainbow. We may have to goose them a bit for that—unless you prefer them all red?"

"Authentic," said Leo, "I want them Earth authentic, as long as you're asking *me*."

"Okay. Tomorrow then," I told Susan. She grinned once more and left.

I sat down at the computer again. Wrote the stuff on the pansy to local memory—then I cleared the screen and called up everything ships' records had on otters.

They didn't eat water lilies and they didn't come eight feet long. Pointing to the genes in question, I told Leo this.

"Does that mean there *is* a monster in the lake?"

"I can't tell you that. I'm not terribly concerned about something that eats water lilies, Leo, but I do want to know if it's chaining up to something else."

"How do we find out?"

"*I* snag a cell sample from the beasties."

Again his lips pressed together in that wry way. "May I offer you what assistance I can?" A sweeping spread of the hands. "I'm very good at keeping out of the way and at following orders. I'm also a first-rate shot with a rifle and I can tell the difference between a monstrosity and a monster. I promise no shooting unless it's absolutely necessary."

"Let me think on it, Leo." Mostly I wanted to ask Elly if what he said was true.

He must have read my mind, because he smiled and said, "Elly will vouch for me. I'll see you in the morning."

That was all. Except maybe I should mention he kissed my hand on his way out. I was beginning to like Leo more and more.

After he left, I did some thinking on it, then I trotted downstairs to talk to Elly. I leaned against the countertop, careful not to get in the way of her cleaning, and said, "Tell me about Leo."

Elly stopped scrubbing for a moment, looked up, and smiled. "Like you," she said.

"That good or bad?"

The smile broadened into a grin. "Both. That means he's stubborn, loyal, keeps a secret *secret*, plays gruff with the kids but adores them just the same."

"Any permanent attachments?" It popped out before I knew it was coming. I tried to shove it back in, but Elly only laughed harder at my attempt.

"Why, Annie! I believe you've got a crush on Leo!" Still laughing, she pulled out a chair and sat beside me, cupping her chin in her hand. "I shouldn't be surprised. All the kids do."

I gave one of Susan's patented sighs.

"Okay, okay," she said, "I'll leave off. I like it, though. I like Leo and I like you and I think you'd get along together just fine."

"Is he as good a shot as he claims to be? And as judicious about it?"

That sat her upright and looking wary.

"No panic," I said firmly. "You *have* got something in

the loch that I want a look at—but it's an herbivore and I doubt it's dangerous. It's big enough to overturn a boat maybe, but—"

"Are you calling in the team?"

"I don't think that's necessary. They could all do with a break—"

"That's what *you* came for. That's hardly fair."

I waved that aside. "Elly, you should know me better by now. I wouldn't have taken this up as a profession if I weren't a born meddler. And I asked about Leo because he offered to give me a hand." I know I scowled. "Money and equipment I can always get—it's the hands we're short."

"You're going to make off with half my kids one of these days."

I couldn't help it. I jerked around to stare at her. She was smiling—and that laugh was threatening to break out all over again. "Annie, surely it's occurred to you that half those kids want to be just like you when they grow up!"

"But—!"

"Oh, dear. Poor Mama Jason. You thought I was raising a whole passel of little Ellies here, didn't you?"

The thing was, I'd never given it any thought at all. More than likely I just assumed Susan and Chris and Ilanith would take over the lodge and . . .

Elly patted my hand. "Don't you worry. Chris will run the lodge and you and the rest can still drop by for vacations."

I felt guilty as hell somehow, as if I'd subverted the whole family.

Elly gave me a big hug. "Wipe that look off your face. You'd think I got chimerae instead of proper kids! The only thing I ask is that you don't cart them off until you're sure they're ready."

"You'll worry yourself sick!"

"No. I'll worry the same way I worry about *you*. Do I look sick?"

She stood off and let me look. She looked about as good

as anybody could. She knew it, too. Just grinned again and said, "Take Leo with you. Susan, too, if you think she's ready. I warn you, *she* thinks she is, but she'll listen to you on the subject."

And that was the end of it as far as Elly was concerned. I walked back to my room, thoughtful all the way.

Damnify knew how I could have missed it. And there I'd been aggravating the situation as well, calling Susan "my assistant," letting her do the gene-read on Leo's pansies. Then I thought about it some more.

She'd done a damn fine gene-read. If she'd heard Leo talk about the pansies, she'd have no doubt thought to try that second as well.

The more I thought, the more I saw Elly was right. It was just so unexpected that I'd never really looked at it.

I crawled into that comfortable bed and lay there listening to the night sounds off the loch and all the while I was wondering how soon I could put Susan to work. I drifted off into sleep and my dreams were more pleased by it all than I would have admitted to Elly.

I woke, not rested enough, to an insistent shaking of my shoulder and opened my eyes to see a goggle-eyed something inches from my face. Thinking the dream had turned bad, I mumbled at it to go away and rolled over.

"Please, Mama Jason," the bad dream said. "Please, I *gotta* talk to you. I can't tell Elly, and I'm afraid it's gonna hurt her."

Well, when a bad dream starts threatening Elly, I listen. I sat up and discovered that the bad dream was only Jen, the nine-year-old. "Gimme half a chance, Jen," I said, holding up one hand while I smeared my face around with the other, trying to stretch my eyes into focus so I could see my watch. My watch told me I'd had enough sleep to function rationally, so I levered myself up.

Jen's eyes unpopped, squinched up, and started leaking enormous teardrops. She made a dash for the door, but by then I was awake and I caught her before she made her exit. "Hold on," I said. "You don't just tell me something's out to hurt Elly and then disappear. Ain't done."

Still leaking tears, she wailed, "It's supposed to be a *secret*. . . ."

Which she wanted somebody to force out of her. Okay, I could oblige, and she could tell the rest Mama Jason *made* her tell. I plopped her firmly on the edge of the bed. "Now wipe your nose and tell me what this is about. You'd think *I* was the chimera the way you're acting."

"You gotta promise not to hurt Monster. He's Susan's."

I did nothing of the sort. I waited and she went on, "I didn't know he was so *big*, Mama Jason!" She threw out those two skinny arms to show me just *how* big, which actually made it about three feet long tops, but I knew from the fingertip to fingertip glance that went with the arm fling that she meant *much* bigger. "Now I'm scared for Susan!"

"What do you mean, he's Susan's?"

"Susan sneaks out at night to feed him. I never saw him, but he must be *awful*. She calls him Monster and he gurgles." She shivered.

I gathered her up and held her until the shivering stopped. Obviously all this had been going on for some time. She'd only broken silence because of Stirzaker's panicky report. "Okay," I said, still patting her, "I want you to let me know the next time Susan sneaks out to feed this Monster of hers—"

She blinked at me solemnly. "She's out there now, Mama Jason."

"Okay," I said. "Out there *where*?"

The bellow off the loch cut me short and brought me to my feet. Unlike Leo, I knew that hadn't been part of a dream. I was already headed for the window when the sound came again. I peered into the night.

Mirabile doesn't have a moon, but for the moment we've

got a decent nova. Not enough radiation to worry about, just enough to see glimmers in the dark.

Something huge rippled through the waters of the loch. I stared harder, trying to make it come clear, but it wouldn't. It bellowed again, and an answering bellow came from the distant shore.

Whatever it was, it was huge, even bigger than the drifted otters I'd seen earlier. Had they chained up to something already? There was a splash and another bellow. I remember thinking Elly wouldn't hear it from her room; she was on the downside of the slope, cushioned from the loch noises by the earth of the slope itself.

Then I got a second glimpse of it, a huge head, a long body. With a shock, I realized that it looked like nothing so much as those blurry flat photos of "Nessie."

I turned to throw on some clothes and ran right into Jen, scaring her half to death. "Easy, easy. It's just me," I said, holding her by the shoulders. "Run get Leo—and tell him to bring his rifle." I gave her a push for the door and that kid moved like a house-afire.

So did Leo. By the time I'd got my gear together, double-checking the flare gun to make sure it had a healthy charge left, he was on my doorstep, rifle in hand.

We ran down the steps together, pausing only once—to ask Jen which way Susan had gone. Jen said, "Down to the loch, she calls it your favorite place! I thought you'd *know*!" She was on the verge of another wail.

"I know," I said. "Now you wait here. If we're not back in two hours, you wake Elly and tell her to get on the phone to Mike."

"Mike," she repeated. "Mike. Two hours." She plopped herself down on the floor directly opposite the clock. I knew I could count on her.

Leo and I switched on flashlights and started into the woods. I let him lead for the time being—he knew the paths better than I did and I wanted to move as fast as possible. We made no attempt to be quiet at it, either. In the dark and shorthanded, I've always preferred scaring the creature off to facing it down.

We got to the boats in record time. Sure enough, one of them was gone. Leo and I pushed off and splashed across the loch, Leo rowing, me with the rifle in one hand and the flare gun in the other.

Nine times out of ten, the flare gun is enough to turn a Dragon's Tooth around and head it away from you. The rifle's there for that tenth time. Or in case it was threatening Susan.

A couple of large things rushed noisily through the woods to our far right. They might have been stag. They might not have been. Neither Leo nor I got a look at them.

"Duck," said Leo, and I did and missed being clobbered by one of those overhanging branches by about a quarter of an inch. Turning, I made out the boat Susan had used. There was just enough proper shore there that we could beach ours beside it.

"All right, Susan," I said into the shadows. "Enough is enough. Come on out. At my age, I need my beauty sleep."

Leo snorted.

There was a quiet crackle behind him and Susan crawled out from the undergrowth looking sheepish. "I only wanted it to be a surprise," she said. She looked all around her and brightened. "It still is—you've scared them off!"

"When you're as old and cranky as I am, there's nothing you like *less* than a surprise," I said.

"Oh." She raked twigs out of her hair. "Then if I can get them to come out again, would you take your birthday present a month early?"

Leo and I glanced at each other. I knew we were both thinking about Jen, sitting in the hallway, worrying. "Two hours and not a minute more," Leo said.

"Okay, Susan. See if you can get 'em out. I'll want a cell sample, too." I rummaged through my gear for the snagger. Nice little gadget, that. Like an arrow on a string. Fire it off

without a sound, it snaps at the critter with less than a fly
sting (I know, I had Mike try it on me when he jury-rigged the
first one), and you pull back the string with a sample on the
end of it.

"Sit down then and be quiet."

We did. Susan ducked into the undergrowth a second
time and came out with half a loaf of Chris's bread. She made
the same chucking noise I'd heard her use to call her otters.
She was expecting something low to the ground, I realized.
Not the enormous thing I'd seen swimming in the loch.

I heard no more sounds from that direction, to my relief.
I wish I could have thought I'd dreamed the entire thing but I
knew I hadn't. What's worse, I picked that time to remember
that one of the Nessie theories had made her out a displaced
plesiosaur.

I was about to call a halt and get us all the hell out of
there till daylight and a full team, when something stirred in
the bushes. Susan chucked at it and held out a bit of bread.

It poked its nose into the circle of light from our flashes
and blinked at us. It was the saddest-looking excuse for a
creature I'd ever seen—the head was the shape of an old boot
with jackass ears stuck on it.

"C'mon, Monster," Susan coaxed. "You know how much
you love Chris's bread. Don't worry about them. They're
noisy but they won't hurt you."

Sure enough, it humped its way out. It looked even worse
when you saw the whole of it. What I'd thought was an otter
wasn't. Oh, the body was otter, all six feet of it, but the head
didn't go with the rest. After a moment's hesitation, it made
an uncertain lowing noise, then snuffled at Susan, and took
the piece of bread in its otter paws and crammed it down its
mouth.

Then it bellowed, startling all three of us.

"He just learned how to do that this year," Susan said, a
pleased sort of admiration in her voice. The undergrowth
around us stirred.

Out of the corner of my eye, I saw Leo level his rifle. Susan looked at him, worried. "He won't shoot unless something goes wrong, kiddo," I said as softly as I could and still be heard. "He promised me."

Susan nodded. "Okay, Monster. You can call them out then."

She needn't have said it. That bellow already had. There were maybe a dozen of them, all alike, all of them painfully ugly. No, that's the wrong way to put it—they were all *laughably* ugly.

The one she'd dubbed "Monster" edged closer to me. Nosy like the otters, too. It whuffled at my hand. Damn if that head wasn't purely herbivore. The teeth could give you a nasty nip from the looks of them, but it was deer family. The ugly branch of it anyhow.

A second one crawled into Leo's lap. It was trying to make off with his belt buckle. Susan chucked at it and bribed it away with bread. "She's such a thief. If you're not careful, she'll take anything that's shiny. Like the otters, really."

Yes, they were. The behavior was the same I'd seen from Susan's otters—but now I understood why the otters had chased one of these away this afternoon. They were recognizably *not* otters, even if they thought they *were*. Like humans, otters are very conservative about what they consider one of them.

Pretty soon the bread was gone. Monster hustled up the troops and headed them out, with one last look over his shoulder at us.

I popped him neatly with the snagger before Susan could raise a protest. He grunted and gnawed for a moment at his hip, the way a dog would for a flea, then he spotted the snagger moving away from him and pounced.

I had a tug of war on my hands. Susan got into the act and so did a handful of Monster's fellow monsters.

Leo laughed. It was enough to startle them away. I fell over and Susan landed on top of me. She was giggling, too, but she crawled over and got up, triumphant, with the sample in her hands.

"You didn't need it, Mama Jason," Susan said, "but I've decided to forgive you. Monster thought it was a good game." She giggled again and added impishly, "So did I."

"Fine," I said. "I hate to spoil the party, but it's time we got back to the lodge. We're all going to feel like hell in the morning."

Susan yawned. "I spose so. They lose interest pretty fast once I run out of bread."

"Susan, you row Leo back."

"You're not coming?" she said.

"Two boats," I pointed out. Susan was sleepy enough that she didn't ask why I wanted Leo in her boat. Leo blinked at me once, caught on, and climbed into the boat with his rifle across his knees.

By the time we reached the lodge, we were all pretty well knocked out. Jen gave us a big grin of relief to welcome us in. But two steps later we ran hard into Elly's scowl, not to mention Chris's, Ilanith's, and a half dozen others.

"I found Jen sitting in the hall watching the clock," Elly said. "She wouldn't go to bed and she wouldn't say why. Once I counted noses, I discovered the three of you were missing. So you"—that was me, of course—"owe me the explanation you wouldn't let her give me."

"There's something in the loch," I said. "We got a sample and I'll check it out tomorrow. Right now, we all need some sleep."

"Liar," said Chris. "Who's hungry? Midnight snacks"— she glanced at the clock and corrected—"whatever, food's waiting."

Everybody obligingly trooped into the kitchen, lured by the smell of chowder. I followed, knowing this meant I wasn't going to get off the hook without a full explanation. That meant no way of covering Susan's tracks.

We settled down and dived ravenously into the chowder.

Chris poured a box of crackers into a serving tray. "There's no bread," she said with finality, eying Susan to let us all know who was responsible for this woeful state of affairs.

Susan squirmed. "Next time I'll take them crackers. They like your bread better, though."

"If you'd *asked*," Chris said, "I'd have made a couple of extra loaves."

"I wanted it to be a surprise for Mama Jason." She looked around the table. "You know how hard it is to think up a birthday present for her!" She pushed away from the table. "Wait! I'll be right back. I'll show you!"

I concentrated on the chowder. Birthday present, indeed! As if I needed some present other than the fact of those kids themselves. If Susan hadn't opened her mouth, Elly would've assumed I'd taken her along with us, as Elly'd suggested earlier. Glancing up, I saw Elly rest a sympathetic eye on me.

Well, I was off the hook, but Susan sure as hell wasn't.

There was a clamor of footsteps on the stairs and Susan was back with a huge box, full to overspilling with papers and computer tapes. Chris shoved aside the pot of chowder to make space for them.

Susan pulled out her pocket computer and plugged it into the wall modem. "I did it right, Mama Jason. See if I didn't."

The photo album wasn't regulation but as the first page was a very pretty hologram (I recognized Ilanith's work) that spelled out "Happy Birthday, Mama Jason!" in imitation fireworks, I could hardly complain. The second page was a holo of a mother otter and her pups. The pup in the foreground was deformed—the same way the creatures Susan had fed Chris's bread to were.

"That's Monster," Susan said, thrusting a finger at the holo. She peeled a strip of tape from beneath the holo and fed it to the computer. "That's his gene-read." She glanced at Chris. "I lured his mother away with bread to get the cell sample. The otters love your bread too. I never used the fresh bread, Chris, only the stale stuff."

Chris nodded. "I know. I thought it was all going to the otters, though."

"More like 'odders,' " Leo put in, grinning. "Two *dees*."

Susan giggled. "I like that. Let's call 'em Odders, Mama Jason."

"Your critters," I said. "Naming them is your privilege."

"Odders is right." Chris peered over my shoulder and said to Susan, "Why were you feeding Dragon's Teeth?"

"He's so ugly, he's cute. The first ones got abandoned by their mothers. She"—Susan tapped the holo again—"decided to keep hers. Got ostracized for it, too, Mama Jason."

I nodded absently. That happened often enough. I was well into the gene-read Susan had done on her Monster. It was a good, thorough piece of work. I couldn't have done better myself.

Purely herbivorous—and among the things you could guarantee it'd eat were water lilies and clogweed. That stopped me dead in my tracks. I looked up. "It eats clogweed!"

Susan dimpled. "It loves it! That's why it likes Chris's bread better than crackers."

"Why you—" Chris, utterly outraged, stood up so suddenly Elly had to catch at her bowl to keep from slopping chowder on everything.

I laughed. "Down, Chris! She's not insulting your bread! You use brandyflour in it—and brandyflour has almost the identical nutrients in it that clogweed has."

"You mean I could use clogweed to make my bread?" The idea appealed to Chris. She sat down again and looked at Susan with full attention.

"No, you can't," Susan said. "It's got a lot of things in it humans can't eat."

Leo said, "I'm not following again. Susan—?"

"Simple, Noisy. Clogweed's a major nuisance. Mostly it's taken care of by sheer heavy labor. Around Torville, everybody goes down to the canals and the irrigation ditches once a month or so and pulls the clogweed out by hand. When I saw Monster would eat clogweed, I figured he'd be worth keeping—if we could, that is."

"Not bad," said Ilanith. "I wondered why the intake valves had been so easy to clean lately." She leaned over to look at Monster's holo. "Two years old now, right?"

"Four," said Susan. "Only one wouldn't have made much difference. Mama Jason, I did a gene-read every year on them. Those're on the next pages. In case I missed something the first time."

I saw that. The whole EC was there, too, along with more holos and her search for matches with ships' records. There were no matches, so the thing was either a Dragon's Tooth or an intermediate. Just this year, she'd started a careful check for secondary and tertiary helices.

She saw how far I'd gotten in her records and said apologetically, "There's a secondary helix, but I didn't have a clue where to look for a match in ships' records, so I had to do it by brute force."

I handed her the sample I'd gotten from Monster little over a half hour ago. "Here, a fresh sample is always helpful."

She took it, then looked up at me wildly. "You mean me? You want me to keep working on it?"

"You want *me* to work on *my* birthday present?" I might just as well have given *her* a present, the way she lit up.

I yawned—it was that or laugh. "I'm going to bed. But nobody's to go down to the loch until Susan's done with her gene-read."

Elly frowned. "Annie? We've got to net tomorrow or Chris won't have anything to cook."

So there was no escaping it after all. "Take a holiday, Elly. There's something in the loch that isn't Susan's clogweed eaters. Leo and I will do a little looking around tomorrow—armed."

"Oh, Mama Jason!" Susan looked distraught. "You don't

think Monster chained up to a *real* monster, do you?" Her eyes squinched up; she was close to tears.

"Hey!" I pulled her into a hug. For a moment I didn't know what else to say, then I remembered the first time Mike had gotten a nasty alternative instead of what he wanted. "I'll tell you just what I've said to Mike: Sometimes you have to risk the bad to get the good."

I pushed her a bit away to see if that had worked. Not really. "Listen, honey, do you know how Mike and I planned to spend our winter vacation this year?"

When she shook her head I knew I had her attention, no matter how distressed. I told her: "Cobbling together something that would eat clogweed. If all we have to do is stabilize your monsters, you've saved us years of work!"

I pulled her to for another hug. "Best birthday present I've had in years!"

That, finally, brought a smile from her. It was a little wan, but it was there.

"So here's the game plan. You load the sample tonight while it's fresh, then get a good night's sleep and do the gene-read tomorrow while *you're* fresh. Leo and I will do a little tracking as soon as it's light enough. Everybody else gets to sleep late."

That did nothing to take the worry out of Elly's or Chris's eyes but I could see they'd both go along with it, though they were still concerned somebody might decide the kids should be evacuated. "Elly," I said, "we'll work something out, I promise."

That eased the tension in her eyes somewhat, even though I hadn't the vaguest idea *what* we'd work out. Still, a good night's sleep—even a short one—was always guaranteed to help. With a few more hugs, I stumbled off to bed.

Morning came the way it usually did for me this time of year—much too early. Leo, bless him, was up but quiet. The first thing I wanted was a good look at the otters' playground. That was near enough to where I'd seen the creature that maybe we could find some tracks. This side of Loch Moose got its sunlight early, if at all. Luckily, the day was a good one and the scenery was enough to make you glad you had eyes and ears and a nose.

I stood for a moment trying to orient myself, then pointed. "Somewhere around here. I'm pretty sure that's where I heard it." We separated.

Something that big should have left visible evidence of its passing. The popcorn tree was my first break. Something had eaten all the lower leaves from it and done some desultory gnawing at its bark into the bargain. That was several days earlier, from the look of the wood, so I didn't find any tracks to go with it.

Now, the popcorn tree's native to Mirabile, so we were dealing with a creature that either didn't have long to live or was a Dragon's Tooth suited to the EC. Still, it was an herbivore, unless it was one of those exceptions that nibbled trees for some reason other than nourishment.

But it was *big*! I might have discounted the height it could reach as something that stood on its hind feet and stretched, but this matched the glimpse I'd gotten by nova light.

Leo called and I went to see what he'd found. When I caught up with him, he was staring at the ground. "Annie, this thing weighs a ton!" He pointed.

Hoofprints sunk deep into the damp ground. He meant "ton" in the literal sense. I stooped for a closer look, then unshipped my backpack and got out my gear. "Get me a little water, will you, Leo?" I handed him a folded container. "I want to make a plaster cast. Hey!" I added as an afterthought. "Keep your eyes open!"

He grinned. "Hard to miss something that size."

"You have up to now," I pointed out. I wasn't being snide, just realistic. I'm happy to say he understood me.

I went back to examining the print. It was definitely not deer, though it looked related. The red deer survived by sticking to a strict diet of Earth authentic, which meant I couldn't draw any real conclusions from the similarities. I was still betting herbivore, though maybe it was just because I was hoping.

I was purely tired of things that bit or mangled or otherwise made my life miserable. Seemed to me it was about time the Dragon's Teeth started to balance out and produce something useful.

By the time we mixed the plaster and slopped it into the print, I'd decided that I should be grateful for Susan's clogweed-eaters and Leo's pansies and not expect too much of our huge surprise package.

"Leo, I think it's an herbivore. That doesn't mean it isn't dangerous—you know what a bull can do—but it means I don't want it shot on sight."

"You wouldn't want it shot on sight if it *were* a carnivore," he said. "If I didn't shoot the first beastly on sight, I'm not likely to shoot *this* without good reason."

I fixed him with a look of pure disgust. The disgust was aimed at me, though. I knew the name Leonov Denness should have rung bells but I'd gotten distracted by the nickname.

Back when he was Leonov *Opener* Denness, he'd been the scout that opened and mapped all the new territory from Ranomafana to Hot Damn! He brought back cell samples of everything he found, that being part of the job; but he'd also brought back a live specimen of the beastly, which was at least as nasty as the average kangaroo rex and could fly to boot. When Granddaddy Jason asked him why he'd gone to the trouble, he'd only shrugged and said, "Best you observe its habits as well as its genes."

The decision on the beastly had been to push it back from the inhabited areas rather than to shoot on sight. Nasty as it was, it could be driven off by loud sounds (bronze bells, now that I thought of it!) and it made a specialty of hunting what passed for rats on Mirabile. Those rats were considerably worse than having to yell yourself hoarse when you traveled through the plains farmlands.

"If you'd jogged my memory earlier," I said, "I wouldn't have bothered to check your credentials with Elly."

"Annie, I didn't think bragging was in order."

"Facts are a little different than brags. Now I can stop worrying about your health and get down to serious business."

Leaving the plaster to harden, I headed him down to the boats. "Two boats today, Leonov Opener Denness. You stake out that side of the loch, I'll stake out this. Much as I'd enjoy your company, this gives us two chances to spot something, and the sooner we get this sorted out the better it'll be for Elly. Whistle if you spot anything. Otherwise, I'll meet you back here an hour after dusk."

We'd probably have to do a nighttime wait, too, but I was hoping the thing wasn't strictly nocturnal. If it was, I'd need more equipment, which meant calling Mike, which meant making it formal and public.

There's nothing more irritating than waiting for a Dragon's Tooth to rear its ugly head, even if you're sure the head's herbivorous. After all these years, I'm pretty good at it. Besides, there were otters and odders to watch and it was one of those perfect days on Loch Moose. I'd have been out contemplative fishing anyhow. This just took its toll of watching and waiting, which is not nearly as restful. Somewhere in the back of my mind, the plesiosaur still swam sinisterly in Loch Ness.

Susan's odders, as ugly as they were, proved in action almost as much fun as the otters, though considerably sillier-looking. And observation proved her right—several times I saw them dive down and come up with a mouthful of lilies or clogweed.

A breeze came up—one of those lovely ones that Loch Moose is justly famous for—soft and sweet and smelling of lilies and pine and popcorn tree.

The pines began to smoke. I found myself grateful to the Dragon's Tooth for putting me on the loch at the right time to see it.

The whole loch misted over with drifting golden clouds of pollen. I could scarcely see my hand in front of my face. That, of course, was when I heard it. First a soft thud of hooves, then something easing into the water. Something big. I strained to see, but the golden mist made it impossible.

I was damned glad Leo had told me his past history, otherwise I'd have worried. I knew he was doing exactly what I was doing at that moment—keeping dead silent and listening. I brought up my flare gun in one hand and my snagger in the other. Even if it was a plesiosaur, a flare right in the face should drive it off. I couldn't bring myself to raise the rifle. Must be I'm mellowing in my old age.

I could still hear the splash and play of the otters and the odders on either side of me. That was a good sign as well. They'd decided it wasn't a hazard to them.

My nerves were singing, though, as I heard the soft splashing coming toward me. I turned toward the sound, but still couldn't see a thing. There was a gurgle, like water being sucked down a drain, and suddenly I couldn't locate it by ear anymore. I guessed it had submerged, but that didn't do a thing for my nerves. . . .

The best I could do was keep an eye on the surface of the water where it should have been heading if it had followed a straight line—and that was directly under my boat. Looking straight down, I could barely make out a dark bulk. I could believe the ton estimate.

It reached the other side. I lost sight of it momentarily. Then, with a surge that brought up an entire float of lilies and splattered water all over me, it surfaced not ten feet from my boat, to eye me with a glare.

I'd thought Susan's odders were as ugly as things came, but this topped them without even trying. Even through the mist, I could see it now.

Like Susan's Monster, it had that same old-boot-shaped head, the same flopping mule ears, streaming water now. What I'd taken for its head in the glimpse I'd gotten the previous night was actually the most unbelievable set of antlers I'd ever seen in my life, like huge gnarled upraised palms. What Stirzaker had taken for grasping hands, I realized—only at the moment they were filled to the brim with a tangle of scarlet water lilies. From its throat, a flap of flesh dangled dripping like a wet beard. It stared at me with solemn black eyes and munched thoughtfully on the nearest of the dangling lilies. The drifting pollen was slowly turning it to gold.

I swear I didn't know whether to laugh or to cry.

For a moment, I just stared, and it stared back, looking away only long enough to tilt another lily into its mouth. Then I remembered what I was there for and raised the snagger. I got it first try, snapped the snagger to retrieve.

The thing jerked back, glared, then let out a bellow that Mike must have heard back in the lab. It started to swim closer.

"BACK OFF!" I bellowed. Truthfully, I didn't think it was angered, just nosy, but I didn't want to find out the hard way. I raised the flare gun.

From the distance came the sound of splashing oars. "Annie!" Leo yelled. "I'm coming. Hang on!"

The creature backpedaled in the water and cocked its head, lilies and all, toward the sound of Leo's boat. Interested all over again, it started that way at a very efficient paddle. I got a glimpse of a hump just at the shoulders, followed by the curve of a rump, followed by a tiny flop of tail like a deer's. The same view Pastides had gotten, no doubt.

Suddenly, from the direction of Leo's boat there came the clamor of a bell. The creature backpedaled again, ears twitching.

With a splash of utter panic, the creature turned around in the water, dived for cover, and swam for shore. I could hear it crash into the undergrowth even over the clanging of the bell.

"Enough, Leo, enough! It's gone!" He shut up with the bell and we called to each other until he found me through the mist. I'm sorry to say by the time he pulled alongside, I was laughing so hard there were tears streaming down my cheeks.

Leo's face—what I could see of it—went through about three changes of expression in as many seconds. He laid aside his bell—it was a big bronze beastly-scarebell—and sighed with relief. He, too, was gold from all the pollen.

I wiped my eyes and grinned at him. "I wish I could say 'Saved by the bell,' but the thing wasn't really a danger. Clumsy maybe. Possibly aggressive if annoyed, but—" I burst into laughter again.

Leo said amiably, "I'm sure you'll tell me about it when you get your breath back."

I nodded. Pulling in the sample the snagger had caught, I waved him toward the shore. When we were halfway up the hill to the lodge, I said, "Please, Leo, don't ask until I can check my sample."

He spread his hands. "At least I know it's not a plesiosaur."

I had the urge again—and found the laughter had worn down to hiccupping giggles.

When we got to the lodge, I didn't have to yell for them—we got surrounded the moment we hit the porch. Elly did a full-body check on both of us, which meant she wound up as pollen-covered as we were.

"Susan," I said through the chaos of a dozen questions at once, "run that for me. Let's see what we've got." I held out the sample.

"Me?" Susan squeaked.

"You," I said. I took Leo's arm, well above the rifle, and said, "We want some eats, and then I want to see Susan's results from this morning."

I cued the computer over a bowl of steaming chowder, calling up the odder sample Susan had been working on. She'd found some stuff in the twists all right.

All the possibilities were herbivorous, though—and I was betting that one of them would match my silly-looking friend in the loch. I giggled again, I'm afraid. I had a pretty good idea what we were dealing with, but I had to be sure before I let those kids back out on the loch.

By the time we'd finished our chowder, Susan had come charging down the stairs. She punched up the results on my monitor—she was not just fast, she was good.

I called up ships' records and went straight to my best guess. At a glance, we had a match but I went through gene by gene and found the one drift.

"It's a match!" Ilanith crowed from behind me. "First try, too, Mama Jason!"

Everybody focused on the monitor. "Look again, kiddo. Only ninety-nine percent match." I pointed out the drifted genes. "Those mean it can eat your popcorn trees without so much as a stomach upset."

Ilanith said, "That's okay with me. Elly? Do you mind?"

"I don't know," Elly said. "What *is* it, Annie? Can we live with it?"

I called up ships' records on the behavior patterns of the authentic creature and moved aside to let Elly have a look. "I suspect you'll all have to carry Leo's secret weapon when you go down to the loch to fish or swim, but other than that I don't see much of a problem."

Leo thumped me on the back. "Damn you, woman, what *is* it?"

Elly'd gotten a film that might have been my creature's twin. She looked taken aback at first, then she too giggled. "That's the silliest thing I've seen in years! Come on, Annie, *what is it?*"

"Honey, Loch Moose has got its first moose."

"No!" Leo shouted—but he followed it with a laugh as he crowded in with the rest to look at the screen.

Only Susan wasn't laughing. She caught my hand and pulled me down to whisper, "Will they let us keep it if it's only ninety-nine percent? It's not *good* for anything, like the odders are."

I patted her hand. "It's good for a laugh. I say it's a keeper." I was not about to let this go the way of the kangaroo rex.

"Now I understand why I found her in that state," Leo was saying. He pointed accusingly at me. "This woman was laughing so hard she could scarcely catch her breath."

"You didn't see the damn thing crowned with water lilies and chewing on them while it contemplated the oddity in the boat. You'd have been as helpless as I was."

"Unbelievable," he said.

"Worse," I told him, "in this case, seeing isn't believing. I still can't believe in something like *that*. The mind won't encompass it."

He laughed at the screen, then again at me. "Maybe that accounts for your granddaddy's monster. It was so silly-looking anybody who saw it wouldn't believe his own eyes."

I couldn't help it—I kissed him on the cheek. "Leo, you're a genius!"

He squeaked like Susan. "Me? What did *I* do?"

"Elly," I said, "congratulations! You now have the only lodge on Mirabile with an *Earth-authentic* Loch Ness monster." I grinned at Susan, who caught on immediately. I swear her smile started at the mouth and ran all the way down to her toes.

Feeling rather smug, I went on, "Leo will make bells so your lodgers can scare it away if it gets too close to them, won't you, Leo?"

"Oh!" said Leo. He considered the idea. "You know, Annie, it might just work. If everybody went to Loch Ness to try to get a glimpse of the monster, maybe they'll come *here*, too. Scary but safe."

"Exactly." I fixed him with a look. "Now how do we go about it?"

He grinned. "We follow our family traditions: we tell stories."

"You think if I hang around for a week or so, that'll make it a safe monster?"

"Yeah, I think so."

"Good," I said. "Susan? What's the verdict? Are you going off to the lab? If I'm going to stay here, *somebody*'ll have to help Mike coddle those red daffodils."

No squeak this time. Her mouth dropped open but what came out was "Uh, yes. Uh, Elly?"

Elly nodded with a smile, sad but proud all in one.

So while they bustled about packing, I had a chance to read through all the material in ships' records on both moose and Nessie. By the time they were ready to leave for town, I had a pretty good idea of our game plan. I sent Susan off with instructions to run a full gene-read on both creatures. Brute force on the moose, to make sure it wouldn't chain up to something bigger and nastier.

Then we co-opted the rest of Elly's kids. Leo gave each of them a different version of our monster tale to tell.

Jen, I thought, did it best. She got so excited when she told it that her eyes popped and she got incoherent, greatly enhancing the tale of how Leonov Opener Denness had saved Annie Jason Masmajean from the monster in Loch Moose.

Leo brought bells from his workshop. They'd been intended to keep beastlies away in the northern territory but there was no reason they wouldn't do just as good a job against a monster that was Earth authentic.

Two days later, the inn was full of overnighters—much to Elly's surprise and delight—all hoping for a glimpse of the Loch Moose monster.

In my room, late night and by nova light, Leo got his first

peek at the creature. Once again it was swimming in the loch. He stared long and hard out the window. After a long moment, he remembered the task we'd set ourselves. "Should I wake the rest of the lodgers, do you think?"

"No," I said, "you just tell them about it at breakfast. Anybody who doesn't see it tonight will stay another night, hoping."

"You're a wicked old lady."

I raised Ilanith's camera to the window. "Yup," I said, and, twisting the lens deliberately out of focus, I snapped a picture.

"Hope that didn't come out well," I said.

KENNY

William F. Wu

 I awoke in total darkness to a ringing phone. The illuminated clock read 1:16:24 A.M. I groped for the receiver, cut off the third ring, and answered while still arising from the oceans of a deep sleep.

"Mm—hello."

"Kenny, *hi.* You busy?"

Kenny, I thought. Only two people still called me Kenny at age thirty-one—my mother, and Angela. Angela Hart.

I swallowed. Angela was in trouble again.

"Kenny Huang, you speak to me! I'm coming right up to see you, okay? Now that I know you're home."

"Listen, where—"

She hung up. Speak to me, she had said.

I lay in the dark, inhaling deeply, trying to wake up. As always, Angela was the last person I wanted to see—even an angry ex-lover would have been more welcome. Anyone but Angela.

And whenever I dealt with Angela, that little kid came alive in my mind.

I threw off the covers and pulled on a pair of jeans. Then I staggered out to the kitchen for coffee, which I normally don't drink. I would need it for Angela's visit.

I had some of the instant stuff around for such an emergency. No more than four minutes after the phone call, I found myself sitting with a steaming cup, slouched on the little green and white couch in my little apartment living room, wondering where she had been when she had called. The late hour wouldn't matter to her, of course, but I go to bed at ten o'clock and rise at six. For me, this was the middle of the night.

I glanced around the darkened room. Light from the kitchen came in at an angle and created a dance of shadows among all the bookcases. I have the couch, two chairs, and then nothing but bookshelves, all full. The shelves start just above the furniture and go to the ceiling. I couldn't remember if Angela had been here or not; I hadn't seen her in several years.

Somewhere around here I had a TV I could show her, and see if she recognized it. Her mother and mine still lived in the two houses where we had grown up across the street from each other. As a child I had been a TV junkie—had grown up by the light of the flickering tube. I didn't watch much television anymore but I had bought an old black-and-white portable from Angela's mother a year before to see what was on these days. None of the programs really interested me, even on public television. I had watched the twenty-four-hour cable news station for a few days.

I sipped the hot coffee and stared blankly into the darkness.

The doorbell rang, the clear happy chimes sounding idiotic in the depth of night. I rose and checked my watch. Only ten minutes had passed since she had phoned. I opened the door.

"Hi, Kenny." Angela smiled brightly, glanced down the hall, and came inside.

I closed the door behind her and backed up a little. "Hello, Angela."

"Well—" She looked sideways at me for a fraction of a second and decided against hugging me. "Well. Nice place, it looks like."

"Come in." I gestured toward the couch.

Angela slid a small red backpack off one shoulder and dropped it. She sank onto the couch and closed her eyes. "Jeez, I need a—oh, I guess you still wouldn't have any alcohol around, would you, Kenny?"

"Sorry. Orange juice?"

"Never mind."

I sat down in a chair across from her.

Angela looked awful and looked great. Her dirty-blond hair was short and matted against her head. She wore a tight mud-splattered rugby shirt with scarlet and gray stripes and blue jeans ragged around the ankles, with both knees completely worn through and ripped out. Her heavy hiking boots were new.

As always, Angela was quite pretty. Her eyes betrayed a prolonged shortage of sleep, but she hadn't lost weight; I recognized the substantial thighs she had first developed playing catcher for a softball team years ago in high school. Her mother had been a minor film ingenue for a short time long ago, and Angela had inherited her striking looks. Any acting ability she had, though, was applied at the con artist level.

Angela was three years younger than I—that would make her twenty-eight now. She looked much the same as she had at eighteen, except for the lack of sleep. I waited for her to say something.

After a while she roused herself enough to take a cigarette and a plastic lighter out of her pack. She had known that I hated tobacco smoke for most of our lives, so I said nothing. Reminding her now was useless.

The lighter flashed in the darkness and the end of her cigarette glowed red and large, then smaller as she stopped inhaling.

"Will you do me a favor, Kenny?" Her voice was pleasant and casual. She blew smoke off to one side, away from me.

"Depends." I always answered her that way, initially.

"I'm in some trouble, I guess."

I grinned and indulged in the luxury of being an old friend. "You're always in trouble, Angela." I laughed gently, comfortable in my old role of disapproving confidant. "You've been in trouble forever."

She smiled down at the cigarette in her hand. "Yeah. You could say that, maybe." She tapped ashes onto my wooden coffee table and looked up at me. "No one else can say it, though."

We both laughed lightly. It was forced amusement.

"What do you want, Angela? This time."

"I've always known I could come to you. This is a big one, though, Kenny. If you won't do it, I'll understand."

She waited for me to say something.

I decided to let her wait. We both had always known she could come to me, though I didn't think she realized that it was not mutual. She lived by short-term solutions—minor deceits, small thefts, skipping towns. Her kinds of solutions only dug her in deeper and took her other acquaintances down with her.

As a child, I had always been considered the good kid in the neighborhood and at school. Something about the way I looked or acted caused adults to like me. I wasn't aware of being an especially good kid, but reading a lot and getting good grades helped my image. Teachers and parents pointed to me and asked other kids, Why can't you be like him? And yet, perhaps because I had never stood up to Angela, she had been my only childhood friend.

I smiled at her shadowed face. "I don't want to be like you, Angela."

She shrugged and tapped ashes onto my couch. "We're even—I don't want to be like you, either. To live like you. Come to think of it, how's your bookstore?"

"Fine." I knew she would return to the subject at hand in her own way. "I only have one partner now. Mark and I bought out the others. We're trying to arrange for a new branch to open up."

"*Oh?* I'm impressed." She smiled nicely. "I take it back, Kenny. Selling books sure beats dealing."

I looked up sharply. She met my eyes with a self-satisfied grin.

"All right," I said. "Dealing what?"

Her eyes stayed on me. "Morphine. Clinic rip-offs."

I slid to the edge of my chair and pointed at her. "If you've brought any in here, then you just—"

"Search me."

"What?"

She kicked her red backpack toward my feet and raised her hands over her head, stretching her rugby shirt even tighter. "I'm clean. Search me if you want."

I didn't believe her. That just meant she'd hidden it in her underwear. She had done the same trick in junior high school with shoplifted cigarettes.

"Skip it, Angela. You know I won't rifle your underwear."

She laughed appreciatively.

"Angela, what do you want?"

"An alibi."

"For what?"

She dragged on her cigarette and blew off to the side again. "You don't want the details, Kenny. Look—just before I called you, I met with my buyer."

I felt sickened. "This guy is a street pusher? And you supply him?"

She smiled tightly, looking off into the shadows of my

books. "We got into a hassle about, uh, well—we argued. I just need a witness to say I was somewhere else."

"What did you do?" I had never known her to carry a gun, but if she had left her fingerprints on one, or on something similar, an alibi wouldn't help her much.

"I did what I had to."

"Then what did he do?"

"That's not the difficulty. Believe me, Kenny, you'd rather not—"

"I won't do anything for you unless you tell me what you did. Tell me or forget it."

She smiled tight-lipped, looking at the floor. "I shoved him in front of a car."

I held my breath.

"He's dead, Kenny, but he really deserved it. He really did."

Murder. She had finally made the big time.

I stared at her, feeling cold and sullen. She had run from a murder scene to me.

"The driver—uh, he died too."

"You know him?" My voice was dry and quiet.

"No."

She had murdered an innocent passerby, also. My Angela. "And you want me to say you were here all night with me." I felt very cold.

"No one can identify me for sure, Kenny. The police'll come for me 'cause his friends saw me as a shadow, but no one saw me clearly. Besides, they'll all be questionable witnesses with police records—not like you."

No. I shook my head and tried to speak. My throat was too dry. I swallowed.

"Nothing will happen, Kenny. You can get me off at the hearings, most likely, or at the grand jury. I won't even go to trial if you speak up."

No. But when I tried to say it out loud, I just couldn't say the word. "I wish, uh . . ."

"Kenny, you . . ." She cocked her head to one side. "What's that?"

"Huh? What?" I listened for police sirens outside.

"Shh." Angela held up a hand, listening, wide-eyed.

I heard it for the first time. It was the sound of voices through a speaker, like a radio or a stereo. They were faint and muffled.

"Kenny?" Angela's tone was hushed. "Kenny, it's in there." She pointed to the door of my living room closet.

"Oh, that's imp—" I stopped, looking at the little flickering line of light beneath the closet door. The voices were coming from the other side of it.

I got up and reached for the knob.

"Kenny, don't."

"Some funny wiring thing, I guess." I opened the door.

The little black-and-white TV was up on the shelf. A couple of kids were playing, as though the show was an old sitcom. There was no sound now.

I stared at it.

Angela crept up beside me and clung to my arm. "What is—" she whispered, and then gasped. "Kenny, it's *not plugged in*."

The bunched black cord, with its plug visible, was hanging down just below the shelf, right in front of us. I stiffened and felt the prickling of fear sweep up my spine to the back of my head.

Those kids looked like Angela and me. Despite my fear, I reached up carefully and took down the set. It remained on as I put it down on the coffee table, with its coiled cord swaying above the floor.

I sat down on the couch, fascinated. Angela, still holding my arm, sat down beside me. Her facade was failing; underneath it, her nerves were shot from what she had done earlier that night.

"You remember this?" My whispered voice was awestruck.

She shook her head, barely enough for me to detect.

I recognized the day. It was the day after Christmas when I was around eleven. We had been playing in the rec room of Angela's house with the little plastic dinosaurs we both had received the day before. That wasn't why I remembered it, though.

As I watched I matched my memories with—whatever we were watching. Angela was bent over the little dinosaurs on the floor, her blond hair falling into her face, keeping the tyrannosauruses and triceratopses for herself and giving me the ones with faces like ducks. I—little Kenny—was sorting my own pile.

Then we both looked off to the side, in response to a sound. I recalled that other neighborhood kids had invited us to play outside with them. The scene shifted to a sunny, snow-covered front yard, with Angela's house in the background.

Angela had snatched up a new baby doll of firm, shiny plastic on the way out of the house. Now she was showing it off to the other kids. As I watched the screen—and remembered—a twelve-year-old neighbor boy came running up to join us waving a toy rifle. He wasn't a bully, but he was the oldest kid in the neighborhood and easily the biggest. With a grin, he swung the rifle around like a club and made a playful motion as though he was going to hit me with it. Angela, out of some strange protective instinct, swung her doll at him and slashed open his forehead. She laughed delightedly, right there on the screen. Then the screen went black, leaving only one tiny spot of white glowing in the center before it, too, disappeared.

I let out a slow breath. The older boy had needed two stitches. Angela's parents had beaten her and locked her in her room all day without food. I had been horrified by her overreaction and horrified again by her punishment.

Kids are kids, though, and the next day we had played together as always.

My past as a TV child had returned to me. And I could feel that child coming alive inside me.

I reached over to my right and turned on a table lamp.

"That's creepy," Angela muttered. "Just coming on all by itself." She smiled weakly.

"You remember that day?"

"What? What day?"

She hadn't recognized us. Chilled again, I changed topics. "Look, I don't want to help a killer. Killing a pusher *might* have extenuating circumstances *if* you were his victim and not his supplier. And killing an innocent guy who just happened along, too—you're just a killer."

"You—you set this up!"

"How? *I* don't know what just happened."

"So—that's my old childhood friend, who won't help me when I ask." Even now, she was too proud to beg.

"I won't turn you in, Angela. I just don't want to help you."

"Kenny, you and I—"

The TV screen came on again.

"What's *that*?" Angela's voice expressed as much confusion as fear.

"I don't . . . say, that's us again." And I realized, somehow, that I had caused—wished—this television to come on.

"Stop it, Kenny. No more tricks. I have enough problems tonight without—"

"It's not a trick, Angela. I don't know how to stop it. But look—that's you there, and this is me."

We were looking at a softball diamond at our grade school, years ago. I was twelve years old, in the sixth grade. Angela was only nine, but she was behind the plate warming up a pitcher and practicing her chatter. This was before any organized softball had come to our area, and the teachers at our grade school had set up mildly competitive teams with both boys and girls. Angela was a third-grade hotshot, big for her age with good coordination. She wasn't a strong hitter, but she hit well for average and could actually throw on target. I—little Kenny—was a short kid standing off to the side with his hands in his pockets, watching. He wore a baseball cap, but his mitt was on the ground at his feet.

Grown-up Angela, next to me on the couch, folded her arms. "You can't tell if that's us."

"Look at it. It's the last inning of the championship game at the end of the year. You and I were on the same team, remember?"

"In *grade* school? How can I remember that?"

I shook my head and kept watching. Our team was behind with one full inning to play. Little Kenny couldn't hit, ran slowly, couldn't catch, and threw weakly. One of the teachers who had acted as plate umpire had suggested one day that he learn to pitch, probably to minimize the amount of damage he could do to his own team. So he had learned, practicing with Angela in the front yard while she practiced her catching and her chattering and threw out imaginary would-be base-stealers. Kenny had the slowest fastball of all the pitchers around, but he had a genuine curve. He pitched in the late innings, usually, and today he had been promised this final inning of the final game—except that his team's rather arrogant starting pitcher had raced to the mound ahead of him just now and was warming up while shy little Kenny stood stonily watching.

As the first batter came up to the plate, Angela stood and cocked her arm to return the ball to the pitcher. She paused, though, looking at Kenny by the first-base line.

"C'mon, Kenny! Get in there!" She threw him the ball.

He bobbled it in his bare hands, but he got it, snatched up his mitt, and trotted to the mound.

The other kid was still standing there, but Kenny stood next to him, slapping the ball into his mitt over and over again, looking at Angela. When the batter stepped up and took a few tentative swings over the plate, the other kid stomped away in disgust.

"C'mon, Kenny!" Angela punched her mitt.

Kenny started without any warm-up pitches. He gave up three hits altogether, and loaded the bases, but he didn't give up any runs. That was all any pitcher could do.

Kenny sat behind the backstop while his team batted. Angela sat on the bench and yelled encouragement, but their team went down, three in a row, and the game was over.

Angela angrily yanked her cap down to her eyebrows and grabbed her mitt. She started in the direction of her house. Kenny hurried up alongside her and said, "Thanks."

She shrugged. "You deserved to pitch. They said you could." She turned and looked up at him from under her baseball visor with eyes I remembered as blue and bright. "Cartoons are gonna be on. Race ya to my house!" And she ran off across the abandoned, dusty field.

Little Kenny kept walking, with his mitt under his arm and his hands in his pockets. I remembered what he was thinking. He was thinking that pitching that single inning was more important to him than anything he could remember. Angela had given it to him. I watched him pull one hand out of his pocket and cross his fingers behind his back. He was wishing. *I wish that someday I get the chance to do a favor for Angela that means as much to her.* Then little Kenny tugged his baseball cap down hard, grabbed his mitt from under his arm, and ran after Angela.

The screen blackened.

I felt another chill.

"They did look like us, sort of," Angela said quietly. "But look, Kenny, I'm in trouble. Will you do me this favor or not?"

I took a deep breath and got it out. "No."

"Kenny, I *need* you. Nobody else could—"

"No. I will not trade one inning of pitching for a phony murder alibi."

"Huh? What are you talk—" She set her mouth hard, suddenly, and scooted back on the couch until she could put both feet against the TV screen. Her strong legs straightened and sent the TV to the carpet with a heavy thud. "There! Now forget about it!"

I clenched my teeth and looked away from the TV set. "You're welcome to spend the night on the couch. You leave in the morning. I won't go to the police, but if they ask me any questions, I'll tell the truth."

She started fumbling around for another cigarette. "All right, all right. What a grouch. I suppose I oughta be thankful for that."

I got off the couch and stepped over the TV set to sit in the chair again.

"Kenny, maybe when the time comes you'll do the right thing." She lit up. "We both know you can get away with it."

"I guess we do."

"I know what everyone else thought—Kenny Huang was a Chinese angel, a proper little egghead who would never do anything wrong and would never, *ever* lie. A regular slant-eyed saint." She watched to see if I would react to her last remark.

"We both know better. The biggest difference between us was that you got caught half the time—I hardly ever got caught at all."

Angela smiled. "I've seen you bluff, Kenny. Remember the time after school, in the school library, when we tried to carve a pumpkin into a jack-o'-lantern? When the librarian got called away to the phone?"

I laughed. "Yeah, I remember. When she came back, you hid in the stacks and left me standing around next to a big pile of pumpkin chunks with seeds and gunk all over them."

"And you talked your way out of it, Kenny. She just *knew* you wouldn't do anything like that."

That was right—I had played stupid and innocent. The librarian let me go, but she found Angela hiding. Angela had to stay after school and later had to pay for the pumpkin. Her mother had used a leather belt on her.

"Angela, I know you got punished for things we both did —even things I did alone. I got away with a lot."

Angela sighed. "That was a long time ago. I don't . . ." She trailed off, staring into the long shadows cast by the bookshelves. Her facade dropped away once again; I could see the fear and strain in her face. If she had been the sort to cry, she would have cried then.

For a moment—no longer than usual—I felt sorry for her. She had never really had a chance. Through all the years I had known her, she had been moving closer and closer to serious crimes. I didn't know what drove her, though, if anything did.

I took a sleeping bag out of the same closet where the TV had been. She got up and we spread it out on the couch.

Angela picked up her pack and started for the bathroom. "You still seeing that Jewish lady, with the black hair?"

"Uh—no. Not for a long time."

"Oh. How 'bout the Chinese one? You still thinking about her?"

"Sometimes, I suppose."

"Too bad." She went into the bathroom and then stuck her head around the door. "Just as well, Kenny. You deserve bigger tits than that." She laughed and swung the door shut.

I escaped to the darkness of my bedroom and closed my own door. The clock read 2:53:04. I hoped I would never have to face her again.

When I awoke around nine the next morning, she was gone. I was annoyed at having slept so late. That stupid TV set was on again, where it lay on its back on the floor. I threw a coat over it without looking at it and started packing. Angela had me just frantic enough not to be too curious.

I called Mark and made vague excuses. He agreed to make my apartment look lived in. I left with the TV still going, now with low muffled sound beneath my coat. Angela would send the police around, and if I stayed, I would see a subpoena with my name on it. She was that certain I would never harm her.

I flew to New York to see book publicists. The ones I met were cheerful dyspeptic drunkards. The first week was fine. Then one night in my hotel room, I shot awake with light flickering and shifting in the darkened room. The TV set had come on, this time in color. I sat up and focused my eyes.

Little Angela and little Kenny were kneeling in the backyard of Angela's house. As I watched, Kenny poured lighter fluid on an anthill and Angela lit it with a match. Offscreen, a grown woman screamed and began yelling obscenities. I saw the two children look up. Then a hand swept down and slapped Angela across the face. The same hand grabbed her hair and pulled her away, shrieking, while little Kenny jumped up and ran away.

The set blackened, leaving me in the darkness. I fumbled for the lamp and got it the third or fourth time. Shivering in a sticky, sweaty chill, I pawed through my suitcase for clean underwear. Instead, I came up with an old blue cap.

It was a small, badly beat-up child's baseball cap. I knew I hadn't packed it—I hadn't seen it in twenty years. On the inside band, I could read *Kenny Huang* in faded ballpoint ink, written in my mother's handwriting.

I threw it into the far darkness of the room and got dressed. Some hours later, I was driving to Maine in a rented car to pick blueberries.

For some weeks, I picked up a hometown paper whenever I could. The innocent driver who had been killed was Curtis Steadman, a geophysicist, aged forty-five. He had been married with one son and one daughter. The street pusher, Higgins, was of less interest. He had a long, violent record. Angela had been arrested, all right, and I followed her progress through the hearings and her indictment on one count of murder one and one count of voluntary manslaughter. Her trial was set to start almost immediately—murder was still rare in my suburban town.

I was buying a shirt in a department store when a TV came on behind me. The cash register was near the entertainment section. Little Kenny was practicing his curveball with little Angela in her front yard.

I grabbed the salesclerk's arm. "Can you see that?"

"What? Well, of course." He pulled his arm free.

"What is it?"

"Oh, some kind of pregame show, I guess. Chinese kid—prob'ly the Taiwan Little League or something. Wonder where that blond girl came from."

"Oh—*thanks.*" Still scared, but somehow relieved, I reached into my wallet to pay him. I tossed down a twenty-dollar bill and a baseball card.

"Say—that's the same kid." The clerk picked up the card. " 'Kenny Huang, age twelve. Relief pitcher. 2–2, 4 Saves. Season ERA, 3.04. Championship ERA, 0.00.' " He whistled and handed back the card. "Cute kid. Your son?"

"No." I finished business, ripped the card to bits, and hurried away in a small whirl of confetti.

I couldn't take any more of this. No, little Kenny was not in favor of murder. He just didn't really grasp it. But if I was ever going to get rid of him—and Angela—I would have to go back, just like I always suspected I would.

When I got home, I found that Mark had set my TV on the coffee table. It was off. I covered it up with my coat again and went to bed.

". . . and nothing but the truth, so help you God?"

"I swear."

"You may be seated."

Another voice, a moment later: "Mr. Huang, Angela Hart has testified that she was in your apartment with you from seven forty-five P.M. on the evening of the crime until nine the following morning when you left town on a prolonged business trip. Is this true?"

"Yes."

That was the important part. He messed around with the

exact times a little, but since the murder had occurred around one A.M., that didn't accomplish much. Then he got nasty and suspicious, so I looked puzzled and ignorant. That kept the jurors on my side. Yes, she had joined me after dinner and had stayed until after breakfast. No, we hadn't watched television —ha!—and no one had called. We had not gone anywhere, together or singly. What had we done all night? I smiled a little, looked embarrassed, and gave him some sophomoric euphemism. Everyone laughed. They were sure this shy, youngish-looking bookworm just couldn't get up on the stand and lie for a murderer.

A friendly voice came around next and asked a few questions about my background. That polished it—no police record, no lively reputation, no high living. I neither drank nor smoked. Mostly, I read a lot of books.

When the questions ended, I walked away erect, with my head held high, smiling slightly at Angela as I passed and casually making eye contact with anyone whose glance happened to meet mine. From the corners of my vision I could see the crowd watching as I left the courtroom.

I was told to wait around in case one side or the other called me back. The trial dragged on and on, but the prosecution had nothing to equal my sworn, convincing corroboration of her alibi. After the jury went out, I maintained my composure as I walked to my car, drove home with shaking hands, and ate a light dinner.

I had done my best to free a killer in the full knowledge of what I was doing. As soon as I finished eating, I vomited up all of my dinner. I cleaned it up and then drank myself into oblivion with a bottle of Scotch I had bought the day before just for that purpose. It was my first liquor purchase.

I awoke in morning sunshine to a ringing phone. The pain in my throbbing head brought me quickly to full consciousness. "Hello," I said hoarsely.

"I've been acquitted, Kenny—you did it! You got me off.

Thanks *so* much. I knew you'd come through for me, Kenny. You always—"

"*Not* for you, Angela. Don't misunderstand. You're scum now, Angela. I don't want you around me. Not now, not ever."

"What—but . . ." Her voice turned angry. "Well, who *did* you do it for, then? Yourself? Don't give *me* that, Mr. Perfect—*you* just perjured yourself for a killer! So who *did* you do it for? Huh?" She slammed down the phone.

I would hear from her again, of course. From now on I would avoid her, reject her, tell her off—I would never do anything for her ever again. But I would always hear from her.

I shoved myself into a sitting position on the bed, hurting all over. No, I certainly hadn't lied on the stand for myself. *I* didn't deserve to be a perjurer. And I hadn't done it for Angela; she didn't deserve acquittal. I swallowed and eased off the bed.

Tentatively, I stretched a little bit. I hadn't done it for little Angela, either. The cute kid with a wild streak had been a true friend, but she was gone—destroyed by the woman she had become. I started for the bathroom.

Somewhere, sitting in the rec room of my mind, hanging back on the edges of the ball field, standing around in the library of all my memories, little Kenny had remembered his promise. He didn't care about grown-up worries; he only knew that I—big Ken—still had a promise to keep. And once I had kept it for him, he disappeared forever.

By the time I sat down on the couch with a cup of steaming tea, I was feeling better. I plugged in the TV and switched it on, just to see for myself. My guilt over Angela was now mixed with a hint of personal satisfaction.

A rerun of some moronic cop show was on. With my sparse history of watching television as an adult, I had no way of recognizing it, and normally I would have shut it off. Now, though, I was ready to see the reliable old network formula.

As I watched, a man came running out of a jewelry store to the sound of a burglar alarm. A squad car with spinning red lights screeched to a halt at the curb. Two uniformed cops jumped out and wrestled the crook to the sidewalk, yelling about how they had set him up and fooled him and book 'im and so on.

This was the mentality I had grown up with but avoided as an adult. Now the familiarity, the sheer predictability, was a great relief. I finally started to understand what most people found so attractive about such shows. I would be safe here.

Then one of the uniformed cops turned to face me in a close-up shot, the badge on his hat shining over a grim, authoritative gaze. "My name is Curtis Steadman," he said. "You never got to know me before. But you will, Kenny—you will."

KITES

Maureen F. McHugh

 The door is flanked by two curtained windows with big flower arrangements in them, it makes the place look more like a discreet and expensive restaurant than a funeral parlor. The first person I see is Orchid—long white hair and black satin quilted jacket with, of course, a huge white silk orchid appliqued across the back. Then Cinnabar, who isn't wearing red. Cinnabar is really Cinnabar Chavez's first name, so I guess he doesn't have to prove anything, he only wears red when he flies.

Some fliers take on their flying name, like Orchid. Everybody calls her Orchid. I don't even know what her name is. But nobody calls Eleni "Jacinth" except the marks. Nobody calls me Gargoyle, they just call me Angel. But everybody calls Johnny B "Johnny B," even though we all know his name is Gregory.

Cinnabar sees me, waves me over. He's a good flier for a guy, a little tall; he's 1.55 meters but so skinny he doesn't mass over 48 kilos. Flying runs in his family, his brother was

Random Chavez—bet you didn't know he even had a last name. Of course, he was killed in that big smash, Jesus, five years ago? I'm getting old. That was the year I started flying the big kites. I was there, I finished that race.

"*Pijiu?*" Cinnabar says. We give each other a hug. There's a spread, a funeral banquet, but I can't eat at funerals. Just as well, since I have to keep my weight at about 39 kilos, and beer has too many calories. Orchid preens, looking strange and graceful as a macaw. I check, no cameras, and, of course, she's not synched. She must do it by habit.

We don't have anything to say to each other. So we stand around the viewing room feeling guilty. The dead can feel virtuous, I suppose. Dead dead dead. That's for all you people who say "passed away."

People die for different reasons; the young ones—the ones with good reflexes—die because they take risks; the older ones die because their reflexes or synapses let them down. Not that we don't all cut up and take risks, it's just that the older you get, the less often you get in positions where you have to, or maybe you know that there's another race.

"Kirin was a nice girl," Cinnabar says.

I didn't really know the deceased all that well. I mean, she'd flown and all but she'd only been riding in the big kites a year or so, and I was out for three months because I tore a ligament in my shoulder. Besides, she was ABC, American Born Chinese, she even had citizenship in China. Opens a lot of doors. ABCs don't have to associate with *weiguoren* from Brooklyn. Especially *weiguoren* having a bad year. Funny, when I was growing up I didn't know that *weiguoren* meant foreigner, because the ABCs were the foreigners to me. I always thought it meant not-Chinese.

"Are you flying tonight?" I ask.

"I'm going down to Florida this afternoon," Orchid says. She goes down there a lot to fly.

"You be out at Washington Square?" Cinnabar asks me.

"If Georgia can get the Siyue off the ground." Georgia's my tech.

"You're still flying a Siyue?" Orchid asks, white eyebrows arching all disdainful.

Cinnabar looks away as if he hasn't heard, to save me face. Last year Citinet dropped me and I've been flying independent. Orchid knows that. *Meiqian,* I'm a poor woman, last year's kite. Bitch. But Orchid isn't going to be dropped, no. Even if she isn't having a good year, she makes a good cover story. Pretty girl, a popular synch.

"Angel," Cinnabar says. "Jai lai tonight on Guatemala Avenue, want to go back to the old neighborhood?"

"Let's see how the race goes."

Cinnabar is such a sweetheart. He comes from Brooklyn, like me. Orchid looks bored, pampered little Virginia girl.

"If you come into money," Cinnabar says, "you pay."

I laugh.

At Washington Square, Georgia and I have got the Siyue working and I lift the kite over my head, holding it so I can feel the wind in the silk. It hums, a huge insect. I'm wired into the half-awake kite and moving in sensory overlap—I have arms and wings both feeding through parallel synapsis, and if I think about which I am trying to move it's like trying to pat my head and rub my stomach at the same time. But I'm lit and my mind is chemical clear. My black silk wings are taut and light above me. I am called *Angel,* with the soft *h* sound of Brooklyn for the *g,* and I am burning, waiting for the race. I stand 1.47 meters tall and weigh 39 kilos but I'm strong, probably stronger than you. My joints are like cables, the ligaments and tendons in my shoulders are all synthetic after the last surgery, strong as spider web, far stronger than steel.

If my kite holds together, there is no one who can beat me. I feel it.

I jog a few meters, and then start to run lightly. There is

the faint vibration of power as the sensors signal that I've reached the threshold between drag and lift and the system trips into active, and when the power feeds through the kite the full system comes on, and I swing my legs up into the harness by habit because I don't even have a body anymore. My body *is* the kite. I feel the air on my silk, I balance on the air. The kite is more than a glider, because it needs a power source that is fueled by my own metabolism, but the original kites—hang gliders—were true gliders; a kite *does* fly. I mean, I'm not a rock. I won't just fall.

I climb in lazy circles, there's two fliers spiraling up above me, one below me. *Loushang* is Medicine, her kite patterned like a Navajo sand painting even from where I see it underneath. *Louxia* I can't see, they are between me and the groundlight, so all I can see is the silhouette of a Liuyue kite. I test the kite, my left shoulder aches like rheumatism. It's an old kite, it has aches and pains.

Then they are starting to form up; eighteen kites, two abreast, I am six back, on the outside. I drop into place, and we do a slow circle of the course. Eighteen triangles of bright silk. The course goes from Washington Square Park to Union Square and back, following The Swath. Over the Square the ground is a maze of lights, then suddenly the groundlights end and there's nothing below us but the undergrowth and debris of the 2059 riots. Off to my right I see the bracelet of lights where Broadway goes under The Swath—I never remember to call it Huang tunnel, it's still Morrissey to me—and then there's nothing but the floaters lighting us until we're over Union Square. Long sweeping turn over Union Square and just as we straighten up, like a long, strung-out New Year's dragon made of kites, we're back over The Swath. Off to my right and slightly behind me now is midtown. I count floaters, there are five, and then we are over Washington Square Park. I catch a glimpse of the betting board but it's too small to read from up here.

I wonder briefly how many people are synched with me. I

used to be self-conscious about the people who are tied in, experiencing what I experience as I fly. Now I don't think of them as separate people much—a teenage boy somewhere in Queens, maybe an old man in the Bronx. If the numbers get high enough, Citinet will sponser me again. But why sponsor someone with last year's kite? Someone who probably won't win? When they dropped me at Citinet, they told me I was too precise a flier. I made all the rational choices, took no chances. I was too cold, no fun.

I told them no one was going to follow *me* down into The Swath, fighting to regain control of my kite, until the automatic cutoff kills the synch just nanoseconds before impact. One of them muttered that at least then I'd be doing something *interesting*.

We come back over Washington Square Park for the second time and the kites begin to pick up speed. We glide past the floater marking the start and already I'm climbing, trying to get altitude. Ten kites are in front of me and I sideslip slightly inside, cutting off Medicine, flying to my left. She's forced to go underneath me, ends up flying *xialou*, my shadow underneath except that my kite is black silk and hers is patterned in red, black, white, and blue. I see Cinnabar ahead, flying third—a scarlet kite with edges that bleed into cinnamon.

And we are over The Swath. I dive. Not hard, just enough to gain speed. A black kite disappears over The Swath, there is only the silver of the lights reflecting like water on my silk. I hang there underneath Kim (whose work name is Polaris but whom I have always called Kim). The dive has put merely the lightest of strain on my frame and the ache in my shoulder is no worse. Still, I wait, to see where everyone is when we flash out over Union Square. I settle in, working steadily. I'm not winded, I feel good. I drink air out of my face mask.

Out over the lights of Union Square.

I am somewhere around fifth, we aren't in neat rows anymore. I feel strong, I've got my pace. I look for Cinnabar. He

has dropped back, but he is high, high above me, *shanglou*.
When my kite was new, I rode up there, *shanglou*. We are a
spume of color, a momentary iridescence over Union Square,
and then we are back over The Swath. I am climbing, forcing
myself up. I feel rather than see someone swoop underneath
me. Not Cinnabar, he's waiting. I push a bit, counting under
my breath as I pass floaters. One, two, three, four, five, and
we are out in the lights again. I have held on to fifth, and am
even with most of the pack, but Cinnabar is above me, and
Riptide has taken low lead. She was the swoop I felt. Kim is
slightly in front of me, and in the light, she dives a bit and
then rises like a sailfish, sprinting forward. She arcs up and
starts to fall into acceleration, but a blue kite flown by some
rookie whose name I don't remember neatly sideslips across
her trajectory, and she must spill air to avoid. And then we
are over the darkness for the second and final circuit. Again I
climb. One, two, three, four, five, and we are over Union
Square. I am higher than Kim and Riptide, but Cinnabar is
somewhere higher above me, so I continue to climb. Something, some sense, tells me just as we are going into the dark
that he is diving, and I dive, too. A kite has to come in at least
200 meters above the ground, that's for safety. I am ahead of
Cinnabar, I don't know how far. Everyone is diving through
the dark, ahead of me I sense the rookie, she is in my arc. I let
my wings catch lift just for a second, feeling the strain, coming just over the top of her, and for a moment I'm afraid I've
cut it too close.

But I'm over her, and I feel her lose it for a second, brake,
spill air, startled and trying to avoid a collision that would
have happened before she had time to react. The wind is so
cold across my wings. I'm taking great gulps of air. My shoulder is aching.

Something moves faster, over me, Cinnabar, and I dive
deeper, but the frame of my kite begins to shudder and I'm
afraid to trust it. I ease up on the dive, trying to power-sprint
forward, but my shoulder twinges and the kite shudders and

is suddenly clumsy. Something has given in the left side of
the kite. Frantic, I spill air, lose speed and altitude as wings
flash around me, over me, under me, but the kite is under
control. I come into the light, crippled, losing altitude. The
others flash across the finish. By the time I get to the finish,
I'm at 150 meters, too low. Cinnabar Chavez is taking his
victory lap as I touch down, running, feeling the strain in my
knees of trying to slow the broken kite, then walking.

Georgia, tall and heavy-hipped, my tech, takes the kite,
lifts it off my shoulders. She doesn't say anything. I don't say
anything. What's to say?

I feel heavy, dirt solid. I take off my face mask and gulp
air. God, I'm tired.

Cinnabar is flushed with winning, he's been having a so-
so year, he's been hungry for a win. But everybody is always
hungry for a win. He comes and finds me where Georgia and I
are packing up my broken kite. It's nice of him to think of
me. He's a little embarrassed to be standing there while we
finish crating it, it takes a long time because part of the frame
is bent and it won't fit.

I compliment him on his win and he says *"Nalinali,"*
making a don't-talk-about-it motion with his hand, looking
away across the park. But he's wound up. "Come meet me, by
my crew," he says, too tense to wait, and why should he
when there are people waiting for him?

So I go to find him, and a bunch of us go out to a place on
La Guardia where we can drink and make a lot of noise. It's
called Commemorative, and fliers hang out there. Cinnabar's
picked up two guys; a blond and an ABC, both clearly bent.
So's Cinnabar. They aren't fliers, of course. Cinnabar has the
hots for the blond, whose name is Peter. He isn't tall, not for,
you know, a non-flier, I'm not good at heights, maybe 1.7?
And not heavy. But next to him Cinnabar looks like nothing
but bone and hair. He's pretty, too. And scrawny Cinnabar is
not pretty.

They're talking about going to see some jai lai, but I figure they don't need me along, so I say I'm tired and have to get up tomorrow to look at the kite. The ABC says he's tired, too, which surprises me.

"How are you getting home?" he asks me. It's the first time he's spoken to me all night, but then Cinnabar and the blond have been doing all the talking.

What's he think, I'm going home by limo? "Subway," I say.

"I'll walk with you," he offers.

There are the usual protestations, the don't gos and if you musts. Then I find myself going down the stairs and out onto the street with this gay ABC in his mirrors and his sharkskin jacket. ABCs all act like their faces are made out of ice. We walk west. I'm not sure of his name, sounded like the blond kept calling him Rafe or something, so I ask and he says, "Zhang," real flat.

Dammit, I think, I didn't ask you to take a walk.

We cross Sixth Avenue, and then all of a sudden he says, "I'm sorry I wasn't synched with you tonight."

I'm a little caught off, so I say, "Were you synched with Cinnabar?"

He shakes his head. "Israel."

Israel? Who the hell is Israel? It must be the rookie. "She'll be okay," I say, "once she has some experience." The kind of stuff one says.

"She was okay until you dusted her," he says.

Neither of us says anything more until we're in the lighted subway. Then to be polite I ask, "What do you do?"

"I'm a tech engineer," he says, which is hard to imagine because he doesn't look or talk like the kind of person who spends his days on construction sites, if you know what I mean. He takes off his mirrored shades and rubs his eyes, adding, "But I'm unemployed," then puts them on.

I mumble something about being sorry to hear it. He's chilly and distant but he keeps talking to me. I can't imagine him wanting me to invite him home, and I sure as hell don't want to anyway. So I look at the track.

Down the track I see the lights of the train.

"When the kite went," he says, "did you think about that *Zhongguo ren*, Kirin?"

The flier that just died. That's why he wanted to be synched to me. "No," I say, "I didn't think about anything but getting it under control. You don't have much time to think. Did you ever fly a kite?" As if I had to ask.

"No," he says.

"It's not a cerebral activity," I say.

The train comes in fast and then cushions to a stop. We get on. He doesn't say anything else except "Bye," when he transfers for Brooklyn.

I always forget that half of the people who watch us fly are waiting to see us die.

I *was* thinking, or rather, I had something in the back of my head, when the kite shuddered. I was thinking of my first year flying the big kites. I was flying in the New York City Flight, it was only my third or fourth big race and it was the biggest race I had ever been in. I was a rookie, the field was huge—26 fliers. I didn't have a chance. And I had a crush on Random Chavez. Five fliers were killed in that race.

That was the first time I ever felt afraid to die. When the kite shudders, whenever something goes wrong and there's that instant of having no control, I'm always back at that race.

I ride the subway home to Brooklyn. It's not far from the subway to my building, but I'm glad to get to the door. Safe in the entry, safer in the elevator. I've been living here for two years, and the building knows me. I have an affinity for machines, call me superstitious but I think it comes of spending some of my waking hours as a kind of cyborg. I think my building likes me. I get in the apartment and the lights come on dim, I get myself something icy and bitter to drink and throw on my rec of that race. The chair hugs me, and I prop my feet up and the apartment darkens. I don't synch in with anyone, so it's like watching it from a floater keeping pace with the race. Like being God. Or maybe God is synched in to everyone. Same thing, though, total objectivity. I'm back in the thick of the pack, flying about ninth. Jacinth has just snapped a connection, and her kite falls behind, then clear, then disappears off the screen. She dropped out just before anything happened.

Fox is in seventh, Random Chavez is in fifteenth; Fox dolphins to rise over Watchmaker and just as she begins the swoop over him she slips it—looks away, loses her concentration, who knows. Anyway, she clips Watchmaker and he waffles, would have pulled out of it maybe but he loses too much speed, and Malachite, in front of me, tries to pull his kite over and they collide, I hear the rip of silk, even though flying is really too noisy to hear anything. I don't remember anything after that, but in the tape I slip sideways, inside, and shoot past them. The pack parts around them but Random is boxed, so he drops nose-first into a steep vertical dive deep into a crack between fliers and is gone underneath all of us, streaking, until he tries to pull up. If his kite had been braced the way they are now he'd have made it, but that's five years ago, and the silk shears under the stress, and he tumbles. And he was dead. And Fox, Malachite, Hot Rocks, and Saffron were dead, and Watchmaker never flew again. And Angel finished seventh.

I run it through a second time, in synch with Random Chavez. I just want to feel the plunge when he saw no way through ahead of him, but being in synch is really not the same as being there. I don't see the space he knew was there, feel only the amusement park sensation of drop, the shoot and cut out when the kite starts to tumble.

The lights start to come up, but I want it dim. I think about my kite, and where I'm going to get money to fix it. Mr. Melman of Melman-Guoxin Pipe is one of my sponsors, I'll go to him, sign a note. Oh damn, I'm so deep in debt already. But it's just a frame and silk, everything else would be all right. And I have silk.

In Chinese, silk is *si*, first tone. Four is *si*, second tone—as in Siyue, April (fourth month). Death is *si*, third tone. Four is a bad-luck number for Chinese. But I'm from Brooklyn.

My synch numbers pick up for the next race, but it's always like that after a crack-up. People like that ABC in Commemorative. I fly a careful race, come in fourth, just out of money. Afterward I think that if I'd flown a more spectacular race—worried less about winning and more about how it synched—I could have picked up my numbers. But how can I go out and fly without planning to win?

It's two weeks before I hit money, and that's only second. Pays rent for Georgia and me. Nights I'm out with Cinnabar. He's been hitting, and his synch numbers are way up, with the requisite loss of privacy. He needs somebody to go places with, he surely can't pick up some bent groupie if a synch crew is likely to come out of the walls and snatch a shot or an impression.

Cinnabar and I share a fondness for kites and a reverence for his dead brother. Late at night, clear out to the vacuum, we talk about how wonderful a flier he was, with that combination of seriousness and hyperbole the sober can't abide.

We go out dancing the night before the New Haven Flight, Cinnabar in his brother's red sharkskin jacket—so what if it's five years out of date—and me in a black dress cut so low in back you can see the copper bruise of the synapsis junction in the base of my spine. We go to someplace way downtown in the area they're reclaiming, you know the place, where you have to fit the mix to get in. The building likes us, I told you I have an affinity for buildings, because we just saunter past all the people it won't let in and *whoosh*, the doors open. Dancing with Cinnabar is nice, on the sultry numbers I don't find myself regarding the middle of his chest and on the fast numbers he isn't as stiff as most straights. Or maybe it's because he's a flier.

We dance a lot, and then get synched, I see the crew from the vid. Some woman from the vid drags us in back for an interview with Cinnabar, and we sit in the kitchen. Cinnabar's soaked with sweat, with his hair all stuck to his face, and I can feel sweat trickling down my back. She asks all the silly questions about racing and if he expects his streak to continue. He just shrugs. It always amazes me that they ask that, what do they expect people to do, say yes?

She asks how he got from Brooklyn to flying kites, and he tells her Random was his older brother. I tell her that the jacket is Random's, I figure it will make good media. The kitchen is environmented, and it's *cold.* Cinnabar puts the jacket around my shoulders and sits with his arm around my waist. I can feel his fingers on my ribs tapping nervously. She asks us if we're ready for the New Haven tomorrow and says she notices we aren't drinking. I tell her it's too many calories. I don't tell her we're iced to the gills (no calories in chemicals). But we're iced enough that we aren't really watching what we're doing.

She asks Cinnabar if he feels he has a good chance for the New Haven, and he makes like to spit over his shoulder, just like they do at home to ward off bad luck, then he says, "Gargoyle's going to beat me."

We all laugh.

Citinet calls me after the synch is on vid next evening, but I'm already out at the park, patching my old Siyue. I'm hoping the vid exposure will raise my synch numbers, but I'm thinking about my kite, not my publicity. I don't even see the vid until later, and in it we look like a couple of seventeen-year-olds cuddling, which hooks all the romantics, and there's that red jacket going from owner to owner to catch all the disaster addicts. Just shows nobody cares about how you race so much as what they think about your life.

There are bunches of people around my pit watching

Georgia and me work, and another synch crew shows up. They want to know what it feels like to be racing against my boyfriend and how serious Cinnabar and I are. I say a race is a race and shrug.

"Do you think Cinnabar is right when he says you're going to beat him?"

I stand up and face the synch crew, put my hands on my hips. "Well, I'm going to try," I say, "but I'm flying a Siyue, and he's flying a Liuyue."

"What's the difference?"

"His is a newer kite," I say. "Now I gotta get ready for a race, *si?*"

They don't stop asking me questions but I stop answering. The pickup chirps, and I leave Georgia testing systems.

"Angel," Cinnabar says, *"está loco aquí."*

"Aquí tambien, amigo. I don't know how I can get anything done." It's so noisy I have to plug one ear with my finger. "We did good, huh?"

"No shit." He laughs. "Synch numbers are going to be great. Got an idea, going to send you the jacket, okay? Make a big fuss. Then, when you fly in that crate tonight, you make it look good, okay? Maybe somebody will pick you up and you can fly a real kite."

"Go to hell, my Siyue is a real kite."

"You like antiques."

"You're doing me a great favor," I say to him.

"Favor hell, the bigger this is, the higher my numbers, *comprende?*"

"Okay," I say.

Fifteen minutes later, as I'm putting on my face mask and getting ready to take the kite out, one of Cinnabar's crew arrives carrying the red sharkskin jacket. I make a big show of staring at it, then put it on slowly. Then I jog the Siyue out.

I'm out early, I need the time to remember I'm flying a race. It's cold up there, it feels good. It's empty, I take a lonely lap out across The Swath and Union Square. For the first time since I got out to the Park I get to think about the race.

I fall into line when I get back out over Washington Square, take one lazy lap with everyone. I'm back at eighth, Cinnabar is second. He'll go *shanglou* and so will Orchid. I haven't a chance against them if I fly their race, not in a Siyue. We flash over Washington Square Park. I climb a bit, but when we go over The Swath I put my kite into a long, flat drive, pumping forward. It's not an all-out sprint, but I'm pushing faster than my usual pace. I ride far out, all the way down till I'm close to the 200-meter altitude limit, and when we flash over Union Square I'm low and way out in front. Everybody is still jockeying for *shanglou,* which is ridiculous, because Cinnabar is going to be the best power diver, at 48 kilos he's got mass on his side. I'm using my light weight— damn few fliers lighter than 39 kilos—and sprinting. I don't expect anyone to dive until we're over The Swath, but Israel breaks and is diving after me. As we go into darkness, the pack breaks above me.

Is that ABC synched with me tonight?

In the darkness, I climb a bit, maybe 25 meters. Kites are diving in the dark, and when we flash over Washington Square the second time, I'm third, and the field is a disaster. People are strung out *shanglou* to *xialou* and Orchid is first. Her kite is pearlized silver. She's in trouble because I know I can out-power her. I'm above her, she's down around bottoming out.

We go back into the dark. I'm pushing, I don't know how much longer I can keep this up. But I've flown this damn race my way. I'm still third when we come out over Union Square, but three people dive in front of me, including Cinnabar. I dive into the middle, still not as low as Orchid. She tries to dolphin up and rises into Medicine. We go into darkness.

It's the worst point of the race under the best of circumstances, because one is half blind and acclimating, and the next floater is too far to see and I don't know what the hell is going on, but I know things are a mess. I feel someone over me, and Medicine and Orchid have to be tangled in front of me. The disaster lights go on and I have just time to see Orchid's kite waffle into Cinnabar and see the silk shred away from the left front strut. Polaris is above me, coming down outside. Israel is coming fast inside me. I take the space in front of me, nose first, and start a screaming, too deep dive.

I know I'm below 200 meters, but I'm more worried about pulling the kite out. My bones/frame are screaming with strain and the cross strut breaks away. I drop out of the harness to provide drag, and come into Washington Square too low, too fast. At 20 meters I try to throw the nose up, no longer trying to save the frame and the silk, and the frame distorts as easily as an umbrella turns inside-out in a high wind. *But the silk holds*, like a slack sail taking up air. I try to land on my feet, the ground makes my foot skip off it, I can't get far enough in front of the kite, the balls of my feet keep skipping off the pavement as I try to run, I tumble, and the ground comes up hard . . .

I come to when they're cutting the harness off. They cut off the sharkskin jacket, too, because I've dislocated my left shoulder. "What happened?" I keep saying. "What happened?"

"An accident," Georgia says, "you're okay, honey."

They've given me something, because I'm way out to the vacuum, and I can't think of the questions I want to ask, so I keep saying, "What happened?"

"Orchid got in. Almost everybody's in," Georgia says.

"Who's not in?"

"Cinnabar," she says, "he went down in The Swath."

Well, of course, you probably remember everything else, since it was all over the media. How Cinnabar Chavez broke his spine. That they did surgery, and that it was a while before they were sure he would live.

He was in bad shape for a long time but he's okay now.

He lives in Brooklyn with his lover, I still see him a lot. He doesn't fly anymore. Surgery is wonderful, so is therapy, and he's still a sweet dancer, but he couldn't trust his reflexes in a race. He has a job as a consultant for Cuo, the company that makes the big kites, and he does commentary for one of the big vid organizations. His income is steady these days.

Mine is pretty good these days too. I fly a big black-and-red kite for Citinet; a Chiyue, the new one. My synch numbers are in the 50s, and my picture's on the front of *Passion* next month. I'm wearing the red sharkskin jacket—I had it fixed—and the article is titled "Gargoyle's an Angel!" which is kind of cute.

I fly better these days. Cinnabar bitches about it, he says I'm too far out in front of myself. Sometimes when he says that, I think of bringing that Siyue in and trying to get in front of it to stop it. But that's what the people want, right?

Besides, I can't say it to him, but I'd rather be dead than not able to fly.

GERDA AND THE WIZARD

Rob Chilson

 The sound of horses and men's voices took her man Hugh out of the house quickly; belatedly Gerda heard the jingle of rich harness. Then they were all dismounting out front. She dithered for a moment between going out to help Hugh and staying in to greet them when they entered. Before she could decide, they were entering the dark, smoky house.

Wealthy men in colorful rich clothes, all seeming younger than she, even the one with gray hair. All tall, sturdy, active, healthy, strong in a different way than she and Hugh were strong. Gerda and Hugh were peasants, strong like oxen; these nobles were strong the way a panther is strong. Gerda counted eight. Three were knights, three esquires, and two servants. Hugh was leading their stamping horses around the house to the mean, fly-filled shed they used as a barn.

Gerda bobbed a curtsy that had a touch of fear in it; never had noble-born been within their dwelling. "May I be of service, Noble Sirs?"

Two of them were openly holding their noses; the rest sniffed disdainfully. They clustered near the feeble light from the door, where the lingering rays of the setting sun entered reluctantly. Behind Gerda the fire was not half so bright. After a moment spent looking around, they had located the obvious hazards to movement; except near the door, there were scarcely more than paths between pieces of rude furniture.

"We shall abide here this night, old woman," said one of the esquires crisply, the knights being too noble to condescend.

They looked at her, though, again with disdain, and Gerda was glad that she was no longer young—and that Maken was married and gone, aye and Ealdgyth, young though she was.

"We are honored," she said, curtsying again. "My man hight Hugh; I am called Gerda."

There was a snort from one of the servants and the esquire spoke loftily: "You entertain the noble Baron Hildimar, Sir Gwilliam of the High Tower, Sir Harold Strong of Stanes, and their noble esquires."

The servants weren't mentioned, and the esquires not named. Gerda curtsyed a third time, saying, "How may we serve you?"

"Perhaps, My Lord, we should save our provender? If so be the carles have anything fit for betters than dogs to eat," said the gray-haired one to one of the middle-aged men.

This handsome fellow was apparently the baron, not the older man as she had thought.

"How say you?" said the esquire to her. "What meat have you to offer us?"

Gerda hesitated a moment. It was a lean time. Of course, such as these would not dream of eating the pease porridge simmering quietly behind her. "Cow's cheese and milk, my lords," she said immediately, to gain time. "Bacon." This would end the flitch, but it was old, ill-tasting. She thought to mention eggs, but it might be best to save them for morning. "Bread. Only rye, my lords. And ale." They'd not finish that, for Hugh had another hogshead buried in the woods.

The noble travelers looked at each other with humorous resignation. "Perhaps the cheese and bread, my lords?" said the esquire. "Washed down by strong country ale, it might save us a meal of our provisions."

There was a general nodding of heads and the third knight spoke: "Let it be so, then, Roger."

The esquire turned to her and barked: "Fetch food then, old woman, and quickly!"

Gerda jumped to obey, as the nobles sorted themselves out and found seats. Another esquire called for candles and she hastily set out her two tallow dips and gave them a brand from the fireplace. Hugh was wealthy as peasants went; there were three stools for the knights and a table big enough, though uneven. The esquires either stood behind their lords, or seated themselves on the two chests Hugh had made. The servants retreated to the straw-tick bed in the angle of the wall—she and Hugh had not slept on the floor since the birth of their first daughter.

However, it was crowded with all these people, for Hugh came from a family of quality. Cattle were never permitted in the house when he was young, and he had held to that. The house was small in consequence. The table, chests, and bed took up most of one end of it, the fireplace and the cupboard most of the other.

Gerda began by pouring ale into every vessel she had: the horn cup, so fabulously expensive, she brought it out only on holidays or when her in-laws were visiting, the two black-jacks, leather cups waterproofed with tar, and the small wooden bowl from which the priest had blessed her six children. The esquires sneered and made haste to produce silvern cups for the three lords, but had to share her plebeian vessels with the servants.

Hugh entered, having bedded and fed the horses, while she was cutting bread and cheese. He made haste to kneel and ask if he could be of further service, having wit enough to keep his unclean hands from the food to be served to the nobles.

Him the knights spoke to directly, sharply inquiring as to how he had cared for their horses. But Hugh had in good times owned horses and knew the lore of their care. Satisfied on that score, they dismissed him and returned to their conversation.

They ate like famished wolves, gulping rye bread and cheese in huge chunks, but then, Gerda thought, they were big men. Hugh might perhaps weigh as much as any but the huge gray-haired fellow, whom she gathered was the famous warrior Sir Harold Strong, of Stanes. Even she had heard vaguely of him. But all these men, even the servants, were taller than Hugh, and none were small.

The esquires served the nobles, and Gerda stood behind to produce the food to be served. Then the esquires drew a little apart from the nobles, as those fell to drinking and talking, and ate their share. After which, the servants ate theirs in the bed corner.

Gerda remained alert to their needs, but a word to Hugh sent him out with a bowl of pease porridge and a wooden spoon, and a half loaf. He was cranky when unfed, and it was no time to have him become surly; it would be like to kill them all if the lords found cause for resentment. Tomorrow, she knew, she'd have to do a half-baking, and began to reckon up in her mind the state of her pantry. Of rye meal there was no lack, and she had sourdough, also some sour milk, and sweet. Salt, lard—perhaps enough.

Around the table they were discussing the Wizard Aelfgar. Of him Gerda had heard, though not by name. He had recently built a dwelling not far from them. His magic had at first generated much fear among the peasantry, and many feats were told of him. But he had harmed none. Babies had not begun to disappear, as some had held would happen; not even young animals of any sort.

Indeed, it was said that those bold enough to offer him cut wood found a ready buyer, and also corn and other foodstuffs. Furthermore, he ground corn for any who dared present it, saving a daylong trip to the village and the baron's mill, to which they were bound by law to bring their corn. Moreover, the Wizard ground the grain for half the baron's price. Few, however, of the peasants in this sparsely populated corner of the land dared have anything to do with him, fearing sanctions of the nobles or the church.

And now the nobles were come to deal with him.

Listening, Gerda learned that the Wizard Aelfgar's chief crime was practicing sorcery, that being forbidden of itself. Secondly, he had threatened the structure of society and led dogs on to look above themselves. (Gerda pretended to be very busy, though Hugh had had no dealings with him.) Finally, he wickedly suborned villeins away from their duties to their liege lords. All of these crimes were punishable by death, and the baron had the power of the high justice. Further, they also had a warrant from the king, and another from the church. Doubly damned, the wizard must die.

Gerda felt a pang. He had to her been nothing but a thing to speak of and wonder at, and henceforth her days would be a little darker for his death.

There was some dispute about their present location. When Hugh reentered and crouched in a corner, Sir Gwilliam of the High Tower turned to him and said, "You, dog, to whom do you belong? My lord Blane, or is it the Count Reddin?"

Gerda felt her heart stop. She could not say who her lord was, could think only of the name of the reeve's man: Otho. But Hugh, to her relief, spoke up, though subdued. "My lord, it is my lord the Baron Blane we owe our duties to."

Gerda did not know that, and wondered if it mattered.

"Ah, it is as I said," said the Baron Hildimar with satisfaction. "We are not yet on the Countee's lands. I should judge that Reddin's demesne begins beyond the wood we saw just ere we descended the hill."

"If so, my lord," said Sir Harold, "then I warrant ye we shall find the wizard within or on the borders of that selfsame wold."

"A fair hazard," said Sir Gwilliam. " 'Tis not so large a copse we cannot search it out in a day, or at most two."

"Mayhap these cattle know aught of interest," said the baron, not turning his head.

Nor did any of them, but Roger the esquire turned to Hugh. Gerda's man had squatted silently, and as still as one tormented by lice and fleas could.

"Say, dog, do you know aught of a wizard new-come to these parts within the past year and oppressing the people thereof?" His look said plainly that he couldn't imagine any oppression lowering the populace.

Hugh rubbed his shock head nervously, said, "My lord, I had from—from a neighbor a word that—that a man had builded a rich house agin' a hill upon the northern side of—of that wood ye spoke of. What we call Culder's Wood. On the north side. A hill called Steep Knob."

"We should be there ere nightfall," said the baron when the esquire had repeated this.

"Best we get our rest now, as our mounts are doing," said Sir Harold. "We shall have need of all our strength if we are to face the wizard after a day's ride."

"My lord," spoke the esquire that had stood behind the baron. "Shall we not rather sleep without than within this foul hut? For these dogs do verily drip fleas."

"It were better we were beneath a roof," said Sir Harold the Strong promptly. The firelight gleamed on his gray hair as he turned to glance at the esquire. "For the wizard surely knows we come to slay him. If the moon or stars shine upon us, it is like he will be able to see us in his dream or perchance in a crystal."

"Then these dogs must sleep under roof also, and there is

scarce room for the eight of us," said Sir Gwilliam. "Else the wizard will wonder why they sleep without."

"Aye, but they have a barn, which perhaps also our servants might use."

But it turned out that none cared to do so, though devoted servants might have slept with the horses as a precaution. When Gerda said as much in the barn to her man, Hugh said in his short way, "They fear the wizard, though they do not admit it."

"Is the wizard dangerous?" she asked.

"Not as ever I heard tell," Hugh said: "Leastwise, not to dogs like us." The last bitterly.

Gerda found sleep difficult despite her weariness; she lay reckoning up her pantry. She hoped the two speckled hens would lay early tomorrow, but doubted they'd have done so by the time the nobles were fain to eat. The horses, too, troubled her; suppose one hurt itself in their barn? Or say horse thieves had followed them, reckoning where they might spend the night?

At length, however, she slept, to awaken well before light. Warm though the summer night had been, she was chill and stiff with lying on the pile of last year's hay. Hugh awakened despite her attempt at silence, rising at once to grope for the meal bin. Gerda left him measuring out rye meal and the black-spotted beans that tasted well enough but were too unsightly to sell. Seizing the buckets, she started for the spring.

It was over a hundred yards to the spring, down hill, but that was close as water went, and she and Hugh were lucky. Gerda's back was bent, her shoulders had been rounded from carrying water before her twentieth birthday. Her bare feet knew the path well enough, and presently she found the spring. They had rocked it around and covered it with a clumsy wooden cover to keep out animals. Even so mice and sometimes rats or squirrels got in through the overflow and drowned. Heaving the cover off, Gerda bent and plunged the buckets in, one at a time.

Filled, made of thick wood, they weighed thirty pounds apiece. Gerda straightened with one in each fist and walked with careful rapid steps back up the hill, her feet feeling the way. But she was used to doing this in the dark. At the house she fumbled the door open as quietly as she might, lest one of the noble warriors hear and spring up with sword in hand.

Inside, she saw in the faint light of the remaining coals that the one called Harold the Strong was indeed awake, watching her. Gerda made him no sign, turning to the fireplace and blowing on the coals, adding bark, until the fire began to blaze up, then piling on split wood. So soon as it was burning, she poured the water into the smaller pot and swung it over the flames.

Turning to go, she saw that the gray-haired knight was again lying with eyes closed; the others had not awakened.

Back down the hill. Hugh had not finished feeding the horses; now he was serving them the remnants of last year's turnips and green onions. His own oxen had to wait. As she went down the path again, Gerda frowned, hoping the nobles wouldn't take the feeding of beans to their horses amiss. It would make them lively, and moreover, would probably make them fart. Still, the horses hadn't time to forage for grass, nor would it provide enough aliment if they did have the time.

This time Gerda poured the water into the water butt outside the door, and went down the hill again. Hugh was chopping wood by the light of a brand lit at the kitchen fire. By the time she had finished the third trip, it was coming on light. It was later than she had expected, and she hurried on the fourth and fifth trips. Fortunately she had not stumbled on any trip.

By the fifth trip the cock was crowing and the men stirring within the house. One of the servants had come without and was cursing the necessity of lying with fleas and other vermin. The water she had brought would have to do. Hugh had rummaged for eggs—he was no fool, was her man—and had found three. These, added to the previous store, might barely do, with the bacon.

The nobles were rising as she entered, Sir Gwilliam disgustedly prodding his esquire with his sheath to arouse him.

"Are the horses cared for?" the baron asked immediately, almost before his eyes were open.

"Aye, and well fed," said Sir Harold, entering behind Gerda so silently that she started.

"Ah, then we have but to eat and ride," said the baron. Glancing at her, and away, he said, "What cheer does this hut hold?"

"There is yet more of the ale, my lord," said Sir Gwilliam. "I think too that there be more bread and cheese."

The esquire called Edwy put the question to Gerda.

"There be eggs, and bacon," said Gerda hastily—there was little enough left of bread or cheese.

"I think this porridge the peasants eat would not be a bad beginning to the day," said Sir Harold Strong. "It is after all more than mere oatmeal; that is pease porridge or I never smelt it. Perhaps some of that bacon in it will make it more palatable to warriors."

"Come, let us wash and let the beldame provide," said Baron Hildimar, stepping past her not discourteously to the fireplace. Sir Harold proffered the wooden basin he had already washed in, in cold water.

"But, eggs, my lord," said Edwy, his esquire. "How can the hinds possibly cook them, lacking pans for the purpose?"

"Boil them, sir squire, in the small pot," Gerda said immediately, and bit her lip for speaking without being spoken to.

Even in the dim light of the fire she could see the united glares of the servants and esquires. But their masters were less conventional.

"Boiled eggs sound well enough," said the baron to Sir Harold. "Hold, though—if we take the heated water with which to wash, the cooking will be delayed. Let the eggs be cooked first. I shall wash with cold water, as I perceive you have done, Sir Harold."

"It is main cold, but not too cold for a warrior, and of a pleasant taste—I ventured to drink."

"Was that wise? I trust you will not suffer a flux," said Baron Hildimar anxiously. A flux would take a warrior's strength down as fast as a wound.

"The peasant avowed he often drank it, sometimes with willow bark for flavor, and never suffered fluxion of the bowels," said Sir Harold as they stepped outside.

Gerda turned her back on the company remaining within, to avoid further notice—she feared at least to be struck for her saucy ways. Dropping the eggs slowly into the boiling water, she listened tensely, but the baron's mild manners, and those of Sir Harold, had apparently disarmed the remaining men. That, or they were eager to breathe the purer air without. She continued at the fire, slicing the end of the rank home-cured bacon into the porridge, as they exited.

It was full light though the sun not yet up when the warriors sat them down to eat. Again they made a meal from the peasant hut, sparing their trail rations. Gerda hoped they would not pass back by this way upon their return, having slain the sorcerer. She could not feed them another meal without arousing their disgust at the victuals. Even now the esquires were contemptuous of the porridge.

Sir Gwilliam High Tower and the Baron Hildimar examined the horses carefully, questioning Hugh on his care of them. They approved mightily, and it seemed, to Gerda listening from within, that they had been disappointed in the care accorded their mounts earlier. To her horror she realized that they desired to carry him with them to the wizard's house, to care for their horses and generally do what work was needful.

"But—My Lord—I am—I am my lord Blane's man," Hugh stammered, standing on one foot and then the other.

"The baron is right," said Sir Harold Strong. "We need

not only a sturdy man to see to our horses, but also a woman to cook for us. You have no son?"

Of the six children Gerda had borne, but three had survived, and Wat, Hugh's only son, had died when the baron Blane called up his feudal levies and rode against the bandits of Fartherlea. Hugh had never been the same man since, and now of course Gerda was too old to bear again.

"Then, my good man, you must come, and fetch your wife," said Baron Hildimar.

"My lord Blane—"

"We shall be pleased to pay you. A broad penny a day," said Sir Gwilliam, drawling distastefull.

Hugh was silent, calculating. He was not avaricious; neither was he fool enough to anger them. Pleasant as the men had been—if only because of her stooped age—if only because the peasants had leapt to serve them—yet Gerda knew that if they were badly crossed they were capable of firing the thatch.

"Let me throw down a mort o' feed for mine oxen, m'lords," Hugh said, and at their nod, was off.

Gerda occupied herself in readying the house for her departure, hoping they would not be gone so long the fire would go out, hoping no one came by in their absence and stole aught, hoping foxes would not destroy their few fowls.

In short order they set off, Hugh before her and Gerda following at the tail of the warriors' march. They walked their horses across lots, and Gerda saw country she had never seen before. Most of it was new to Hugh also. Over hill and dale, making east. They passed three houses whose occupants came forth and stared at them from a distance. The first was their neighbor Till Hud's son's house, and Gerda hoped his daughter Tilby would think to go down and watch her house. But she could not call out while with the lords, and so said nothing.

Presently, nearing the borders of the wood, the houses were left behind. All this was fallow land, as the war of a generation or two before had so wasted the country that it was abandoned, and the peasants had not yet spread back into it. Also, it was as she heard still disputed at law between the baron and the count.

The shadows were growing long when they came upon Steep Knob and saw the smoke going up. Chopped wood was visible here and there in Culder's Wood, and they heard the ring of axes. Presently the nobles drew rein before the most imposing house Gerda had ever seen, far more so than the blacksmith's in the village, her only standard of comparison.

Big though it was, it was obviously digged back into the hill, for windows looked out of turfy banks, and above, on the slope, stone chimneys placidly vented smoke, as if above thatch, not forest floor. The nobles murmured, for the windows were partly closed, yet one could see through them, as if through ice. Strips of gauzy cloth hung down on either side of them, and people could be seen going to and fro in rooms behind, busy as a castle.

Even as they stared, a tall, commanding figure stood in the open door. He was gray, with a neatly trimmed gray beard, a mild eye, wore a soft loose robe that shimmered yellow even in the shaded doorway.

"Enter, my noble friends, and be welcome," he called.

After a moment she heard Sir Harold say, "He seems not to meditate mischief, my lord. Let us do even as he bids, and seek to learn his weaknesses."

Hugh hurried forward to gather their reins, and Gerda shifted the bag of provisions she had brought for the horses and hurried to help him. They stood puzzled for a moment when the nobles and their servants had gone, for there was no stable or other outbuilding visible. However, someone in glittering armor came out of a side door in the turfy bank of Steep Knob.

The horses began to jerk at the reins in a panicky manner and she and her man had much ado to hold them. Then Gerda saw the armored one more clearly and nearly dropped the reins, her heart hammering with fear. For this was no mortal woman who stood before them, but a thing made as if by coppersmith all of brass, in the shape of a woman.

The brazen woman said, "If you follow me, I will lead you to a place for the horses." Her voice was as mellow as a horn. Her eyes glinted in her gleaming face like the glitter of mica in certain rocks.

She turned and dumbly they followed her, staring as though their eyes would protrude. Belatedly Gerda thought shame to her for going about unclothed, but this was buried in the wonder of the working of the woman's joints. It was hard to think of her as a magical being, easy to assume she was a girl in brazen armor. But her face was brazen also, and her voice; it could not be.

The horses had to be urged into the room in the hill, and they entered shuddering and rolling their eyes. Here were more brazen women and men, who stood back and watched with glittering eyes while the horses were tied by their reins to posts. Like the women, the brazen men were nude, but like them had no sex. Gerda could not guess the purpose of the room, but it was not for horses. There was a stone-flagged floor that engaged her admiration. It was spotlessly clean, and did not even have rushes on it.

As they were tying up the horses, she became aware that every flea and louse on her body was suddenly on the move. A few breaths passed, and the vermin moved more wildly. Then one, and another, and all of them ceased to move entirely. She said nothing but looked in amaze at Hugh, who looked back big-eyed. Then he pointed mutely at a horsefly that had come in with them. It lay upside down on the floor, desperately yet weakly buzzing its wings and moving its legs. It died as they watched.

Neither spoke of it. Hugh measured out the beans and oats they had brought onto the floor, a sufficiency before each horse, Gerda holding the bag. Then they looked round uncertainly.

The brazen woman who first had approached them stepped forward again. "If your duties be fulfilled, then you may follow me. First you should wash, then you shall be fed."

It had been a long day, and Gerda had had but little time to eat pease porridge that morning. The thought of food did not overcome her fear of the magics of this place, but the brazen woman had spoken only kindly to them. The others had not spoken at all, even to each other. Back farther into the hill, where to their wonder great round stones gave forth light like the sun, yet no heat or smoke, they were shown to a room with troughs in the floor.

Quickly the brazen people fetched flat things woven of straw or perhaps rushes, flimsy walls they might have been, like nothing Gerda had ever heard of. These were set up around two of the troughs, Gerda and her man in separate little rooms. The brass woman in her room did things to the metalwork at the end of the trough, and water began to rush steaming into it, causing Gerda to jump.

It came upon her that she was to wash in that. With wonder, and some hesitation, she doffed her heavy linen dress and let down her graying hair. In summer it had been her custom as a girl to bathe monthly with the other girls in the river, and as a young wife she still continued the custom till she and Hugh moved from the Littledale. Now she was a sober old woman, thirty-eight and a grandmother, and washed partially from a basin from time to time. It was years since she had been in all over.

The brazen woman took her dress and handed it out to one who waited without, and Gerda regarded them with alarm, standing stiffly beside the trough. But the woman of brass said, "Fear not, it shall be returned to you when it is clean. Get you into the water, and take this."

She handed to Gerda a square of coarse cloth with a flower embroidered on it—no, woven artfully into it. "Wash yourself all over with that—its magic will get you clean in a trice."

Wonderingly Gerda did as she was bid, hearing through the screen similar words spoken to Hugh. And indeed, in moments only, the wetted cloth left her skin white where it was not browned by the sun. It even cleaned her wetted hair, and to her amazement, and partly to her disgust, Gerda saw the corpses of all the vermin that had infested her that day floating on the water. She arose cleaner than perhaps she had ever in her life been. The brazen woman did something else and all the water in the trough rushed out, carrying the dirt and dead vermin away.

Her dress had been returned to her, clean and smelling warm and piney. The woman of brass seated Gerda on a stool and brushed out her hair with a brush that, in moments, left it untangled and faintly scented. Then she braided it properly and put it back up on Gerda's head. Gerda submitted dumbly, thinking that nothing could amaze her more than this service.

When she went looking for Hugh, however, she found that a brazen young man had just finished trimming his hair and beard. Her man now looked like a short, broad-shouldered nobleman; even his skin looked soft after his bath, like a noble knight's. From his mute look she must have seemed as strange to him.

The brazen woman led them into a nearby room and urged them to be seated at a small table. "Food will be served directly," she said.

"Oh, no," said Gerda. "W-we are b-but peasants—"

"Your masters are even now finishing their baths and will soon be served with our master in the main dining room. Their servants will be served in the smaller dining room. Here, you will be served."

"B-but it is not meet—" Gerda could not continue: a brazen man was carrying in a wooden platter on which were two bowls and bread.

They were served clear yellow soup that smelled of chicken. The good meat smell of it started Gerda's stomach, and she hesitated only a moment more. In each bowl—of fine earthenware with a blue flower painted in it—was a spoon made of some metal as shiny and bright as silver, but by the look and feel, not silver. They ate abashedly, Hugh after a few trials abandoning the spoon and dipping the bread—white bread, not rye or black—into the broth. Finished, Gerda still felt hungry, but it had been very good.

Then the man of brass brought in another platter with two tranchoirs of earthenware, each with a smoking steak on it. Gerda was horrified; the metal ones had become confused and were serving them their masters' meal. It took some persuasion to convince her and Hugh that all was well. They ate the steaks, and a pie was brought in. It was filled with meat and gravy and many vegetables, green peas and beans and turnips. They ate it too, with gusto; everything tasted so very good. And with each course save the first, wine milder than their ale, though not so nourishing, was served.

"Do you require more food?" the brazen woman asked.

They signified not.

"You have bathed and fed. How else may we serve you?"

Gerda looked at Hugh. She could think of nothing. After a moment he nudged her and whispered, "Ask."

Gerda thought a moment, and said hesitantly, "Will you tell us why there are no flies or other vermin within this house?"

"Our master, the wizard Aelfgar, has devised a magick that slays all vermin of any nature that enters the dwelling."

"Whence came the water that we bathed in? Who carried it, and how far?"

"It came from a well, below the hill. But the rest is easier to show than tell. Come."

They followed her a short distance under those wonderful glowing stones, up two flights of stairs that made them wonder again, into a room. A thing like an iron tree stump rose from the floor, from which limbs leapt sideways to pierce the walls.

"Here is the well. This mass of stone is magick, and is called an attractive. Watch." The woman of brass flipped back the lid on the stump, disclosing a shaft that dropped into darkness. She swung the "attractive" stone over the hole.

After a prolonged moment there was a gurgle from below that caused Gerda to start; standing next to Hugh's clean shirt, she felt his heart pound.

"The water is rising," said the brazen woman, and as the liquid tone altered, she said, "Now it is flowing through the side pipes into the tanks. These are huge cauldrons from which water may be let down into the rooms below."

"But the water was warm," Gerda said, awed. "Is there a fire beneath these cauldrons?"

"Nay. There is a great fire in the center of this dwelling, and in it are all manner of magicks. There are firestones in it, and so long as these small stones be within the fire, then the greater firestones shall be hot, and give off heat. The water is poured over these stones in its course to the bathing troughs, and other uses."

Gerda could think of nothing more to say. Awed, she reached out and touched gently the stony attractive. Hugh nudged her and murmured, "No horses?"

Clearing her throat, Gerda said, "Do you have no horses?"

"Nay, we automatons do what work is needful, and be strong as any horse. Neither need we eat nor sleep, and so require no food or bedding."

"How then do you live?" Gerda asked faintly. Hugh's whole life was spent in getting food, shelter, and clothing for himself and her.

"We do not live, any more than does a waterwheel."

The brazen woman conducted them back to the horses, where Hugh nervously assured himself they were doing well. Indeed, they were now as calm as if raised among brazen people. But they had scattered their feed so, they had not eaten a third of it, and were trying to lick it up from the clean flags like cattle.

"We need buckets or troughs," he whispered to Gerda, vainly trying to rake piles of feed together.

Hesitantly she said so to the brazen people, and immediately sturdy wooden buckets were brought. The horses ate contentedly while Hugh and Gerda rubbed them, loosening the saddles to work under them.

Presently a brazen woman stepped forward to say, "Your masters will require their horses very soon."

Quickly Hugh went round, tightening their cinches, punching one horse in the belly, while Gerda removed the buckets. Ready, they led the horses out by the door they had entered, took them to the shade of the trees, and waited for some little time, while flies again attacked the stamping horses.

Presently the warriors began to exit from the house under Steep Knob, the knights and baron lingering to bid their host farewell. Crossing to the horses, they mounted swiftly and walked them along a path out of sight of the house in the wold. Then they halted and all drew near Sir Harold the Strong.

"How say you, Sir Harold? Can we overthrow him? I had no idea he was so mighty a wizard," said the baron.

"I think it may be done, my lord," said Sir Harold confidently. "From what I saw, the chiefest of his magick derives from that great fire we saw at the center of his hall. Remember that cauldron with the complicated engine within, its parts turning like a waterwheel? What said he of it?"

"That it gave animation to his automatons."

"Indeed. Whiles that fire burns and that cauldron bubbles, then so long shall the brazen beings move. But should it be stifled, then so shall they. And I make no doubt that they are the chiefest defense of the wizard's house."

"A mighty defense, indeed," said Sir Gwilliam, subdued. "Men or women, these brazen people are of the doughtiest sort that ever I saw. For they tire not, neither can they be wounded, to be weakened by loss of blood. How might we battle through them to douse this fire?"

"That should not be necessary, as I shall show," said Sir Harold. "That fire is the one whose smoke vents from the central chimney, upon the hill. Needs only to have water poured down upon it to douse it effectually."

There was a general chorus of understanding and approbation. "Will you then rede us your plan, Sir Harold?" the baron asked. "For you are by far the most experienced in war of us here, and have also dealt with sorcerers."

"None like to this. All of you give thought to what we do, for it is by no means likely that the automatons are the whole of Aelfgar's magicks," said Sir Harold. "Hesitate not to make suggestions."

The plan, as it shaped, was that the warriors should stand in three groups, the baron and his esquire on the right, Sir Gwilliam and his esquire on the left, Sir Harold, his esquire, and the two servants in the middle.

"For the servants have some knowledge of arms, though they be not well practiced," he said. "Whereas this dog-peasant is a better horse-handler than they, at any day. He then shall stand among the trees with our horses. The old woman shall carry water up the hill and pour it down upon the fire. So soon as the smoke ceases to rise, or we see the automatons cease to move, we shall all raise a shout and storm the house."

This sounded good to them all, but it was the esquire Roger of all people who spoke the thought that was in Gerda's mind: "How shall the old woman carry water, lacking buckets? Must we borrow them of Aelfgar?"

Sir Harold glared at him, but the baron said, "She shall use the leathern horse-buckets in my saddlebags." He reached back and took from his bags a pair of leather buckets that collapsed like hosen when not full of water. "They are for carrying dry stuffs, but will hold water well enough."

"Good!" said Sir Gwilliam. "I saw a spring upon the farther slope of the hill as we approached the house. Let us forth, then!"

When the party had halted, Gerda was given the buckets and she and Hugh went wordlessly to find the spring. He was as gloomy as she over being involved in nobles' battles. Perhaps he was thinking, as she was, that this was how their son Wat died. Gerda filled the buckets and paused, looking at him. Hugh stood looking solemnly back, looking noble and handsome despite his gnarled age, in his cleanliness. Gerda felt quite an old peasant woman beside him.

For a moment she remembered him like this, when young, and remembered the ardency of their yearning for each other. She had not remembered that for ages; the old wild yearning was gone, replaced by a stolid content and reliance. Now she felt a touch of it again. But she did not know what to say.

And in the end, there was nothing to say.

They nodded to each other, and she turned to trudge up the slope of Steep Knob. Behind her, she heard nothing for several seconds, then Hugh turned and plodded back to the waiting warriors.

The climb was three times her usual water carry, and as she toiled panting up the hill, Gerda remembered the attractive. A pity she had not that now. A pity she had no such thing at home. That, she supposed, would be for nobles only, if ever it escaped the wizards. Yet—

Gerda had spent her whole life carrying water. Her daughters, not yet twenty, were already beginning to be bent and hunched from carrying water. Her granddaughters—they were born straight, as her daughters had been. But that would not last, for they too would spend their lives carrying water. And now Gerda knew it was not necessary.

Atop the hill, she readily identified the chief chimney that Sir Harold had spoken of. She paused to rest, the leather strings of the buckets cutting into her palms. The chimney was a little taller than she, and she was puzzled how to climb it. Finally Gerda hung one bucket on a limb and scrambled up on the chimney with the other bucket in one hand.

White wood smoke poured easily, calmly, from it. Gerda, panting, thought of the fireplace below, of the magical heart of the brazen woman beating swiftly in boiling water, of the woman's calm, kindly voice, of the dying vermin on her skin, of the kindly way the wizard, who never saw her or knew her, had had her entreated.

Spilling the water, flinging the bucket away, Gerda lifted herself over the chimney. Catching a breath of pure air, she put her face over the smokehole and cried, "Halloooo! Halloooo! Bewaaaare! Bewaaaare! Bewaaaare!"

Then she leapt down from the chimney, panting, red-faced, smoke in her hair, and ran to the other bucket, which also she emptied. For good measure she threw both buckets down the fireplace, then hurried down the farther side of the hill.

Gerda could think of nothing to do but go home.

They caught her in late dusk, four tired and wounded men on three horses. One of the horses fell even as they shouted at her. Gerda made no effort to flee farther, stood facing them apathetically. Sir Harold the Strong, of Stanes, was not with them. Perhaps well for her; then she realized it did not matter.

Baron Hildimar and Sir Gwilliam had survived, as had Edwy the esquire and one of the servants. Hugh was not with them, and Gerda experienced a pang. But that, too, did not matter.

For the first time a noble spoke to her directly.

"Bitch! Betrayer!" they shouted, cuffing her. "Why did you betray us?"

At length they calmed themselves. Sir Gwilliam said to the baron, "My lord, we should waste no time on her. Let us slay her and be on our way. Pommers hath died, and is not like to be the last horse we will lose, while the wizard may yet be hard upon our trail."

"I shall not dirty my steel with the dog's blood of her," snapped the baron.

"Nay, nor I; nor is such a death meet for a dog. Rather she should be burned at the stake for having holpen the wizard—"

"Nay, there be no time to gather faggots."

"Nor have we a rope, wherewith to hang her. Let her be given to the servants to be beaten," said Sir Gwilliam.

"Aye. But let it be quick."

Edwy and the other servant approached her, dropping the bags they had gathered from the fallen horse. Edwy undid his belt, the servant picked up a half-rotten limb, and they fell hastily upon her, striking and kicking as Gerda fell.

Gerda hunched upon the forest floor under an oak and readied herself for death. The blows fell thickly and fast; she heard the whistling breath of the frightened and exhausted servant. She made a distance between herself and the pain, thinking of Hugh. She hoped he had not thought unkindly of her as he died.

The beating ended before unconsciousness came. Fear of pursuit, exhaustion, defeat, worked on her oppressors. She heard the horses make off, followed by the stumbling men. Gerda continued to lie there, dully conscious of pain, thinking of her house. She hoped they would not fire it as they passed by. Flagstones for the floor, then an attractive for the water, but she could not see how the upcoming water could be guided up the footpath.

Footsteps approached, and for a moment she feared it was the nobles returning, or perhaps Sir Harold following the baron. Then came the hope it might be Hugh, impossible as that could be. With an effort that brought forth screams of pain from her back and ribs, she raised and turned her head.

A brass face bent above hers. For a moment she thought it was the woman who had served them; then she saw that it was a brazen man. He turned his head and in his deep bronze voice called, "Here she be!"

Kneeling, he gathered her up while Gerda bit back groans. "My master, the wizard Aelfgar, but wishes to know one thing, good woman. Why did you warn us of enemies without?"

He was a sparkling face lined against black-green oak leaves in the night. Even as she looked, the sparkles separated, pulsed, coalesced, separated again. Never before had she been called a good woman. She knew then that she had not guessed wrong about the wizard. Gerda croaked, "For my granddaughters."

Then the darkness took her.

EXORCYCLE

Joan D. Vinge

 It's a pleasure to live in southern California—
TAN YOUR HIDE IN OCEANSIDE, as the Chamber of
Commerce billboard across the street proclaims.
And it's a pleasure to be here in the off-season,
to have a decent breakfast on the sunny patio
and time for the morning mail. I stripped the
brown wrapper off of my latest selection from the book club
and turned it over: yet another in the seemingly endless
stream of "inside" accounts of the late, great government
scandals. But this one: As I read the title I felt an odd shiver
run up my spine. Just then Pewter bounded up into my lap,
purring loudly for no obvious reason. I greeted him with my
usual sneeze, and groped for a napkin. "Damn it!" I put my
hands fondly around his thick gray neck. "I'm going to make
violin strings out of you, cat."

"Sean, how can you say that," my wife Marge chided
absently; her red curls and freckled hand appeared in the pass-
through from the kitchen. She gave me a glass of milk. "He's
just kidding, Pew."

"Don't count on that forever," I muttered. "You know, Marge, I wonder what really became of Prentice—"

"Prentice who?" Marge called. "Oh, that Prentice; the actor. How do you want your eggs?"

"Not raw. *That* Prentice, who made the Queen's Own Players the rage of two summers in the park, earned us fame and renown, as if you could forget Prentice. . . ." Marge *tsk*ed. And yet, as much as I admired him as an actor, personally he probably was the most forgettable man I ever knew; maybe that was why he was so good. He could have been another Olivier—if only he hadn't gone into politics. Pewter looked up at me through slitted emerald eyes, drooling sentimentally as he kneaded the title page, inflicting tiny puncture wounds. He assumed, like all cats, that whatever you were doing could not possibly be as interesting as he was. He was wrong. I sneezed again and wiped my eyes, deciding that I could forgive Prentice anything but that cat.

The cat had come strolling down the pier to meet us, as matter-of-fact as fate, on the foggy night we first saw the two of them. I'd come to the beach with Marge, to let the astringent air of a Pacific evening ease away the trauma of directing summer theater, to drown Shakespeare in the sibilance of the waves, and possibly to do a little necking. We strolled hand in hand along the pier, above the rushing water in the seagreen twilight; we were entirely alone, or so I thought. I was just about to suggest that we stop against the rail, when down the pier an enormous slate-gray cat materialized, marching toward us and yawping insufferably.

"Oh, look, Sean," Marge said, automatically putting out a hand. "Kitty, kitty, kitty—" She shared the opinion all cats had that they were irresistible, anytime, anywhere.

I leaned against the splintery rail, shoving my hands into the back pockets of my jeans and wondering if this was why Mother always told me not to get involved with actresses.

The cat came to Marge and wound ingratiatingly around

her ankles. She picked him up and nuzzled him; I sneezed, getting splinters, as the residue of loose cat hair settled into my hyperallergic nose.

"Lips that touch feline shall never touch mine," I said stuffily.

Marge groaned her contrition, dropping the cat and wiping her mouth on the sleeve of her work shirt. "Rats." She gave me a Kleenex. "Sorry. But look, he must belong to that man fishing down there. Let's take him back before he wanders away." She picked the cat up again. Obviously delighted, he settled across her shoulder and pinned me with an inscrutable gaze, before he looked away down the pier. Marge started walking.

I followed, wondering how I could have overlooked the fact that someone else was down there. Or the fact that he was quoting Shakespeare: " 'Oh, that this too, too insubstantial flesh would melt . . .' " Misquoting, I thought sourly, hearing his voice soar above the waves.

But Marge caught at my arm. "Hey, listen. God, he's *good*, he sends shivers down my spine!" And even if he did own a cat, I had to admit that much was true.

"Excuse me—" Marge said meekly, as we came up behind him.

He started and looked back at us almost guiltily. The cat began to purr in Marge's arms, blinking at him smugly. "Pewter," he said, his voice suddenly fading into the wind, "what have you done now?"

That confirmed my worst suspicions, but Marge only held him out reluctantly, saying, "We were afraid he'd get lost."

The stranger took the cat and draped him over a shoulder. "No—we're inseparable, really. But thank you." His clothes were nondescriptly hip, and he had a lean and hungry look. Such men are dangerous. . . . I wondered whether he turned Marge on. But he also looked like he wished we'd go the hell away. The feeling being mutual, I was about to suggest it, when Marge burst out:

"We heard you reciting. If you don't mind my saying so, it was tremendous. Are you an actor?"

"I don't mind." He smiled vaguely. "I have been . . . off and on." I harrumphed, placing a hand firmly on Marge's shoulder; she is a chronic victim of the Fallen Sparrow Syndrome. But she pressed on stubbornly, "Are you looking for a job? We're with the Queen's Own Players, we do Shakespeare in the summer, and contemporary drama through the year, here in Oceanside. We're having auditions this week. This is Sean Haley, our director. I'm Margaret Gillespie."

"Elwyn Prentice—"

Marge shook his hand heartily, and then I did. He had a weak grip. I said, "Pleased to meet you," insincerely; and before I quite knew what was happening we seemed to have invited him out for coffee. As we walked back down the pier, my plans for the evening sinking slowly in the west, Marge asked him, "Um, say—you weren't thinking of jumping, Elwyn, were you?" I winced, but somehow Marge manages never to offend anyone. It's a knack I've often wished I had.

Prentice only shook his head, looking morose. "Nay . . . no, it wouldn't have done any good."

It was hardly what I'd have called an auspicious beginning. But Prentice wound up—inexorably, perhaps—as one of the Queen's Own Players, and I was forced to admit to Marge (as she twisted my arm) that she'd been right after all. He was one hell of an actor. He was also just about the strangest man I'd ever met; and when you work with actors that's saying a lot. Immersed in a character he was totally real and believable, but offstage there was an insubstantial quality about him, a fuzziness around the edges that was somehow more than psychological: his ability to merge into the background was a subject of morbid fascination for us all. I could never remember what he looked like for more than half a minute at a time; it was even possible to forget he was in the room. I wish I could have said the same for his cat. We seldom saw Prentice outside of rehearsals. He didn't seem to have any interest in the things that usually interest actors, or human beings generally—"he hated public appearances," he said. He rented a picturesque hovel out by the beach, and it didn't surprise me at all when the neighbors told me nobody lived there. Someone in the cast summed it up well, once, when he said, "Prentice who —?" I think Prentice affected everyone that way.

But it was partly his lack of character that made him such a good actor—he could play anything, several parts in the same play, and lose himself in them completely. I'd hired him initially for stand-ins and bit parts, since the leads were already filled; but it seemed to be all he wanted. He was content to be the perfect spear-carrier, onstage as well as off of it, and he virtually avoided the spotlight like the plague: even his vanity was invisible. He had an early–Gene Wilder quality: he was totally inoffensive, a director's dream.

And yet he could have been co-director, if he'd been interested (and if my vanity had been invisible). He seemed to know every line Shakespeare had ever written, he must have had a mind like a tape recorder—and his promptings to the less blessed were somehow so perfectly tuned in that only a blank mind would receive him. His interpretations of Shakespearean dialogue and byplay had an authentic feel that once led Marge to remark, admiringly, "You'd think he was a personal friend of the Bard."

"In that case," I snapped, "he's too old for *you.*"

Partly because he was her discovery, he fascinated Marge; she was drawn to him as the moth is drawn to the flame. Or so I assumed, and proposed to her to be on the safe side, even though he never seemed to be more than pleasantly distant. Because there was something about Prentice, if you looked hard enough, that was haunting in the poetic sense—a shadow of bedevilment, a restlessness that somehow hinted at secret sorrows. He had, in a way, the mournful dignity of a down-at-the-heels tragic hero, and the faintly archaic speech patterns to match.

That may have been why he was so good at tragedy; and maybe it also had something to do with the thing that really made him remarkable on stage—his Shakespearean ghosts. Whether his inspired performances came out of skeletons in his closet or bats in his belfry, I'm still not quite sure. I probably never will be. But in any case, we did *Hamlet* that first summer; and, with a certain instinct for type-casting, I picked Prentice for the ghost of Hamlet's father. It was my casting coup of the year. As Hamlet walked the battlements at rehearsal, there appeared before him a hideous ectoplasmic manifestation that would have turned Christopher Lee green with envy. Its voice turned Hamlet as white as his father's ghost; and, raising a trembling hand, he said, "Eeek." His father's ghost fed him his lines. Later that night, catching Prentice as he drifted out the side door, I asked him how the devil he'd *done* that? He only swelled with rare offstage presence, and smiling conspiratorially, said, "Trade secret." He disappeared into the foggy street, trailing Pewter on an invisible umbilical, whistling an Elizabethan tune.

The public, it turned out, was as impressed as we were by Prentice's ghost: In a way, it gave the perfect touch of reality—or unreality—to charge the atmosphere of the play and transport the playgoers back into Elizabethan times, when ghosts were as real a fear as muggers. Our summer season was an unmitigated success; Hamlet's ghost made the theater page of *Time,* and set us on the road to national fame and artistic fortune.

The next summer, knowing a good thing when I saw one materialize, I scheduled *Macbeth* and cast Prentice as the ghost of Banquo. The season's success topped all our wildest dreams of glory: we actually outdrew San Diego's Shakespearean Festival; and in July we received a request for a special, end-of-season performance at the western estate of the President of the United States.

Marge and I got married that summer and blew our honeymoon on a pointless trip to Disneyland, before we slid back into the endless stream of sunburned, blue-and-golden days, and nights of chilling mayhem on the stage. Life had never been more beautiful.

And then, after one Saturday matinee, Prentice squeezed into my broom-closet office, his cat and costume making him look like Dick Whittington come to London. He appeared to be more morose than usual. Pewter, on the other hand, bounded gleefully up onto my desk, scattering scripts and knocking over cola cups. I wondered what practical joker had started the rumor that cats were graceful. He sat down in my correspondence heap and tried to rub his face along the edge of my chin. I sneezed, ruffling his fur. He protested in aggrieved tones. "Are you sure," I asked again, "that this cat isn't going to run off some day, and get hit by a truck?" Prentice said something but it was lost in another sneeze. I blew my nose on a used napkin; Pewter leaped down from the desk, taking a stack of books with him. "What did you say?"

Prentice picked up a book and whacked his cat in passing, before he rebuilt the stack on my desk. Pewter removed himself to a corner and began to wash, twitching indignantly. Prentice swept coats and dungarees off the guest chair and sat down. "Sean, I want to quit."

"My God," I said, "that's what I thought you said. Do you want more money? Bigger parts? Starting in the fall—"

He shook his head. "Nay. It's not that."

I began to pull on my beard. "But I even agreed to let your cat do a walk-on with the Three Weird Sisters—"

"I know." He laughed, looking uncomfortable. Pewter crept out of exile and settled under his chair, squinting up at me like an appraising jeweler. "You've been a real friend, Sean. Not like some. I don't know how to explain this to you. . . ."

"Is it the Presidential Performance coming up? You're the last person I'd expect to *get* stage fright, frankly."

"It's not that, either." He shrugged. " 'Tis no worse than the Queen's command performance. . . ."

"You've performed for Queen Elizabeth?" I gaped, forgetting the point.

He blinked back into focus, looking mildly surprised. "Not for a long time."

"Then you must know what an honor it is to perform for a president. You're the real reason he's asked us to come. Where's your artistic integrity—hell, man, where's your conceit? You can't walk out now!"

He tied a lace on his doublet. "There's a thing I have to do. Something I've been needing and wanting to do for years, and now the time has come. I wouldn't do this to you, Sean, but I can't resist it." He looked up, and for half a second I wondered who he was, figuratively and literally.

"It can't wait another couple of weeks?"

"I'm just tired of acting."

I stopped pulling on my beard and started in on my hair. If there's anything I hate it's vagueness; or maybe it's actors. "You've got to do better than that, if you're going to snatch fame and fortune out of my greedy little hands. How can you be tired of acting after two years—two years of greatness?"

"More like four hundred years, of obscurity." He sighed. "How much Shakespeare can a man stand?"

"Come again?"

He hesitated. "Well . . . you remember Marge saying I must have been a personal friend of the Bard? She was right. I was in the original productions." He swept off his feathered cap. "Elwyn, the 'prentice actor, at your service. My credentials are authentic."

"Oh. I see," I lied, glancing at the door and wondering whether he got violent when contradicted.

"You wanted to know how I did my ghosts so realistically." He looked faintly indignant at my expression, whatever it was. "Now you know."

"You mean because you're—authentically Shakespearean?"

"No . . ."

I thought for a moment. "You mean you're—"

"An 'ectoplasmic manifestation.' A ghost. A departed spirit—except that I never departed properly, for wherever I was supposed to go. 'I ain't got no-body,' as they say."

"Ah," I managed, wishing I'd brought my fifth of Scotch down to the theater. "How did this—come about?"

"I died, but something didn't work out. The energy half of my matter-and-energy whole failed to dissipate when the bond was broken, perhaps." He looked apologetic. "It's only a theory. I try to keep up with the literature. It's all academic, anyway. I'm *here*, drifting helplessly through eternity . . . a lost soul." He sighed again, melodramatically. "Always trying to get in out of the cold."

It occurred to me that he always seemed to be standing in a draft; and I'd studied enough horror films to know what *that* meant. "How—uh, how does one do that?"

"By taking over someone else's body . . . nay, don't worry, not yours." I wondered whether to be relieved or insulted. "I only choose strangers. But that's my real problem. The cycle is almost complete again, and the urge to inhabit someone is getting to be irresistible. I don't know if I can finish the season."

"Now you're telling me that you're a demon." I couldn't help sounding a little petulant. "That you really take over someone else's mind and body, you make them commit vile deeds, and humiliate themselves, and all that? That's a little hard for me to believe. Especially of you, Elwyn. What in hell —er—would make you want to do anything like that?"

"It's hard to explain, to a 'mere mortal.'" He grinned ruefully. "But I'm not exactly ye Ideal Demon—I've always been a failure at real, diabolical creativity. I'm only good at causing gourmets to spill wine in expensive restaurants, or forcing decent people to show their friends home movies of their baby's drool . . . I've always lacked the inspiration of a Classic Demon.

"It's not even the classic Evil that makes you do it, some devil with a pitchfork tail; or at least I don't think so. But it is a kind of damnation, to be stranded alone forever between here and there. It warps your perspective. It makes you jealous, it makes you bitter . . . and it makes you competitive. You resent that happy soul secure in its body; you want to dominate it and take over, you want to take out your frustrations on it. It's like a punching bag."

"What happens if you win?"

"I don't know. I've never gotten a chance to find out. Like I said, I've always been a—hopeless failure. I've been thrown out of more bodies than I can count."

"Exorcised?" I whispered.

He nodded.

"But if you're not classic Evil, how can you be tossed out by classic Good?"

"I don't know that, either. Maybe there is something to the classical definitions." He leaned back in the chair and stretched his booted feet; I noticed that the chair hadn't creaked. "It just seems to set up vibrations that I can't tolerate, like scratching your nails on the blackboard. Except that in my state it's more serious, it disassociates me, or polarizes me, or something like that. The longer I resist and stay in the body, the more damage it does—I can't inhabit another body until I've spent time this way, sometimes *years*, getting myself back together again."

"So what you're trying to tell me is that this cycle you mentioned is up again, and that's why you want to go out and inhabit somebody else?"

"Yea. And this time I feel that at last it's going to be a success! I'm fed up with being a bush-league demon, getting cast out like an old shoe. I'm very grateful to you, Sean, more than I can say, for the chance you've given me to prove myself. Working with the troupe—it's been like old times again, the best of times. It's renewed my faith in myself, after so many humiliating failures: I have self-confidence again. This time I'm going to do something grandiosely—Evil. I'm going to find someone whose goals and needs and nature truly match my dark desires. This time I'm going to succeed, thanks to you, Sean!"

I looked back over my shoulder at the window, feeling a little like an arcane Norman Vincent Peale. The eucalyptus trees rustled reassuringly in the theater courtyard outside; life went on as before. "Well, I'm going to level with you, Elwyn . . . I don't know if you're crazy, or I am." I laughed, nervously. "I—almost—believe you really intend to go out and bedevil the world. And frankly, I don't give a damn. What I give a damn about is the fact that you want to do it *now*, and our biggest performance is coming up in two weeks. If I've really done so much for you, will you do just this one thing for me? Just stay through that performance. Then you can fly up the flue if you want to, it won't really matter. And we'll be forever grateful to you."

He shifted in his seat, like a soul in torment. "I just don't know if I can wait that long. . . ."

"I took you in when you were a—lost soul, remember." I leaned forward, hearing the pencil can fall off my desk. "And think of the president! You can't walk out on him, it's unprofessional . . . it's probably even unpatriotic." Inspiration came to me from above; or below. "You performed for the Queen of England as a mere apprentice in the trade. How can even you pass up the chance to perform now as the real star, before our president and his top officials? Some of the most important men in the world, all waiting for *you*?"

"Ah . . ." His eyes gleamed like red glass in the late afternoon light; I felt a sudden desire to crawl under my desk and look for pencils. "Zounds, 'tis perfect! 'The play's the thing, in which to catch the conscience of the king—' You're right. I'll stay."

I sighed, with relief or something less comfortable.

"But you must swear never to reveal what I've told you, to anyone."

"Your secret's safe with me," I said sincerely, having no more desire to be put away than the next person.

"*Swear*—" He rose from his chair, swelling into night's dark agent, and swept from the room on peals of maniacal, theatrical laughter.

I told one person—Marge—since I felt it was only fair to let her know, and since she was my wife and didn't count, because she couldn't testify against me. It was the sort of thing you have to tell someone. Besides, she'd wanted to know what had happened to all the Scotch. She listened soberly, and then told me that I didn't have to make up tales about Prentice, she'd always liked me best anyhow.

Our final grand performance, Prentice's farewell appearance, was flawless: when Banquo's ghost came billowing down the dining hall Macbeth turned green, as he invariably did, and three Secret Service men fainted in the second row. And after the performance, Prentice disappeared without a trace, true to his word. We never saw him, or heard from him, again. The only thing he left behind was Pewter, yowling forlornly in the empty hall. He wound himself inextricably around my legs, peering up at us with the eyes of an abandoned child. "Sean, do you suppose it was true?" Marge said softly. I shrugged, but against my better nature I picked him up, and we took him home.

"Your eggs are petrifying, Seanie. Eat, eat!" Marge removed the book from Pewter's grasp and looked at the cover. "What, yet another book about red faces in high places? Good Lord, is there no end?"

"Goodness had nothing to do with it, my dear. Not that I

haven't always thought most politicians were crooks; I'm inured to that. But, my God, at least they're usually competent crooks, and don't get caught at it. . . . But you know, maybe this really is the definitive confession." I stared again at the title: *The Devil Made Me Do It.*

"You still think Prentice was serious about that, after all this time?" She pulled on her sweater and sat down. "Just think: We knew him when."

"That we did. Too bad he wasn't as good a politician as he was an actor."

"You don't think the present political follies were exactly what he had in mind, huh?"

I shook my head. "Nope. He wanted to be behind grandiose evil. But I'm afraid he's still a bush-league demon." Pewter raised his head and peered up at me, his whiskers quivering, and slowly closed his eyes.

CHRISTMAS WITHOUT RODNEY

Isaac Asimov

 It all started with Gracie (my wife of nearly forty years) wanting to give Rodney time off for the holiday season and it ended with me in an absolutely impossible situation. I'll tell you about it if you don't mind because I've got to tell *somebody*. Naturally, I'm changing names and details for our own protection.

It was just a couple of months ago, mid-December, and Gracie said to me, "Why don't we give Rodney time off for the holiday season? Why shouldn't he celebrate Christmas, too?"

I remember I had my optics unfocused at the time (there's a certain amount of relief in letting things go hazy when you want to rest or just listen to music) but I focused them quickly to see if Gracie was smiling or had a twinkle in her eye. Not that she has much of a sense of humor, you understand.

She wasn't smiling. No twinkle. I said, "Why on Earth should we give him time off?"

"Why not?"

"Do you want to give the freezer a vacation, the sterilizer, the holoviewer? Shall we just turn off the power supply?"

"Come, Howard," she said. "Rodney isn't a freezer or a sterilizer. He's a *person*."

"He's not a person. He's a robot. He wouldn't want a vacation."

"How do you know? And he's a *person*. He deserves a chance to rest and just revel in the holiday atmosphere."

I wasn't going to argue that "person" thing with her. I know you've all read those polls which show that women are three times as likely to resent and fear robots as men are. Perhaps that's because robots tend to do what was once called, in the bad old days, "women's work" and women fear being made useless, though I should think they'd be delighted. In any case, Gracie *is* delighted and she simply adores Rodney. (That's *her* word for it. Every other day she says, "I just adore Rodney.")

You've got to understand that Rodney is an old-fashioned robot whom we've had about seven years. He's been adjusted to fit in with our old-fashioned house and our old-fashioned ways and I'm rather pleased with him myself. Sometimes I wonder about getting one of those slick, modern jobs, which are automated to death, like the one our son, DeLancey, has, but Gracie would never stand for it.

But then I thought of DeLancey and I said, "How are we going to give Rodney time off, Gracie? DeLancey is coming in with that gorgeous wife of his" (I was using *gorgeous* in a sarcastic sense, but Gracie didn't notice—it's amazing how she insists on seeing a good side even when it doesn't exist) "and how are we going to have the house in good shape and meals made and all the rest of it without Rodney?"

"But that's just it," she said, earnestly. "DeLancey and Hortense could bring *their* robot and he could do it all. You *know* they don't think much of Rodney, and they'd love to show what theirs can do and Rodney can have a rest."

I grunted and said, "If it will make you happy, I suppose we can do it. It'll only be for three days. But I don't want Rodney thinking he'll get every holiday off."

It was another joke, of course, but Gracie just said, very earnestly, "No, Howard, I will talk to him and explain it's only just once in a while."

She can't quite understand that Rodney is controlled by the three laws of robotics and that nothing has to be explained to him.

So I had to wait for DeLancey and Hortense, and my heart was heavy. DeLancey is my son, of course, but he's one of your upwardly mobile, bottom-line individuals. He married Hortense because she has excellent connections in business and can help him in that upward shove. At least, I hope so, because if she has another virtue I have never discovered it.

They showed up with their robot two days before Christmas. The robot was as glitzy as Hortense and looked almost as hard. He was polished to a high gloss and there was none of Rodney's clumping. Hortense's robot (I'm sure she dictated the design) moved absolutely silently. He kept showing up behind me for no reason and giving me heart failure every time I turned around and bumped into him.

Worse, DeLancey brought eight-year-old LeRoy. Now, he's my grandson, and I would swear to Hortense's fidelity because I'm sure no one would voluntarily touch her, but I've got to admit that putting him through a concrete mixer would improve him no end.

He came in demanding to know if we had sent Rodney to the metal-reclamation unit yet. (He called it the "bust-up place.") Hortense sniffed and said, "Since we have a modern robot with us, I hope you keep Rodney out of sight."

I said nothing, but Gracie said, "Certainly, dear. In fact, we've given Rodney time off."

DeLancey made a face but didn't say anything. He knew his mother.

I said, pacifically, "Suppose we start off by having Rambo make something good to drink, eh? Coffee, tea, hot chocolate, a bit of brandy—"

Rambo was their robot's name. I don't know why except that it starts with R. There's no law about it, but you've probably noticed for yourself that almost every robot has a name beginning with R. R for *robot*, I suppose. The usual name is Robert. There must be a million robot Roberts in the northeast corridor alone.

And frankly, it's my opinion that's the reason human names just don't start with R anymore. You get Bob and Dick but not Robert or Richard. You get Posy and Trudy, but not Rose or Ruth. Sometimes you get unusual R's. I know of three robots called Rutabaga, and two that are Rameses. But Hortense is the only one I know who named a robot Rambo, a syllable combination I've never encountered, and I've never liked to ask why. I was sure the explanation would prove to be unpleasant.

Rambo turned out to be useless at once. He was, of course, programmed for the DeLancey/Hortense menage and that was utterly modern and utterly automated. To prepare drinks in his own home, all Rambo had to do was to press appropriate buttons. (Why anyone would need a robot to press buttons, I would like to have explained to me!)

He said so. He turned to Hortense and said in a voice like honey (it wasn't Rodney's city-boy voice with its trace of Brooklyn), "The equipment is lacking, madam."

And Hortense drew a sharp breath. "You mean you *still* don't have a robotized kitchen, Grandfather?" (She called me nothing at all, until LeRoy was born, howling of course, and then she promptly called me "Grandfather." Naturally, she never called me Howard. That would tend to show me to be human, or, more unlikely, show *her* to be human.)

I said, "Well, it's robotized when Rodney is in it."

"I daresay," she said. "But we're not living in the twenti-eth century, Grandfather."

I thought: How I wish we were—but I just said, "Well, why not instruct Rambo how to operate the controls. I'm sure he can pour and mix and heat and do whatever else is necessary."

"I'm sure he can," said Hortense, "but thank Fate he doesn't have to. I'm not going to interfere with his program-ming. It will make him less efficient."

Gracie said, worried, but amiable, "But if we don't inter-fere with his programming, then I'll just have to instruct him, step by step, but I don't know how it's done. I've never done it."

I said, "Rodney can tell him."

Gracie said, "Oh, Howard, we've given Rodney a vaca-tion."

"I know, but we're not going to ask him to *do* anything; just tell Rambo here what to do and then Rambo can do it."

Whereupon Rambo said stiffly, "Madam, there is nothing in my programming or in my instructions that would make it mandatory for me to accept orders given me by another robot, especially one that is an earlier model."

Hortense said, soothingly, "Of course, Rambo. I'm sure that Grandfather and Grandmother understand that." (I no-ticed that DeLancey never said a word. I wonder if he *ever* said a word when his dear wife was present.)

I said, "All right, I tell you what. I'll have Rodney tell *me*, and then I will tell Rambo."

Rambo said nothing to that. Even Rambo is subject to the second law of robotics which makes it mandatory for him to obey human orders.

Hortense's eyes narrowed and I knew that she would like to tell me that Rambo was far too fine a robot to be ordered about by the likes of me, but some distant and rudimentary near-human waft of feeling kept her from doing so.

Little LeRoy was hampered by no such quasi-human restraints. He said, "I don't want to have to look at Rodney's ugly puss. I bet he don't know how to do *anything* and if he does, ol' Grampa would get it all wrong anyway."

It would have been nice, I thought, if I could be alone with little LeRoy for five minutes and reason calmly with him, with a brick, but a mother's instinct told Hortense never to leave LeRoy alone with any human being whatever.

There was nothing to do, really, but get Rodney out of his niche in the closet where he had been enjoying his own thoughts (I wonder if a robot has his own thoughts when he is alone) and put him to work. It was hard. He would say a phrase, then I would say the same phrase, then Rambo would do something, then Rodney would say another phrase and so on.

It all took twice as long as if Rodney were doing it himself and it wore *me* out, I can tell you, because everything had to be like that, using the dishwasher/sterilizer, cooking the Christmas feast, cleaning up messes on the table or on the floor, everything.

Gracie kept moaning that Rodney's vacation was being ruined, but she never seemed to notice that mine was, too, though I *did* admire Hortense for her manner of saying something unpleasant at every moment that some statement seemed called for. I noticed, particularly, that she never repeated herself once. Anyone can be nasty, but to be unfailingly creative in one's nastiness filled me with a perverse desire to applaud now and then.

But, really, the worst thing of all came on Christmas Eve. The tree had been put up and I was exhausted. We didn't have the kind of situation in which an automated box of ornaments was plugged into an electronic tree, and at the touch of one button there would result an instantaneous and perfect distribution of ornaments. On our tree (of ordinary, old-fashioned plastic) the ornaments had to be placed, one by one, by hand.

Hortense looked revolted, but I said, "Actually, Hortense, this means you can be creative and make your own arrangement."

Hortense sniffed, rather like the scrape of claws on a rough plaster wall, and left the room with an obvious expression of nausea on her face. I bowed in the direction of her retreating back, glad to see her go, and then began the tedious task of listening to Rodney's instructions and passing them on to Rambo.

When it was over, I decided to rest my aching feet and mind by sitting in a chair in a far and rather dim corner of the room. I had hardly folded my aching body into the chair when little LeRoy entered. He didn't see me, I suppose, or he might simply have ignored me as being part of the less important and interesting pieces of furniture in the room.

He cast a disdainful look on the tree and said, to Rambo, "Listen, where are the Christmas presents? I'll bet old Gramps and Gram got me lousy ones, but I ain't going to wait for no tomorrow morning."

Rambo said, "I do not know where they are, Little Master."

"Huh!" said LeRoy, turning to Rodney. "How about you, Stink-face. Do you know where the presents are?"

Rodney would have been within the bounds of his programming to have refused to answer on the grounds that he did not know he was being addressed, since his name was Rodney and not Stink-face. I'm quite certain that that would have been Rambo's attitude. Rodney, however, was of different stuff. He answered politely, "Yes, I do, Little Master."

"So where is it, you old puke?"

Rodney said, "I don't think it would be wise to tell you, Little Master. That would disappoint Gracie and Howard who would like to give the presents to you tomorrow morning."

"Listen," said little LeRoy, "who you think you're talking to, you dumb robot? Now I gave you an order. You bring those presents to me." And in an attempt to show Rodney who was master, he kicked the robot in the shin.

It was a mistake. I saw it would be that a second before and that was a joyous second. Little LeRoy, after all, was ready for bed (though I doubted that he ever went to bed before he was *good* and ready). Therefore, he was wearing slippers. What's more, the slipper sailed off the foot with which he kicked, so that he ended by slamming his bare toes hard against the solid chrome-steel of the robotic shin.

He fell to the floor howling and in rushed his mother. "What is it, LeRoy? What is it?"

Whereupon little LeRoy had the immortal gall to say, "He hit me. That old monster-robot *hit* me."

Hortense screamed. She saw me and shouted, "That robot of yours must be destroyed."

I said, "Come, Hortense. A robot can't hit a boy. First law of robotics prevents it."

"It's an *old* robot, a *broken* robot. LeRoy says—"

"LeRoy lies. There is no robot, no matter how old or how broken, who could hit a boy."

"Then *he* did it. *Grampa* did it," howled LeRoy.

"I wish I did," I said, quietly, "but no robot would have allowed me to. Ask your own. Ask Rambo if he would have remained motionless while either Rodney or I had hit your boy. Rambo!"

I put it in the imperative, and Rambo said, "I would not have allowed any harm to come to the Little Master, madam, but I did not know what he purposed. He kicked Rodney's shin with his bare foot, madam."

Hortense gasped and her eyes bulged in fury. "Then he had a good reason to do so. I'll still have your robot destroyed."

"Go ahead, Hortense. Unless you're willing to ruin your robot's efficiency by trying to reprogram him to lie, he will bear witness to just what preceded the kick and so, of course, with pleasure, will I."

Hortense left the next morning, carrying the pale-faced LeRoy with her (it turned out he had broken a toe—nothing he didn't deserve) and an endlessly wordless DeLancey.

Gracie wrung her hands and implored them to stay, but I watched them leave without emotion. No, that's a lie. I watched them leave with lots of emotion, all pleasant.

Later, I said to Rodney, when Gracie was not present, "I'm sorry Rodney. That was a horrible Christmas, all because we tried to have it without you. We'll never do that again, I promise."

"Thank you, Sir," said Rodney. "I must admit that there were times these two days when I earnestly wished the laws of robotics did not exist."

I grinned and nodded my head, but that night I woke up out of a sound sleep and began to worry. I've been worrying ever since.

I admit that Rodney was greatly tried, but a robot *can't* wish the laws of robotics did not exist. He *can't*, no matter what the circumstances.

If I report this, Rodney will undoubtedly be scrapped, and if we're issued a new robot as recompense, Gracie will simply never forgive me. Never! No robot, however new, however talented, can possibly replace Rodney in her affection.

In fact, I'll never forgive myself. Quite apart from my own liking for Rodney, I couldn't bear to give Hortense the satisfaction.

But if I do nothing, I live with a robot capable of wishing the laws of robotics did not exist. From wishing they did not exist to acting as if they did not exist is just a step. At what moment will he take that step and in what form will he show that he has done so?

What do I do? What do I do?

HOME FRONT

James Patrick Kelly

 "Hey, Genius. What are you studying?"

Will hunched his shoulders and pretended not to hear. He had another four pages to review before he could test. If he passed, then he wouldn't have to log onto eighth grade again until Wednesday. He needed a day off.

"What are you, deaf?" Gogolak nudged Will's arm. "Talk to me, Genius."

"Don't call me that."

"Come on, Gogo," said the fat kid, whose name Will had forgotten. He was older: maybe in tenth, more likely a dropout. Old enough to have pimples. "Let's eat."

"Just a minute," said Gogolak. "Seems like every time I come in here, this needle is sitting in this booth with his face stuck to a schoolcomm. It's ruining my appetite. What is it, math? Español?"

"History." Will thought about leaving, going home, but that would only postpone the hassle. Besides, his mom was probably still there. "The Civil War."

"You're still on that? Jeez, you're slow. I finished that weeks ago." Gogolak winked at his friend. "George Washington freed the slaves so they'd close school on his birthday."

The big kid licked his lips and eyed the menu above the vending wall at the rear of the Burger King.

"Lincoln," said Will. "Try logging on sometime, you might learn something."

"What do you mean? I'm logged on right now." Gogolak pulled the comm out of his backpack and thrust it at Will. "Just like you." The indicator was red.

"It doesn't count unless someone looks at it."

"Then you look at it, you're so smart." He tossed the comm onto the table and it slid across, scattering a pile of Will's hardcopy. "Come on, Looper. Get out your plastic."

Will watched Looper push his ration card into the french-fry machine. He and Gogolak were a mismatched pair. Looper was as tall as Will, at least a hundred and ninety centimeters; Looper, however, ran to fat, and Will looked like a sapling. Looper was wearing official Johnny America camouflage and ripped jeans. He didn't seem to be carrying a school-comm, which meant he probably was warbait. Gogolak was the smallest boy and the fastest mouth in Will's class. He dressed in skintight style; everyone knew that girls thought he was cute. Gogolak didn't have to worry about draft sweeps; he was underage and looked it, and his dad worked for the Selective Service.

Will realized that they would probably be back to bother him. He hit Save so that Gogolak couldn't spoil his afternoon's work. When they returned to Will's booth, Looper put his large fries down on the table and immediately slid across the bench to the terminal on the wall. He stuck his fat finger into the coin return. Will already knew it was empty. Then Looper pressed Select, and the tiny screen above the terminal lit up.

"Hey," he said to Will, "you still got time here."

"So?" But Will was surprised; he hadn't thought to try the selector. "I was logged on." He nodded at his comm.

"What did I tell you, Loop?" Gogolak stuffed Looper's fries into his mouth. "Kid's a genius."

Looper flipped channels past cartoons, plug shows, catalogs, freebies, music vids, and finally settled on the war. Johnny America was on patrol.

"Gervais buy it yet?" said Gogolak.

"Nah." Looper acted like a real fan. "He's not going to either; he's getting short. Besides, he's wicked smart."

The patrol trotted across a defoliated clearing toward a line of trees. With the sun gleaming off their helmets, they looked to Will like football players running a screen, except that Johnny was carrying a mini-missile instead of a ball. Without warning, Johnny dropped to one knee and brought the launcher to his shoulder. His two rangefinders fanned out smartly and trained their lasers on the far side of the clearing. There was a flash; the jungle exploded.

"Foom!" Looper provided the sound effects. "Yah, you're barbecue, Pedro!" As a sapodilla tree toppled into the clearing, the time on the terminal ran out.

"Too bad," Gogolak poured salt on the table and smeared a fry in it. "I wanted to see the meat."

"Hey, you scum! That's my dinner." Looper snatched the fries pouch from Gogolak. "You hardly left me any."

He shrugged. "Didn't want them to get cold."

"Stand-ins." A girl in baggy blue disposables stood at the door and surveyed the booths. "Any stand-ins here?" she called.

It was oldie Warner's granddaughter, Denise, who had been evacuated from Texas and was now staying with him. She was in tenth and absolutely beautiful. Her accent alone could melt snow. Will had stood in for her before. Looper waved his hand hungrily until she spotted them.

"Martin's just got the monthly ration of toilet paper," she said. "They're limiting sales to three per customer. Looks like about a half-hour line. My grandpa will come by at four-thirty."

"How much?" said Looper.

"We want nine rolls." She took a five out of her purse. "A quarter for each of you."

Will was torn. He could always use a quarter and he wanted to help her. He wanted her to ask his name. But he didn't want to stand in line for half an hour with these stupid jacks.

Gogolak was staring at her breasts. "Do I know you?"

"I may be new in town, sonny"—she put the five on the table—"but you don't want to rip me off."

"Four-thirty." Gogolak let Looper take charge of the money. Will didn't object.

Martin's was just next door to the Burger King. The line wasn't bad, less than two aisles long when they got on. There were lots of kids from school standing in, none of them close enough to talk to.

"Maybe she got tired of using leaves," said Gogolak.

Looper chuckled. "Who is she?"

"Seth Warner's granddaughter," said Will.

"Bet she's hot." Gogolak leered.

"Warner's a jack," said Looper. "Pig-faced oldie still drives a car."

Most of the shelves in aisle 2 were bare. There was a big display of government surplus powdered milk, the kind they loaded up with all those proteins and vitamins and tasted like chalk. It had been there for a week and only three boxes were gone. Then more empty space, and then a stack of buckets with no labels. Someone had scrawled *Korn Oil* on them: black marker on bare metal. At the end of the aisle was the freezer section, which was mostly jammed with packages of fries. Farther down were microwave dinners for the rich people. They wound past the fries and up aisle 3, at the end of which Will could see Mr. Rodenets, the stock boy, dispensing loose rolls of toilet paper from a big cardboard box.

"How hard you think it is to get chosen Johnny America?" Looper said. "I mean really."

"What do you mean, really?" said Gogolak. "You think J.A. is real?"

"People die. They couldn't fake that kind of stuff." Looper's face got red. "You watch enough, you got to believe."

"Maybe," Gogolak said. "But I bet you have to know someone."

Will knew it wasn't true. Gogolak just liked to pop other people's dreams. "Mr. Dunnell swears they pick the team at random," he said.

"Right," Gogolak said. "Whenever somebody gets dead."

"Who's Dunnell?" said Looper.

"Socialization teacher." Will wasn't going to let Gogolak run down Johnny America's team, no matter who his father was. "Most of them make it. I'll bet seventy percent at least."

"You think that many?" Looper nodded eagerly. "What I heard is they get discharged with a full boat. Whatever they want, for the rest of their lives."

"Yeah, and Santa is their best friend," Gogolak said. "You sound like recruiters."

"It's not like I'd have to be J.A. himself. I just want to get on his team, you know? Like maybe in body armor." Looper swept his arm down the aisle with robotic precision, exterminating bacon bits.

"If only you didn't have to join the army," said Will.

Silence.

"You know," said Looper, "they haven't swept the Seacoast since last July."

A longer silence. Will figured out why Looper was hanging around Gogolak, why he had not complained more about the fries. He was hoping for a tip about the draft. Up ahead, Mr. Rodenets opened the last carton.

"I mean, you guys are still in school." Looper was whining now. "They catch me, and I'm southern front for sure. At least if I volunteer, I get to pick where I fight. And I get my chance to be Johnny."

"So enlist already." Gogolak was daring him. "The war won't last forever. We've got Pedro on the run."

"Maybe I will. Maybe I'm just waiting for an opening on the J.A. team."

"You ever see a fat Johnny with pimples?" said Gogolak. "You're too ugly to be a vid. Isn't that right, Mr. Rodenets?"

Mr. Rodenets fixed his good eye on Gogolak. "Sure, kid." He was something of a local character—Durham, New Hampshire's only living veteran of the southern front. "Whatever you say." He handed Gogolak three rolls of toilet paper.

Will's mom was watching cartoons when Will got home. She watched a lot of cartoons, mostly the stupid ones from when she was a girl. She liked the Smurfs and the Flintstones and Road Runner. There was an inhaler on the couch beside her.

"Mom, what are you doing?" Will couldn't believe she was still home. "Mom, it's quarter to five! You promised."

She stuck out her tongue and blew him a raspberry.

Will picked up the inhaler and took a whiff. Empty. "You're already late."

She held up five fingers. "Not till five." Her eyes were bright.

Will wanted to hit her. Instead he held out his hands to help her up. "Come on."

She pouted. "My shows."

He grabbed her hands and pulled her off the couch. She stood, tottered, and fell into his arms. He took her weight easily; she weighed less than he did. She didn't eat much.

"You've got to hurry," he said.

She leaned on him as they struggled down the hall to the

bathroom; Will imagined he looked like Johnny America carrying a wounded buddy to the medics. Luckily, there was no
one in the shower. He turned it on, undressed her, and helped
her in.

"Will! It's cold, Will." She fumbled at the curtain and
tried to come out.

He forced her back into the water. "Good," he muttered.
His sleeves got wet.

"Why are you so mean to me, Will? I'm your mother."

He gave her five minutes. It was all that he could afford.
Then he toweled her off and dressed her. He combed her hair
out as best he could; there was no time to dry it. The water
had washed all her brightness away, and now she looked dim
and disappointed. More like herself.

By the time they got to Mr. Dunnell's house, she was ten
minutes late. At night, Mr. Dunnell ran a free-lance word-
processing business out of his kitchen. Will knocked; Mr.
Dunnell opened the back door, frowning. Will wished he'd
had more time to get his mom ready. Strands of wet, stringy
hair stuck to the side of her face. He knew Mr. Dunnell had
given his mom the job only because of him.

"Evening, Marie," Mr. Dunnell said. His printer was
screeching like a cat.

"What so good about it?" She was always rude to him.
Will knew it was hard for her, but she wouldn't even give Mr.
Dunnell a chance. She went straight to the old Apple that Mr.
Dunnell had rewired into a dumb terminal and started typ-
ing.

Mr. Dunnell came out onto the back steps. "Christ, Will.
She's only been working for me three weeks and she's already
missed twice and been late I don't know how many times.
Doesn't she want this job?"

Will couldn't answer. He didn't say that she wanted her
old job at the school back, that she wanted his father back,
that all she really wanted was the shiny world she had been
born into. He said nothing.

"This can't go on, Will. Do you understand?"
Will nodded.

"I'm sorry about last night."

Will shrugged and bit into a frozen fry. He was not sure what she meant. Was she sorry about being late for work or about coming home singing at three twenty-four in the morning and turning on all the lights? He slicked a pan with oil and set it on the hot plate. He couldn't turn the burner to high without blowing a fuse, but his mom didn't mind mushy fries. Will did; he usually ate right out of the bag when he was at home. He'd been saving quarters for a french fryer for her birthday. If he unplugged the hot plate, there'd be room for it on top of the dresser. He wanted a microwave too —but then they couldn't afford real microwave food. Someday.

His mom sat up in bed and ate breakfast without looking at it. The new tenants in the next bedroom were watching the war. Will could hear gunfire through the wall.

Normally this was the best time of day, because they talked. She would ask him about school. He told her the truth, mostly. He was the smartest kid in eighth, but she wasn't satisfied. She always wanted to know why he was not making friends. Will couldn't help it; he didn't trust rich kids. And then she would talk about . . . what she always talked about.

Today, however, Will didn't feel much like conversation. He complained halfheartedly that Gogolak was still bothering him.

"I'll bet you have him all wrong, Will."

"No way."

"Maybe he just wants to be your friend."

"The guy's a jack."

"It's hard on him, you know. Kids try to use him to get to his father. They're always pumping him for draft information."

"Well, I don't." Will thought about it. "How do you know so much anyway?"

"Mothers have their little secrets," she said with a sparkle. He hated it when she did that; she looked like some kind of starchy sitcom mom.

"You've never even met him."

She leaned over the edge of the bed and set her empty plate on the floor. "I ran into his father." She straightened up and began to sort through her covers. "He's worried about the boy."

"Was that who you were with last night?" Will threw a half-eaten fry back into the bag. "Gogolak's dad?"

"What I do after work is none of your business." She found her remote and aimed it at the screen. "We knew him before—your father and I. He's an old friend." A cartoon robot brought George Jetson a drink. "And he does work for Selective Service. He knows things."

"Don't try to help me, Mom."

"Look at that," she said, pointing to the screen. "He spills something and a robot cleans it up. You know, that's the way I always thought it would be when I was a kid. I always thought it would be clean."

"Mom—"

"I remember going to Disney World. It was so clean. It was like a garden filled with beautiful flowers. When they used to talk about heaven, I always thought of Disney World."

Will threw the bag at the screen and fries scattered across the room.

"Will!" She swung her legs out of bed. "What's wrong with you today? You all right, honey?"

He was through with her dumb questions. He didn't want to talk to her anymore. He opened the door.

"I said I was sorry."

He slammed it behind him.

It wasn't so much that it was Gogolak's dad this time.

Will wasn't going to judge his mom; it was a free country. He wanted to live life too—except that he wasn't going to make the same mistakes that she had. She was right in a way: it was none of his business whom she made it with or what she sniffed. He just wanted her to be responsible about the things that mattered. He didn't think it was fair that he was the only grown-up in his family.

Because he had earned a day off from school, Will decided to skip socialization too. It was a beautiful day and volleyball was a dumb game anyway, even if there were girls in shorts playing it. Instead he slipped into the socialization center, got his dad's old basketball out of his locker, and went down to the court behind the abandoned high school. It helped to shoot when he was angry. Besides, if he could work up any kind of jumper, he might make the ninth basketball team. He was already the tallest kid in eighth, but his hands were too small, and he kept bouncing the ball off his left foot. He was practicing reverse lay-ups when Looper came out of the thicket that had once been the baseball field.

"Hey, Will." He was flushed and breathing hard, as if he had been running. "How you doing?"

Will was surprised that Looper knew his name. "I'm alive."

Looper stood under the basket, waiting for a rebound. Will put up a shot that clanged off the rim.

"Hear about Johnny America?" Looper took the ball out to the foul line. "Old Gervais got his foot blown off. Stepped on a mine." He shot: swish. "Some one-on-one?"

They played two games and Looper won them both. He was the most graceful fat kid Will had ever seen. After the first game, Looper walked Will through some of his best post-up moves. He was a good teacher. By the end of the second game, sweat had darkened Looper's T-shirt. Will said he wouldn't mind taking a break. They collapsed in the shade.

"So they're recruiting for a new Johnny?" Will tried in vain to palm his basketball. "You ready to take your chance?"

"Who, me?" Looper wiped his forehead with the back of his hand. "I don't know."

"You keep bringing it up."

"Someday I've got to do something."

"Johnny Looper." Will made an imaginary headline with his hands.

"Yeah, right. How about you—ever think of joining? You could, you're tall enough. You could join up today. As long as you swear that you're fifteen, they'll take you. They'll take anyone. Remember Johnny Stanczyk? He was supposed to have been thirteen."

"I heard he was fourteen."

"Well, he looked thirteen." Looper let a caterpillar crawl up his finger. "You know what I'd like about the war?" he said. "The combat drugs. They make you into some kind of superhero, you know?"

"Superheroes don't blow up."

Looper fired the caterpillar at him.

Will's conscience bothered him for saying that; he was starting to sound like Gogolak. "Still, it is our country. Someone has to fight for it, right?" Will shrugged. "How come you dropped out, anyway?"

"Bored." Looper shrugged. "I might go back, though. Or I might go to the war. I don't know." He swiped the basketball from Will. "I don't see you carrying a comm today."

"Needed to think." Will stood and gestured for his ball.

"Hey, you hear about the lottery?" Looper fired a pass.

Will shook his head.

"They were going to announce it over the school channels this morning; Gogo tipped me yesterday. Town's going to hire twenty kids this summer. Fix stuff, mow grass, pick up trash, you know. Buck an hour—good money. You got to go register at the post office this afternoon, then next month they pick the lucky ones."

"Kind of early to think about the summer." Will frowned. "Bet you that jack Gogolak gets a job."

Looper glanced at him. "He's not that bad."

"A jack. You think he worries about sweeps?" Will didn't know why he was so angry at Looper. He was beginning to like Looper. "He's probably rich enough to buy out of the draft if he wants. He gets everything his way."

"Not everything." Looper laughed. "He's short."

Will had to laugh too. "You want to check this lottery out?"

"Sure." Looper heaved himself up. "Show you something on the way over."

There was blood on the sidewalk. A crowd of about a dozen had gathered by the abandoned condos on Coe Drive to watch the EMTs load Seth Warner into the ambulance that was parked right behind his Peugeot. Will looked for Denise but didn't see her. A cop was recording statements.

"I got here just after Jeff Roeder." Mrs. O'Malley preened as she spoke into the camera; it had been a long time since anyone paid attention to her. "He was lying on the sidewalk there, all bashed up. The car door was open and his disk was playing. Jeff stayed with him. I ran for help."

The driver shut the rear doors of the ambulance. Somebody in the crowd called out, "How is he?"

The driver grunted. "Wants his lawyer." Everyone laughed.

"Must've been a fight," Jeff Roeder said. "We found this next to him." He handed the cop a bloody dental plate.

"Did anyone else here see anything?" The cop raised her voice.

"I would've liked to've seen it," whispered the woman in front of Will. "He's one oldie who had it coming." People around her laughed uneasily. "Shit. They all do."

Even the cop heard that. She panned the crowd and then slammed the Peugeot's door.

Looper grinned at Will. "Let's go." They headed for Madbury Road.

"He wanted me to get in the car with him," Looper said as they approached the post office. "He offered me a buck. Didn't say anything else, just waved it at me."

Will wished he were somewhere else.

"A stinking buck," said Looper. "The pervert."

"But if he didn't say what he wanted . . . maybe it was for a stand-in someplace."

"Yeah, sure." Looper snorted. "Wake up and look around you." He waved at downtown Durham. "The oldies screwed us. They wiped their asses on the world. And they're still at it."

"You're in deep trouble, Looper." No question Looper had done a dumb thing, yet Will knew exactly how the kid felt.

"Nah. What are they going to do? Pull me in and say 'You're fighting on the wrong front, Johnny. Better enlist for your own good'? No problem. Maybe I'm ready to enlist now, anyway." Looper nodded; he looked satisfied with himself. "It was the disk, you know. He was playing it real loud and tapping his fingers on the wheel like he was having a great time." He spat into the road. "Boomer music. I hate the damn Beatles, so I hit him. He was real easy to hit."

There was already a ten-minute line at the post office and the doors hadn't even opened yet. Mostly it was kids from school who were standing in, a few dropouts like Looper and one grown-up, weird Miss Fisher. Almost all of the kids with comms were logged on, except that no one paid much attention to the screens. They were too busy chatting with the people around them. Will had never mastered the art of talking and studying at the same time.

They got in line right behind Sharon Riolli and Megan Brown. Sharon was in Will's class, and had asked him to a dance once when they were in seventh. Over the summer he had grown thirteen centimeters. Since then she'd made a point of ignoring him; he looked older than he was. Old enough to fight.

"When are they going to open up?" said Looper.

"Supposed to be one-thirty," said Megan. "Hi, Will. We missed you at socialization."

"Hi, Megan. Hi, Sharon."

Sharon developed a sudden interest in fractions.

"Have you seen Denise Warner?" said Will.

"The new kid?" Megan snickered. "Why? You want to ask her out or something?"

"Her grandpa got into an accident up on Coe Drive."

"Hurt?"

"He'll live." Looper kept shifting from foot to foot as if the sidewalk was too hot for him.

"Too bad." Sharon didn't look up.

"Hey, Genius. Loop." Gogolak cut in front of the little kid behind Looper, some stiff from sixth who probably wasn't old enough for summer work anyway. "Hear about Gervais?"

"What happened?" said Sharon. Will noticed that she paid attention to Gogolak.

"Got his foot turned into burger. They're looking for a new Johnny."

"Oh, war stuff." Megan sniffed. "That's all you guys ever talk about."

"I think a girl should get a chance," said Sharon.

"Yeah, sure," said Looper. "Just try toting a launcher through the jungle in the heat."

"I could run body armor." She gave Looper a pointed stare. "Something that takes brains."

The line behind them stretched. It was almost one-thirty when Mr. Gogolak came running out of the side door of the post office. The Selective Service office was on the second floor. He raced down the line and grabbed his kid.

"What are you doing here? Go home." He grabbed Gogolak's wrist and turned him around.

"Let go of me!" Gogolak struggled. It had to be embarrassing to be hauled out of a job line like some stupid elementary school kid.

His dad bent over and whispered something. Gogolak's eyes got big. A flutter went down the line; everyone was quiet, watching. Mr. Gogolak was wearing his Selective Service uniform. He pulled his kid into the street.

Mr. Gogolak had gone to the western front with Will's dad. Mr. Gogolak had come back. And last night he had been screwing Will's mom. Will wished she were here to see this. They were supposed to be old friends, maybe he owed her a favor after last night. But the only one Mr. Gogolak whispered to was *his* kid. It wasn't hard to figure out what he had said.

Gogolak gazed at Looper and Will in horror. "It's a scam!" he shouted. "Recruiters!"

His old man slapped him hard and Gogolak went to his knees. But he kept shouting even as his father hit him again. "Draft scam!" They said a top recruiter could talk a prospect into anything.

Will could not bear to watch Mr. Gogolak beat his kid. Will's anger finally boiled over; he hurled his father's basketball and it caromed off Mr. Gogolak's shoulder. The man turned, more surprised than angry. Will was one hundred and ninety centimeters tall, and even if he was built like a stick, he was bigger than this little grown-up. Lucky Mr. Gogolak, the hero of the western front, looked shocked when Will punched him. It wasn't a very smart thing to do but Will was sick of being smart. Being smart was too hard.

"My mom says hi." Will lashed out again and missed this time. Mr. Gogolak dragged his crybaby kid away from the post office. Will pumped his fist in triumph.

"Run! Run!" The line broke. Some dumb kid screamed, "It's a sweep!" but Will knew it wasn't. Selective Service had run this scam before: summer job, fall enlistment. Still, kids scattered in all directions.

But not everyone. Weird Miss Fisher just walked to the

door to the post office like she was in line for ketchup. Bobby Mangann and Eric Orr and Danny Jarek linked arms and marched up behind her; their country needed them. Will didn't have anywhere to run to.

"Nice work." Looper slapped him on the back and grinned. "Going in?"

Will was excited; he had lost control and it had felt *great.* "Guess maybe I have to now." It made sense, actually. What was the point in studying history if you didn't believe in America? "After you, Johnny."

TRAVELING WEST

Pat Murphy

 I was ten years old when my father sold our farm and packed our belongings into a wagon that he had spent all winter building. He hitched up a team of oxen, tied the horse and mule behind, and turned our steps westward, to California.

The year before, his brother had emigrated to California. My father had received only one letter from my uncle. It told of beautiful valleys that begged to be planted, a temperate climate where snow never fell, a paradise on earth.

And so, in the spring of 1849, we headed west. It took almost a month for us to cross Iowa and reach the banks of the Missouri River. I remember the first part of the trip as a cozy sort of adventure. To me, the wagon was a wonderful place: a moving house carrying all that my father, my mother, and I could ever need. I lay in the wagon, watching the slabs of smoked bacon that hung from the crossbeams swaying with each jounce.

At Council Bluffs, we reached our jumping-off place, where we left civilization behind. We joined a group of wagons waiting to be ferried over the Missouri River. While my father went to talk with the ferryman, my mother and I stayed with the wagon. I saw my first Indian wandering among the waiting wagons. He was a wild-looking man with a half-shaven head and a painted face. He wore a bit of red calico wrapped around his bare shoulders like a shawl, and he returned my stare with eyes as hard and shiny as wet pebbles. I saw buckskin-clad mountain men, squatting on the Missouri River's muddy bank and playing some sort of gambling game.

"Hello, little girl," one of them called to me. "Where are you going?"

"California," I called from the seat of the wagon. "We're bound for California." My mother put a hand on my shoulder to stop me from bouncing up and down on the seat in excitement.

The mountain man approached, taking off his broad-brimmed hat and holding it respectfully in both hands. "No disrespect, ma'am," he said to my mother. "It's late in the season to be setting out. You'd best be careful."

My mother just smiled at him and nodded. "Thank you for your concern," she said.

My father returned then, with news that we could join a company bound for California. We left the mountain man and his advice behind, but I waved as the oxen pulled us slowly away.

An uncertain-looking wooden raft ferried our wagon across the river; the oxen, the horse, and the mule followed, swimming across the muddy water. On the far side, we joined the other wagons in our company—five families in all. The captain of the company, a bluff man, clapped my father heartily on the shoulder, saying that they needed more brave men, since they were heading through Indian country.

The day we set forth was sunny—brave and hopeful weather. I walked beside the wagon and searched for wild flowers among the prairie grasses. I picked the brightest flowers and brought them to my mother, who exclaimed with delight. In the evening, we circled the wagons and made camp. It was like a picnic; I was safe with my mother and father.

We followed the ruts that other wagons had worn in the prairie grass, heading always westward. Once we passed three graves, marked with crude wooden crosses. The wolves had been at them, leaving a scattering of fresh dirt across the trail. My mother turned her head away as we passed.

The next morning, I woke to the sound of steady rain on the canvas wagontop. More than once that day, the wagon bogged down in mud and we all had to climb out and stand in the wet while the oxen and the men labored to rock the wheels free. By the day's end, when we reached the Loup Fork of the Platte River, we were all soaked to the skin and cold to the bone.

The Loup Fork was known for its treachery. The river bottom was laced with deep channels and pockets of quicksand that some said could swallow a wagon and team. It took the best part of a day, working in the rain and mud, to get our wagon train across. We forded the river at a narrow point, where the river bottom was thought to be solid, hitching a double team of oxen to each wagon to haul it across, then swimming the oxen back to haul another wagon. When our turn came, my mother and I clung to the wagon, watching the water lap at the wagonbed. But the wagonbed was solidly built and carefully caulked. It floated like a boat and carried us across to safety.

Even so, the day was a miserable one. My father worked valiantly, helping others in the train long after my mother advised him to rest. At suppertime, he sat in the wagon, wrapped in a blanket, trying to warm himself.

The next day, he fell ill, a fever brought on by the chill he had caught. That day, he rode in the wagon. I sat with him while my mother drove the team. The fever was a bad one—

he tossed in his bed and moaned each time the wagon jounced over a rut.

After a day of that, my mother insisted that we stop to nurse him back to health. Given the lateness of the season, the others of the wagon train refused to stop. The captain advised that we continue with the train and put my father's fate in God's hands. But my mother was a stubborn woman.

I stood beside her as the wagon train departed, leaving our solitary wagon behind. The weather had cleared; the sky was blue above us. The prairie spread around us, flat and smooth, a sea of grass, lacking trees or anything that could properly be called a hill. The Platte River flowed beside us, a placid, slow-moving current of muddy water. The river marked our trail westward. When my father recovered, we planned to follow the river, hurrying after the wagon train and catching them, we hoped, the next time they stopped for a day to rest the oxen.

That was not to be. My mother nursed my father tenderly, soothing his fever with rags cooled in river water, dosing him with whiskey and tea. Despite her efforts, he died in his bed on the second day after the wagon train left us. My mother, weary from her nursing, fell ill that same day, and I tended her as she had tended my father. She lay in the wagon, not four feet from his dead body, and I sat by her side and prayed that God would not leave me an orphan.

That first night, I sat by my mother's side until just after sunset. She had been sleeping fitfully, but she opened her eyes then and asked for a cup of tea.

Encouraged to see her looking better, I left the stuffy confines of the wagon, stepping out into the evening breeze. The full moon was rising; the prairie grasses looked gray in its pale light. The horse and mule, picketed nearby, looked up with interest and nickered, hoping for a handful of grain. The oxen were tethered not far from the wagon. By the light of the full moon, I built a fire of dried buffalo chips and weeds and heated river water to a boil.

I was pouring boiling water from the kettle into the teapot when I saw a gray shadow move among the grazing oxen. As I watched, the shadow lifted its head and met my gaze with eyes that reflected yellow in the moonlight. A great gray wolf, as big as I was, stared at me.

I froze, terrified. I had never seen a wolf, but I had heard them howling in the night; their wails made me shiver and draw the covers up over my head. I had nothing to defend myself with but a teapot and a kettle of boiling water. I stared back at the beast, my heart pounding.

"Sarah Ann!" my mother called from the wagon. "Sarah Ann!"

At the sound of my mother's voice, the beast pricked up its ears. With a glance in the direction of the wagon, it trotted away, moving with an uneven gait, as if one of its paws were injured.

I hurried to my mother's side, bringing her a cup of hot tea. Not wanting to add to her worries, I did not tell her about the wolf; I just said that the fire had been difficult to start. She did not ask much. It took all her strength to sit up in bed and sip the tea. When I let her be, she lay down and did not move again.

I slept that night wrapped in a blanket by my mother's side. She moaned in her sleep and tossed fitfully. Once, she called for water and I brought her a dipper from the bucket. When she drank, she looked at me with wild and feverish eyes, as if she did not recognize her own daughter.

In the morning, when sunlight shining through the canvas of the wagon woke me, my mother was not breathing. Her eyes were open and staring. Her skin, when I touched her, was cold and stiff. I backed away, not knowing what to do. God had not answered my prayers. I climbed out of the wagon, staring around me wildly.

The wind blew across the open prairie, making the grass whisper and sway. In all directions, there was only the grass: not a wagon, not a person, not even a tree standing above the flatness. The bell on the lead ox's neck rang softly as he moved his head, searching for the best grass. I was alone in the wilderness and there was no one to help me. I had spent my childhood under the protection of my mother and father, but that protection was gone.

I'm not too proud to say that I sat in the grass and wept. I was ten years old and there was nothing else to do. When my tears ran dry, my pain and panic gave way to a kind of numbness. I knew my duty to my parents. I had to bury them as deep as I could, so that their bodies would be safe from wolves.

I took the shovel from the back of the wagon and I walked to the bluff beside the river. The soil was baked hard in the sun, and I scratched at the unyielding earth for an hour without making a very big hole. At one point I realized that I was not wearing my sunbonnet and my mother would be angry. Then my tears came afresh, because I knew that my mother would never be angry with me again.

I was wiping away my tears when I heard the sound of a human voice, a woman's voice, I thought, raised in song. The words were not in English; the tune, a rollicking melody, was not familiar. I looked up and saw a figure on a horse, riding along the riverbank. A scout for another wagon train, I thought, and I waved. "Hello," I cried. "Hello there."

The stranger rode on a spotted horse, the kind I had seen Indians riding near Council Bluffs. I dropped my hand then, suddenly remembering stories of children who had been captured by Indians and scalped or raised as savages. But I was too late; the stranger had seen me.

The voice had sounded like a woman, but the stranger was dressed like a man: in deerskin trousers, a plain brown shirt, and a broadbrimmed black hat. The stranger rode near, pushing back the hat and squinting at me in the sunshine. Though the face beneath the hat was tanned by the sun, the chin was beardless and the features were feminine.

"Please," I said. "Is your wagon train coming?"

"I'm not with a wagon train." A woman's voice. She spoke with an accent that reminded me of some German farmers we had met, but her voice was more lilting and musical. "I travel alone." She glanced at our wagon and the grazing animals and then looked toward the horizon, as if she were eager to be on her way. A bedroll and saddlebags were tied behind her saddle; she carried a rifle and wore a pistol at her belt.

"Please," I said again, the words spilling out in a rush. "My mama and papa are dead. I'm digging their grave." Then tears stopped me from saying more. I hid my face in my hands.

I heard the woman swing down from her horse. I thought for a moment that she would stop to comfort me, but she walked past. I glanced up and saw her peer into the back of the wagon and mutter something in a foreign language. I rubbed my eyes with the back of my hand, and lifted my head to meet her eyes as she returned.

She was a small woman, only a little taller than me. Young, I thought—no more than eighteen years old. Her face had been browned by the sun until she was as dark as an Indian. Like some of the Indians I had seen, she wore her long, dark hair pulled back in a single braid. She smelled of horse sweat and dust and campfire smoke.

As she took the reins of her horse in her right hand, I noticed that she was crippled. There was a mass of white scar tissue where the smallest two fingers should have been. The scar tissue continued a pale line that extended from the palm to disappear into her sleeve.

As I studied her, she looked me over. By her expression, she found me wanting. I have no doubt that I was a sight: my dusty face streaked with tears, my hands filthy and blistered from digging. But something about the look she gave me cut through my numbness and sorrow, raising anger in its place.

"Do you have any kin?" she asked me brusquely.

"My uncle lives in California," I said. "That's where I'm

going." It was only in that moment that I realized that I was going on to California alone. Always before, I had said "We are going to California."

"Are you now?"

I nodded. "I have to catch up to the wagon train. They left us three days ago."

"Can you ride?"

"Yes," I lied. "But I can't saddle the horse by myself."

"I see." She kept looking at me. I knew that I had not convinced her, but she did not question me further. "I can help you," she said—reluctantly, I thought. "We will catch your wagon train and get you on your way to California."

I suddenly realized that I did not know her name. "I'm Sarah Ann," I said.

"My name is Nadia." She held out her maimed hand and I shook it gingerly. She did not notice my reluctance, taking my hand firmly in hers. I could feel the rough scar tissue against my palm.

She started to turn away, heading toward the horse. I clutched the shovel and did not move. She glanced back at me.

"I have to bury my mama and papa," I said. "I can't just leave them here."

She studied me again, as if revising her original assessment. "You are a stubborn child," she said. Her tone had changed—I think she approved of my stubbornness. But the expression on her face did not change.

In the end, she did most of the digging. That afternoon, we buried my mother and father in shallow graves by the riverside. She did not talk much, and I did not want to talk. I worked in a daze, gathering rocks from the riverbank and heaping them on top of the graves to discourage Indians and wolves from digging up the bodies.

Late in the afternoon, when the sun was low in the sky, I asked Nadia if we could make a marker for the graves. She used my father's saw to cut the handle of the shovel into two pieces. She lashed one to the other to form a crude cross, which she planted at the head of the grave.

When the cross was in place, I looked at the grave and suggested that we pray. Nadia shrugged. "I don't pray," she said. "But you do as you like."

I stared at her. This admission was even more startling than her peculiar way of dressing and her strange accent. I did not know anyone who did not pray. "Why don't you pray?" I asked her.

"Your God doesn't listen to me," she said casually.

I wondered at that. What other God was there, if this one was mine? Besides, God often didn't listen to me either. He had taken my parents and left me an orphan, despite my prayers.

Still, my mother and father had always told me to pray. I knelt down and thought for a while. Then I asked God to take care of Mama and Papa and to guide me on my way. Nadia stood nearby, looking out over the smooth water of the Platte. When I was done, she walked with me back to the wagon.

"Tomorrow we will be on our way," she said. "We'll pack what we need on the oxen and leave the wagon behind. Too much trouble for us if we hope to catch your wagon train."

I nodded, willing to abandon the wagon as long as she did not leave me behind.

That night, I made fruit compote from the dried apples and pears that my mother had been saving for a special occasion. We cooked biscuits and chipped beef over a fire that Nadia built using some wood from the wagon. "Might as well burn what we need," she said. "We won't be taking it with us."

It felt strange to see the wood burning. Ever since we set out on the plains, wood had been so precious. Exhausted from the long day, I sat beside Nadia and watched the flames dance along the seasoned hardwood slats. The pale moonlight cast dark shadows on the prairie grass. Nadia's shadow shifted and swayed with the movement of the grasses in the night wind.

In the distance, a wolf yipped once, then howled. Its wailing cry was joined by others, a wild chorus that made me shiver. I sat with my legs up, my arms wrapped around them. I missed my mother; I missed my father. I felt unprotected and alone. I glanced at Nadia and found her watching me.

"You don't care for the music?" she said.

"Music?" I shook my head, puzzled by her words.

"The music of the wolves."

"They sound like they want to come tear us apart."

"Have you ever seen a wolf?" She looked at me as if she already knew the answer.

I nodded.

"And that wolf, did she come tear you apart?" Her eyes challenged me.

I shook my head.

"You don't understand the wolves," Nadia said softly. "They are calling to the moon. The world is a big and empty place. They cry out and listen for an answer." She listened to the chorus rise again, then tipped her head back, barked once, and let loose a howl that echoed across the empty land. When the wolves answered, she smiled at me for the first time, a quick flash of white teeth in a brown face.

I was fascinated. For a moment, I forgot my loneliness. "Would they answer me if I howled?"

"Try," Nadia suggested.

Cautiously, I barked once, a small sound that was barely louder than the croaking of the frogs in the river.

"You bark like a puppy," she said contemptuously. "You can do better."

I barked again, louder and deeper this time.

"Better," she said. "Now howl. Let the moon hear you."

I fixed my gaze on the moon's pale face and howled. The sound began small and then swelled, as if it had been waiting, deep inside me, for this moment. All I had to do was release it. Nadia joined me with a deep wail that made the air ring.

The distant wolves answered, and I felt Nadia's hand on my shoulder. "They heard us," she said.

The wind blew, making the fire flare. The shadows shifted in the moving grass. I barked again, then wailed, my howl rising on the wind.

That night, Nadia laid her blankets beside the fire, saying that she preferred sleeping in the open to the confines of the wagon. At first, I climbed into the wagon, thinking to spend one last night in my familiar bed. Though I was very tired, I could not fall asleep. Finally, I slipped from the wagon, taking my blanket with me, and I lay down beside Nadia. My footsteps must have awakened her. Her eyes glimmered in the moonlight. I fell asleep, listening to the steady rhythm of her breathing.

The next day, Nadia packed the mule and the oxen with goods that she deemed most valuable for trade: my father's rifle and pistol, his pouch of tobacco, my mother's silver-handled mirror (an heirloom from her grandmother), the bacon, the coffee, a bag of dried beans, two bags of flour, two bolts of cloth. She let me select the things that I wanted to take: my mother's Bible, my father's buck knife, a bag of hard candy. The letter from my uncle in California was tucked in the Bible, and I took that, too.

Nadia saddled the horse and boosted me into the saddle. I had my dress awkwardly tucked around my legs so that I could ride astride, and I clung to the saddlehorn desperately, but I stayed on. The horse was an even-tempered beast, bred for the plow rather than the saddle, and he ignored my presence on his back. Nadia tied my horse's lead rope to the back of her saddle and tied the mule and the oxen behind my horse in a long train.

We rode in silence at first. Every now and then, Nadia would speak, telling me of things that I had not noticed before. "That fellow," she said, pointing high in the sky where a bird soared. "Prairie falcon. He's hunting now. There." The bird dove, disappeared for a moment in the tall grass, and then reappeared, flapping its wings and bearing something—a mouse, Nadia said—in his talons.

"Antelope," she said another time, pointing to a flicker of movement, vanishing into the tall grass. "Half dozen of them."

When we passed a prairie dog town, the small rodents stood up on their mounds and barked at us. Nadia barked back, and the prairie dogs all dove into the safety of their holes, emerging only after we were long past.

That first night, as we made camp, Nadia sniffed the breeze. "We'll have fresh meat for dinner," she said. Taking her rifle, she walked away from camp, her head held high as if she were catching a scent. I was on my way to the river to fill the kettle with water for tea, when I heard a shot. I headed toward the sound. Not far away, I found Nadia, disembowling an antelope. The entrails steamed in the evening air.

Nadia's attention was on the work at hand. She did not hear me coming up behind her. She flipped the body to one side to let the blood drain from the body cavity. As I watched, she got to her feet, holding her knife in one hand and a bloody piece of meat in the other. With an air of relish, like a child with an unexpected treat, she sliced off a bit of meat, still warm and bloody, and popped it in her mouth.

"Nadia," I called, startled.

She turned to face me, licking a drop of blood off her lips. She studied me for a moment, her face expressionless. "Fresh meat for dinner," she said.

I took a step back, momentarily frightened, but she remained motionless.

"Come and help me carry it to camp," she said.

I hesitated for a moment, and then I went to her. That night, I chopped the antelope meat for stew. When Nadia wasn't looking, I tasted a bit of the raw meat. Salty and harder to chew than cooked meat, but not so bad.

The sun was high the next day when I saw the white canvas of a wagon in the distance. I pointed to it, calling to Nadia in my excitement. I could make out only one wagon clearly, its canvas bright in the sunlight. There were others beyond it, but something was wrong with them. Their canvas had been stripped away, I thought, but why would anyone do that? As we rode closer, we saw that the wagons were motionless. Some of them had been burned black by fire.

Nadia reined in her horse, and mine bumbled to a stop. She held her head high, sniffing the air, then urged her horse forward at a walk. A little farther on, a man's body was sprawled across the trail. Buzzing flies rose from the body.

Nadia stopped again and glanced at my face. "I know him," I said. "He is . . . he was the captain of the wagon train." I stared down at the body.

Nadia untied my horse and gave me the lead to hold. "Stay here," she said, and rode toward the stationary wagons, leaving me to watch the flies lazily circle the captain's body while my horse cropped grass. I tried not to look at the dead man. I kept my gaze on Nadia. She peered into the back of each wagon, and then turned and rode back to me.

"Indian attack," she said, frowning. "I wonder what provoked it."

I glanced down at the captain's body again. "He said . . . he used to say that he would kill himself some wild Indians when he got out West," I told her.

Her expression was grim. She nodded. "Stupid man," she said callously. "Maybe he thought he could kill an Indian and pay nothing for it." She reined her horse to the side, leaving the trail and leading me in a wide circle around the wagons. When the wagons were far behind us, she said, "There are men who think they have the right to kill anything they choose. They are surprised to learn otherwise. I expect your captain was surprised when he died." I stayed silent, cowed by her disapproval.

When we had left the wagons far behind, I gathered my courage and asked Nadia what we would do, since I could not rejoin the wagon train. "There'll be other wagon trains," she said grimly. "There are always more white men heading west." She glanced at me, her expression softening, but she said nothing more.

Each day, we rode beside the river; each night, we slept under the stars. I grew used to Nadia's unpredictable moods. I did not follow her, when she went hunting; I waited until she brought the meat to the campfire. Sometimes, on mornings when she was silent and frowning, I was afraid to talk to her, afraid she might decide to leave me alone on the plains. But other times she seemed to welcome my company. Sometimes, I thought she liked me.

One night, when Nadia sniffed the air and said that a thunderstorm was coming, we put up her tent of heavy canvas. The rain came, with winds that shook the tent and drove water in through every seam. The prairie grasses whipped and danced in the high wind. Small rivers flowed down the tent's canvas sides. The lightning flashed, revealing the oxen standing with their heads down, soaked by the pelting rain. The thunder frightened me, but Nadia put her arm around my shoulders and laughed. "Frightened by the growling from the sky?" she said. "Don't be foolish." She sang me a lullaby in her own language. The chorus reminded me of wolves howling, a sound that was no longer frightening. I fell asleep to her singing.

I lost track of the days. There was a dreamy, timeless quality to our travel. The scenery did not change as we traveled: one bend in the river looked much the same as the last. We passed landmarks that I had heard of: Court House Rock and Chimney Rock rose in the distance, unmistakable. Antelope bounded away from us. A herd of buffalo watched us pass. We saw no other wagons, and eventually Nadia stopped talking about when we would find another wagon train. I thought she might have forgotten, and I was willing to forget with her.

As we rode, Nadia sometimes sang snatches of song in her native language. She taught me the lullaby she had sung the night of the storm. At the end of my first lesson, I could sing one verse, though my tongue tripped over the unfamiliar words and Nadia laughed at my pronunciation.

She translated for me. "Sleep well, little one. The moon is up and your father is hunting. Sleep well and be safe." And then the chorus of wolf howls.

Each night, the wolves came closer to our camp. In the twilight, when Nadia and I sat by our tiny campfire, they drifted among the oxen like the silent clouds that blew past the face of the moon. When I asked Nadia about them, she just smiled. "They know me. They know they are welcome here."

"Aren't you afraid that they'll kill the oxen?" I asked.

"They're not hungry. Look at them. If they were hungry, they'd be off with the buffalo herds, not prowling around this tame meat." She leaned back, her face ruddy in the firelight, and told me about how the wolves hunted the buffalo.

"What's the best smell you can imagine?" she asked me.

I hesitated. "My mama's bread, fresh from the oven."

"Imagine that smell, thick around you, a warm living scent that draws you near. That's what the buffalo smell like to the wolves. The smell calls to them." She inhaled deeply, as if she could smell buffalo on the wind. "Their shaggy fur is dusty and they move as if they were part of the earth, the hills come alive." She fell silent, but I prompted her.

"What happens when the wolves see the buffalo?" I asked.

"The wolves test the herd, running at the buffalo. Some buffalo shift nervously, and a few start to trot away. The wolves run at them again, and some buffalo spook. When the herd begins to gallop, you can feel the earth trembling underfoot, trembling with excitement at the chase. One buffalo, maybe an old bull, falls behind the others, and the wolves nip at his heels, tear at his haunches, slash at his legs. Maybe he turns and makes a stand, facing the pack with his horns, trying to trample them beneath his hooves. The wolves circle behind him, nipping and tearing and dodging his kicks. Again he runs, leaving splashes of hot blood behind in the grass. The warm smell of fresh blood fills the air."

She glanced down at me and laughed. She was in one of her happy moods. "Don't look so fearful, little one. I just wanted you to understand why the wolves have no interest in tame meat."

"How do you know so well how it is?" I asked her.

She smiled. "I know," she said. "I have been there."

I nodded, not trusting myself to say anything.

As the days passed, my dress grew tattered and grimy. After struggling to find a way to ride while wearing it, I tore the skirt so that I could ride astraddle. My arms and legs were brown from the sun; my skin was rough from the constant wind. Nadia taught me to load and shoot my father's pistol. I had to hold it with both hands, and even then the kick made me stagger. I was proud the first time I managed to hit the boulder I was aiming at.

With each passing day, the moon grew thinner, wearing itself down to a half-moon, a quarter-moon. With the waning of the moon, Nadia grew restless. Twice that week, when a sound in the night woke me, I opened my eyes to see her silhouetted against the stars, gazing outward into the darkness. During the day, she said nothing of her late-night wakefulness. She wore her hat pulled low, but she could not hide the dark circles beneath her eyes. She would slump in her saddle. She no longer sang as we rode.

We reached the fur-trading post known as Fort Laramie on July 9. Nadia stood beside the tall, clay-brick walls and shouted that we had supplies to trade. A Frenchman with hair as long as an Indian's opened the gate and let us into the central courtyard. Indians and traders, reclining at ease on the low roofs of the buildings within the walls, stared down on us. They ignored me, concentrating on Nadia. But after a few minutes, she lost her fascination and they returned to their gambling game. By the open doors of the buildings, squaws sat in the shade. Some of them were engaged in needlework, stitching moccasins or garments of buffalo hide. Everywhere, there were children: dark-faced and curious, most of them half naked.

"Will we stay here tonight?" I asked Nadia.

"Here?" She looked up at the walls and wrinkled her nose as if she smelled something bad. "I'd as soon spend the night in prison."

She tied the horses and the mule to a post and told me to watch them. I sat in the shade nearby, while Nadia talked with the Frenchman. The children swarmed around me, and I glared at them, warning them away.

Nadia spoke enough French that I could barely follow the conversation. Negotiating the trade took a long time. Nadia praised the oxen and the goods they carried. The Frenchman said that the beasts looked sick. Some of the traders and Indians climbed down from the roof to join the discussion, surrounding Nadia and the Frenchman. At one point, Nadia started to lead the oxen away, shouting to me, "We'll do no business here. Come along, Sarah Ann." But then the Frenchman called her back and the circle of traders closed around her again. There was much shouting in French and English. A young Indian boy ran to and fro. First, he brought an odd assortment of bundles and bottles to the Frenchman. Then he ran away and returned, leading a small Indian pony.

Nadia called to me and beckoned me to join her among the traders and Indians. I did not like these men—they stared at me and smelled of tobacco and whiskey. But Nadia was there to protect me.

"Here now," she said, holding up a pair of buckskin trousers. She measured them against me. "They'll fit well enough, I reckon." She handed me a shirt and moccasins as well, and jerked her head toward the doorway where a squaw sat. "Go put them on."

In the darkened interior, under the watchful eyes of the squaw and her children, I tugged off my dress. The new clothes smelled of dust, and the shirt was far too large, but I tucked it into the pants.

I swaggered into the sunshine, happy to be wearing pants rather than a skirt. Nadia boosted me onto the pony's back. The beast shied and then steadied. I gripped it with my knees and clung to the buckskin strap that girdled its belly.

"Good enough," Nadia said to the Frenchman. The pony stood docilely, head hanging low in the afternoon heat, while Nadia loaded the other packages onto the back of the mule and the most docile of the oxen.

"The last wagon train through here was days ago," she said as she tied the pack. "I don't think we can catch it."

"That's good," I said. At that moment, I did not want to catch a wagon train. I wanted to go on traveling with Nadia, singing her songs and riding on my pony by her side.

She glanced up at me, her expression unreadable. "What's this, little one? You don't want to travel with the white men?"

"I want to travel with you."

She wet her lips, staring up at me, then she looked away. "We'd best be going," she said. "Put some distance between us and this place before night." She swung up onto her horse, chirped to the animal, and started out the gate.

Though she had said nothing, I thought that she wanted me to stay. She was lonely too, I think. I took her silence as agreement and I was happy for the rest of that day.

That night, after I had wrapped myself in my blanket to sleep, I heard Nadia get up and go to the pack. In the darkness, I heard liquid splash into a tin cup. Then I caught a whiff of whiskey. Nadia sat alone by the ashes of the fire. I could not see her face in the darkness. She lifted the cup and drank.

The horses shifted and their harness jingled. I lay in my blanket, watching Nadia drink. After a time, I heard her pour another cup of whiskey. The moon hung just above the western horizon, a crescent of white as delicate and pale as the rim of a china cup. Nadia's hat shielded her face from its dim light. Her head was down, her shoulders bowed.

I sat up, but she took no notice. With my blanket wrapped around me, I went to sit beside her. She did not look at me.

"What's wrong, Nadia?" I asked her. I was afraid of her, just then. But she looked so mournful that I could not stay away.

She shrugged and shook her head. "I don't even like the taste of it," she said, her voice harsh. "But it will help me sleep."

I waited. She was halfway through the cup when she spoke again. "It's the moon," she said. "Wearing itself down to a splinter and leaving us in the darkness."

"It will get big again soon enough," I told her. It was as if I were the older of us two, comforting her in the darkness.

"It will," she said. "But the full moon is so far away. I can't wait so long." She drained the cup and poured another. "It was easier when my mother and father were with me."

"What happened to your mother and father?" I asked her. "Where is your family?"

"Dead," she said. "Killed every one of them." She looked up and met my eyes. "My father was shot when he was out hunting deer. In the thrill of the chase, he did not see the other hunter."

I shook my head. "Why would a hunter shoot him for chasing deer?"

"He didn't look like a man," she said softly. "A hunter would shoot a wolf for no reason at all. A wolf, he would just shoot for being a wolf. No reason." She leaned back, looking up at the sliver of a moon. "You know, I tracked the hunter and one day, I shot him. Just like that. I told him that I was killing him for my father's death, and he didn't understand. He didn't understand at all.

"My mother and I headed west. But after my father's death, I don't think my mother cared if she went on living. She grew careless. Not so long after my father's death, she was caught in a trap. The steel jaws closed on her leg, breaking the bone and holding her fast. She might have escaped at dawn, but the trapper walked his line before the sun came up. He found her there and shot her. I killed him, too, shot him through the heart early the next day. But my mother was gone."

Nadia did not look at me. "I've been careless too." She held up her maimed hand. "I was lucky. The trap was old; its spring was weak. It did not break my leg, just caught and held it. I managed to pull free of it. I lost a few fingers, but I survived." Her voice was flat and even.

I watched her, not speaking, scarcely breathing. Her eyes were focused on the cup in her hands.

"Do you understand, Sarah Ann?"

I nodded, afraid to trust my voice.

She glanced at my face. "My parents brought me to this country when I was just a child. My mother used to tell me about the old country. The villages were so close together; the wild animals had long since fled. My family lived on the edge, between the village and the wild lands, part of both. As the wild lands went away, there was no space for us, no space at all. There, people blamed the wolves for killing sheep."

She waved a hand at the horizon. "Here, there is space. But still men kill wolves. They say wolves are vicious; wolves are dangerous. Always the men who say these things are vicious men, dangerous men, men who like to kill." She shook her head and drained her cup of whiskey. "Go to sleep, little one. You can do nothing for me."

I reached out and touched her hand. "We can be sisters. We'll be family to each other. Don't be sad."

For a time, we sat together. I woke in the daylight with my blanket tucked around me. Nadia had built a fire and was heating water in the kettle. She said nothing of our late-night conversation, and I did not mention it either.

Each night after that, when I was wrapped in my blanket, she rose from her bed and drank. Some nights, she paced away from the camp, wandering out into the darkness. I worried about her, but I dared not follow.

The moon grew larger, but Nadia's restlessness did not fade. If anything, it increased: a nervous excitement that seemed somehow unhealthy. On the evening when the moon would be full, we made camp early. She claimed she was hungry, but I noticed that she ate little, barely touching the stew or the biscuits. Well before our usual hour, when the sun was just down, she lay down and suggested I do the same. Tired as always from the day's journey, I dozed off.

When I woke, Nadia was no longer beside me. The fire had burned to embers and the moon illuminated the prairie with its cold white light. Nadia's shirt and trousers and boots and hat had been neatly placed on her blanket.

I sat up and looked around. Our horses stood motionless a few feet away. "Nadia?" I said. There was no answer. "Nadia?" This time, my voice was touched with panic.

I shook off my blanket and walked to the river bluff. I could hear the placid murmur of the water and the creaking of frogs on its bank. No human sound disturbed the silence. The night wind raised ripples on the smooth water.

I returned to camp and poked the fire until it flared, the flames licking at the dry grass that I piled on the embers. With my blanket wrapped around my shoulders, I kept watch, holding my father's pistol in my lap. I don't know what I had expected. I suppose I expected that somehow Nadia would take me with her when she went hunting. It was too much to be left alone again. I cried a little, worrying that she would not come back, she would never come back. I must have drowsed then, my eyes closing of their own accord.

I woke suddenly and saw Nadia, silhouetted against the dawn glow in the eastern sky. She was naked. Her body was sturdy and square-shouldered. I could see her muscles moving beneath her skin as she strode through the grass.

Unconcerned with her nakedness, she stopped by her blanket and stretched, reaching up to the sky. When she saw me watching her, she smiled down at me, amused by something I could not understand. "It was a fine night for hunting," she said. "You look fierce, little one. Have you been sitting up with a pistol all night?"

"I woke up and you were gone," I said.

Her smile faded then, and she squatted in front of me and took my chin in her hand. "When the moon is full, I go hunting," she said. "You understood that." She studied my face, and for a moment I was afraid of her. She let me go, and then reluctantly pulled on her trousers and shirt.

"We'll spend a few days here," she told me. Without another word, she wrapped herself in her blanket, pulled her hat low over her eyes, and went to sleep.

I could not go back to sleep. I got up, went away from the camp, and scrambled down the bank to the shore of the river. On the muddy bank, I noticed footprints: my prints from the day before. Crossing my prints were pawprints: the track of a wolf. The animal's right front paw was missing two toes.

I sat on the riverbank for a while, watching the frogs that lived in the slow eddies by the river's edge. If I sat still, the frogs forgot that I was there and came swimming to sit on the muddy shore. But if I turned my head or moved to scratch an itch, they all fled, leaping for the safety of the water. Each escaping frog left rings of spreading ripples. The ripple patterns intersected, making an intricate design, like elaborate lacework.

I was sitting very still when all the frogs jumped at once.

Nadia came up behind me and sat beside me on the muddy bank. She didn't speak at first. I didn't look at her.

"I'm sorry," she said at last.

I nodded, my eyes on the spreading ripples. For a long time, she didn't say anything else. I glanced up at her. She was staring at her hands.

I reached out and took her crippled hand. "It's all right," I said.

We sat together on the bank, and after a time, the frogs came back.

We spent three days by the river. On the fourth day, when we set out on our journey again, Nadia was singing and happy. The trail left the riverside and gradually climbed to the South Pass that led through the Rocky Mountains. We reached the northern end of the Colorado Valley in early August. It took several days for us to cross the valley; many of the springs and water holes there were dangerous. Nadia sniffed the air near each one. Sometimes she insisted we keep moving, looking for safer water and feed for the horses. Often we didn't make camp until well after dark.

But I did not mind that. Nadia and I sat by the campfire and looked up at the stars, howled and listened to wolves answer. I thought I would be with her forever. I had never had a sister, but surely we were sisters. There was nothing we couldn't do together.

We crossed the ridge that divided the Colorado Valley from the Great Salt Lake Basin. My surefooted pony made his way along the winding trail, and I was grateful that we had left the wagon behind. On clear days, I could see snow on the peaks high above us. It was a wild and unforgiving place, and I loved it.

At least, by day I loved it. At night, after the campfire had burned low, I felt lonely again. I thought about my mother and my father and I wept, trying to sob quietly. Once,

Nadia woke up and heard me crying. She rocked me in her arms and sang me the lullaby of the wolves until I slept again.

"Sarah Ann," she asked me the next morning. "Why do you cry at night?"

I ducked my head, embarrassed that she had mentioned my tears, which I regarded as a foolish weakness. "I guess I just miss my mama," I said.

She studied me thoughtfully. "You miss your people."

"Only sometimes," I said quickly. "Only at night."

"I miss my people, too," she said. "I understand."

As we rode over the pass, Nadia taught me another song in her language, this one about a woman and a man who fell in love. The woman, the song said, had "wild blood," and the man did not. In the end, she left him behind, even though she loved him. I remember the chorus, where the woman sang to her lover: "Leave me now, for I must wander. I have no place to call my home." I didn't like this one as well as I liked the lullaby. The melody was plaintive.

I asked Nadia why the woman left the man, even though she loved him. She shrugged, looking sad. "That is the way of things," she said. "They were not of the same people."

"I don't think that's the way things have to be," I said. "Couldn't she change? Couldn't she change him?"

She shook her head. "There's no changing the way things are."

In the Great Salt Lake Valley, Nadia sniffed the wind and led the way to a spring where hot water bubbled from the ground. There, we washed away the grime of the trail, repeatedly filling the kettle with steaming water and pouring it over each other's heads. We scrubbed ourselves with handfuls of grass and I felt clean for the first time in more than a month.

The next day, I saw the Great Salt Lake far below. Its waters glittered in the light of the setting sun. Behind it, the mountains rose up; in front were the houses and gardens of a small city. "One day's travel," Nadia said, reining her horse in beside me.

After the days and nights of solitude, the city by the lake was overwhelming. Too many people; too many houses. A Mormon woman looked up from her vegetable garden to watch us pass, her eyes lingering on Nadia's trousers. Nadia asked her where the wagon companies camped, and the woman pointed to the west side of town.

I rode close by Nadia's side, following her to the place where the wagons camped. As we rode past a wagon encampment, I could see a family like my own. The mother was shelling peas for their dinner, doubtless the first fresh vegetables they had eaten for many weeks. A little girl played at her feet with a rag doll. A girl my own age watched me from her mother's side. Beneath the brim of her sunbonnet, I could see her eyes. She gawked at me and my pony as if we were a circus curiosity.

I dug my heels into my pony's sides and caught up with Nadia. She glanced at my face. "What's wrong?" she asked me.

"Nothing's wrong," I said. "Just the sun in my eyes." I wiped a few tears away and would not look at her.

We camped not far away. The moon was just a sliver in the sky, and Nadia drank whiskey with dinner. She did not talk much. I did not try to draw her out. Soothed by the whiskey, she fell asleep by the fire.

For a time, I sat by the fire, looking up at the stars. In the distance, I heard music: not the howling of wolves, but the homey sound of a harmonica. I recognized the tune as one that my father used to play. As I listened, voices raised in song joined the harmonica music.

I crept away from the fire and made my way to the outskirts of the circle of wagons. I stood beside one of the wagons, where I could watch and listen. The firelight shone on the faces of the travelers. The woman who had been shelling peas sat in the firelight with a child in her lap, singing with the others.

I was so caught up in the music that I did not hear the girl until she was right beside me.

"Hello," she said. "What are you doing here?"

I took a step back, startled. "Just watching."

"My name's Mary. What's yours?"

"Sarah Ann."

She looked me up and down. "How come you're dressed like a boy?"

"It's easier to ride like this."

She shook her head, not accepting the explanation. "Is that your mama, riding with you?"

I shook my head. "My mama's dead," I said, and the words stuck in my throat.

The girl looked thoughtful. "Where's your papa?"

"He's dead too. They died of fever."

"Mary?" The woman from the fireside was coming our way. I shrank back into the shadows, strangely fearful. "Who is that you're talking to?"

"Sarah Ann," Mary said.

The woman came close to us. Something about her—her smell, the rustle of her skirts, the way she carried herself—something reminded me of my mother.

"I was just listening to the music, ma'am," I managed to say.

"There's nothing wrong with wanting to hear music, child," the woman said. "There now, what's wrong?" She stooped down and put one arm around my shoulders. "What is it, child?"

"She's an orphan," Mary announced matter-of-factly.

"There now," Mary's mother said. "There now." She patted my back and had Mary fetch a clean handkerchief from the wagon. The handkerchief's strong scent of laundry soap reminded me of home and made the tears flow afresh. She rocked me in her arms and I told her how my father had died and my mother had died. I told her about traveling with Nadia, about trading at Fort Laramie.

I did not know that I was making a choice. I did not intend to make a choice. I had been happy in the mountains with Nadia. But the music of the harmonica lured me close.

Mary's mother soothed and comforted me. "You should stay with us tonight," she said. "You can sleep here with Mary." She wiped my face clean with the handkerchief and put me and Mary to bed. It was comforting to sleep in a wagon again. But I did not understand that I was making a choice. I thought I would wake early the next day and hurry back to Nadia.

The next morning, when the first light of dawn touched the wagon's canvas sides, I slipped from bed and climbed out of the wagon. My pony was picketed beside the wagon. The pack that held my things was on the ground beside the pony. I looked at these things for a moment, without understanding. Then I ran to the camp where I had left Nadia. The camp was empty; the fire was cold. She had left before dawn, packing my belongings and leaving them beside the wagon.

Mary's mother and father took me with them to California. They were good people, generous people, though they took away my trousers and made me wear a sunbonnet and a dress. When we reached California, they found my uncle. He and his wife adopted me as their own daughter. I came to call my uncle "Papa" and his wife "Mama." But I never forgot how to shoot and sometimes, when I could get away with it, I rode my pony astride, like a boy.

Eventually, I married. I had children of my own. When I was a young mother, I sometimes amused my babies by howling and letting the wolves answer. If there were wolves, they always answered. They knew that I was calling out in loneliness, and they always replied.

Over the years, I wondered what happened to Nadia. Now that I am older, I understand better why she left me. She could not take the responsibility for taking a child who lacked the wild blood. She did not want to ruin my life. But she did not know that the seeds of wildness had already taken root. Though I tried to fit into my uncle's family, I never felt comfortable. I had grown too big for the space allotted me. It was as if I were caught between the wild lands and the village, belonging to neither.

But all this was long ago. My husband and I live in town now. The surrounding land has been plowed for farming. I do not howl, and if I did, the wolves would not answer. There are no wolves here now.

THE SCORCH ON WETZEL'S HILL

Sherwood Springer

 Today, by merest chance, I heard a word, a single word that immediately began clattering up and down the corridors of my mind, knocking on every door.

It was an unfamiliar word, and there was a bothersome urgency about the sound of it. I tried rolling it off my tongue, but that only strengthened the certainty that I had never spoken the word before, or heard it used. Why, then, that feeling of unease about it, of something far back in my memory that stirred ominously?

Nothing would surface, however, and, brushing off the mood, I attempted to resume the pattern of my day. But the effort met resistance and soon I found myself merely going through the motions of resuming my pattern, while that accursed word nagged me insistently for attention. All of us, at some time or other, have to face it: Some things are bigger than we are. I should have given up at the beginning and consulted Webster.

It was there, all right, on page 658, all four tricky syllables of it. And, surprisingly, it was a word I *had* used in my childhood, but Noah's accent marks changed the pronunciation so drastically, it was no wonder the correct usage had borne no familiarity for me. Just another example, I thought, of the many mispronunciations my mountain-bred father had handed down to me, some of which had required years to get rooted out of my vocabulary. So this was merely one more—

But as I closed the dictionary, my heart was pounding strangely. Someone besides my father had mispronounced that word. Someone who . . .

Have you ever stepped on land after being seaborne for days, and felt the solid earth sway beneath your feet?

Mr. Porter! But he . . .

Memories long since categorized and properly stored away suddenly started to slide from their safe little niches and tumble into new order, like the jolting change in a kaleidoscope.

In shock I realized—too late by more than forty years—that on a summer day long ago I had had it in my power to solve the mystery of the Scorch on Wetzel's Hill. And just as suddenly I knew for the first time that I had walked, as a ten-year-old on that long-gone day, into the shadow of what television viewers call the Twilight Zone.

Two generations or more have grown up and gone away from my hometown since then—it was that kind of hometown—and only the oldsters will remember there ever was a mystery on Wetzel's Hill. But there was, and it was there when I was a boy, and even the professors from State College floundered in their efforts to explain it.

First let me tell you about the Hill, then about the events on that day in my boyhood, and finally about the singular word that fell on my ears today which so devastatingly changed the pattern and meaning of those events.

Forty miles west of Shikelamy, the great stone face on the Susquehanna River where the Indian was fabled to have leapt to his death screaming, "She killa me!" lie sprawled the

Seven Mountains. From them a procession of valleys fan out like wrinkles in the tortuous foothills of the Alleghenies: Poe Valley, Decker Valley, High Valley, Brush Valley, and Sugar Valley.

The mountains crowd the valleys forebodingly, and some obscure poet once visioned them as "waiting" when he wrote:

> *Across the valley hill on purple hill*
> *Loom somberly and dark against the stars,*
> *Like wooded backs of ancient dinosaurs*
> *That lie there buried . . . sleeping . . . still . . .*

One of these is known as Thunder Mountain, and just to the west of Jackpine Gap it rises slightly in a dome called Bald Knob. From this elevation it pitches in a precipitous jumble of rocks and gnarly red pine to a crescent-shaped apron about a hundred feet above the waters of Jackpine Creek. This level apron, about two acres in extent and overlooking the valley on one side, is known as Wetzel's Hill.

Fifty years before I was born (my father told me), a man named Grover Wetzel came out of the east and saw the hill. It was mountain land then, and untillable, but he liked what he saw and he purchased it on the spot. Soon afterward he brought his wife and two young sons from Hummels Wharf or Whomelsdorf or some such place—Pennsylvania is full of towns like that—and set to work clearing the land.

Grover Wetzel was a giant of a man. Some say he was kin to Lewis Wetzel, the famed Indian hunter of pioneer days. Be that as it may, he and his sons worked a miracle on the hill. Boulders, trees, and brush melted before their labors, a cabin was built and a garden planted. A small spring, common in that country, gurgled from a crevice in the mountain behind the cabin, and water was plentiful.

As the seasons passed, more and more of the land was

cleared, potatoes, corn, and greens were harvested, and chickens, hogs, and a cow shared the hill with the Wetzels.

But the decades passed, too, and the sons grew up and found wives in the valley. One of them moved to Ohio and settled in Akron or Cleveland or someplace, and the other found a job in town. Grandchildren were born, and Grover Wetzel and his wife found themselves growing old on the hill.

They must have been over eighty when it happened.

Maggie Gephardt said later that a green ball of fire had come slanting in over Shriner Mountain to the east of Bald Knob and landed smack on Wetzel's Hill with a splash of fire. But Maggie Gephardt was famous for seeing things like that, and nobody took any stock in her story. She was still living when I was a boy of fourteen, and I can remember clearly her directions for finding the wreck of the mail plane that carried pilot Harry Ames to his death somewhere west of Hell's Gap.

She had seen the plane come down, she said, and soon she had our entire troop of Boy Scouts combing the ridge between Turpentine and Spigelmyer's Hollow in a dripping fog. There's no need to add that the flier's body was later found a full twenty miles to the northwest, beyond so many ridges that Maggie Gephardt couldn't possibly have seen anything connected with the crash.

But there was no doubt at all about the tragedy that occurred on Wetzel's Hill that January night about five years before I was born. One of the Edmonds boys was driving home in his sleigh about three o'clock in the morning after a late date with some girl in Brush Valley. He saw the cabin ablaze as he came through the gap and started arousing neighbors along Jackpine Creek. One of them telephoned John Stover in town. As chief of the volunteer fire department he was able to rout many townsmen from their beds. But it was a futile effort. The roof of the cabin had already fallen in, and the walls were on the point of collapse when the first neighbor with his bucket reached the crest of the hill. Later the bodies of Grover and Ruth Wetzel were found burned beyond recognition on the remains of what had once been their bed.

It was a tragedy, of course, but not unique in those days of fireplaces, wood stoves, and coal-oil lights. Not in the dead of winter, anyway. People shook their heads in sadness, but they were not mystified. The mystery was to come later.

The Wetzel boys and their children's families were there for the funeral. They disposed of the livestock that had survived, and the feed and tools that were in an outlying barn, but the land they did not offer for sale. Some years later, when they finally did put it on the market, it was too late.

For a curse had come to Wetzel's Hill.

It did not come overnight. The following spring was like any other spring. My father told me that if anyone at all had noticed anything strange on the hill that year he certainly didn't mention it. And my father was in a position to know since he was tollkeeper, and our house was by the old tollgate just inside the gap and right around the bend from Wetzel's Hill. When you're a tollkeeper, my father said, you hear everything that happens in both valleys, and what you don't hear isn't worth knowing.

Maybe the grass and weeds up on the hill didn't grow as high that year, and maybe they did burn brown earlier under the August sun, but it wasn't until the following year that it really was noticeable.

Some said later it was the half-wit called Pasty Pumpernickel who first noticed the change. "It looks to me," he said one day, "like it got scorched up at the old Wetzel place."

Pasty probably would have been the first to see it, just by the nature of his existence. He wandered the mountains and the town like some friendly, homeless dog, ungainly and unlettered, sleeping in barns, accepting meals where they were offered, doing odd jobs sometimes, and perennially being made the butt of schoolkids' jokes. But if you grew up in my home town, you already know about Pasty Pumpernickel.

At any rate, a landmark was born, and even before June

had merged into July people for miles around were commenting on the "Scorch."

Many climbed the hill to see for themselves. They walked around, kicked the dusty lumps of earth and shook their heads. Grass that had sprouted in March and April was already dead. The ground was powdery, just as if there hadn't been a drop of rain since the snows melted. This was the peculiar part, for it had been a wet spring, and the valley and mountainsides were lush and green. What could have happened to Wetzel's Hill?

"It's the Lord's doing, and none of our affair," some folks said. But there were others who had a different explanation. "Somebody's put a hex on that patch," they said, pausing to look warily over each shoulder. And children were warned to keep their distance. These hills, you know, are not beyond the limits of the old Pennsylvania hex country, and disturbing memories linger there.

But the mystery, however, remained a mystery, in spite of an investigation made by the county agent and some professors from State College several years later. They poked around on the hill one whole afternoon, made soil tests, and later collaborated on a report that ran—it was said later—more than twenty thousand words. What this report boiled down to was that a roughly oval area about two hundred feet long on Wetzel's Hill wasn't getting any rain. Even Pasty Pumpernickel could have told them that.

As the years went by, however, and the Scorch remained bare, people referred to it only in the nature of a landmark, and so it remained for fifteen years, or until that day in summer when I was a ten-year-old boy.

So much for the hill.

Now I must tell you what led up to that day—and the coming of Mr. Porter.

It has long been my opinion that almost any child can become a prodigy if his interest in a particular subject can be sufficiently aroused and sustained. In my case my father made sure of that. Before I was eight years old I could name on sight every species of wild flower and tree that grew within a mile of our house. By the age of ten I was a prancing encyclopedia on the subject (although I must confess that now, forty years later and living in another clime, I would be hard put to distinguish a mimosa from a cyclamen). It was this precocious learning that led me into the series of events that followed.

Only a small truck patch separated our house from Jackpine Creek—and if you happen to be a fisherman, you already know there are few better trout streams in the whole state. And although my father kept many a salty word on tap to prove his low estimate of fishermen in general, and of those who left boot tracks in his garden in particular, for my part I kept a cunning eye cocked toward their flashing fly rods. Hemlocks, birches, and alders crowded the stream and, with hungry branches waiting to snag an unwary line, there was many a nickel to be earned by a boy who could shinny up trees.

And that was how I met the newspaperman from Philadelphia. While I freed his hook from a branch he stood knee-deep in the riffles and cussed the "damn spruce trees."

"This is a hemlock, mister," I said. "Spruce trees don't grow around here."

"Well, damn the hemlocks then," he said. "What makes you think this isn't a spruce tree?"

"It don't have spruce needles, that's why."

Whatever answer he was expecting, it wasn't that. His jaw opened for comment, closed again, and then he burst into laughter. I remember how I liked his crinkly eyes.

After a minute he said, "By God, that makes sense. The world could use some of it. Come down here and tell me about the needles."

Well, we sat on the bank at the edge of the truck patch and I showed him how the hemlock needles grew all along the twigs. Spruce needles, I told him, grow in bunches. I ran to a white pine that stood farther upstream and brought back a switch. "See, like this," I said. "White pine needles grow five in a bunch, sorta long. Red pine has three, and they're shorter. Up on the ridge we got southern yellow pine, that has two and they're awful long. We also got jack pine and table mountain pine around here, but no spruce trees—unless you go and buy one from the tree man."

"What's your name?" he asked, and he rooted in his coat for a scratch pad and a stubby pencil. I told him my name, and we sat there while he made notes as I reeled off answers to his queries. Along the line somewhere I volunteered the information there was a place to go if he got caught in the rain—the Scorch.

I swear I never met a man with so much curiosity. Right away he wanted to know all about the Scorch, and before you know it he had stowed his fishing gear in the car, slung a camera around his neck, and we were climbing up the side of Wetzel's Hill. He made some more notes, and took pictures of me and the Scorch. Later when he said goodbye I thought that was the end of it.

But it wasn't.

On a Sunday morning about two weeks later, our phone began to ring. And it didn't stop ringing all day. All of a sudden I was a celebrity. I guess everybody in town called up to say how they'd seen my picture in the *Philadelphia Inquirer.* Along about four o'clock my father said he wouldn't stop much and take the damn receiver off the hook and leave it off. But we had a party line, and you can't do a thing like that, my mother said—as if anybody else on our line had a chance to use it that day anyway. So the calls continued, and when I went to bed that night I couldn't sleep, thinking how it was the biggest day of my life.

But even the greatest splash in a pond has to subside. Only in this case one of the ripples penetrated an obscure crevice. I wasn't to realize how obscure until more than forty years had passed.

It began about a week later with another telephone call. It was Bill Kerstetter, who ran the Union Hotel in town.

"There's a man here from Philadelphia," he told my mother, "wants to see Sherwood about hunting wild flowers and stuff. He's some kind of perfessor."

And that's how Mr. Porter entered my life. He came driving up after a while in an old Ford and spent some time talking to my father. He was a naturalist from the Museum of Natural History, my father told me, and probably quite famous. He wanted to go hiking the next day and hoped I would do him the favor of showing him around.

Well, after he drove away, my mother had plenty to say on that subject.

"Any man his age," she said, "with that bad heart and all, has no business traipsing up and down these mountains with a child. He could keel over dead."

"How can you tell he got a bad heart?" I asked.

"Blue lips, that's how. Blue lips mean a bad heart, as anybody knows. And look at his skin, just like cheese. Poor circulation."

I had to admit Mr. Porter did have a funny look, at that, with his curly white hair, bushy eyebrows, and those glasses he wore. His eyes looked half pinched shut behind lenses the color of coffee.

But my father wouldn't listen to any objection. "Mr. Porter's old enough to know what he's doing, and Sherwood knows every inch of these mountains. If something happens and he needs help, he'll come for it." And that was that.

So next day Mr. Porter and I started up the Watery Road, which winds up the hollow back of our house. It was only a sort of road, although my father said wagons used to use it in the old logging days. Alders, laurel, and rhododendron choked it in many places, and a gurgle-size stream wandered back and forth across it as if it had forgotten where its channel was. When we got to the Landing, where the old log slide used to be, we cut up the steep bank to the hogback; and although both of us were puffing by the time we reached the top, Mr. Porter sure didn't look to me like he was about to keel over with a bad heart.

I was acting as if I'd had a few hookers of dandelion wine under my belt. All a ten-year-old prodigy needs is an audience, and this was my day. Looking back now across the years, it seems incredible that it never occurred to me there was anything peculiar about our conversation. It would be logical to assume a boy in the presence of a famous naturalist would try to absorb additional knowledge, but don't bet on it. In this case the one doing the lecturing was the one in knee pants.

We were too late for the hepaticas, the skunk cabbage, bloodroot, and spring beauties; but other flowers were in bloom to take their place. I showed him adder's-tongues with their mottled leaves, rue anemones, Solomon seals, pipsissewas, columbines, yellow wood violets, and my special favorite, the weird lady's slipper.

"And if you get lost and hungry," I explained, "you go to work and eat sassafras leaves." To demonstrate this life-saving information, I tore several mitten-like leaves from a nearby tree and stuffed them in my mouth. "They're good, too."

Mr. Porter smiled and also sampled the leaves, nodding his head in assent.

Then he said a very strange thing.

"Isn't that odd? The leaves are not all the same shape."

"That's sassafras for you," I said. "Some are plain, some have one thumb and some have two—that's the way they grow. But they all taste alike."

We were standing now on the upper end of the hogback just before it merged into the bulk of Thunder Mountain below Bald Knob. Behind us to the northwest stretched a rolling expanse of wooded ridges, below us lay the gap that provided exit for the shimmering waters of Jackpine Creek, and to the east the ponderous Shriner Mountain rose up and began its unbroken march to the distant Susquehanna.

Mr. Porter was looking at his watch for the third time. When he had hauled it out the first time, I thought from its shape it was a compass. But then I heard it tick, and who ever heard of a compass that ticked? It even ticked funny for a watch.

He put it away and stared down toward the gap, where the brown tip of the Scorch could be seen through the trees. Something must have been on his glasses, for he took them off and began cleaning them with a handkerchief.

"I never will become used to the brightness of your sun," he said, and I noticed he kept his eyes closed until the glasses were back on his nose. Then he nodded toward Wetzel's Hill.

"Interesting," he said. "What is down there?"

So I had to explain to him all about the Scorch.

"I'd like very much to see it," he said.

"That ain't gonna be easy from here," I said. "You get into a lot of rocks and thorn bushes, and you gotta look out for rattlesnakes. We oughta go all the way back to the house, and around below."

"That would take longer, wouldn't it?"

"Yep, it sure would."

"Then let's try the rocks and thorn bushes," he said.

So we started down, and I have to admit for an old man he sure could handle the rough going. It was no picnic, and I had scratched arms and a tear in my shirt before we reached the bottom. But by some miracle Mr. Porter, who had scrambled down behind me, didn't seem to have a mark on him.

We stood on Wetzel's Hill, and Mr. Porter drew a line in the powdery dust with the toe of his shoe.

"Strange," he said. He looked at this watch again and I could have sworn it was ticking louder and faster than it had before. "What's that over there?"

"That's the ruins of the old Wetzel place," I said. "Come on, I'll show you."

The dust swirled in eddies as we clumped across the Scorch toward the jumble of charred timbers and foundation stones that marked the tragedy of fifteen years before. We walked halfway around it, and I pointed to what was left of the old cellar hole. Some of the rocks had fallen in, and a rough-hewn beam partially blocked the opening, but I got down on my hands and knees and peered into the darkness.

"Here's my hideout," I said. "It's good and cold in there on a hot day."

"Cold?" he said.

"Like ice," I said. "Ain't much room, but if you want to try and crawl in, I'll show you."

Mr. Porter looked at his clothes and shook his head. "I don't think that will be necessary."

He extended his hand to help me out of the cellar hole, and there was an odd little smile on his lips. "How far is it back to your home?" he asked.

"Don't you want to look for more wild flowers?"

"No, we've had quite a hike today. I'm not a youngster anymore."

"OK," I said, with some disappointment. "I'll show you where the path goes down to the road. Then it's just around the bend."

So we returned to my place, and Mr. Porter talked to my father awhile, telling him of some of the things we had seen. Then he thanked me and, winking, slipped a shiny silver dollar into my palm. Wow!

Saying goodbye then, he climbed into the old Ford and took off down the road. And that was the last time in my life I was ever to see Mr. Porter, the naturalist from Philadelphia.

And, except for the occasional times my father mentioned his name in the year or two that followed, I have never even thought of him.

Until today.

Today I heard a word pronounced, and nothing—for me—will ever be quite the same.

I could hear my father's voice again. He was a widely read man but self-educated, and the hallmark of the self-educated is weevily pronunciation. I remember, for instance, a print of "La Cigale" that hung on our living room wall. My father always referred to it as "Lacy Gale." As I grew up and braved the outside world, many were my vocal mannerisms that needed rectifying.

But the word I heard today was the name of a wild flower, one that I have never used or heard used since the day I left the hill country.

The television set was blabbing away—as it usually is in our home, whether anyone is watching or not. The program must have been some sort of nature study. As I passed the screen my ear caught the single word, "Po-LYG-a-la."

This was the word that stopped me in my tracks, that sent worried messengers to probe my memory banks. Its ring was reminiscent of Caligula, the Roman tyrant; but nothing at all in my memory matched its syllables. But though my ear had been tricked, the dictionary revealed the truth of it. "Polygala," it said.

Of course, I thought. In my youth I had called the flower "fringed polly-galla," which you must admit is a far cry from "polyg-a-la." My father had pronounced it "polly-galla." Why, even Mr. Porter—

With vivid clarity I saw him conversing with my father after our hike. As if it were yesterday I heard his voice: "Columbines we found, and Solomon seals and fringed polly-gallas . . ."

But Mr. Porter was a highly educated man, and nature study was his profession. Would he copy my father's mispronunciation? Unless—

Another memory spurted into my brain: His surprise at the inconsistent shapes of the sassafras leaves. Then, as if they had waited forty years to coalesce, a horde of other memories screamed furiously for attention and new evaluation: the blue lips, the ticking compass, Maggie Gephardt's

green ball of fire, the icy cellar hole, Mr. Porter's loss of interest in flowers after we had seen the Scorch . . . and then,
thunderingly, what came after.

For something did come after, and never had I dreamed
there was a connection. A month must have passed before I
next visited my hideout. From above, the cellar hole looked
to a casual eye just as it had always looked. But when I got
down on my belly to crawl under the beam my face knitted
into a puzzled frown. The entrance was gone. Timbers and
stones had become rearranged somehow, and I wondered if
some old black bear had been messing around my hideout.
Even the cold air no longer seeped through the crevices, but
how a bear could have managed *that* feat didn't bother me
then. I got to my feet, kicked some dirt awhile, and finally
shrugged the whole thing off. I had other hideouts.

But it took the entire valley to shrug off the next wonder.
For that fall it began to rain again on Wetzel's Hill, and after
fifteen years grass and weeds started growing on the Scorch. It
was green the next year, as green as Thunder Mountain. And,
for that matter, it's green today.

But for me, suddenly, these are no longer mysteries. I
know now that something did fall from the sky that long-ago
winter night—an object, a mechanism of unguessable description—and, until someone secretly retrieved it, it lay buried for fifteen years beneath the ruins on Wetzel's Hill.
Among its attributes was some form of radiation that could
vaporize rain before it reached the ground, a radiation that
registered on my companion's "watch," and that my body at
close range translated into degrees of cold.

I perceived another attribute: The object was of incalcu-
lable importance to someone. The arrival of Mr. Porter so
soon after the newspaper story of the Scorch could have been
no coincidence. He or "they" must have been searching—
perhaps for fifteen years. Ergo, the mechanism must have
fallen to earth accidentally. But who, in those days, had any
craft that could reach the altitude necessary to produce the

scorching velocity of its fall? Surely not our own government. Surely no European or Asiatic power.

With a start I remembered Mr. Porter's words as he cleaned his glasses:

"I will never become used to the brightness of your sun."

Our sun!

WINDWAGON SMITH AND THE MARTIANS

Lawrence Watt-Evans

 I reckon most folks have heard of Thomas Smith, the little sailor from Massachusetts who turned up in Westport, Missouri, one day in 1853 aboard the contraption he called a windwagon. He'd rigged himself a deck and a sail and a tiller on top of a wagon, and just about tried to make a prairie schooner into a *real* schooner. Figured on building himself a whole fleet and getting rich, shipping folks and freight to Santa Fe or wherever they might have a mind to go.

Well, as you might have heard, he got some of the folks in Westport to buy stock in his firm, and he built himself a bigger, better windwagon from the ground up, with a main-mast and a mizzen both, and he took his investors out for a test run—and they every one of them got seasick, and scared as the devil at how fast the confounded thing ran, and they all jumped ship and wouldn't have more to do with it. Smith allowed as how the steering might not be completely smooth yet, though the idea was sound, but the folks in Westport just weren't interested.

And last anyone heard, old Windwagon Smith was sailing west across the prairie, looking for braver souls.

That's the last anyone's heard till now, anyways. A good many folks have wondered whatever became of Windwagon Smith, myself amongst them, and I'm pleased to be able to tell the story.

And if you ask how I come to know it, well, I heard it from Smith himself, but that's another story entirely.

Here's the way of it. Back in '53, Smith headed west out of Westport feeling pretty ornery and displeased; he reckoned that the fine men of Westport had just missed the chance of a lifetime, and all over a touch of the collywobbles and a bit of wind. Wasn't any doubt in his mind but he could find braver men somewheres, who would back his company and put all those mule-drawn freight wagons right out of business. It was just a matter of finding the right people.

So he sailed on, and he stopped now and then and told folks his ideas, and he was plump disconcerted to learn that there wasn't a town he tried that wanted any part of his windwagon.

He missed a lot of towns, too, because the fact was that the steering *was* a mite difficult, and he didn't so much stay on the trail as try to keep somewhere in its general vicinity. He stopped a few times to tinker with it, but the plain truth is that he never did get it right, not so as one man could work it and steer small. After all, the clippers he'd learned on didn't steer with just a tiller, but with the sails as well— tacking and so forth. If Smith had had more men on board, to help work the sails, he might have managed some fine navigation, instead of just aim-and-hope.

After a time, though, he had got most of the way to Santa Fe, but had lost the trail again, and he was sailing out across the desert pretty sure that he was a good long way from where he had intended to be, when he noticed that the sand was getting to be awfully red.

The sky was getting darker, too, but there wasn't a cloud anywhere in it, and it wasn't but early afternoon; it just seemed as if the sun had shrunk up some, and the sky had dimmed down from a regular bright blue to a color more like the North Atlantic on a winter morning. The air felt damn near as cold as the North Atlantic, too, and that didn't seem right for daytime in the desert. What's more, Smith suddenly felt sort of light, as if the wind might just blow him right off his own deck, even though it didn't seem to be blowing any harder than before. And he was having a little trouble breathing, like as if he'd got himself up on top of a mountain.

And the sand was *awfully* red, about the color of a boiled lobster.

Well, old Windwagon Smith had read up on the West before he ever left Massachusetts, and he'd never heard of anything like this. He didn't like it a bit, and he took a reef in the sails and slowed down, trying to figure it.

The sand stayed red, and the sky stayed dark, and the air stayed thin, and he still felt altogether too damn light on his feet, and he commenced to be seriously worried and furled the sails right up, so that that windwagon of his rolled to a stop in the middle of that red desert.

He threw out the anchor to keep him where he was, and had a time doing it, because although the anchor seemed a fair piece lighter than he remembered, it almost took him with it when he heaved it over. Seemed like he had to be extra careful about everything he did, because even the way his own body moved didn't seem quite right; of course, being a sailor, he could keep his feet just about anywhere, so he got by. He might have thought he was dreaming if he hadn't been the levelheaded sort he was, and proud of his plain sense to know whether he was awake or asleep.

Just to be sure, though, he pinched himself a few times,

and the red marks that that left pretty much convinced him he was awake.

He stood on the deck and looked about, and all he saw was that red, red sand, stretching clear to the horizon whichever way he cared to look. The horizon looked a shade close in, at that; wasn't anything quite what it ought to be.

He didn't like that a bit. He climbed up aloft, to the crow's nest up above the main topsail, and he looked about again.

This time, when he looked to what he reckoned was west, he saw something move, something that was blue against the blue of the sky, so he couldn't make out just what it was.

It was coming his way, though, so he figured he'd just let it come, and take a closer look when he could.

But he wasn't about to let it come on him unprepared. After all, there were still plenty of wild Indians around, and white men who were just as wild without any of the excuses the Indians had, seeing as how they hadn't had their land stolen, or their women either, nor their hunting ruined. They could be just as wild as Indians, all the same.

He slid down the forestay and went below, and when he mounted back to the maintop he had a sixgun on his belt and a rifle in his hand.

By now the blue thing was closer, and he got a good clear look at it, and he damn near dropped his rifle, because it was a ship, a sand ship, and it was sailing over the desert right toward him.

And what's more, there were three more right behind it, all of them tall and graceful, with blue sails the color of that dark sky. Proud as he was of his work, old Windwagon had to admit that the ugliest of the four was a damn sight better-looking than his own windwagon had ever been, even before it got all dusty and banged up with use.

They were quieter, too. Fact is, they were near as silent as clouds, where his own windwagon had always rattled and clattered like any other wagon, and creaked and groaned like a ship, as well. All in all, it made a hell of a racket, but these four sand ships didn't make a sound—at least, not that Smith could hear yet, over the wind in the rigging.

He was pretty upset, seeing those four sand ships out there. Here he'd thought he had the only sailing wagon ever built, and then these four come over the horizon—not just one, but four, and any of them enough to burst a clipper captain's heart with envy.

If they were freighters, Smith knew that he wasn't going to get anywhere near as rich as he had figured, up against competition like that. He began to wonder if maybe the folks back in Westport weren't right, but for all the wrong reasons.

The sand ships' hulls were emerald green, and the trim was polished brass or bone white, and above the blue sails they flew pennants, gold and blue and red and green pennants, and they were just about the prettiest thing Smith had ever seen in his life.

He looked at them, and he didn't know what the hell they were doing there or where they'd come from, but they didn't look like anything wild Indians would ride, or anything outlaws would ride, so he just watched as they came sailing up to his own ship—or wagon, or whatever you care to name it.

Three of the sand ships slowed up and stopped a good ways off, but the first one in line came right up next to him.

That one was the biggest and the prettiest, and the only one flying gold pennants. He figured it must belong to the boss of the bunch, the commodore or whatsoever he might be called.

"Ahoy!" Smith shouted.

He could see people on the deck of the sand ship, three of them, but he couldn't make out any faces, and none of them answered his hail. They were dressed in robes, which made him wonder if maybe they weren't Indians after all, or Mexicans.

"Ahoy!" he called again.

"Mr. Smith," one of them called back, almost like he was singing. "Come down where we can speak more easily."

Smith thought about that, and noticed that none of them had any guns that he could see, and decided to risk it. He climbed down, with his rifle, and he came over to the rail, where he could have reached out and touched the sand ship if he stretched a little.

He was already there when he realized that the strangers had called him by his right name.

Before he could think that over, the stranger who had called him said, "Mr. Smith, we have brought you here because we admire your machine."

Smith looked at the strangers, and at the great soaring masts and dark blue sails, and at the shiny brass and the sleek green hull, and he didn't believe a word of it. Anyone who had a ship like that one had no reason to admire his windwagon. He'd been mighty proud of it until a few minutes ago, but he could see now that it wasn't much by comparison.

Well, he figured, the strangers were being polite. He appreciated that. "Thanks," he said. "That's a sweet ship you have there, yourself."

While he was saying that, he noticed that the reason he hadn't been able to make out faces was that the strangers were all wearing masks, shiny masks that looked like pure silver, with lips that looked like rubies. The eyes that showed through were yellow, almost like cat's eyes, and Smith wasn't too happy about seeing that. The masks looked like something Indians might wear, but he'd never heard of any Indians like these.

He said, "By the way, I'd be mighty obliged if you could tell me where I am; I lost my bearings some time back, and it seems as if I might be a bit off course."

He couldn't see which of the strangers it was that spoke, what with the masks, but one of them said, "My apologies,

Mr. Smith. It was we who brought you here. You are on Mars."

"Mars?" Smith asked. He wasn't sure just how to take this. "You mean Mars, Pennsylvania? Down the road a piece from Zelienople?" He didn't see any way he could have wound up there, and he'd never heard tell that Pennsylvania had any flat red deserts, but that was one of the two places he'd ever heard of called Mars, and he didn't care to think about the other one much.

"No," the stranger said, "the planet Mars. We transported your excellent craft here by means that I am unable to explain, so that I might offer you a challenge."

Now, Smith knew something about the planets, because any sailor does if he takes an interest in navigation, and he knew that Mars was sort of reddish, and the red sand would account for that nicely. He looked up at that shrunken sun and that dark blue sky, and then at those sand ships like nothing on Earth, and decided that one of three things had happened.

Either he'd gone completely mad without noticing it, and was imagining all this, which didn't bear thinking about but which surely fit the facts best of all; or somebody was playing one hell of a practical joke on him, which he didn't have any idea how it was being done; or the stranger was telling the truth. For the sake of argument, he decided he'd figure on that last one, because the second seemed plumb unlikely and the first wasn't anything he could figure on, never having been mad before and not knowing just how it might work. Besides, he'd simply never judged himself for the sort of fellow that might go mad, and he wasn't in any hurry to change his mind on that account.

So he figured the stranger was telling the truth. Whether it was magic, or some sort of scientific trick, he didn't know, but he reckoned he really was on Mars.

And he didn't figure he'd ever find his way back to Earth by himself.

"What sort of a challenge?" he asked.

He sort of thought he saw the middle stranger smile behind his silver mask.

"I," the middle stranger said, "am Moohay Nillay, and I am the champion yachtsman of all Teer, as we call our planet." Smith wasn't any too sure of those names, so I may have them wrong. "I have the finest sand ship ever built, and in it I have raced every challenger that my world provided, and I have defeated them all. Yet it was not enough; I grew bored, and desired a new challenge, and sought elsewhere for competitors who could race against me."

Smith began to see where this was leading, but he just smiled and said, "Is that so?"

"Indeed it is, Mr. Smith. Unfortunately, our two worlds are the only two in this system bearing intelligent life, and your world has not produced many craft that will sail on sand. I am not interested in sailing upon water—our planet no longer has any seas, and I find the canals too limiting. I might perhaps find better sport on the seas of your planet, but the means by which I drew you here will not send me to Earth. I have been forced to wait, to search endlessly for someone on your planet who would see the obvious value of sailing the plains. To date, you are only the second I have discovered. The first was a man by the name of Shard, Captain Shard of the *Desperate Lark*, who fitted his seagoing ship with wheels in order to elude pursuit; I drew him here, and easily defeated his clumsy contrivance. I hope that you, Mr. Smith, will provide a greater test."

"Well, I hope I will, Mr. Nillay. I'd be glad to race you." Smith didn't really think he had much of a chance against those sleek ships, but he figured that it wouldn't hurt to try, and that if he were a good loser, Mr. Nillay might send him back to Earth.

And of course, there was always the chance that his horse sense and Yankee ingenuity might just give him a chance against this smooth-talking Martian braggart.

Well, to make a long story a trifle less tiresome, Smith and the Martian agreed on the ground rules for their little competition. They would race due south, to the edge of a canal—Smith took the Martian's word for just where this canal was, since of course he didn't know a damn thing about Martian geography. Whoever got there first, and dropped a pebble into the canal without setting foot on the ground, would win the race.

The Martian figured it at about a two-day race, if the wind held up, and he gave Smith a pebble to use—except it wasn't so much your everyday pebble as it was a blue jewel of some kind. Smith hadn't ever seen one quite like it.

If Smith won, he was to have a big celebration in the Martian's home town, and would then be sent back to Earth, if he wanted. If he lost, well, he wouldn't get the celebration, but if he had put up enough of a fight, made it a good race and not a rout, the Martian allowed as he might consider maybe sending him back to Earth eventually, just out of the goodness of his heart and as a kind gesture.

Smith didn't like the sound of that, but then he didn't have a whole hell of a lot of choice.

"What about those other folks?" he asked, figuring he needed every advantage he could get. "I'm sailing single-handed, and you've got two crewmen and three other ships."

The Martian allowed as how that might be unfair. Captain Shard had had a full crew for his ship, and Mr. Nillay hadn't been sure whether Smith had anyone else aboard or not, but since he didn't, since he was sailing alone, then Mr. Nillay would sail alone too. And the other three ships were observers, just there to watch, and to help out if there was trouble.

Smith couldn't much quarrel with that, so after a little more arguing out details, the two ships were lined up at the starting line, Smith's windwagon on the left and the Martian sand ship on the right, both pointed due south.

One of the other Martians fired a starting pistol that didn't bang, it buzzed like a mad hornet, and the race was on.

Old Windwagon yanked the anchor aboard and started hauling his sheets, piling on every stitch of canvas his two little masts could carry, running back and forth like a lunatic trying to do it all by himself as fast as a full crew, all the while still keeping an eye on his course and making sure he was still headed due south.

Those sails caught the wind, and before he knew it he was rolling south at about the best speed he'd ever laid on, with nothing left to do but stand by the tiller and hope a crosswind didn't tip him right over.

When he was rolling smooth, he glanced back at the Martian sand ship, and it wasn't there. He turned to the stern quarter, and then the beam, and he still didn't see it, but when he looked forward again there it was, a point or two off his starboard bow, that tall blue sail drawing well, full and taut, and that damn Martian yachtsman standing calm as a statue at the tiller.

And although it wasn't easy over the rattling and creaking of his own ship, Smith could hear the Martian sand ship make a weird whistling as it cut through that red sand.

Well, seeing and hearing that made Smith mad. He wasn't about to let some bossy little foreigner in a mask and a nightshirt beat him *that* easily, no sir! He tied down the tiller and ducked below, and began heaving overboard anything he thought he could spare, to lighten the load and help his speed.

Extra spars and sails, his second-best anchor, and the trunk with his clothes went over the after rail; he figured that he could come back and pick them up later if he needed them. When the trunk had hit the ground and burst open, he turned and looked for that Martian prig, and was about as pleased as you can imagine to see that he was closing the gap, gaining steadily on the Martian ship.

Then he hit a bump and went veering off to port, and had to take the tiller again.

Well, the race went on, and on, and Smith gained on the Martian little by little, what seemed like just a few inches every hour, until not long after sunset, while the sky was still pink in the west, the two ships were neck and neck, dead even.

It was about at this point that it first sank in that they weren't going to heave to for the night, and Smith began to do some pretty serious worrying about what might happen if he hit a rock in the dark or somesuch disaster as that. He hadn't sailed his windwagon by night before.

He wasn't too worried about missing a night's sleep, as he'd had occasion to do that before, when he was crewing a clipper through a storm in the South Pacific, or spending his money ashore in some all-night port, but he *was* worried about cruising ahead under full sail across uncharted desert in the dark.

It helped some when the moons rose, two little ones instead of a big one like ours, but he still spent most of that night in a cold sweat. About his only consolation was that the crazy Martian was near as likely to wreck as he was himself.

It was a mighty cold night, too, and he wrapped himself in all three of the coats he still had and wished he hadn't been so quick to throw his trunk over.

About the time when he was beginning to wonder if maybe the nights on Mars lasted for six months, the way he'd heard tell they did way up north, the sun came up again, and he got a good look at just where he stood.

He'd pulled ahead of the Martian, a good cable's length, maybe more. He smiled through his frozen beard at that; if he just held on, he knew he'd have the race won.

So he *did* hold on, as best he could, but something had changed. The wind had died down some, and maybe the Martian had trimmed his sails a bit better, or the wind had shifted a trifle, but by the middle of the afternoon Windwagon saw that he wasn't gaining any more, and in fact he might just be starting to lose his lead. He wasn't the least bit pleased, let me tell you.

He started thinking about what else he had that he could throw overboard, and he was still puzzling over that when he topped a low rise and got a look at what lay ahead.

He was at the top of the longest damn slope he'd ever seen in his life, a slope that looked pretty near as big as an ocean, and down at the bottom was a big band of green, and in the middle of that green was a strip of blue that Smith knew had to be the canal.

And it was downhill almost the entire way!

The green part wasn't downhill, he could see that, but that long, long red slope was. It wasn't steep, and it wasn't any too smooth, but it was all downhill, and that meant he didn't want to lighten the ship any more at all.

He tied down the tiller again and hung down over the side, pouring on the last of his axle grease so as to make the most out of that hill.

When he got back up on deck and looked back he could see that he was gaining quickly now, pulling farther and farther ahead of the Martian's lighter ship. And that canal was in sight, straight ahead! He figured he just about had it won.

And then the wind, which had been just sort of puffing for a while, up and died completely.

By this time he was rolling hell-for-leather down that hill, at a speed he didn't even care to guess, and he didn't stop when the wind died—but that flat stretch of green ahead suddenly looked a hell of a lot wider than it had before.

He pulled up the tiller entirely, to cut the drag; after all, the canal stretched from one horizon to the other, so what did he need to steer for? He could still maneuver the sails if he had to.

He went bouncing and rattling down that hill, thumping and bumping over the loose rocks and the red sand, praying the whole way that he wouldn't tip over. He didn't dare look back to see where the Martian was.

And then he was off the foot of the slope, crunching his way across that green, which was all some sort of viney plant, and his wagon went slower, and slower, and slower, and finally, with one big bounce and a bang, it came to a dead stop —a hundred feet or so from the canal.

Smith looked down at those vines, and then ahead at that blue water, and then back at the Martian sand ship, which wasn't much more than a dark spot on the red horizon behind him, and he just about felt like crying. There wasn't hardly a breath of wind, just the slightest bit of air, enough to flap the sails but not to fill them.

And what's more, the vines under his wheels weren't anywhere near as smooth as the red sand, or the prairie grass back on Earth, and he knew it would take a good hard tug to get the old windwagon started again.

If he could once get it started, he figured that he could just about reach the canal on momentum, without hardly any wind; the vines sort of petered out in about another twenty feet, and from there to the canal the whole way was stone pavement, smooth white stone that wouldn't give his wheels the slightest bit of trouble.

But he needed a good hard push to get off those vines and get moving, and the wind didn't seem to be picking up, and that Martian was still sailing, smooth and graceful, closer and closer down the slope.

And thinking back, Smith recalled that the sand ship had a blade on the front. He hadn't seen much use for it back on the sand, but he could see how it would just cut right through those vines.

He looked about, and saw that a dozen or so Martians, in their robes and masks, were standing nearby, watching silently. Smith wasn't any too eager to let them see him lose. If there was ever a time when he needed some of that old Yankee ingenuity he prided himself on, Smith figured this was it.

He looked down at the vines again, and thought to himself that they looked a good bit like seaweed, back on Earth.

He was stuck in the weeds, just like he might be on a sandbar or in shoal water back on Earth.

Well, he knew ways of getting off sandbars. He couldn't figure on any tide to lift him off here, but there were other ways.

He could kedge off. He hauled up the anchor, and heaved it forward hard as he could—and the way his muscles worked on Mars, that was mighty hard. That anchor landed on the edge of the pavement, and then slid off as he hauled on it, and bit into the soft ground under the vines.

That was about as far as he could haul by hand, though. For one man to move that big a wagon, even on Mars, he needed something more than his own muscle. He took the line around the capstan and began heaving on the pawls.

The line tautened up, and the wagon shifted, and then inched forward—but he couldn't get up any sort of momentum, and he couldn't pull it closer than ten feet from the pavement, where it stopped again, still caught in the vines. When he threw himself on the next pawl the anchor tore free.

He hauled it back on board and reconsidered. Kedging wasn't going to work, that was pretty plain; he couldn't get the anchor to bite on that white stone. So he was still on his sandbar.

He thought back, and back, and tried to remember every trick he'd ever heard for getting a ship off a bar, or freeing a keel caught in the mud.

There was one trick that the men-o'-war used; they'd fire off a full broadside, and often as not the recoil would pull the ship free.

The problem with that, though, was that he didn't have a broadside to fire. His whole armory was a rifle, two sixguns, and a couple of knives.

He looked back up the slope, and he could see the sand ship's green hull now, and almost thought he could see the sun glinting on Mr. Nillay's silly mask, and he decided that he was damn well going to *make* himself a broadside—or if not a broadside, at least a cannon or two.

The wind picked up a trifle just then, and the sails bellied out a bit, and that gave him hope.

He went below and began rummaging through everything he had, and found himself his heavy iron coffeepot. He took that up on deck, and then broke open every cartridge he had and dumped the charges into the pot; he judged he had better than a pound of powder when he was through. He took his lightest coat, which wasn't really more than a bit of a linsey jacket anyway, and folded that up and stuffed it in on top of the powder for a wad. He put a can of beans on top for shot, and then rolled up a stock certificate from the Westport and Santa Fe Overland Navigation Company and rammed it down the coffeepot's spout for a fuse.

The sails were filling again, but the wagon wasn't moving. Smith figured he still needed that little push. He wedged his contraption under the tiller mounting, and touched a match to the paper.

It seemed to take forever to burn down, but finally it went off with a roar like a bee-stung grizzly bear, and that can of beans shot out spinning and burst on the hillside, spraying burnt beans and tin all over the red sand. The coffeepot itself was blown to black flinders.

And the wagon, with a creak, rolled forward onto the pavement. The sails caught the wind, feeble as it was, and with rattling and banging the windwagon clattered across that white stone pavement, toward the canal.

And then it stopped with a bump, about ten feet from the edge, just as the wind died again.

Smith just about jumped up and down and tore at his hair at that. He leaned over the rail and saw that there was a sort of ridge in the pavement, and that his front wheels were smack up against it. He judged it would take near onto a hurricane to get him past that.

He looked back at the Martian sand ship, with its long,

graceful bowsprit that would stick out over the canal if it stopped where he was, and he began swearing a blue streak.

He was at the damn canal, after all, and the Martian was just now into the vines, and he wasn't about to be beat like that. He knew that he had to *drop* the pebble, not throw it, so he couldn't just run to the bow and heave it into the water. He was pretty sure that that old Martian would call it a foul, and rightly, if he threw the confounded thing.

And then that old horse sense came through again, and he ran up the rigging to the mainyard, where he grabbed hold of the starboard topsail sheet and untied it, so that it swung free. Hanging on to the bottom end, he climbed back to the mizzenmast, up to the crosstrees, still holding the maintopsail sheet, and dove off, hollering, with the pebble-jewel in his hand.

He swooped down across the deck, lifting his feet to clear it, and then swung out past the bow, up over the canal, and at the top of his swing he let the pebble drop.

It plopped neatly into the water, a foot or two out from the canal wall, while that Martian yachtsman was still fifty feet back. Windwagon Smith let out a shriek of delight as he swung wildly back and forth from the yardarm, and a half-dozen Martians applauded politely.

By the time Smith got himself back down on the deck, Mr. Nillay had got his own ship stopped on the pavement, and he was standing by the edge of the canal, and even with his mask on Smith thought he looked pretty peeved, but there wasn't much he could do.

And then a few minutes later the whole welcoming committee arrived, and they took Smith back to their city, which looked like it was all made out of cut glass and scrimshaw, and they made a big howdy-do over him, and told him he was the new champion sailor of all Mars, the first new champion in nigh onto a hundred years, and they gave him food and drink and held a proper celebration, and poor old Mr. Nillay had to go along and watch it all.

Smith enjoyed it well enough, and he had a good old time for a while, but when things quieted down somewhat he went over to Mr. Nillay and stuck out his hand and said, "No hard feelings?"

"No, Mr. Smith," the Martian said, "no hard feelings. However, I feel there is something I must tell you."

Smith didn't like the sound of that. "And what might that be, sir?" he asked.

"Mr. Smith, I have lied to you. I cannot send you back to Earth."

"But you said . . ." Smith began, ready to work himself up into a proper conniption.

"I did not believe I would lose," the Martian interrupted, and his voice still sounded like music, but now it was like a funeral march. "Surely, a sportsman like yourself can understand that."

Well, Smith had to allow as how he *could* understand that, though he couldn't rightly approve. It seemed to him that it was mighty callous to go fetching someone off his home planet like that, when a body couldn't even send him back later.

Old Nillay had to admit that he had been callous, all right, and he damn near groveled, he was so apologetic about it.

But Smith had always been philosophical about these things. It wasn't like he'd had a home anywhere on Earth; all he'd had was his windwagon, and he still had that. And there on Mars he was a hero, and a respected man, where on Earth he hadn't been much more than a crackpot inventor or a common seaman. And the food and drink was good, and the Martian girls were right pretty when they took their masks off, and those big yellow eyes could be mighty attractive. What's more, what with Martians being able to read minds, which they could, that being how they could speak English to Smith, the women could always tell just what a man needed to make him happy, and folks were just generally pretty obliging.

So Windwagon Smith stayed on Mars and lived there happily enough, and he raced his windwagon a few more times, and mostly won, and all this is why he never did turn up in Santa Fe and why he never did find any more investors after that bunch in Westport backed out.

And I know you may be thinking, well, if he stayed on Mars, then how in tarnation did I ever hear this story from him so as I could tell it to you the way I just did, and all that I can say is what I said before.

That's another story entirely.

TO HELL WITH THE STARS

Jack McDevitt

Christmas night.

Will Cutler couldn't get the sentient ocean out of his mind. Or the creature who wanted only to serve man. Or the curious chess game in the portrait that hung in a deserted city on a world halfway across the galaxy. He drew up his knees, propped the book against them, and let his head sink back into the pillows. The sky was dark through the plex-idome. It had been snowing most of the evening, but the clouds were beginning to scatter. Orion's belt had appeared, and the lovely double star of Earth and Moon floated among the luminous branches of Granpop's elms. Soft laughter and conversation drifted up the stairs.

The sounds of the party seemed far away, and the *Space Beagle* rode a column of flame down into a silent desert. The glow from the reading lamp was bright on the inside of his eyelids. He broke the beam with his hand, and it dimmed and went out.

The book lay open at his fingertips.

It was hard to believe they were a thousand years old, these stories that were so full of energy and so unlike anything he'd come across before: tales of dark, alien places and gleaming temples under other stars and expeditions to black holes. They don't write like that anymore. Never had, during his lifetime. He'd read some other books from the classical Western period, some Dickens, some Updike, people like that. But these: what was there in the last thousand years to compare with this guy Bradbury?

The night air felt good. It smelled of pine needles and scorched wood and bayberry. And maybe of dinosaurs and rocket fuel.

His father might have been standing at the door for several minutes. "Good night, Champ," he whispered, lingering.

"I'm awake, Dad."

He approached the bed. "Lights out already?" he asked. "It's still early." His weight pressed down the mattress.

Will was slow to answer. "I know."

His father adjusted the sheet, pulling it up over the boy's shoulders. "It's supposed to get cold tonight," he said. "Heavy snow by morning." He picked up the book and, without looking at it, placed it atop the night table.

"Dad." The word stopped the subtle shift of weight that would precede the gentle pressure of his father's hand against his shoulder, the final act before withdrawal. "Why didn't we ever go to the stars?"

He was older than most of the other kids' dads. There had been a time when Will was ashamed of that. He couldn't play ball and he was a lousy hiker. The only time he'd tried to walk out over the Rise, they'd had to get help to bring him home. But he laughed a lot, and he always listened. Will was reaching an age at which he understood how much that counted for. "It costs a lot of money, Will. It's just more than we can manage. You'll be going to Earth in two years to finish school."

The boy stiffened. "Dad, I mean the *stars*. Alpha Centauri, Vega, the Phoenix Nebula—"

"The Phoenix Nebula? I don't think I know that one."

"It's in a story by a man named Clarke. A Jesuit goes there and discovers something terrible—"

The father listened while Will outlined the tale in a few brief sentences. "I don't think," he said, "your mother would approve of your reading such things."

"She gave me the book," he said, smiling softly.

"This one?" It was bound in cassilate, a leather substitute, and its title appeared in silver script: *Great Tales of the Space Age*. He picked it up and looked at it with amusement. The names of the editors appeared on the spine: Asimov and Greenberg. "I don't think we realized, uh, that it was like that. Your mother noticed that it was one of the things they found in the time vault on the Moon a couple of years ago. She thought it would be educational."

"You'd enjoy it, Dad."

His father nodded and glanced at the volume. "What's the Space Age?"

"It's the name that people of the classical period used to refer to their own time. It has to do with the early exploration of the solar system, and the first manned flights. And, I think, the idea that we were going to the stars."

A set of lights moved slowly through the sky. "Oh," his father said. "Well, people have had a lot of strange ideas. History is full of dead gods and formulas to make gold and notions that the world was about to end." He picked up the book, adjusted the lamp, and opened to the contents page. His gray eyes ran down the listings, and a faint smile played about his lips. "The truth of it, Will, is that the stars are a pleasant dream, but no one's ever going out to them."

"Why not?" Will was puzzled at the sound of irritation in his own voice. He was happy to see that his father appeared not to have noticed.

"They're too *far*. They're just too far." He looked up

through the plexidome at the splinters of light. "These people, Greenberg and Asimov: they lived, what, a thousand years ago?"

"Twentieth, twenty-first century. Somewhere in there."

"You know that new ship they're using in the outer System? The *Explorer*?"

"Fusion engines," said the boy.

"Yes. Do you know what its top recorded speed is?"

"About a hundred fifty thousand miles an hour."

"Much faster than anything this Greenberg ever saw. Anyhow, if they'd launched an *Explorer* to Alpha Centauri at the time these stories were written, at that speed, do you know how much of the distance they would have covered by now?"

Will had no idea. He would have thought they'd have arrived long ago, but he could see that wasn't going to be the answer. His father produced a minicomp, pushed a few buttons, and smiled. "About five percent. The *Explorer* would need another eighteen thousand years to get there."

"Long ride," said Will grudgingly.

"You'd want to take a good book."

The boy was silent.

"It's not as if we haven't tried, Will. There's an artificial world, half built, out beyond Mars someplace. They were going to send out a complete colony, people, farm animals, lakes, forest, everything."

"What happened?"

"It's too *far*. Hell, Will, life is good here. People are happy. There's plenty of real estate in the solar system if folks want to move. In the end, there weren't enough volunteers for the world-ship. I mean, what's the *point*? The people who go would be depriving their kids of any kind of normal life. How would *you* feel about living inside a tube for a lifetime? No beaches. Not real ones anyhow. No sunlight. No new places to explore. And for what? The payoff is so far down the road that, in reality, there *is* no payoff."

"In the stories," Will said, "the ships are very fast."

"I'm sure. But even if you traveled on a light beam, the stars are very far apart. And a ship can't achieve an appreciable fraction of that kind of velocity because it isn't traveling through a vacuum. At, say, a tenth of the speed of light, even a few atoms straying in front of it would blow the damned thing apart."

Outside, the Christmas lights were blue on the snow. "They'd have been disappointed," the boy said, "at how things came out."

"Who would have?"

"Benford. Robinson. Sheffield."

The father looked again at the table of contents. "Oh," he said. He riffled idly through the pages. "Maybe not. It's hard to tell, of course, with people you don't know. But we've eliminated war, population problems, ecological crises, boundary disputes, racial strife. Everybody eats pretty well now, and for the only time in its history, the human race stands united. I suspect if someone had been able to corner, say,"—he paused and flipped some pages—"Jack Vance, and ask him whether he would have settled for this kind of world, he'd have been delighted. Any sensible man would. He'd have said *to hell with the stars!*"

"No!" The boy's eyes blazed. "He *wouldn't* have been satisfied. None of them would."

"Well, I don't suppose it matters. Physical law is what it is, and it doesn't much matter whether we approve or not. Will, if these ideas hadn't become dated, and absurd, this kind of book wouldn't have disappeared. I mean, we wouldn't even know about *Great Tales of the Space Age* if someone hadn't dropped a copy of the thing into the time capsule. That should tell you something." He got up. "Gotta go, kid. Can't ignore the guests."

"But," said the boy, "you can't really be *sure* of that. Maybe the time was never right before. Maybe they ran out of money. Maybe it takes all of us working together to do it."

He slid back into the pillows. His father held up his hands, palms out, in the old gesture of surrender he always used when a game had gone against him. "We could do that *now*, Dad," Will continued. "There's a way to build a *Space Beagle. Somehow.*"

"Let me know if you figure it out, son." The lights died, and the door opened. "You'll have to do it yourself, though. Nobody *else* is giving it any thought. Nobody has for centuries."

The snow did not come. And while Will Cutler stared through the plexidome at the slowly awakening stars, thousands of others were also discovering Willis and Swanwick and Tiptree and Sturgeon. They lived in a dozen cities across Will's native Venus. And they played on the cool green hills of Earth and farmed the rich Martian lowlands; they clung to remote shelters among the asteroids, and watched the skies from silver towers beneath the great crystal hemispheres of Io and Titan and Miranda.

The ancient summons flickered across the worlds, insubstantial, seductive, irresistible. The old dreamers were bound, once again, for the stars.

AFTERWORD:
DIGGING AROUND
IN THE FUTURE

Sheila Williams

Joan D. Vinge once described archaeology as the anthropology of the past and science fiction as the anthropology of the future. Curious about what came before and what will come later, we look for ways to explore both. Archaeologists dig up fragments of past cultures and piece together what they were like. From the study of fabric preserved in a peat bog or pottery shards and flint knives harvested from the earth, we form a picture of the daily lives and beliefs of long-dead people, their rites and their celebrations. While anthropologists model the past from these clues, science fiction writers often look at the artifacts of the present to determine how societies may evolve in the future.

Science fiction writers cannot literally "dig" up the future, but they can take a close look at how transformations in common objects may affect life in the years to come.

These artifacts may be as mundane as televisions, radios, and computers. They are inventions and innovations still in or even before the drawing board stage. And as important as registering what new things may evolve under the sun is taking note of those aspects of human nature that never seem to change: love and hate, loyalty and betrayal, cowardice and bravery.

Science fiction writers use what they know of past and present to make an archaeological dig out of which a picture of the future emerges. Their own homes are sites where they can excavate the future with the trowels and brushes of their imagination. In "TV Time," by Mark L. Van Name, the television, for most people a comforting electronic security blanket, takes on overwhelming attributes and dimensions. No longer merely a small box that simply dominates a room in the house, the author's futuristic set has swallowed up an entire wall and threatens to engulf the lives of its viewers as well.

If your parents find modern-day computers baffling and a bit frightening, imagine how they'll react to Eileen Gunn's vision of computers and society in "Computer Friendly," a not-so-friendly look at the possible effects of computers on human consciousness. People solve moral issues with the same techniques programmers bring to devising algorithms, or as though they were as amenable to equations as simple arithmetic problems.

At the site of Isaac Asimov's archaeological dig, we encounter something that is still only a gleam in the eyes of electronic engineers: the robot who handles everyday chores and problems with the adeptness of P. G. Wodehouse's butler, Jeeves. In Asimov's amusing tale of an elderly couple's "Christmas Without Rodney," we find that home economics has become a lost art. Without their robot, these people can hardly boil water—let alone cook a fancy dinner. Asimov provides us with an image of what life might be like after the introduction of the robot, and he gives us an idea of what life might be like if that robot were then taken away. His characters are not unlike people of today who rely entirely on the hand-held calculator for solutions to simple math problems.

Of all the stories in this anthology, the author who takes us the farthest into the future is Janet Kagan. The people in "The Loch Moose Monster" don't live on the Earth or even in our solar system. Scientific discoveries about genetics and interstellar travel have vastly outstripped our present-day knowledge. Yet despite these amazing advances, Mama Jason has a great deal in common with historical pioneers. Like the early American settlers, the people who now make their home on Mirabile can never return to the world they left behind. Despite the advantages of time, they, too, must rely on their own pluck, courage, and intelligence to survive, and to make their new land home. Janet Kagan deftly explores a fascinating future where, despite a multitude of discoveries, certain basic human characteristics remain unchanged.

Although most science fiction stories look to the future, their authors feel little compunction about invading the traditional terrain of archaeologists and anthropologists—the past—or about taking a close look at the present. That's one reason why you'll also find stories in this anthology about peasants and knights from the Middle Ages, pioneers from the American past, and ghosts in today's TV set.

Science fiction doesn't claim to be a predictive literature. The French are more precise when they call this genre the "literature of anticipation." It is unlikely that any picture of the future simply cobbled from present-day facts is nearly as representative of the real future as the archaeologist's schema of the past. We live in a world that is made up of, and that has evolved from, hundreds of richly diverse cultures. Not one of these cultures may end up resembling the futures described in the stories gathered here. Yet, by reading science fiction, we can imagine where we might be headed if certain factors hold true, if certain discoveries are made. Science fiction writers, like archaeologists and anthropologists, remind us that we are all—our ancestors and our contemporaries—

builders of a road that extends from our distant beginnings to the unforeseen future. Our hope is that one day this road will take us to the stars, that one day future archaeologists and anthropologists will build their images of the past not from this world alone, but from the innumerable ones that await us.

Even the past will not yield all of her secrets to the diligent archaeologist; she only offers us hints and clues about what might have been. Science fiction, too, is a guidepost. It won't tell us exactly where we are headed, but it does give us some insight into the adventures that lie ahead.

ABOUT THE CONTRIBUTORS

Mark L. Van Name ("TV Time"):
Mark L. Van Name's first professional fiction sale was to *Isaac Asimov's Science Fiction Magazine*'s original anthology, *Tomorrow's Voices*. One of his most recent stories, "Desert Rain," is a collaboration with Pat Murphy (the author of "Traveling West") for *Full Spectrum III*. He cofounded the Sycamore Hill Writers' Conference, where he first showed "TV Time," and he is the author or coauthor of more than five hundred computer articles. Mr. Van Name lives in Raleigh, North Carolina, with his wife, baby daughter, more than forty computers, and a *large*-screen TV.

Mary Rosenblum ("Water Bringer"):
When she was eleven, Mary Rosenblum discovered a stack of old *Galaxy* magazines in the closet of the house her family was renting. Reading them was the beginning of a lifelong love affair with science fiction. Ms. Rosenblum has worked as a horse trainer, an endocrine researcher, and a commercial

cheese maker. She became a full-time SF writer after attending the Clarion West Writers' Workshop in 1988. Her fiction has appeared in *Isaac Asimov's Science Fiction Magazine (IAsfm), The Magazine of Fantasy & Science Fiction, Pulphouse,* and various anthologies. Ms. Rosenblum resides in Portland, Oregon, with her two sons, three large dogs, and assorted livestock.

Eileen Gunn ("Computer Friendly"):

Eileen Gunn, of Seattle, Washington, is a former young person herself, and a two-time Hugo Award nominee. While she was writing her 1990 Hugo finalist, "Computer Friendly," she decided to call in two consultants to help her end the story. She took her nieces, Erin and Kelsey—then eight and five years old—and stuffed them full of ice cream. "They preferred what I thought was the most horrifying of the possible endings. So, shamed by the moral courage of children, and fortified by mandarin orange chocolate, I let Elizabeth (in the story) do what she thought was right. I've never regretted it."

Janet Kagan ("The Loch Moose Monster"):

Five cats graciously allow Janet Kagan and her husband, Ricky, to share their home in Lincoln Park, New Jersey, with them. Ms. Kagan's novels include *Uhura's Song (Star Trek #21)* and *Hellspark* (Tor Books). Other stories about the irrepressible Mama Jason and the folks at Loch Moose can be found in her latest book, *Mirabile* (Tor Books). Ms. Kagan's short stories have appeared in *Pulphouse, Marian Zimmer Bradley's Fantasy Magazine, Starshore,* and *Isaac's Universe II.* In 1989 "The Loch Moose Monster" won the *IAsfm* Readers' Award Poll for Best Novelette. The following year, one of this story's lively sequels, "Getting the Bugs Out," also received the award.

William F. Wu ("Kenny"):

William F. Wu lives in El Mirage, California, which is out in the Mojave Desert. He isn't far from Palmsdale, where the space shuttles and stealth planes are made, or from Edwards Air Force Base, where the shuttle comes down. In 1984 his short story "Wong's Lost and Found Emporium" was nominated for the Nebula, Hugo, and World Fantasy awards, and it was later filmed for an episode of *Twilight Zone*. One of his most recent novels, *Hong on the Range* (Walker), was a Young Adult Editor's Choice from the American Library Association.

Maureen F. McHugh ("Kites"):

Although Maureen F. McHugh currently lives in Loveland, Ohio, she has lived in New York City and in Shijiazhuang in the People's Republic of China. Both China and New York have been important to her life and to her writing. Their influence can be seen in her first novel, *China Mountain Zhang* (Tor Books), which is set in the same world as "Kites."

Rob Chilson ("Gerda and the Wizard"):

Rob Chilson's empathy for his characters in "Gerda and the Wizard" evolved directly from his own experience. At eleven, his family moved to a place where there was neither a well nor electricity. For three years he hauled water for washing uphill from a spring, trip after trip, night after night. He started reading about barbarian swordsmen in his teens, and while he enjoyed those stories, it occurred to him early on that swordsmen didn't do much to solve the problems of the world. It was the wizards who seemed far more likely to invent things like water pumps, bright lights, medicines, flea powder, and so on, so he began to root for them. Mr. Chilson's latest novel, *Queanes of Faerie*, will remind readers of the story in this anthology. His other publications include *Rounded with Sleep* and *Men Like Rats*.

Joan D. Vinge ("Exorcycle"):

Joan D. Vinge's background in anthropology and her work in salvage archaeology have contributed a great deal to her science fiction. She says that the two disciplines are similar because they both offer fresh viewpoints for looking at "human" behavior—"archaeology is the anthropology of the past and science fiction is the anthropology of the future." Ms. Vinge has twice been the recipient of the Hugo Award: in 1977 for her novelette "Eyes of Amber," and again in 1981 for her novel *The Snow Queen*. Another novel, *Psion*, was named a Best Book for Young Adults by the American Library Association. Ms. Vinge's most recent book, *The Summer Queen* (Warner), is the third in her "Snow Queen Cycle." She lives in Chappaqua, New York, with her husband and their two children.

Isaac Asimov ("Christmas Without Rodney"):

The word *robotics* was introduced into the English language by Isaac Asimov, and millions of people owe their own introduction to robots and science fiction to his classic works. His outstanding books include *I, Robot*, the Foundation series, and *The Gods Themselves*. He was named a Grand Master by the Science Fiction Writers of America, and his work was honored with four Hugo and two Nebula Awards. He was well known for his mysteries and for his wide-ranging books on the sciences. Other nonfiction works include books on humor, Shakespeare, Gilbert and Sullivan, and the Bible. Dr. Asimov died in April 1992.

James Patrick Kelly ("Home Front"):

James Patrick Kelly is one of *IAsfm*'s most popular authors. He has received two of the magazine's Readers' Awards for his fiction and one for poetry. His story "Home Front" was written shortly after he finished a ten-week writing residency with eighth-graders at a middle school in his home town, Durham, New Hampshire. He tried to make the kids in this story talk and act like the kids he had just worked with. This Nebula and Hugo Award finalist's novels include *Freedom Beach, Look into the Sun,* and *Wildlife.*

Pat Murphy ("Traveling West"):

"Traveling West" is the first in a series of stories this multiple-award-winning author plans to write around the character Nadia. One of Ms. Murphy's earlier tales for *IAsfm,* "Rachel in Love," finished first in the Readers' Award Poll and won the 1987 Nebula Award. She also won the 1987 Nebula Award for her novel *The Falling Woman,* and her newest book, *Points of Departure,* was the first short-story collection ever to win the Philip K. Dick Award. Ms. Murphy lives in San Francisco, California.

Sherwood Springer ("The Scorch on Wetzel's Hill"):

Although the author has taken some liberties in describing the hill, and has changed some names, "The Scorch on Wetzel's Hill" is based on his home town in central Pennsylvania. As a boy, he, too, shinned up trees to untangle lines for fly fishermen. Mr. Springer is a retired newspaperman who now lives in Hawthorn, California. His fiction appearances include *IAsfm, The Saturday Evening Post,* and *Omni.*

Lawrence Watt-Evans ("Windwagon Smith and the Martians"):

According to Lawrence Watt-Evans, "Windwagon Smith and the Martians" is "an attempt at a new American tall tale, combining the historical character Thomas 'Windwagon' Smith [who, though a subject of previous tall tales, really did exist] and the Mars of Ray Bradbury." Mr. Watt-Evans is another popular *IAsfm* author. His "Windwagon" story won the

1989 Readers' Award Poll, and an earlier tale, "Why I Left Harry's All-Night Hamburgers," captured both the Readers' Award and the prestigious Hugo Award for Best Short Story. Mr. Watt-Evans lives in Gaithersburg, Maryland, with his wife and two children.

Jack McDevitt ("To Hell with the Stars"):

When he's not writing science fiction, or working as a training officer for the United States Customs Service in Brunswick, Georgia, Jack McDevitt can often be found coaching his sons' Little League baseball team. Mr. McDevitt has been a finalist for both the Nebula and the Hugo Awards. He is the author of *The Hercules Text*, *A Talent for War*, and a third novel, *Gomorrah, Farewell*, which is just out from Berkley. His most recent short story appearances include tales for *When the Music's Over*, *Full Spectrum III*, *Sacred Visions*, *Alternate Wars*, and *IAsfm*.

Sheila Williams joined *Isaac Asimov's Science Fiction Magazine* in 1982 and she has been the managing editor there since 1986. She received her bachelor's degree from Elmira College in Elmira, New York, and her master's degree from Washington University in St. Louis, Missouri. During her junior year she studied at the London School of Economics.

In addition to *The Loch Moose Monster: More Stories from IAsfm*, Ms. Williams has co-edited two other anthologies for young adults and *Isaac Asimov's Robots*, recently out from Berkley. She also co-edited *Writing Science Fiction and Fantasy* (St. Martin's Press) with the editors of *IAsfm* and *Analog*. She lives in New York City with her husband, David W. Bruce.